In the Shadows

AMY CRONIN

POOLBEG
CRIMSON

Published 2024 by Poolbeg Press Ltd.
123 Grange Hill, Baldoyle,
Dublin 13, Ireland
Email: poolbeg@poolbeg.com

ISBN 978-1-78199 681-2

www.poolbeg.com

About the Author

Amy Cronin lives by the sea with her husband and young children in Cork, Ireland. A former tutor at Munster Technological University, she worked in the Irish Civil Service for a number of years, before pursuing her passion for writing crime fiction.

She has published two crime thrillers, *Blinding Lies* and *Twisted Truth* with Poolbeg Press. *In The Shadows* is the final instalment in the 'Anna Clarke' trilogy.

You can follow Amy online @AmyCroninAuthor (X) & amyjcauthor (Instagram)

Acknowledgements

Thank you, dear reader. This is the final instalment in the trilogy and I truly hope you have enjoyed the journey.

I am eternally grateful to Paula Campbell of Poolbeg Press for the opportunity to bring *Blinding Lies, Twisted Truth,* and now, *In the Shadows* to readers.

To Gaye Shortland, a huge thank-you.

To David Prendergast and the wider team at Poolbeg Press, heartfelt thanks.

I'm grateful and lucky to have people in my life that know things I don't – Sandra, Gary, Alan. Any mistakes in the crafting of this book are mine.

To the people of Cork – this is a work of fiction, and certain places either don't exist or have been tweaked slightly for the sake of the story. Thank you for understanding and for your enthusiastic queries about when this book might be published. I really appreciate your support!

Thank you to my fellow authors, in Cork and beyond, for your encouragement and camaraderie.

Huge thanks to John Breen of Waterstones in Cork, and all booksellers who join the link between writers and readers so seamlessly.

To librarians – for your help in guiding a little girl to hidden treasures a long time ago, and for your enthusiasm for *all* stories – thank you.

To my friends and family – your support is so appreciated. Especially Kevin … *thank you.*

To Laura-Jane, Stacey and Shauna, with love

Prologue

Mijas, Spain

Isaac flipped the chairs over, one at a time, their spindly wooden legs arcing in the crisp morning air. The tiles felt sticky under his shoes but their blue and white chequers gleamed in the sunlight, and the scent of lemon perfumed the café. Camila had been here since sunrise, cleaning even though it was already spotless, before heading to the bakery at the back of the small building. Now she would focus on their mother's recipes, her efforts selling out before lunchtime. He smiled, picturing his sister moving from counter to oven, over and over, her floured hands labouring, her brow furrowed in concentration. Even in the springtime, when the tourists were not as plentiful, their little bakery was spoken about throughout the region … or so he liked to tell anyone that would listen. His uncle had said he was a fool to buy the small, white-washed building, hidden among the cobbled backstreets. But the aroma of his sister's skill drew customers looking for a reprieve from the sun and a sweet treat to pass the time.

Foreigners amused Isaac. He spoke English well and, from what he had learned from their customers, most people came to the little village of Mijas to escape. A stressful job, a harassing ex-wife, a depressing climate; a multitude of complaints. Yet all of them made the same mistake, in his opinion. Rather than soothe their tired soul

1

in the tranquillity offered by an Andalusian morning – the birdsong, the chorus of cicadas, the otherwise stillness of a quiet village – they sought coffee and a stranger to listen to their woes. Always wanting to speak about themselves. Well, Isaac was happy to listen, securing his future with each nod of his head and refill of their coffee.

The tinkling bell over the door had been Camila's idea. It grated on him in the beginning, but he had grown to love it. Each tinny rattle of the bell was a customer, a profit to make their lives more comfortable. He offered coffee, pastries and a willing ear; in return the customers helped him pay off his loan and live his dream. It was a fair exchange and life was good.

It was March, and cooler than the tourists liked, but the bell rang steadily that morning, over and over, louder than the burst of air from the coffee machine and the stilted conversation Camila endured with the customers.

When she answered the ringing telephone she quickly shook her head in frustration.

"Isaac, puedes coger esta llamada? Está en inglés!"

He smiled and took the receiver from her hand, intrigued. Only suppliers or their uncle rang the coffee shop phone, and they never spoke in English.

"*Hola!* Good morning. Can I help you?"

"Yes. I hope so."

He waited, his pulse a little quicker than before, the chill morning air blowing in through the open door lifting the hairs on his arms.

"A woman calls to your café. Short dark hair, green eyes. She is accompanied by another woman, her sister, and two red-haired little girls. They speak English."

"*Sí?*" His heart was rattling now inside his ribcage and he had no idea why, except that the caller's voice was hushed and urgent.

"If you see her today, I need you to give her a message. Please! It's very important."

He knew the people the caller spoke about. Every day for almost three weeks the children drank little cups of hot chocolate and munched on Camila's chocolate-dipped churros while the women sipped coffee and spoke quietly, their heads so close together they were almost touching. He had wondered about them. They were not Spanish – they spoke English to each other – but they were not Americans, he was sure. They spoke Spanish well enough though. They favoured the darkest corner of the café and never stayed long, always bringing pencils and colouring books for the children and shushing them whenever they spoke. The little girls were exuberant and playful, squealing when Camila placed their treats on the table, giggling as their little legs swung on the café chairs. He guessed they were maybe four years old. They beamed at him each morning, while the women with them seemed to want to stay invisible. In fact, the women had gasped in alarm one morning when one of the little girls had loudly called out *Aunty Kate!*"

Today, they arrived at quarter past eleven, a little later than usual. While one woman settled the children, the one with the shorter, darker hair, the one he thought was called Kate, approached the counter to order. She smiled at him, her eyes bright-green and friendly. Before she had a chance to speak, he interrupted.

"I received a message for you this morning. On the telephone." He spoke in English, trepidation making his hands tremble a little underneath the counter.

She looked at him in surprise, the freckles on her cheeks disappearing in the creases of her smile.

3

"Are you sure it's for me?"

Her smile was broad and warm, reassuring. He couldn't return it.

"*Sí*. The caller described you and the others." He gestured to where the children and other woman sat. "I wrote it down."

Relief steadied his hand as he gave her the piece of paper, torn from an order book. He watched the woman intently. He didn't understand the message, but knew it carried a threat, and he was glad to have been able to pass it on and warn her. As she read his alarm grew. She seemed to shrink into herself, doubled over, her breath drawn in sharply, one arm wrapped around her stomach. She gripped the countertop with one hand and swayed a little, her eyes screwed tightly closed. When she opened them, her eyes were glazed, the green dull now. He wanted to offer help and he reached out a hand, but she turned and walked stiffly to the table where the others sat. No words were exchanged. It was as though a code passed between them. Cardigans were pulled around the little girls' shoulders and colouring books and pencils stuffed quickly into a backpack. Without a sound they left the darkest corner of the café, his eyes following them out the door.

She had left the written message on the countertop and Isaac screwed it into a ball, stuffing it into his pocket as he moved to settle the chairs at their table. He wanted to hide it, to diminish the threat it carried, but he knew it would stay with him for the rest of the day. He also knew he'd never see the women and little girls again. She hadn't said a word, but her physical reaction told him everything. The message was a warning, and she was going to heed it.

They would not be back.

Isaac had never carried the burden of his customers' problems before. Once he shut the door to the café and turned the key in the lock, pulled the shutters down, that was it – that part of his day was over. But this was different. This felt like a *real* problem, not the first world-privilege whining his usual customers spouted in between mouthfuls of coffee and cake. The woman's reaction to the words on the slip of paper gnawed at him all day. And her lack of surprise – she had been expecting it.

Before he closed the café that night he pulled the note from his pocket and read it once more.

Tom has found you. You need to run.

1

Cork

One Day Before

Earth fills her nose and mouth. She can feel it in her ears too, clogging up the space, pressing its grainy residue against her skin. Its heavy weight covers her, holding her in place. Moving is impossible; she is compacted on all sides. Her lungs are empty but there is nothing to inhale and her eyes are sealed shut by the weight pressing on her lids. Worse still is the wriggling sensation against the cheeks on her face, against her lips and her closed eyelids – maggots, writhing in search of a way in. A scream builds inside her and she can no longer bear it.

"*Anna! Anna!* For God's sake *wake up!*"

Her eyes snapped open and she gasped, burning her lungs with air. She swallowed hard, pushing sour-tasting bile down her throat, which ached with a familiar rawness.

"I'm sorry!" she whispered, the words automatic, her mind groggy. She propped herself up on her elbows. "Sorry, Vivian! Was I screaming again?"

Her friend switched on the lamp on the bedside locker and sat heavily on the edge of the bed. Her blue eyes were red-rimmed and watery, her pale skin shining in the half-light. Vivian was exhausted. "You were, you poor thing!" She passed Anna a mug and the aroma of fresh coffee was so strong her stomach lurched. "That's the third time this week."

Anna squinted at the alarm clock on the bedside locker; it read 6:10. She sighed. Her friend smiled at her kindly but the shadows under her eyes betrayed her tiredness.

"Vivian, I ... I don't know what to say except I'm sorry!"

"I'm not looking for an apology," Vivian rubbed Anna's arm, "but I think you need to get some help."

"I'm fine!" It was an instinctive response, easily given, and entirely untrue.

They both knew it.

"OK," Vivian said lightly and hopped off the bed. She smiled from the doorway. "I really hope so."

Anna sat up, resting her shoulders against the wooden headboard, and sipped the coffee. The hiss of the shower reached her; Vivian getting ready for work. Too often lately she had woken her friend this way – she felt heat sting her face and was intensely grateful to Vivian for not making a big deal of it. What was going on with her? Screaming in her sleep was a drama her friend didn't deserve to deal with.

Her heart was racing in her chest, either from the caffeine or the nightmare, or maybe the embarrassment of the last few minutes. Waves of nausea pummelled her and she gripped the mug, anchored by its heat. The dream had happened enough times now to be classed as 'recurring' and was upsetting enough to elicit screams from her in the middle of the night. Anna knew she needed to sort this out. She just wasn't sure how to go about it. She'd had therapy, insisted upon by her supervisor at work. It had helped. By day she kept herself busy, training, chatting to her brother on his daily telephone call and tried to immerse herself in the files on her desk at work. But by night her memories crept from her subconscious and played out in her dreams, leaving her shattered and breathless as dawn broke.

The stillness of her bedroom was unnerving. As she sipped the hot drink, her eyes found the dark corners of the room and her heart began to race faster again. Lurking shapes in the dark ... boxes of all her possessions lined the walls, a reminder that she had fled her home. Images flicked like the pages of a photo album through her mind and she pushed the covers back, swinging her legs to the floor. She could hear the kitchen radio had been switched on now – how long had she been sitting still? – could hear Vivian humming to a song as the coffee machine whirred again ... familiar sounds, comforting and reassuring. Yet her heart still hammered loudly inside her chest and her thoughts refused to come together.

Her toes nudged into the thick carpet at her feet. This wasn't her bedroom, not really. It was a borrowed space until she found a new home. Because the house she had grown up in was full of painful memories. And, lately, her experiences in the house had been so terrifying that she was taking refuge here. A part of her felt sad it had come to this. But she knew she needed a fresh start.

Her legs dragged heavily as she walked to the bathroom. Wiping steam from the mirror, she recoiled a little at her reflection. She had never seen her brown eyes this dull, nor her skin. The counsellor she had seen had said Anna should expect to feel this way. After a trauma it is perfectly normal to feel detached, to suffer nightmares, to feel as Anna did.

Half alive.

She didn't bother with breakfast, just a glass of water. Her training gear was ready in a bag by the front door and she called goodbye to Vivian as she swung it over her shoulder. As she opened the front door the chill spring air pushed the last of the sleepy fog from her brain and she jogged quickly down the flight of concrete steps to her car, feeling her energy return somewhat.

She passed Blackrock Castle as she edged into traffic, its stone tower less imposing this morning, encased in a dense mist. She wound down the window and let the air sting her face, keeping her alert.

The morning DJs on the local radio station were alarmingly upbeat for this hour, she thought, turning up the volume, smiling a little at their energy. As the news anchor was introduced and the headlines read out, her smile dropped quickly and she gripped the steering wheel tighter.

"*Gardaí continue to search a sealed-off area of remote farmland north of Portlaoise in the search for the remains of Michael and Helen Clarke, suspected victims of a violent –*"

Her hand darted out and she snapped off the radio. The bitter taste of vomit flooded her mouth again and she swallowed hard, flexing her foot on the accelerator.

Jason was waiting in the hotel gym in Kinsale, with a smile that managed to be both friendly and concerned. Anna greeted him quickly, bending to pull on her sparring gear, not wanting to look at his face. Or not wanting him to see *her* face, the haunted one full of shadows that had looked back at her from the mirror this morning.

Her Taekwon-Do trainer for over ten years, now in his late-fifties, tall and rangy, his dark hair still full and thick, Jason had been her father's best friend. His and Michael Clarke's shared love of martial arts had cemented their friendship and now Anna thought of him as *her* friend. His muscles were subtle, his movements quick as he warmed up in front of her. She felt herself relaxing as he made idle chat, the nightmare fading fully from her memory.

When her parents had disappeared, Jason and Taekwon-Do training had kept her focused, given her a way to expel her feelings and move forward. He had helped her reach black belt level, and they shared the teaching for his Taekwon-Do Tykes classes once a week. In truth, he left her take charge of those classes; he knew how much she loved it.

They usually worked out together five mornings a week, sparring and training, focusing on her progress. Those skills had kept her alive in the last few months. Now that they knew Anna's parents were dead, the gardaí searching for their bodies, the intensity of their training had stepped-up. Jason knew she needed the physical release, and if it helped her mentally as well, as it had before, he was glad to do it. His presence in her life was an anchor and she was grabbing on tightly.

"Do you need a warm-up?"

She flexed her neck. "Nope."

"Alright." He picked up two red pads. "We've done enough patterns this week – we're going to have some fun this morning!"

The familiar rush of adrenaline unfurled the last of her tense muscles. "Let's go!"

Over and over she kicked the pads, and when Jason called for her to switch it up, she punched them instead. Jason staggered backwards at one point but re-steadied himself; she needed this. They both did. She had a list of names inside her head that ran on repeat. With each hit she recited each syllable, pummelling again and again.

Robert Evans – Roy Eastly – Dean Harris!
Robert Evans – Roy Eastly – Dean Harris!

2

Tom Gallagher thought they would have made more of the place, considering the amount they charged per week. The facility looked like a rundown nursing home from the front. A drab pebble-dashed cluster of bungalows, in need of a good power-wash. The short driveway, lined with a scattering of bare trees, was a disappointment as well. But it was rumoured to be the best treatment centre in the country and was far enough out of Cork city to offer complete discretion. In truth, this wasn't rehab, more a middle ground between a health spa and full-on mental-health treatment. A hybrid afforded only to the very wealthy ... not that you'd know it from the outside.

The inside wasn't a good deal better in Tom's opinion. He guessed the scratched hardwood floors were supposed to be rustic and earthy. Mae would have wrinkled her nose at the reception chairs in rich tartan patterns, if she was in any fit state to take anything in. But, after her discharge from hospital, she hadn't protested at being dropped off and left in the care of the attendant who was young enough to be her daughter. Tom had understood that at that time, Mae hadn't given a damn about anything at all.

She was waiting for him in what was called the Day Room. He hadn't seen this part of the facility before – it lifted his spirits. It was a large octagonal conservatory, with shafts of the morning sunlight streaking the tiled floor. Windows were pushed open and cold air filtered through, diluting the sharp smell of bleach that had filled his nostrils when he'd come through the front door. Several wicker chairs with thick floral cushions were scattered around the room; they looked ominously frail and spindly to Tom, and he wondered if they'd hold his weight. A coffee table in the centre offered a choice of magazines, there was a water cooler in the corner and, overall, an air of optimism he hadn't expected.

He approached his wife with some trepidation. Dressed in a cashmere jumper and shirt and dark jeans, he'd made sure to wear her favourite cologne. His dark hair was jelled back, slick and neat as usual. He couldn't hide the dark shadows under his eyes, but he'd done his best. Months ago he'd promised her there'd be no treatment facility; outside intervention went against everything he stood for. The Gallaghers solved their own problems. Quickly, quietly, brutally. And he'd never broken a promise to his wife, until now. He'd last seen Mae when he left her here for the first time; then, he hadn't felt he had much choice.

There had been no solving Mae's depression. He'd stood by as she drank through the days after their son David's death. It was understandable; her grief was unbearable. Back then, he'd been sure it was a phase that would pass. Everyone said time healed all ills, and who was he to argue? He'd focused his energy on finding the woman who shot David ... Kate Crowley. Tom had promised his wife he would bring Kate to her to do with as she pleased. The light in Mae's eyes when he spoke those words was enough − his wife was still there, underneath her grief she was fighting to get out, and he would rip the earth apart to free her.

A man like Tom, with vast resources and contacts in the darkest corners of the world, only had to be patient. Kate could only have gone so far, surely – a woman on the run, with two young children in tow, she was a walking target. But the little bitch was as slippery as she was cunning. She'd shot their son, evaded the gardaí, and encouraged her sister to flee too, with *their* granddaughters, no less. France, now Spain … he wondered how she had managed it. She had money, he knew that much. She had stolen thousands from David. It stood to reason she had found someone willing to help her get passports or other false documents – the world was full of people willing to bend the rules of law for easy money. It was a lifestyle he understood. He knew now that they were travelling through Europe, the little group of four. He thought Kate might be beginning to relax, smiling to herself that she was safely hidden from him.

But not for much longer. He had underestimated her for the last time. He thought of Kate when he saw his wife – surely this news would rally her. He wanted her home.

Mae was sitting alone, her face turned away from him to the light outside and the gardens he had noticed as he walked in. A manicured lawn, benches around a small fishpond, residents chatting on low concrete seats. More like what he imagined the place to be. Her hand on the armrest of the chair was steady, not trembling like it had been since David's death last November. Fleetingly he wondered if she was angry with him for leaving her here. He rested his hand on hers and was reassured to find it warm.

"Mae?"

She turned to him, surprise in her eyes. He stifled a sob that threatened to explode from his chest. Her blonde hair was streaked with grey around the temples and at the centre parting, but it shone in the morning sunlight. The blue in her eyes seemed brighter, and she smiled, though it faltered around the edges.

"Tom. They said you were coming to see me."

He felt like he could punch the air in triumph at the strength in her voice. It had been *months* since she had sounded so much like her usual self. He lowered himself carefully into the wicker chair, pausing to test its sturdiness, and folded his long legs beneath it as best he could.

"How have you been, my love?"

She pulled the sleeves of her sweater down over the dressings at her wrist.

"Fine. Much better." She focused her eyes on his, found his doubt and fear there. "Honestly, Tom, I'm getting there. There's no alcohol here, obviously. A doctor called and gave me tablets for the pains, you know."

She lowered her eyes and he sensed she felt embarrassed. He gripped both her hands in his, willing her to keep talking, careful not to put any pressure on her injured wrist.

"I'm seeing a lovely lady. A counsellor. Her name's Susan. She makes a lot of sense." Mae pulled her hands back then, her voice fading.

"Well, you look much better, and you sound … I just want you home, Mae."

She whipped her head up to look at him again, her eyes alarmed.

"I'm not ready, Tom! Susan said it will be a while before I can go home. The other doctor too – it's best I stay here!"

"I know! There's no rush, love. You take your time."

"How's … how's John?"

Tom drew air into his lungs; how exactly would he answer this? What had happened to John, their older son, was the reason she was here. The catalyst that pushed her dependence on alcohol into a suicide attempt. John had been shot by one of their own, one of Tom's most trusted men. The betrayal by Ely Murray paled in comparison to knowing that John would probably spend the rest of his life in prison. Raising a son that engaged in serious criminal activities was hardly a surprise. But he had kept his ... project ... a secret from them. Arranging to have people murdered for a criminal ring run on the dark web, to be viewed and rated by voyeurs, John had expected to make a fortune. Instead, he was lucky to be alive, and Tom and Mae had yet to really speak about the horrifying details of his crimes. Perhaps they never would.

"John is healing well!" He hoped he sounded optimistic. "He's much better and I expect he'll be leaving hospital soon. It's been a month; his doctor says it won't be long before he's well enough to be transferred to ... well, to prison. Who knows when his trial will be, but don't worry, I have the best men on his defence."

Mae nodded and he saw her throat bob around the sobs that threatened to derail her composure.

"And you? Have the gardaí called you in?" Her voice was just a whisper.

He noticed her eyes were wide and fearful, her hands trembling on the armrests of the chair. He cursed under his breath; he shouldn't have come here. She was making progress, that was plain to see, and he was damned if he was going to derail that!

"Nothing I can't handle, love. Don't you be worrying yourself unnecessarily. Sure you know me, always in control. Listen, Mae, I have good news!" God knows she needs some good news, he

16

thought. "I've found Crowley. Kate and Natalie have been staying in Spain. I've a man watching a little village in the north, and we know they're there. I've photographs – it's them!"

He pulled a brown A4 size envelope from inside his jacket, eyes darting around the empty room as he passed it to her – old habits die hard. Always wary, always watching for someone that was watching him.

Mae took the envelope and slid the photographs out, studying them carefully, her eyes flicking over the faces. Natalie, once the closest thing to a daughter-in-law, Rachel and Rhea their granddaughters, and then Kate.

Tom noticed that the photograph was fluttering in Mae's hand, as though caught in a non-existent breeze, and saw his wife's chest rise and fall in quick bursts. He reassured himself this was the right thing to do, despite what seeing the images was doing to her – this could be the boost she needed.

"Where is this?" she demanded in a hoarse whisper.

"Mijas, in Spain. A small town. It seems they've lived there for a few weeks, made a little routine for themselves."

She traced one finger over the centre of the photograph, over their granddaughters' faces. "What is this building? Where is this?"

Tom leaned over, saw the small white structure he was familiar with, having studied the photographs already.

"Just some coffee shop. *Sueños.* It means 'dreams' or something … who cares? My guy says they go there every day, spend about an hour killing time at the back, and leave again. The second photo – there, see? – that's their apartment. We have her, Mae! And the girls, *David's* girls … they'll settle in with us in time. They'll *remember* us! I can make this happen."

He shifted in the wicker chair, his excitement at the prospect of making his wife happy, of ending this nightmare, making it impossible to sit still. The wicker creaked and groaned at the joints but he barely heard it.

Mae nodded, her face completely impassive, and Tom's heavy dark brows drew together in confusion – he wasn't expecting this reaction. Or lack of one. For months she had begged him to find her granddaughters. They wanted their son's children back. And they wanted Kate dead.

This had been their plan all along, and now Mae was sitting quietly, unmoved, as if he had just told her the weather report. When she finally spoke her gaze was out the window again, into the garden.

"That's nice. I miss the girls."

"*Nice*?" The heat in his face felt like all the blood in his veins was pooled there now. "It's fucking great! You said you wanted Kate, your hands around her throat! You wanted the girls back! We *both* do! It's what Kate deserves, Mae. For David!" Lowering his voice was impossible and part of Tom expected the door to open with some nosy staff member any second, wondering what all the fuss was about.

Mae turned to him and put one hand to his cheek. "Yes, I know." She smiled slowly, her mouth twitching around the now unfamiliar movement, "I know." It sounded like she was soothing him, placating a child. She turned her whole body in the chair, into the morning light, and folded her hands in her lap. He could see the white edge of the bandages on her wrist under the sleeve of her sweater and remembered that night, finding her in her bed, the sheets soaked in blood.

The elation he had felt earlier at bringing her this news fizzled and died.

She said nothing else for the duration of his visit. He spoke of her sister, that she had been calling him non-stop and wanted Mae to call her when she felt up to it. He told her Marco's mother had died; he told her every bit of gossip he could think of, but she didn't react to anything he said. Before, she would have fussed over the news of Marco's loss, mothering over his muscleman, his longest employee. She would have asked a multitude of questions about the death and the funeral and lamented on the fact she had missed it. He had expected her then to wonder if he had driven here himself and was he sure that was wise. He had many enemies and had preferred to have Marco drive his car and stay by his side for almost his whole adult life. Hazard of the job.

Today, she didn't seem to care.

They must have her drugged, Tom reasoned, she must be spaced out. He went through the motions of conversation, a loving husband, a willing participant in her recovery. But he couldn't reach her – he was plodding through quicksand to find a connection and the wife he remembered was still so far out of reach.

As he exited the driveway thirty minutes later he couldn't remember feeling as dejected in a long time. He was inching onto the country road, his view hampered by hedgerows, when he saw them. An unmarked Garda car, he assumed, a dark-blue Toyota Avensis, idling a little way down the road past the treatment centre. They had tailed him from Cork, as they had been doing for weeks now. He lifted one hand and raised his middle finger. The driver had the audacity to wave back and smirk.

Back in the good days, they wouldn't have dared. Tom could have marched over to the car, hauled the man out and smashed his head into the bonnet, and the gardaí wouldn't have been able to touch him. And, if anyone dared to follow him, he would have had a car following *them,* following them home that night, teaching them a lesson that could never be traced back to him.

With gritted teeth and his hands clamped tightly on the steering wheel, he eased the car onto the road and headed for home. The shrill yell of his ringing mobile further jangled his nerves and he swore loudly into the empty car.

"How is she?" The woman's voice was clipped, impatient.

"Hello to you too. And I'm fine, thanks for asking!"

"Cut the shit, Tom! I want to know how my sister is!"

He exhaled heavily, shoulders slumping.

"She not herself. Spaced out on meds, I'd say. But she looks better."

"Better to be away from you!"

The line went dead before he could reply. Even if she had given him a chance to, he doubted he could have convinced his sister-in-law otherwise. And, if he was honest with himself, he agreed with her.

3

Detective Sergeant William Ryan stuffed his sunglasses into his overcoat pocket as the buzzer sounded and pushed open the door to the city morgue. He was familiar with the smell – disinfectant and other chemicals, and more odours he really didn't want to think about – yet it still clogged up his nostrils and coated his throat. His shoes clipped softly on the tiles as he made his way to the reception desk and showed his ID, barely able to muster a greeting. He really hoped the cadaver was who he wanted it to be …

"Sergeant Ryan, a pleasure to meet you."

William thought that was a pretty weird thing to say and nodded curtly. He couldn't manage a smile. Patrick O'Shea introduced himself and remained standing a few inches away, not offering a hand. At average height he was still half a foot shorter than William and, as he led the way down the corridor, he offered as much information as he could. William kept up the man's hurried pace easily, aware of a sticky-suction sound with each step on the tiles as they wound deeper into the building, his eyes searching in vain to find an open window in the narrow space. He was beginning to feel lightheaded.

"I haven't met you here before. Unusual situation this really, we don't get many John Does. The body was found on French Church

Street yesterday morning, in a shop doorway. Gave the young girl opening up a fright! The autopsy hasn't been performed yet, but it's pretty obvious how the man died. We just have no clue who he is. He was robbed apparently; there's not a thing on him. I'm told your lot ran his facial profile through the missing persons and didn't get a hit."

William knew all this and he had seen the images of the deceased, but he wanted to be sure. As sure as a man who has seen with his own eyes. He offered no further information as O'Shea snapped on gloves and pulled open the handle to the refrigerated compartment, sliding out the mortuary tray containing the deceased. As the white sheet was lowered to rest on the man's neck, William's eyes narrowed in concentration and he sucked in a deep breath. *Please*, he prayed. Quickly his eyes flicked over every inch of the dead man's face and head.

The crumpling of the skull bones drew his attention first. Blunt force trauma to the head – a term often used. The force it took to shatter a man's skull was entirely underestimated. Stretched, pale skin, dark hair, eyebrows thick over protruding brow bones. Strong jaw, nose angled to the left, long-ago broken. High cheekbones … the man's bone structure was distinctive. His body under the sheet looked shorter than average for a middle-aged man, his shoulders narrow.

This wasn't him.

William frowned, a quick flash of movement before his face was impassive again.

"Not who I'm looking for. Thank you for your time."

In the car he punched the steering wheel and exhaled heavily, resting his head back, eyes screwed shut. This was *his* fault. Dean

Harris was missing for almost a week now, and William knew he had played a part in that. His eyes roamed the car park, searching, always searching.

Where was he?

The only thing moving in the carpark around his car was litter, wrappers blowing in the brisk spring breeze. He felt unnaturally hot, sweat gathering along his collar line and between his shoulder blades. He shrugged out of his overcoat and suit jacket and dumped them on the passenger seat, opened the top button on his shirt and pulled his blue tie aside.

"*Fuck you, Harris,*" he muttered, starting the engine.

The first week of Dean Harris's release on bail had been smooth, uneventful. The man signed on daily at his local Garda station and kept his head down. He stayed with his mother in a well-kept bungalow in the outskirts of the city, walking her fluffy white Bichon Frise twice a day, strolling to the chemist to collect remedies for whatever ailed her and to the shop for one bag of groceries before noon. William knew all this because he tailed the man or made sure someone else did. He wanted twice daily reports and he wanted specifics – where he went, what he bought, who he spoke to, how did he look?

He was one of the most dangerous men William had met in his career as detective. Not just because he preyed on vulnerable women, waiting until they were alone before he subjected them to his sadistic attacks in the dead of night. And not just because the man was an opportunist, using his job installing house alarms to find his victims. It was because he believed in his own absolute *right* to do this.

The woman who had stopped him in his tracks, ending his three-year spree of random, violent attacks, was currently sitting at her desk in the clerical pool downstairs from his own cubicle in the Lee Street Garda station. Anna Clarke. She was about to start a two-week stint of annual leave that day, forced on her by their Chief Superintendent. William didn't usually agree with Frank Doherty, but this time the chief super was right. Anna needed a break – the last few months had been tough, not helped by Harris preying on her, intent on making her his eighth victim.

As he pulled into traffic at the Wilton roundabout, William smiled – an involuntary reaction whenever he thought of the night Dean Harris broke into Anna's house. It amused him hugely that Harris had so underestimated her; the short, slight young woman had fractured his jaw when he tried to attack her. William had enjoyed arresting the man in his hospital bed the following morning, had relished being the detective to close the case on the three-year spate of unsolved attacks. But it had all blown wide open – an alcoholic in the forensics lab had made mistakes, and Harris's solicitor had pounced on the opportunity to see his client released. William had consoled himself that it was a straightforward babysitting case until the evidence was properly secured for trial – Harris signed on every day and kept to his bail conditions, until that one day William stepped too far into Harris's face.

And that miscalculation had led him here.

Harris had been queueing in a hardware store when William stepped into line behind him. He was a tall man but William still looked down onto the top of his head, onto the bald patch and sprinkle of silver running through the brown hair. As the queue shuffled forward Harris had become aware of a presence and, on turning, had jumped almost a foot to the left in shock. William had been unable to keep the smirk from his face at the man's bulging eyes and the colour flooding his cheeks.

"Hello, Dean. What are you buying there?"

"Just bits and pieces."

William was surprised the man spoke at all. His voice was unexpectedly high-pitched for a middle-aged man, and it was thick with teenage-angst defensiveness.

He had hunched his shoulders around himself as he eyed William, whose own hands were wedged into the pockets of his suit pants. "What are *you* doing here?"

"Shopping. Same as yourself."

"No, you're not! You're harassing me! There are laws against this! I know my rights!"

The queue had moved forward again and Harris moved with it, next in line to pay, keeping a firm grip on the items in his hands.

William had barely concealed his disgust, but had managed to keep his voice low, a hiss between clenched teeth, and his hands in his pockets – safer that way.

"You don't have any rights, Dean, remember? You lost those when you started attacking women, at least in my eyes anyway. Tell me, what do you want that rope for?" He had nodded to the coiled brown bundle in Harris's arms and the man stepped backwards until he touched the edge of the wooden service counter, his back so hunched he was almost bent over.

"None of your damn business! I don't have to tell you. I know my rights!"

"So you said."

"I'm telling my solicitor about this! This is harassment!" Harris then turned one-eighty degrees, his eyes darting around him, looking at the customers milling around the shop.

William remembered thinking the man was growing in confidence, his surly demeanour replaced with a cockiness that unfurled his back and squared his shoulders.

He had dared to jab a finger into William's chest. "*You* can't do this to *me!*"

William stepped closer, closing the gap between them. He was close enough to see the open pores on Harris's greasy forehead. Adrenaline had made his teeth chatter so he clamped them tight around his words. "It's only a matter of time, Dean." Though there were no customer standing close enough to hear him, his voice had been soft and low, a discreet conversation for Harris's ears only. "No-one's disputing the evidence and once the paperwork is straightened out, it's back where you belong. In the meantime, I'm watching you. We all are. So you make sure to keep one foot in front of the other, got it? Not one step out of line."

He'd stepped back as his peripheral vision registered customers milling too close, and he'd winked at Harris, bid him a good day. Fear had descended like a veil over the man's face – the threat of a return to prison obviously something he found unbearable – and William had gone about his day with a spring in his step. He'd returned to his desk and his case files feeling less bogged-down by the weight of Harris's release.

But, later that evening, Anna Clarke had burst through the door to his office level, had run to his desk, her brown eyes wide and terrified. Harris had given his watchers the slip and had made an approach to her niece. He had found the housing estate where her brother lived in Kinsale, had waited for the five-year-old, and told her to deliver a message.

To tell her Aunty Anna her friend Dean said hello.

As Anna staggered into a seat beside his desk, William had felt as though he were drowning in freezing water, surrounded by the crushing weight of it, his lungs bursting for oxygen. While his heart thudded threateningly inside his chest, he had snatched up the desk phone, calling garda after garda, all telling him the same thing – Harris was missing.

William had practically camped outside Harris's mother's house since then. The chill wind and stinging rain were his penance for pushing the man too far. Old Mother Harris seemed to be the only person he had cared about, but she didn't know where he was. All week long her little Bichon Frise remained unwalked. Harris's solicitor was baffled, his previous victims warned to be vigilant, and the woman he blamed for his incarceration, Anna Clarke, was on high alert.

As William drove back to the Lee Street station through the city streets, passing the grounds of the university on his right, his eyes scanned the pathways. Groups of students, some joggers, a man pausing to light a cigarette, hunched against the wind – none of them Harris.

The man was loose in Cork city and the streets were a lot more dangerous because of it. Whether it was William's fault or not, he wouldn't stop searching until Harris was back in custody. Whatever, and however long, it took.

4

Anna heard the familiar ring of her mobile phone from across the room where she was filing some paperwork, crossed the open-plan office quickly and snatched it up. She was due to clock-off in ten minutes for a two-week break from work, and hoped the call was nothing urgent. Every time her phone rang these days, her heart thumped loudly in her chest. On seeing the caller was her brother, the dread of impending news was a pounding rush in her ears.

"Hi, Alex."

"How's it going?"

Her brother's voice was warm and casual and she smiled. His tone reassured her there was nothing to report, no update on the search for their parents. For once she felt grateful for the lack of news on their disappearance. Even though she knew they were dead, and she needed this to end, she dreaded to hear the words that their remains had been found.

"I'm good! Any progress there?" She had to ask the question – it was a part of their daily conversation now – and she winced as she waited for his answer.

"Nothing new since yesterday. It's a huge operation, Anna – you should see the machinery and all the gear. It's really impressive – infra-red this, ultra-violet that, scanners, the works. The detective overseeing the search updates me as much as she can."

Anna exhaled loudly and flexed her neck from left to right, gripping the edge of her desk as she lowered herself into her chair.

"Well, that's good, I guess."

"Detective Neilson keeps reiterating that this might not be a successful search, that it's over ten years since Eastly and Evans buried their bodies and the whole operation is based on what they can remember. But it's a start and hopefully will lead to something."

Anna stayed silent, not trusting herself to speak just then. She knew it would be utterly heart-breaking if the search yielded nothing. And equally heart-breaking if it was successful.

"It's today you're finishing up work, isn't it?" Alex asked.

She could hear voices near him and rustling, and she sensed he was walking to a quieter area to speak to her.

"Yeah. I really think I'd be better off busy." Her chief super had insisted on her taking her annual leave. "How are you all? The in-laws getting used to you three invading their space yet?"

Anna understood that her brother's decision to temporarily relocate to Dublin was two-fold. In the first instance, he wanted to be near the search-site, the area the gardaí were focusing on to find their parents. They had both lived with the unbearable reality that their parents were missing for so long that the pain had become a part of them, like an unhealing wound their bodies had grown around. Now that they knew they had been murdered, and why, Anna felt strangely detached from it all. She had feverishly searched for answers, thinking they would be the oxygen to save her. But now that she had them she only felt the suffocation weigh heavier. She didn't know how Alex could bear to be so close to where this all would end – to stand with the detectives watching the painstaking process of trying to locate two bodies while preserving the evidence. She felt guilty for not being there with him, but she just couldn't make herself go. She knew he was working in the mornings, keeping his accountancy practice going, and liaising with the detectives intermittently, driving for over an hour to the search-site, hoping each new day brought them closer to the end of the nightmare that had hung over their heads for almost eleven years.

The second reason he had hastily packed up his family and moved in with his wife's parents was the threat Dean Harris posed. Alex wouldn't risk losing any more of the people he loved. While Anna moved in with Vivian in Blackrock, almost an hour-long drive away from her home in Kinsale, Alex took his pregnant wife and young daughter to Dublin, finally trusting that his sister could look after herself.

"Ah, Sam's parents are grand! Chloe is still loving all the fuss and Sam gets to put her feet up every night – it's working out great really. Chloe likes it at her new playschool – so far so good!"

"So you haven't outstayed your welcome yet then? You're very lucky Bill doesn't mind his son-in-law turning his man-cave into an office!"

Alex laughed. "No, he's cool with it. Hopefully it won't be for much longer though. Once we get back to Cork I'll come to the site at weekends if the search is still going on. Will you come with me?"

She swallowed, guilt reducing her voice to a whisper, and tried to push enthusiasm into her answer. "Of course."

"Will you visit Myles on your time off from work?"

Anna smiled. Thinking about her boyfriend always had that effect on her.

"No … he's busy working on a project day and night. He hopes to have time off soon though."

"Fair enough. You know where I am if you change your mind and want to join me here."

"Alex, I –"

"There's no pressure, Anna. *Um* … has there been any sign of Harris?"

The hard edge to his voice, one she had grown familiar with over the last few months, had returned. She knew Alex wouldn't return home until the man was in custody.

"Nothing. It's like he's disappeared into thin air. DS Ryan is freaking out."

"I don't blame him. Keep me posted, OK?"

"Sure. And … you too. Anytime."

He agreed and ended the call quickly.

All her pushing for answers had led to this. Searching online for names, asking Myles to dig deep using his work contacts and computer skills – he had helped them find the truth. It had led them to Robert Evans, a dying man keen to confess his sins. Yet Anna sometimes wondered if she had done the right thing.

She became aware of a presence beside her desk and she looked up into the eyes of Chief Superintendent Frank Doherty. His jaw clenched as he ground something between his teeth. His bulk towered over her as she stood up, pulling her jacket from the back of the chair.

"Are you finishing up now?" he asked.

"Yes, unless there's something you need me to do?"

He shook his head. Yet his mouth was twisted in the fashion of a man with something to say, and the red colour that was flooding his neck and face made him look increasing uncomfortable. Anna drew in a deep breath, her apprehension rising. As she opened her mouth to speak he silenced her with a meaty hand on her shoulder.

"You take care of yourself, OK? Rest and relax for the fortnight and I'll see you back here soon. And keep your wits about you, as the saying goes."

With a parting nod he turned and strode to the stairwell door, clearing his throat gruffly, his gaze darting around the room to each of her colleagues, daring anyone to meet his eye. Everyone kept their heads bent over their work until he was gone. When the doorway swung back on its hinges behind him, the staff in the room exhaled in collective relief.

"He's as weird as ever!" Anna's colleague Lauren hopped from her chair and pulled her into a hug. "This isn't fair! I'm barely back from my honeymoon and you're taking time off. I'll really miss you! Who'll bring me coffee every morning?"

Anna laughed and rubbed her friend's arm, then pointed out the window at the side of their open-plan office.

"Do you see that building, Lauren? It's called Victus – it's a coffee shop. That's where you can buy yourself a coffee for the ten working days I'm not here!"

They laughed together and Lauren hugged her quickly again, keeping her hands on her arms as she spoke. "Doherty's right. Rest. Relax. But ring me if your brother has any news, OK? And I'll be in touch if there's anything happening here with," she lowered her voice, "that pervert Dean Harris. But, to be fair, DS Ryan will have you in the know the second they find him, I'm sure."

"I really hope so!"

"It won't be long more, Anna. Life will go back to normal soon."

32

She pushed her glasses back into place as she returned to her desk.

Anna smiled at her fondly. She would miss her friend over the next two weeks – her steadfast optimism was something she had come to rely on.

A little while later, as Anna clocked out and pushed open the door to the reception area of the Lee Street Garda station, she smiled in surprise to see Vivian waiting for her.

"Vivian!"

Her friend's long brown hair was swept into a stylish bun, her jeans and knee-high boots under her long grey wool coat a more casual look than Anna was used to. Vivian had worked as a freelance journalist until last month. Her sharp suits and crisp white blouses were relegated to the back of her wardrobe in her new role, at least until she was in front of the camera. She was now an investigative reporter for a new production company, Banba Productions, and currently researching for a documentary series, working her way through stacks of paperwork at home in her apartment when she wasn't at her desk in an office block on the South Mall.

Her friend grinned. "I thought I'd surprise you. Dinner is on me. And maybe we could take a little walk first. I want to show you something."

Feeling curiosity edge out the trepidation she'd carried since the phone call with her brother, Anna wound her scarf around her neck and followed Vivian into the cool spring afternoon.

5

"What's so special about here?"

They stood on the flight of concrete steps on the east side of the Cork Courthouse on Washington Street. The building dwarfed them. Anna gazed upwards at the limestone columns and large sculpture resting on the pediment. She remembered her mother suddenly, and their conversation here a long time ago, shopping bags resting on the ground at their feet. Helen Clarke had pointed to the sculpture and told Anna it had been designed by a man named Thomas Kirk, and that it featured Hibernia, Lady Justice and Commerce. She gazed at it, shielding her eyes, unable to make out the scales held by Lady Justice in the glaring afternoon sunlight.

The footpath was busy, a rushing river of bodies wrapped in coats and scarves moving alongside them. Traffic hummed nearby, punctured by the occasional beep of a car-horn. Vivian stepped closer to Anna and when she spoke her voice was low, her tone grave.

"Here is where Bernard O'Meara died in 1977."

Anna turned to face her friend. "Why do I know that name? Is it a famous case?"

Vivian nodded, a gleam of excitement in her eyes. "It's the subject of my first cold case documentary for Banba Productions."

Guilt flooded Anna's face, her cheeks pink. Vivian had spent the last few weeks poring over documents every evening while Anna scrolled through her mobile phone, sitting beside each other on the sofa in Vivian's apartment, yet their focus was miles apart. Anna had been preoccupied with everything she had learned about her parents' fate, and almost nothing had been able to penetrate that.

A search had begun for her parents' bodies in the same week that Dean Harris had approached her niece Chloe, and Anna had silently brooded, carrying her fears into her nightmares each night. Vivian had told her the story of the murder she was planning to feature in the programme, even showing her the newspaper articles her new employer had commissioned to generate hype about the company and their new investigative reporter. Yet Anna had been existing behind a veil. Nothing could penetrate her worry about where Dean Harris might be, and what the gardaí would find in their search for two skeletal remains in a field off a narrow backroad near Portlaoise.

She felt ashamed now for her lack of interest in her best friend's new career.

"Vivian, I'm so sorry! I've been completely preoccupied and I … I don't remember much of what you told me about Bernard O'Meara. I feel awful!"

The wind had picked up and was blowing loose strands of hair around Vivian's face. She tucked them behind her ears as she smiled at Anna and rubbed her arm.

"Don't worry about it! I know you've a lot on your mind right now. And I'm hoping to distract you for the next two weeks."

"How so?"

"I need an assistant."

Anna laughed, a short burst of surprise, the sound drowned by the din of the passing traffic on Washington Street. "You need me to help you with the documentary?" She was a statistician, a data-collator for the gardaí. Vivian was the creative one, confident when difficult questions had to be asked and truth teased from hints and clues. Why would she need her help? Her laughter died in the air as she saw her friend's grimace, noted her eyes wet from the wind or something else …

Vivian placed her hands on Anna's shoulders and spun her around.

"You are now standing on the third step of the courthouse, which is where Bernard O'Meara drew his last breath. According to witnesses and the old Garda reports anyway. Paramedics were called but he died right here. Right where he was assaulted."

With her eyes on the concrete step underfoot, Anna felt a profound rush of sadness. She had seen enough crime-scene photos over the last three years to be able to picture the man's dead body lying on the steps. She pulled the belt on her coat tighter.

"What happened to him?"

"He was beaten to death. It happened on the 7th of November. Bernard O'Meara was an elderly man, he was seventy-one, and minding his own business when he was attacked."

"God, that's awful! Did he have business in the courthouse?"

"No, he was just walking by. He was a retired school principal, walking in the city while his wife and daughter browsed the shops. His daughter Eileen is still alive – she supports the documentary, she wants answers. He was assaulted by a young man in what is assumed was a random, unprovoked attack. He was beaten so savagely he died before he could be taken to hospital."

"That's horrible!"

"It really was. Crimes like that were much less common back then. We are used to hearing about things like this now, so much so that it barely registers on our personal radars. We assume it's drugs or whatever and move on to the next story. When I worked as a reporter, stories like this got a day on the front page, tops, and the next day, the pages were recycled or littering the streets. But this one was different. The situation was pretty unheard of, in the first place, and what happened afterwards gripped the public for months. It was a national scandal."

She bent down and rubbed her fingertips on one step, over and back, seemingly lost in the detail of all she had researched. When she stood up, she looked westward.

"That's when things got even more interesting. In one way, it was a second tragedy to befall Cork that day. In another, it was a huge Garda error that shouldn't have happened. The media reports weren't kind. Come on – I'll show you."

She linked arms with Anna and together they began to walk down Washington Street toward the Western Road. The gates of University College Cork were ahead of them on the left, Anna knew, but not yet visible. She had studied there for over four years; her qualifications in mathematics and statistics satisfying her need for reason, for order. She'd always thought it was the disordered frenzy of the weeks and months after her parents' disappearance that had set her on that educational path. Numbers were predictable – they did what they were supposed to, never presenting shocks or surprises. Statistics too; logic and reasoning appealed to her. It was *people* that were unpredictable – the story of Bernard O'Meara's death enveloping them as they walked was proof of that.

Vivian outlined the facts of the case to Anna, a grim story she recounted in a low voice.

"So, back to 1977 – someone called the gardaí and an ambulance and a young man was arrested at the scene, at the courthouse. Reports say he was estimated at eighteen, maybe nineteen years old, but he could have been younger. The Garda squad car pulled up as he was stamping on Bernard O'Meara's head."

"*Jesus!*"

"He was pulled off the victim and handcuffed. But, as he was being led to the car, he overpowered the garda and ran. Witnesses say he ran down Washington Street, onto the Western Road, and jumped into the river. They said he didn't resurface. There were a few passers-by and they stopped at the sight of a boy running from the gardaí and jumping over the wall, as you'd expect. But the witnesses interviewed were adamant he didn't break the surface of the water again. His body was never found."

They reached the wall that ran alongside this branch of the River Lee. Vivian stopped and rested her hand on it, where green moss grew between cracks in the cement blocks. It was cold and slick to the touch. They both peered into the river churning underneath them, rushing and galloping fast away from them. The water was brown, full of mud and debris dislodged in heavy rainfall over the last few days.

"Why on-earth would he jump, with his hands cuffed?"

"He had just murdered a man. I assume he was desperate to get away from the scene."

"So he drowned?" Anna asked, eyes still on the water. "I mean, he must have. He ran, what, three hundred metres in this direction and jumped into the water, with his hands cuffed." She looked back at Vivian, eyes narrowed. "Cuffed at the front? Or behind his back?"

A hint of a smile played on Vivian's lips. "You see, *this* is why I want your help. This eye for detail, for logic. Was he cuffed in front or at the back? Because it's a variable that changes things and, truthfully, I don't know yet. The Garda report is scant on fine detail and it isn't mentioned. But maybe it wouldn't normally be?"

Frustration borne of unanswerable questions edged into Vivian's voice. Anna realised she was searching for more than what information was available to her, needing to read between the lines of the reports on the crime to fully understand. Asking a friend, who was experienced in writing up and collating criminal reports for help, was a sensible move.

"Maybe a person could survive it," Anna said quietly, as though to herself. "He was young. He could have been an experienced swimmer. He could even have floated. What were the weather conditions that day?"

"It was cold, showery, nothing unusual for November."

"How did the witnesses describe the river?"

"The adjectives used by the witnesses include 'rushing', 'swelling', 'dirty', and 'full'. The Lee is tidal, of course, and at the time the boy jumped the water level was high, and it was brown with debris and mud, much like it is now. It was winter, there'd been a lot of rainfall."

Anna pinched her lips, lost in thought, and Vivian grinned.

"I can tell you're hooked on the story already! Let's get some dinner. And wine, on me. I need your help with this one, Anna. The deeper I dig the less confident I feel that I have all the facts. And there's a thought in my head that just won't quit – what if this young guy survived? It's a strong possibility. He could be still alive

– imagine it! He could be living in the shadows of the city all along. I want to find out one way or another if he's alive or dead. I want to interview people again, those that are still alive anyway, talk to some experts, really dig deep into this. There are so many unanswered questions."

They fell into step beside each other, walking back towards the heart of the city, in search of a cosy corner, dinner and a bottle of wine.

"I could use your logical brain on this one, Anna. There's a lot to go through, and I feel the answer lies in the boxes of documents I have at home." Vivian had made copies of what was in the office, going over and over the details. "I just … I need fresh eyes on this. Plus, I think it could be a good distraction for you."

Anna thought of her nightmares and the screams that woke her friend several mornings a week lately and had to agree she might be right. Her brother was away, her boyfriend working overseas … this case could take her mind off waiting for news, waiting to pass time until she felt she could move on.

She was intrigued by the mystery of the young man who had jumped into the river. What a desperate thing to do! Could he possibly have survived and be still alive, hiding in the city's shadows, as Vivian had said? She spent her days at the Lee Street Garda station immersed in reports on crimes across the city and county – it would be familiar territory for her to read through the data Vivian had and help her decipher the clues contained in it.

However, as they turned left onto the Grand Parade she eyed her friend suspiciously. Vivian was a skilled reporter. Only last month she had reported exclusive after exclusive on the "serial killers" terrorising the city, linking the facts faster than any other journalist in the press-conference DS William Ryan had run. He had called her a pain in the neck, and Anna had been surprised by the level of her friend's tenacity, at her dogged hunt for the truth. So why did she seem nervous now?

"So what's the other reason you want my help?" she prompted as she pulled open the heavy glass door at the entrance of their favourite restaurant in the Coal Quay.

Vivian ignored the question, waiting until they were seated with tall, shiny menus in front of them before she answered.

"You asked why I need your help ... to be honest, I think I might need your butt-kicking skills."

"Come again?"

Vivian grinned. "Those serial killers never stood a chance in your living room last month. And that detective you worked with, what was her name again? Whatever. Your Taekwon-Do skills are something I'm lacking and I think I might need them."

"But why?"

"Because someone sent me this." She pulled a creased sheet of paper from her handbag and passed it across the table.

Anna noted her friend's folded hands and tense shoulders, her apprehension flowing across the table in waves. Waiting for Anna's reaction, for her to confirm she was right to be scared. She picked up the small note and scanned it quickly.

Hell is empty and all the devils are here. Tread carefully.

"Whoever sent it didn't even bother with punctuation marks! I mean, it's a quote, for heaven's sake!" Vivian groaned in disgust. Poor punctuation was a major peeve of hers.

"Shakespeare ... *The Tempest*," Anna murmured, the paper shaking slightly in her fingers. The lack of punctuation was the least thing that concerned her. "Who sent you this?"

"No clue."

"Have you told anyone else? Your boss, or the gardaí?"

Vivian made a face. "I told my executive producer, Luke Daly. He said the company would look into it."

"Which means what?"

Vivian shrugged.

"When did you get this?"

"Yesterday. The day after Banba Productions ran that newspaper feature about me and the details of the documentary."

The newspaper feature Anna hadn't paid any attention to because she was so caught up with her own problems.

A waitress approached their table. Anna met her eyes and quickly shook her head. Not yet.

"So let me get this straight – one day after the company announces you're looking into the death of Bernard O'Meara and the disappearance of the man responsible, you receive a warning note? How was it delivered?"

"In an envelope to my work address, left in the mailbox on the building's outside wall."

"Postmarks?"

"No. Just my name on the front."

"It must have been hand-delivered. It sounds like someone is warning you off."

"Which is precisely why I need you to help me out!" Vivian said lightly, picking up the menu, her smile of relief easy and warm. "With you by my side I'll solve this faster, and safer too."

"I don't know, Viv … this seems dangerous."

Vivian reached across the table and grabbed Anna's hands.

"You know what it's like not to know the truth, Anna! That's the case for Mr O'Meara's daughter. We have a chance to end her pain, to find the answers to who did this! And if the killer *did* manage to survive the jump, he should be brought to justice! We both know the statute of limitation doesn't apply to crimes like this."

Anna thought of the men held in custody over her parents' death … yes, she understood what the family of Bernard O'Meara must be going through. She knew their longing for the truth, for justice, wouldn't have diminished over time. She raised her hand and beckoned the waitress over.

"Do you have clear plastic bags, like the ones used for leftover food? Yes? Could I have one, please?"

"What are you doing?" Vivian asked, as the waitress nodded and walked away.

"You need to get this to Lee Street. It's not ideal that you've had it stuffed inside your bag, but there might still be something useful on it."

"OK, I hadn't thought of that. See – you're helping already! I'll tell my boss you're involved but no-one else, I don't want you getting threatening messages too! That note proves to me someone out there knows something, something worth keeping hidden. Whoever sent it thinks they can scare me off. Well, I don't scare that easily! But I do know when I need to call in reinforcements! So will you help me or not?"

6

"What do you mean, gone?"

"Gone as in *gone*. Not there anymore. Left. Should I go on?"

Tom Gallagher hurtled the phone across the room and felt little relief from his anger as it smashed against the wall. His office felt claustrophobic now. The large oak desk seemed to be penning him in, the walls inching closer. He grabbed at his tie, not even sure why he was wearing it anymore, save to show the detectives he was better than them. Not rattled. In control. In a fit of anger he pulled at it with both hands until the knot was undone and he tossed it onto the desk.

He'd spent hours answering questions about his business, the same questions over and over, just worded differently, the detectives hoping he'd slip up. As if that would ever happen! Yet still they interviewed him, his solicitor insisting that this time he should cooperate, that thanks to John's actions there was nothing he could do …

John had practically handed the gardaí his father on a plate. For years Tom had evaded their scrutiny because nothing could ever be definitively linked to him – his club was legit, everything was properly accounted for, down to the last cent. To dig deeper could reveal a shadowy pool of filth and misdeeds, but no-one ever got to dig because Tom was always too careful to keep everyone at arm's length. It was how he had survived this life for over thirty years. It was a game really and he always held the top trump.

He was a businessman, nothing more, often persecuted by Cork city's gardaí when they needed a fall-guy. It was a story he almost believed himself. David, his younger son, had danced too close to the flame of attention each time he assaulted his partner Natalie. When her sister Kate had shot him, the family had come under extreme scrutiny. But the drugs and stolen goods remained holed away and too far out of reach. Business carried on.

But John … his older son had got involved in something that kept Tom awake at night, trying to comprehend the draw to it, the workings of the operation. Two killers had stalked the city for over a week, killing at random, disguising their appearance and filming the murders. The newspapers had reported that it was all done for money. A crime ring operating on the dark web, with John Gallagher at the helm of the Cork operation. John hadn't been named, initially. But as soon as the rags got hold of his identity everything changed.

"PROMINENT BUSINESSMAN'S SON LINKED TO MURDERS"

"CORKMAN RUNS ONLINE MURDER GANG"

The headlines had broken Mae's heart. Tom had banned newspapers from the house, hoping that shielding her from the worst of it would help somehow. But the damage was done.

There were few things in his life that had left Tom Gallagher dumbfounded, but his son's involvement in this was top of the list. It would have ended with the death of Anna Clarke – after interrogating her on the whereabouts of Kate Crowley, John had planned to make her the final victim – but things had taken a sinister turn. John had been shot. He survived, but remained in Garda custody, pending trial.

The house, the club, everything was turned upside down. Tom had to stand by and watch while the city's detectives rubbed their hands together in shared glee – finally, they could search the house and business premises of the man they had long-suspected of running a criminal ring around them. John had unwittingly provided the ammunition, and they would happily blow a giant hole in Tom's world.

But there was nothing to find. Dissatisfaction set in and questions kept coming, interviews his solicitor, Victor White, asked him to cooperate with. The detectives remained frustrated – there was no connection between Tom's businesses and John's crimes.

Tom wondered how long that would last …

He knew John was lucky to be alive. Shot in the chest, his youth and fitness had kept him breathing and allowed him to recover. Tom had learned that his intended victim, Anna Clarke, was probably the reason he was alive. She'd applied pressure to the wound and alerted the gardaí using a panic button. Saving her own skin, but still. Her actions had allowed Tom to speak to his son again, not to see him in the city morgue like when David was shot. And it allowed John to tell his father that he had recognised his would-be assassin …

Tom thought of Ely Murray often. Once his number two, the man who had killed on command, who gave his whole life over to Tom and never asked any questions. Like a true turncoat he had seized an opportunity – shooting John, cleaning out the safes and warehouses, leaving Tom with nothing but his reputation on the street in tatters, his life collapsing like a tower of cards.

The detectives were finally finished with the house. What hadn't been taken away in their small cardboard boxes had been returned to its rightful place. In a leather bound notebook in his desk drawer, one he was satisfied would stay hidden from prying eyes, Tom had written a list. There were several names on it, battling for top position. All had his wrath coming. When the nights were long and cold, his bed empty of his wife, his house empty of his sons, he took out that notebook, reread the list. It soothed him.

Ely Murray
Alan Ainsley
Kate Crowley

He thought about adding the name Anna Clarke to the list, but he remained undecided. To his knowledge, all she was guilty of was helping out a friend in need, Kate Crowley. Anna had saved John after all. And if the RTÉ news reports were accurate, she was familiar with the loss of loved ones … they had that in common.

The man leading the hunt across Europe for Kate Crowley had a smart mouth and a quick temper. Tom knew him only as Vinnie, a stupid cliché bad-guy name, if ever he heard one. It probably wasn't his real name, and Tom didn't give a damn. Vinnie was being well paid to track Crowley across Europe and, so far, he had been effective. He'd found her and her sister, and Tom's granddaughters. He'd sent photographs and waited on further instruction, because apparently hired muscle like Vinnie were unable to act on initiative. He had been told only to locate her and report back, so he stalked her through the streets, hiding behind his sunglasses and tourist attire, blending into the shadows cast by the Andalusian sun.

But as Vinnie had told him this evening, she was gone. How she had managed to give him the slip, Tom could only guess but, then, she had evaded his men on the streets of Cork before. He looked at the metal fragments of his phone lying on the floor and cursed. An outburst of temper was useless – he had built himself up from nothing by containing his rage. But it always simmered, a volcano waiting to expel its fire uncontained...

He pulled another phone from a drawer in his desk and sent a message to Victor White. Instructions to Vinnie to restart the search, and to spare no expense. Kate Crowley *had* to be found. *Again*. He had done it once, and she couldn't have gone too far.

A soft knock on his office door drew his attention and he grunted loud enough to be heard. Jessica, his housekeeper, opened the door a fraction but didn't step inside. He could sense her fear. Her large brown eyes were wide and bright, her hands clasped together over her blue buttoned-up coat.

"Will there be anything else, Mr Gallagher?"

His eyes roamed over her, over the fabric stretched across her chest and when he met her eyes he found he enjoyed the look of anxiety there.

"Nothing else, Jessica."

He smiled at her, the smile of a man who can take whatever he wants whenever he wants it, and she bowed her head slightly, turning away from him, her heels a quick snap on the tiles.

Tom pushed away from his desk as Jessica slammed closed the front door of his house. The clang echoed in the empty hallway. He walked slowly, aimlessly through the house, feeling restless. His club was closed – that once would have provided respite from his loneliness, liquor to burn his throat and dancers to watch and fuel his imagination. Now, he had nowhere to go and no-one to share a drink with.

He thought of Kate, how her actions had started the wheel of his misfortune to turn.

"Not long now," he spoke to the silence around him and flexed the muscles in his neck, rolling his shoulders.

If nothing else, he was an optimistic man.

7

The taxi journey to Vivian's apartment in Blackrock passed in a blur, the raindrops on the car windows twinkling from the glow of the city lights. They each sat silently, staring out at the night, the driver thankfully engrossed in a sports review on the radio, sparing them the usual small talk.

Anna thought about the note her friend had received. They had called into the station again after dinner. Lauren was working late and had promised to pass it on to the forensic analysis team. Anna knew a conviction could be hampered by how the note had been handled, if it ever came to that, but it was still possible to collect fingerprints and DNA samples.

Vivian had admitted she had discarded the envelope that had contained the note in a wastepaper bin beside her desk. The office cleaner had definitely removed it by now. Her producer had promised to deal with it, but Vivian didn't know if he had checked the building's CCTV, to determine if the post-box was covered in the footage, and to review the footage if it was. Anna advised her to escalate things to her boss, and to make a complaint to the gardaí. Vivian had frowned, reluctant to take that step.

"Just let me talk to Luke first."

When the taxi pulled up at the apartment block, Anna realised she hadn't thought of her parents or the whereabouts of Dean Harris for the whole journey. She was already gripped by the mystery Vivian had presented. Perhaps she *would* spend her annual leave from work helping her friend, to keep her mind off everything, if nothing else.

As Vivian paid the driver, Anna waited beside her, peering around at her new home. There were twenty-four apartments set in a crescent shape around a large grassy area. It seemed to her that every resident in the occupied apartments worked long hours; they had yet to meet most of their neighbours. The grey brick and white-pebble dash of the buildings were mostly set in darkness now, save for a few sensor-lights that illuminated the area sporadically. She imagined passing cats were setting them off; there was nothing else she could see. The lights of Blackrock Castle drew her eyes, like a guiding beacon in the darkness. It was quiet here by night – quieter than she had expected it would be, being so close to the city. After days of rainfall, the earlier bright shine had been welcome. But now, she dipped her head into her collar and hunched her shoulders against fresh falling rain. They hurried up the flight of concrete steps to Vivian's first-floor apartment, both tired now, heads bent low. The next-door neighbour's door opened a fraction as they neared the top step. Anna met Vivian's eyes and they both groaned.

"Evening, girls!" Dermot poked his head around the door, his porch light illuminating the dome of his bald head. "Been out late, have we?" His cat weaved between his legs before darting inside.

"Goodnight, Dermot!" Vivian said firmly as they walked straight past him.

Tutting and muttering, he glared at them and shuffled back inside his apartment.

"Trust me to own an apartment next to the nosiest man in Cork!" Vivian grumbled as she pushed her key into the lock.

They hadn't lived there long, but the man next door had already become a source of irritation, always seeming to open his door just as they were passing. They had been friendly to Dermot in the beginning – he seemed lonely and was a lot older than them – and they had expected casual exchanges, quick greetings and remarks about the weather, the way most conversations went with someone you hardly knew. Dermot had other ideas; his disapproving eyes roamed over them whenever they met, assessing what they were wearing, asking questions about where they were going and what they were up to.

As she followed Vivian into the apartment, Anna's phone rang loudly in her bag and she pulled it out quickly.

"Myles!" she answered, a grin flashing on her face. She darted to her bedroom and pushed the door closed. A wave of sadness pressed around her – it felt like a very long time since she'd seen him.

"Hello, you, how are you?"

"Hello you, too! I'm good. And I've no news. No update from Portlaoise and no sighting of Dean Harris." She spoke quietly, pulling off her coat, and sat down heavily onto the bed. "How's the project going?"

He yawned loudly and she pictured him stretching, lifting his glasses to rub his eyes the way he did when he was tired. She missed his bright smile, missed running her fingers through his curly black hair. A long-distance relationship was harder than she had thought it would be.

"I've another hour to go here."

"It must be close to midnight where you are!" Brussels – she thought – he was always pretty vague about where he was working.

"Ah sure, it has to be done. I'll ring you tomorrow for a longer chat, OK? But, tell me, what are your plans for your break from work?"

Anna thought of Vivian and the conversation they'd had over dinner but decided to keep this to herself for now. "Oh, nothing major – I'll probably spend some quality time with Viv." She quickly reasoned she wasn't lying – she would never lie to Myles – but rather sparing him from worrying.

After they said goodbye she stayed in her room for a little while, turning her mobile phone over and back in her hands. She missed him. She barely knew him but she ached to see him, to hug him again. Vivian was sitting on a patio chair on the balcony, a small space that jutted off the living area. Anna pulled open the sliding door and was momentarily speechless.

"Vivian!"

Her friend coughed in surprise and waved a hand in front of her face to disperse the nicotine fog before shrugging sheepishly. She brought the cigarette to her lips again and inhaled deeply.

"*Uh*, don't judge me! I've fallen off the wagon, OK! It's this documentary … anyway, don't worry about it, I'll quit again, I promise! How's Myles?"

"Fine." Anna stepped to the balcony railing and looked out into the shared concrete yard where the residents housed their refuse and recycling bins. It occurred to her that if anyone wanted to get onto this balcony, he wouldn't even need a ladder. He could just push the bins against the wall of the apartment below and climb up. Depending on that person's height they could easily hoist themselves up and over the metal railing … Dean Harris was taller than her by several inches, she was sure of it. He could easily …

"*Hello?* Earth to Anna! Are you with me?"

She jerked back from the railing and smiled, wrapping her arms around herself. Too many gruesome crimes in her life lately, too many reports typed up, too many nights worrying. She shook her head – enough! She needed to escape her thoughts.

"I was asking about Myles. What's an intelligence analyst, or whatever he does in the Department of Justice, doing in Brussels for so long, or will you have to kill me if you tell me?" Vivian rubbed the end of the cigarette onto the concrete floor of the balcony and stood up, stretching her arms overhead and yawning loudly. "Actually, don't answer. What Myles does for the EU is his business. I'm just glad he makes you happy. Come on, I promised you all the details of the case. Let's get more wine and I'll tell you everything I know."

8

Casares, Spain

Kate double-checked the details on her phone – the guesthouse was listed as two-star, but that seemed generous. Chipped floor tiles gave the ground a spider-webbed look, a suction sound as their sandals walked to the bed making her heart sink. The bathroom was separated from the main sleeping area by a shower curtain too narrow to cover the door frame. She recoiled at the stale tobacco and musty odour wafting from the curtains when she moved them aside to watch the street below. They could afford somewhere better – the money she had taken from David Gallagher was enough to cover their living expenses for two years at least, in far nicer places than this. But as the bus trundled away from the hilltop town of Mijas she had opened a Google search on her phone, keeping her head low in the window-seat, and this was the first accommodation listed with a vacancy in Casares. It was another beautiful, whitewashed, rural village, the type of place where she had once thought they could disappear. But now she knew she was wrong and they wouldn't be staying long.

Natalie had bargained for over an hour with Rachel to lie down and rest. The twins were long overdue a nap, but Rachel has resisted, her agitation at being confined to the small space of a bus for almost four hours palpable. She cried and fought until sleep eventually overtook her. But it was her sister Rhea that Kate was truly worried about – she walked quickly without prompt now, her green eyes flitting around them nervously everywhere they went. Even though Kate and Natalie had never discussed their situation within earshot of the girls, Rhea seemed to feel their tension. When a nap was suggested she didn't argue but turned her back on them all, her blue teddy bear tucked under her chin, and stared silently at the pockmarked wall until she fell asleep.

Natalie moved away from the double bed where the twins were sleeping and sat beside Kate on the bed they would share.

"What do we do now? We can't stay here. Can we even stay in Spain if the Gallaghers know where we are?"

Kate held up her hands. She needed Natalie to calm down, fast. But her sister was spiralling again – she began to sob loudly, gulping gasps of air, one hand at her throat as though to soothe herself, the other bunching the off-white bedsheet underneath her. Kate knew she should comfort her, should put an arm around her shoulders, anything. But she pushed off the bed, needing to be away from this space, this room, all this *responsibility*.

"Get some rest, Natalie," she said softly, picking up her small backpack. "I'll get some food and be back soon."

As usual these days, Natalie did what her sister told her to do – she curled into a ball on the bed, her fist at her mouth in an attempt to muffle the sound of her sobs.

Kate closed the door firmly behind her.

There was a café two streets away from the guesthouse, with tables under yellow parasols that offered a view of the winding streets around it. Kate sat outside with her back to the door and her eyes on the street. Her espresso arrived in a tiny white cup and saucer; the china cup rattled as she lowered it back into place after her first swallow of coffee. Looking at her trembling hands, she cursed under her breath.

Gallagher had found them. She had gone through so much to be here, to have Natalie and the girls safely away from David Gallagher, and she had never really thought his father would track her to Spain. The day she shot David was never far from her mind. She had no regrets. Even now, hiding here, waiting until it was safe, she would do it all over again.

Once Natalie wanted out of the relationship – and it had taken her far too long in Kate's opinion – she was ready. They had planned how to leave safely for weeks, taking David's ill-gotten money to fund their escape. By the time David realised what was going on and barged into Kate's house, Natalie and the twins were already on a flight to Paris and, when he threatened her, Kate had nothing left to care about. In the days after she shot David in her living room she had hidden from his family in hotels in Cork city … she had been terrified every waking second. Hiding from the Gallagher family, from the gardaí, she'd lain low in the city, resisting the pull of familiar places. The English market, where the wonder of the sights, sounds and smells had enthralled her and her nieces, had to be avoided. Too crowded, especially as Christmas approached. So too was the main thoroughfare, Patrick Street. No more window-shopping on Saturday afternoons with her sister, no browsing clothing stores and Waterstones bookshop, no chance to while away hours discovering treasures in the city library. Instead, her last few days in the city had been spent alone, walking hurriedly along narrow backstreets with her head down, desperate not to be seen.

Christmas in Cork city had come and gone without them. She and Natalie had an annual routine with the girls: a trip to Brown Thomas for hot chocolate and a new Christmas decoration for the tree, then to Santa's Grotto where the twins could shyly whisper what they hoped to receive on Christmas morning, before the annual pantomime in the Cork Opera House. They had even planned a trip to Glow in Bishop Lucey Park, to see the lights and the Christmas elves, before a ride on the Ferris wheel. It was easy to capture the magic of the season in the city.

But they had missed it all and now they could never go back.

Europe had seemed an accessible option for them and, far enough away from Cork, she had convinced herself they were safe. She'd been wrong. Their mother lived in America but it was a long time since Kate had reached out to her … she would only do so now if she truly had no choice.

She wondered how Tom Gallagher had found them, and how long it would take his men to find them again. And she wondered who had left her a message to run. Someone was on their side – could it be Anna? Perhaps her old friend was still trying to help. Her hands massaged the back of her neck, working at tension knots, her fingertips trailing the tips of her short hair. It wasn't so long ago that she had looked identical to Natalie, the same fiery red curls, same bright green eyes. Cutting and dying her hair had seemed like a good idea when she was hiding out in Cork, and it was still dark now, the curls dried straight each morning before frizzing again in the growing humidity. She had kept her hair this way – until she felt completely safe, she would not be *that* Kate again, the girl whose biggest concern was how to convince her sister to dump her loser boyfriend. *This* Kate was weighed down by the responsibility of her sister and nieces, of keeping them all alive. *This* Kate walked a little less tall, slept a lot less well and never stopped watching. If it was the price she had to pay for getting them away from David Gallagher, then so be it.

She watched the people moving between the café tables and on the narrow streets around her. Her breath came a little easier as she registered tanned skin and relaxed body language, clothing more suited to the warm Spanish spring evening – locals, or foreigners who had made Casares their home. She finished her coffee, her hands still shaking – that would take longer to remedy.

Back in the guesthouse she found the twins still sleeping. Natalie was awake, kneeling on the bed against an open window, staring into the space outside the hotel. Kate sat down beside her.

"What did you bring?" A white plastic bag rested on the blanket between them.

"Sandwiches and drinks. And these," she pulled a child-sized baseball hat and some clothes from the bag; blue shorts and a red T-shirt with a T-Rex roaring on the front. Natalie looked at her quizzically.

"They're looking for two women and two little girls. One of the twins has to dress like a boy. No more dresses and cardigans. They can take turns maybe. What do you think?"

Kate thought Natalie nodded but it was difficult to tell in the dim light. She was used to her sister not speaking much. The carefree, vibrant person she once was had been eroded by David Gallagher over the last few years, and she had grown quieter since they left Ireland. Not for the first time Kate wondered if her sister was suffering some sort of post-traumatic stress from all she had gone through.

"What about me?" Natalie whispered.

Kate pulled a bottle of peroxide from the bag.

"You go blonde. Red curls are too noticeable. We need to change as much of our appearance as possible."

She pulled a map of Spain from the bag and spread it on the bed. They needed a new destination, somewhere they could hide a little longer. Maybe somewhere they could make their home. Fear trickled along her skin like running ants and she scratched at them furiously. Gallagher was one step behind them, but she had to remember they had come this far. He may have found them yesterday, but tonight they were safe.

Tomorrow, perhaps they would run again.

9

Cork

Anna held out her hand for the glass of wine Vivian offered without looking up. She sipped it absentmindedly, her eyes on the manila folder spread open on her lap.

"These injuries … that poor man! Bernard O'Meara suffered an awful assault! And he didn't make it to the hospital …" Her voice trailed off, her eyes roaming the report.

Vivian was sitting in the grey armchair beside her, her legs folded underneath her, a pale-blue blanket wrapped tightly around her shoulders. A map of Cork harbour was spread on the coffee table in front of them, several files and scattered pages beside it.

"He had several broken ribs but the worst of his injuries were to his face and head. His jaw was broken, a cheekbone shattered, his skull was fractured in two places. He died as the ambulance personnel were pulling up at the scene." Vivian recited the man's injuries, the case clear and fresh in her memory, her voice soft.

"And it was definitely an unprovoked attack?" Anna closed the file, placed it on the coffee table in front of them and gripped her wine glass with both hands. The horror of the man's injuries was starting to make her feel very uneasy. It was a long time ago, and Vivian had said assaults of that nature were less common then – she was right. If Anna were to type up a report like this at work, she would assume the guilty party was high on some cocktail of drugs, or that it was a gang-related revenge attack. What else could make someone do such a thing?

"Witnesses at the time said Mr O'Meara was walking in the direction of the city centre when he was approached by a youth coming from the opposite direction. A young man, possibly in his late teens or early twenties. There were a few words exchanged and the young guy punched Mr O'Meara, who then fell backwards onto the courthouse steps. The young guy continued beating him until passers-by started to shout and yell, and one man tried unsuccessfully to pull him off. Two gardaí were on the scene pretty quickly, and then, well, you know the rest."

"Yes," Anna nodded, "he was arrested, cuffed, then overpowered the female garda and fled, later seen jumping into the river." She sat up straighter. "Could those witnesses have been mistaken? The ones that saw him jump?"

Vivian shook her head emphatically.

"No, it was definitely him and he definitely jumped. He was being chased by the two gardaí. People were literally stopped in the street, staring at them. Several people said they saw him jump the wall and into the river. There's no doubt about it."

Anna sipped her wine, thinking. Several eye-witnesses saying the same thing was usually taken as truth, and it didn't surprise her none of the witnesses were able to give a clearer description of the guy. She had observed it many times in the reports at work, and William Ryan had once called it the Bizarreness Effect, explaining that witnesses would often remember the more bizarre elements of the scene rather than the more common characteristics, such as what a person was wearing. In this case, the witnesses were sure of the man's actions but were so vague about what he looked like that Anna wasn't surprised a clearer image of the young man hadn't been generated.

"It was raining that day. Most of the witnesses were carrying an umbrella which could have hampered their view of what happened. They all described the man as young, tall, possibly dark-haired or wearing a dark hat or had a hood up. That's basically it!"

"No DNA evidence?"

"Nothing. No trace of the attacker left on the victim. Most of the damage he inflicted was with his boots, kicks to the head and so on."

Anna winced. "What about CCTV from the businesses on the street?

Vivian sighed. "It was a different time. What *was* available was so grainy that all that could be seen were moving bodies." Her eyes clouded, staring into the middle distance, her brows knotted together in frustration.

Anna could feel her friend's irritation at the lack of clear information. She leaned forward, setting her glass on the table, and began to study the map of Cork harbour. Vivian had marked a large red X where she believed the young man had entered the river.

"This map is quite comprehensive."

Vivian's eyes refocused and she sat forward too. "Yes! I hope to get real detail about where the current would have taken the guy, and maybe how he could have survived."

"You really think he could be still alive?"

"Well, he was never found. Bodies that enter the water usually do turn up. After I present the facts in the documentary, I'm going to focus on that element, the mystery: did the boy survive the jump into the water and, if so, where has he been all these years?"

She sat back heavily again and pulled the blanket around her shoulders, her fingers then fiddling with a slim gold watch on her wrist, a gift from her birth-mother.

Anna reached for a second folder, opening it to reveal photocopies and printouts of newspaper articles from the days and weeks after the killing. Photographs of the crime-scene and the point on the Western Road where the young man had entered the river were blurred, the lack of clarity reminding Anna of images from an old film reel. Her eyes scanned the articles quickly, skimming the detail.

"*Wow*, the press really went to town on this!"

Vivian's eyes were heavy with tiredness. "Yes," she said softly. "The journalists were obsessed with the story and with finding out who he was. One paper called him 'The Boy Who Jumped' and it stuck. He became a celebrity even though no-one knew his identity! Bernard O'Meara got lost in it all. It's sad really."

Anna placed the folders back on the table and studied her friend. She could tell the journalist in Vivian was hooked on the story – perhaps a little bit of the obsession from 1977 had seeped into her.

"What made you choose this?" Anna asked, "this series of documentaries. Cold cases, I mean. What made you want to dig into past crimes?" She thought she knew the answer.

Vivian looked at her apologetically. "I think, and I hope you take this in the spirit that it's meant, but it's something to do with being your friend all these years, watching you search for answers about your parents." She took a deep breath and smiled sadly, hoping Anna would understand. "Since we were teenagers, since they disappeared after the car crash, I've seen what that did to you.

Birthdays, Christmas each year, and the anniversary of their crash – I saw how you *needed* answers. I guess it's something like my own search for my mother when I found out I was adopted; wanting to know everything about the truth of my own life. So I think searching for the truth is the draw to this, hoping to find answers and bring peace of mind. Actually, I had a conversation with Bernard O'Meara's daughter Eileen a few weeks ago, and she reminded me of you."

"She did?"

"Well, she's a lot older, obviously! She's in her seventies now, but she was in her thirties when her father was murdered, and she *still* doesn't know by who, or why. She's lived with that all her life. The way you lived with the disappearance of your parents for ten years. Even now, even though you know the truth, you still don't have *all* the answers. I suppose I just want to try to offer Eileen and the extended O'Meara family an end to the constant questions, if I can."

She reached across the small space between them and wiped at Anna's cheek.

Bringing her hands to her face, Anna was surprised it was wet with tears. She smiled at her friend – she understood – but didn't say anything. Words seemed to be stuck in her throat.

Vivian rose and took their wine glasses to the sink. "Let's get some rest. Tomorrow I'll take you to Bernard O'Meara's grave. There's something else in the grounds nearby, something very interesting. Something that makes me sure this case needs reopening!"

10

Wakefulness seeped in slowly with the growing sunlight. The realisation that she had slept peacefully all night and hadn't disturbed her friend by screaming through her nightmares was a welcome relief for Anna. She had wondered if she might dream of the case, of Bernard O'Meara and the hooded young man. But she had slept deeper than she had in weeks – perhaps there was something to Vivian's theory about taking her mind off her own problems.

She had insisted Jason take the weekend off – he had a family of his own and, though she knew he wanted to keep an eye on her with Alex in Dublin, he relented. Still, the need to do something to release her physical tension was strong and she decided to run the Blackrock to Mahon route. The five-mile stretch alongside the river was popular with people from all over the city and county and was an added bonus to living with Vivian. Anna had taken to running it often when her head was full of thoughts she desperately needed respite from, and when her body felt coiled with the pressure of waiting on an update from her brother or DS William Ryan.

Even though it wasn't yet nine in the morning, the wide path was busy with joggers and cyclists, babies in buggies pushed along by parents keen to get in their step count before the day really began. She ignored the scenic harbour views, clear and calming in the morning sun, and kept her eyes straight ahead. She imagined there would be birdsong at this hour, and perhaps squeals from the babies and toddlers being pushed quickly along the route. But she needed to drown out any chance of thought filtering through and she secured her earbuds in place.

For the last ten years of her life her favoured music choices had been her mother's. If she were out for a run she would have listened to orchestral cello, Bach's opening strings drawing her back to her childhood. Once that sound had filled Anna with a warm familiarity; it was her mother's favourite of the classical instruments, the sound of it firmly encased in her memories. It had offered comfort, had kept her close to her mother in some way. Now she knew her mother had been an accomplished cellist in the Soviet Union, and had fled her father's control, disappearing from her family in 1978. Anna's father had been running from his past too. Now Alex stood for hours each evening in the cold, waiting for news that their bodies had been recovered. Now that she knew the truth, each time she heard the deep resonance of the cello she turned the music off – it was too painful. This morning she opted for a noughties-classics playlist and let her feet pound the concrete in time to the beats, her breath fogging in front of her face.

Vivian was up and brewing coffee, dressed in jeans and a warm wool jumper, when Anna arrived back at the apartment. Her eyes were ringed by dark shadows but, as she passed a mug to Anna, she grinned.

"You look fresh! And I think you slept well?"

"Very well!" As she blew steam from the hot liquid Anna sat heavily on the barstool at the breakfast counter. She had pushed herself hard this morning, stretching the boundaries of her fitness.

She felt revived and ready for whatever Vivian had planned for the day.

"You've time for a quick shower before we head to Bernard O'Meara's grave. I hope you don't mind a long drive? It's near Skibbereen. Just beyond it actually."

Anna raised her eyebrows. That could be almost two hours' driving, depending on traffic.

"Then we are meeting a former harbour master in the afternoon," Vivian went on. "I want some real detail about where a body should go, in theory, if you jump into the water. Christopher O'Callaghan is an old friend of my dad's. He was in the Navy, and after that he worked as a marine engineer. I couldn't get anyone from the Cork Harbour Commissioners to agree to speak to me, yet, but Luke is working on it. Christie is the next best thing."

"Right … sounds fun," Anna murmured, wincing as the coffee burned her tongue.

"Well, it's necessary, I promise. And tonight we'll liven things up!" Seeing Anna's raised eyebrows, she explained. "It's the Banba Productions official launch party, so you can get your glad rags on. By day, we talk death and despair!" She placed the back of her hand on her forehead and fake-swooned theatrically. "By night, we party!"

They rode the bus to town to retrieve Anna's car from the Lee Street carpark. The bus was busy, standing room only, and condensation on the windows obscured their view of the route into the city. When they alighted Anna inhaled a deep lungful of fresher air. The carpark was a short walk from the bus stop and, upon reaching it, her eyes scanned the space for William Ryan's Hyundai. It wasn't there.

"He'll ring you when they find Harris," Vivian said pointedly as she climbed into the passenger seat. "Try to focus on the job at hand – I need you at the top of your game!"

"Aye-aye, captain!" Anna saluted ironically and they smiled at each other.

Anna turned up the heating and rubbed her hands together before setting off.

"OK, here's the Eircode for the graveyard." Vivian jabbed at the buttons on the dash-mounted screen. "Shit, it doesn't look like your satnav can take those! I mean, I know the way of course, I've been there, but I'm not so good with giving directions!" Her voice rose, laced with panic.

"It's OK, it takes coordinates. Are you OK? You seem stressed out."

Vivian sighed and rubbed her temples. "I didn't sleep much last night, to be honest. I kept waking and thinking about Bernard O'Meara. In some ways, I wish I'd never started this. It's so awful, the details are horrible to keep rereading and I can't switch off thinking about it. But I can't turn back now, it's too late. Do you know what I mean?"

Anna nodded. She thought of the last few months, of everything she had learned about her parents, how she had pushed her brother to help her find the truth, had asked Myles to use his computer skills again and again … and she wished now she could turn the clock back and un-know the truth. In many ways, she knew exactly what Vivian meant.

Vivian looked around the front of the car, rooting through the storage compartment between their seats. "Have you any headache tablets in here?"

"Try the glovebox."

Anna's migraines were a plague she had suffered for years, ten years to be precise. Since her parents had vanished from her life. It had occurred to her the headaches might disappear now that the mystery of what had happened to them was almost solved, the pain of wondering almost over. She hoped her subconscious wasn't swapping the migraines for nightmares.

Vivian found a silver tablet packet and popped two into her palm, fishing water from her bag. After she had swallowed she exhaled heavily.

"Remind me not to mix wine and work-stress again – it's a pure myth one cancels out the other!"

Anna laughed, manoeuvring her car into the Saturday morning traffic. The city was always busy, the traffic a quick pulse beating steadily on the city streets. She eyed the map on the dashboard – her destination was a graveyard she had never heard of before, set beyond Skibbereen. As they waited at traffic lights on the Grand Parade, she turned the heat down a little.

"Have you heard anything from Gareth?"

Vivian shook her head. "Nope. He's still angry with me. And still not speaking to me!"

"God, that's so ridiculous!"

Vivian and her brother Gareth were both adopted as infants. A while back, both had made contact with their birth parents. While Vivian had formed a strong bond with her biological mother Brenda, Gareth hadn't been so fortunate. The woman he contacted was an old friend of his parents and wrote to him only once. She was glad he'd had a good life, was grateful to her old friends for adopting him and she wished him well. But she told him she had "no room for him" in the new life she had made for herself. He had taken it badly and, for reasons they couldn't understand, Vivian had become the focus of his anger. After months of taunts and angry outbursts vented in her direction, he had now cut off contact, refusing to speak to her.

Vivian turned in her seat now to face Anna.

"You might think this is crazy but I've been thinking – what if Gareth is the one who sent the warning note? Banba Productions have run a big marketing campaign about me, their 'shiny new star reporter', about the cold case documentaries and the O'Meara murder. Gareth is bound to know all the details, and I *know* him. My success must be driving him nuts!"

Anna shifted gears, looking at her quickly before turning her attention back the road and the moving traffic.

"You're right – that *is* crazy!"

"But think about it! The Shakespeare quote? He's doing a PhD in Shakespeare Studies with the University of Birmingham!"

"He is?"

"Yeah, he's doing it by distance learning. Mum told me. So, like, that quote is obviously familiar ground for him."

"A lot of people are familiar with Shakespeare. It's forced on us in school, remember, and it sticks! Even *I* recognised the quote, and English literature is not my strong suit. I really doubt your brother is sending you threatening messages, Viv!"

Vivian sat back into the seat, looking somewhat defeated.

"Well, it *could* be him," she muttered, so low Anna thought she could be talking to herself. She reached for the radio dial, selecting CD mode. The deep, mellow sounds of a cello filled the small space in the car.

Without a word, without explanation, Anna switched to radio, and their journey continued.

11

Vivian was brooding. Perhaps it was a combination of her wine-induced headache, the death of the man long-ago buried in the graveyard they were en route to, or a niggling worry about the threatening note. Anna left her to her thoughts for a while, concentrating on navigating the journey.

Skibbereen was a place she was familiar with, having travelled through the town many times with her parents en route to the ferry to Sherkin Island at Baltimore. She was more used to the winding backroads from Kinsale, used to being a back-seat passenger with her brother, listening to their mother outline the daytrip that lay ahead of them. She hadn't been this far west since they had died. Pushing her memories away, she gripped the steering wheel. She should relax, should focus on helping Vivian – the route from the city seemed straightforward, the roads mostly broad and even, their destination well signposted.

"You OK, Viv?" she asked after too long spent in her friend's uncharacteristic silence.

"Yeah, I guess so." Vivian shifted in her seat to face Anna. "Just a lot on my mind. A lot of pieces to slot into place in this puzzle. I can't get this case out of my head. I really need your help – with everything – including being my chauffeur!" She managed a smile.

"For which I am very grateful, thank you! This week we'll focus on interviewing witnesses."

"Are there many still alive?"

"Several, actually. There were some children on Washington Street that day, although I'm not sure what they'll remember. Still, Luke says it makes for good optics to speak to people that were there on the day and to hear their memories in their own words. I'm not hopeful of new information to be honest. I'm doing preliminary interviews with the two gardaí this week as well. I need to convince them to appear on film."

"Are they refusing to take part in the documentary?"

"Wouldn't you? Even after all this time, it's an embarrassing mistake. So far, one is reluctant and the other is completely refusing. They've agreed to speak with me, at least off the record, but I get the impression it's to get me off their backs. I'll have to try to convince them. Luke is keen to start filming soon so I need to get the interviewees on board and signing paperwork, fast. I'm starting to feel the pressure, to be honest. Carol said she'll help if I need it."

"That's your boss, right? See – I have been paying attention!"

"Carol is amazing – you'll meet her tonight. Are we nearly there?"

"Almost. Not long to go."

The sea was visible on their right. The roads began to narrow, flanked by overgrown ditches and small roadside bungalows. Anna returned her attention to following the map on her car and watching the signposts, and Vivian leaned her elbow against the door, cradling her head in one hand, lost in her thoughts again. As the approach to Skibbereen loomed closer, she sat up straight.

"We need to pass through the town and out the other side. Then it's just a couple of kilometres after that. But Luke said it's nearly impossible to find the graveyard. Blink-and-you-miss-it!" She peered out the windscreen, excitement replacing her earlier dense mood. They were almost there.

Eventually, after a turn-off to the left up a winding road that was best described as a boreen, the graveyard was visible, set off the road on their right. Anna pulled in slowly, bringing the car as close to the high stone wall as possible, concerned that it would protrude into the narrow road. She climbed across to the passenger seat and hopped out after Vivian, both happy to stretch their legs after so long in the car. Vivian circled her arms over her head and looked around.

"God, I'd kill for a decent coffee!" she groaned. "Where's a converted horsebox when you need one?"

Anna ran her fingers along the stone wall. It looked unsafe, crumbling in some parts with pieces of stone on the ground beside it. Even the sturdier sections were marred with cracks, some wide enough to push her finger through.

"How old is this graveyard?"

Vivian shrugged. "I've no idea. But Luke said there are some famine graves in here, so about two hundred years old, or even longer." She put her hand on the metal grills of a narrow gateway set into the wall. "Are you ready?"

The gate screeched loudly in protest as she swung it open. The graveyard stretched out in front of them in a wide rectangle dotted with faded and crumbling headstones. Several trees stood to their left, bare branches reaching to the sky. Two crows perched on one branch and squawked loudly before taking flight, disturbed by their presence. They met eyes, a giddy grin on Vivian's face.

"It's eerie, isn't it? I'm glad you're here with me, especially after that note from Gar – well, from whoever sent it. Luke and the camera crew were down here during the week – he thinks we'll do some filming here among the graves to add to the sombre tone of the documentary."

"Clever," Anna murmured, her eyes scanning the area ahead, though she thought the story was sombre enough already. An image of her brother, standing at what they hoped was their parents' graves, darted in front of her – imagined, of course – she had no idea what the field looked like. But for a brief moment she regretted her decision to help Vivian – how was trawling through a graveyard, searching for a killer, much different to what she had done lately to find answers about her parents?

Vivian moved ahead of her on a narrow pebbled pathway, overgrown grass and cracked headstones to their left and right. Something scurried into the undergrowth a few feet away from them, the grass shaking briefly, and Anna shuddered, walking faster to keep up.

"This graveyard is no longer in use – the County Council mow the grass from time to time but the area is largely neglected. His daughter Eileen hasn't been out here in over ten years – she's been in bad health. She was an only child and she didn't marry, so there's been no-one to look after her parents' grave. It's badly in need of some TLC."

They reached a single plot, a long dead pot-plant the only hint that someone had cared for it once. The grass was long overdue a cut and weeds along the nearby path spilled onto the grave undeterred. It was the headstone that saddened Anna the most – the words were so faded they were almost impossible to read. She leaned closer, and Vivian called out what she already knew was written there.

"'*Bernard O'Meara 1906–1977, beloved husband and father. Joan*

O'Meara, 1909–1981, treasured wife and mother.' That's it – not much of an epitaph. They were modest people, I suppose, but still … It's sad, isn't it?"

There was a lump in Anna's throat and she swallowed hard. The case felt very real now, seeing the name of the man whose violent death she had read about last night etched into the crumbling headstone. The wind whipped at her legs, ruffling the end of her coat, and strands of her short blonde hair danced in front of her face – when she pushed them behind her ears her hands were shaking. She felt the injustice of what Mr O'Meara had suffered, what his daughter must have gone through. She blinked water from her eyes as they roamed over the headstone, over the simple words on it, the record of a birth and death but little more. It remained an unsolved crime – she had experience with those. Her heart beat a little too fast for comfort as she crouched low and ran her fingers over the blades of long grass around the grave, silky smooth and still slightly damp from last night's rainfall.

Eventually, she stood up and turned to Vivian, who was watching her with her arms folded, her eyes curious.

"Are you in? Do you want to help me gather as much information as I can to bring this back into the public's memory? I know it's not exactly a relaxing way to spend your break from work, and there's no hard feelings if you want to walk away."

"No, I'm in," Anna said firmly, her eyes travelling the length of the small graveyard. "I want to help. Mr O'Meara deserves justice."

Vivian smiled, visibly relaxing. "The next time we come here we'll bring flowers and a clippers, tidy the place up. But after the filming. We want to jolt someone's memory and get people talking, so everything needs to look as bleak as possible."

Anna nodded and moved toward her, glad to be leaving.

"I think I've seen enough. Are you ready to go?"

"No, I told you – I have something else to show you." Vivian turned to the left and pointed, shielding her eyes with a hand. "Can you see it?"

Anna strained to see what she was pointing at and, when she spotted it, she walked quickly until she was standing right in front of it. She couldn't believe what she was looking at.

Another headstone. Engraved in the centre, the outlines of the letters blurred with time, was 'The Boy Who Jumped, 7th November 1977'.

"*What the hell?*"

"Exactly!" Vivian was suddenly by her side, bouncing on her feet. "Someone had this headstone engraved and erected, even though no body was ever buried here."

"Sorry?"

Vivian grinned in satisfaction. "You should see your face! And can you picture the viewers' reaction when they are reminded about this? It's been largely forgotten. This headstone was erected sometime in early 1978."

"By whom?" Anna stepped back. She felt this headstone was tainted, a mocking tribute resting so close to the victim's own. It was a thin slab of concrete, less sturdy than the others around it, and slanted ominously to the side, as though it had been haphazardly pushed into the ground.

"I was in touch with a representative from the County Council office," Vivian continued. "There was never any recorded application to buy a plot, or to erect a headstone. It just appeared overnight a few months after the murder of Bernard O'Meara.

Officially, it was assumed someone obsessed with the killer had it put here and, believe me, there were plenty of people in that category! He was like a celebrity, as I said. Eileen O'Meara tried to have it removed but, by then, there were groups of people obsessed with the boy, holding vigils at the headstone and so on."

"*Vigils?* It's unbelievable!"

"The press coverage of the headstone appearing overnight fuelled the obsession again. It was assumed the killer was local to the area, but that theory was abandoned eventually. The guards investigated but times were different and ultimately the fuss died down and it's been left here. Bottom line – we're no closer to finding out who put up the headstone for the killer. For The Boy Who Jumped."

There were many questions swirling inside Anna's head. It was clear to her that someone knew the identity of the killer, someone who wanted to commemorate the date he jumped. To his death? Or to a new life, one where he escaped justice? Few crimes were ever committed without witnesses, or without loved ones that suspected something and eventually figured it out, and many cases had been solved by the weight of a guilty conscience propelling those people forward. But erecting that headstone felt like *celebrating* the killer.

Vivian's obsession was contagious. Anna balled her hands into fists, her heart pounding. The truth of this case was close and she was determined to find it.

12

Tom couldn't decide what it was about the Crawford Art Gallery on Emmet Place that drew him back each week. It was a new interest for him, browsing the sculptures and artwork. Now he was going every Saturday to pass the time and to get out of the house, and out of his own head. He relished the peace inside the heritage building, the chance to gain perspective. If he was a deep thinker he would have pondered that the solitude there was a balm for the chaotic turn his life had taken, and that his soul needed this. Today, though it was busy, the air inside was tranquil, the energy in each chamber of the building soothing. People moved noiselessly through the rooms, walking reverently on the wooden floors, afraid to disturb the quiet admiration of those appreciating the art. There was respect within these walls, not earned, but expected nonetheless. That, alone, appealed to him.

He moved among the Greek and Roman sculpture casts on the ground floor, his hands in the pockets of his chinos. He couldn't pretend to appreciate such things properly – Mae could have educated him if he had ever accompanied her here. She had suggested it many times; to browse the art and have coffee after, maybe grab dinner before he headed to his club, the Oracle. But those days were over. He regretted it now, never indulging his wife in her interests.

So while he was without her he did it alone instead, and when she was better they would do it together, with their granddaughters in tow. The future Rachel and Rhea would enjoy would be filled with art and culture. Mae would like that – they could start over.

He moved through the rooms, up the wide staircase and into an area housing a variety of paintings and other works. He didn't pause at the information plaque detailing this exhibition but saw enough to know it reflected the darkness and light within a person. Interesting. If he had to categorise himself and his family, they would fall on the side of darkness. He had always been the bad guy. He looked like one too, if anyone cared to look close enough. Slicked-back dark hair, tall with broad shoulders, a physically imposing presence, with the eyes of a man used to knowing where all the exits were. A restless energy that kept him alive but made it impossible for him to ever live in the moment truly. Even now, dressed more casually than usual, relaxing in the quiet ambience, he found himself scanning the room, watching, waiting.

For what?

He was never sure. Last November had been the only time in over thirty years that his business had suffered a security breach so big his whole life had fractured. Things seemed to have spiralled since then, and all he could think about was taking back control.

As he walked slowly around the room, exploring the exhibition, he pondered whether someone being good or bad was all about context. If he was wrong to bring the men who mutilated his son to justice, so be it. Should Kate go unpunished for shooting David? For leaving him to die alone? Tom didn't think so. A man had to protect his family and all he had worked for. Such philosophical questions always came to him in here; perhaps it was the intellect and talent in the works, perhaps such things had leaked through to the very air inside the building and were infused into the visitors.

Or perhaps he was just going mad.

He looked around the room, observing detail, a habit he was well-practised in now. A family, the parents and three kids, all too young to appreciate the art around them, made a quick circuit of the artwork. They must be tourists to the city, he decided, keen to pass an hour. Two women whispered to each other intimately in front of one painting, their hands touching, and one giggled. A man walked slowly, his jeans too long and dragging on the ground, headphones over a shaved head. And another solo male, in dark trousers and jacket, his hands in his pockets, was standing a few feet away, a look of complete disinterest on his face as he stared at a large painting. That guy doesn't fit in here, Tom thought, and turned to go. But he stopped suddenly in the doorframe.

That man didn't fit in here one bit.

Tom moved back to stand beside the man, his footsteps soft and quiet. He was shorter than Tom and stocky, and he kept his hands in his trouser pockets, his eyes on the painting, yet Tom could feel a subtle shift in the energy around him. He was alert now.

"Do I know you, friend?"

The man wasn't surprised to be spoken to. When he turned to face him, Tom realised he was younger than him by about twenty years, maybe in his early forties. He returned his eyes to the painting and spoke out of the side of his mouth.

"I'm not your friend."

Tom placed his accent to the midlands, Tipperary maybe.

"I'm here to tell you Ely Murray sends his regards and wants to arrange a meeting."

One of the children from the family of five collided with the back of Tom's leg with a loud squeal. His mother grabbed his upper arm and yanked him away, her eyes darting to Tom's face as she prepared an apology. It never came. She recoiled in muted fear at his expression and bent to scoop up the child, rushing back to her husband, whispering urgently.

Tom barely registered that they were hurriedly leaving the room. He felt heat in his face, as though his skin were on fire, and a tremor had started in his hands. He fought to stay calm, relaxed, in control. It was how he had built up the business and how he always got out on top. It was how he was still alive, and he was damned if he would show the man beside him the effect his words had had. The effort of it now made his jaw tremble, but his voice stayed smooth and strong.

"Ah, Murray. Too yellow-bellied to come back to Cork himself so he sent a messenger boy?"

The man turned to face Tom again with an exaggerated, impatient smile twisting his features.

"He'll come – Murray knows there's nothing to fear in Cork. Most of your crew have deserted you and your son is about to do a long stretch."

"So why send *you* here?"

"He's a busy man. He wants to arrange a meet. He has a proposal for you."

"So he plans to repay his debt?" Tom's rising voice echoed on the walls and his eyes flicked about the room. A few heads turned quickly away as they met his eyes. He would have to contain his anger here, in public – a clever meeting-point.

Ely Murray had earned his place by Tom's side over three

decades, and shattered the trust placed in him over the course of one night. Tom understood he had been vulnerable – one son dead, another damaged – but Ely had pushed the knife in so deep, metaphorically speaking, it still took Tom's breath away. In many ways, Tom owed the man a pint – after he had robbed Tom there was hardly anything for the guards to find when they bullishly searched everything he owned trying to gather evidence of John's crimes. But Ely's betrayal would never be forgiven.

Understood, maybe, but never excused.

The man beside Tom now crossed his hands over his stomach, like a bouncer outside a nightclub. "As far as Mr Murray is concerned, he took what *he* was owed. He has formed an alliance with a family from London ... you know who I'm talking about." His eyes, like dark pebbles embedded in the flesh of his face, darted to left and right. "It's better for you that you know that. He wanted you to be aware that any attempt on him will naturally be taken by them as an attack on the group. He wants to make you an offer. For old time's sakes."

Tom licked his lips. Inside his pockets his fingernails were leaving crescent-shaped indents in the soft flesh of his palms. He was familiar with the British gang the man mentioned; they would have welcomed the cash and gear Murray provided to buy his passage in. The rumour mill reported that they were growing every month, moving more drugs into Ireland than Tom would ever have dared, and they handled any would-be aggressors in a manner more savage than his imagination could stretch. Murray and the men that had gone with him were better off being part of something with bigger ambitions; it was a smart move. It meant Tom couldn't touch him.

"I'm listening." Better to hear the messenger out, to gather all the facts. He could feel pain in his chest, as though his arteries were constricting. He subtly gulped a deep breath and stayed still.

"Murray wants Cork city. He's worked the streets long enough and he wants what's his. He'll expand into Munster from here."

The breadth of Murray's ambition was staggering, more than Tom had ever dared. He assumed the man had Dublin in his sights too, maybe Belfast. The details of the painting in front of Tom became just a blur, the colours blending into the cream wall behind.

"I must have misheard you," he whispered through gritted teeth.

"Murray is still respected among the men who chose not to follow him last month. He'll offer them a way back in, no grudges. It's time for you to step aside."

"Why the fuck would I want to do that?"

The man turned to face him, a Cheshire cat smile stretched across his face. He squared his shoulders with the confidence of a man with the winning hand.

"Because it's the price of staying alive. You give up Cork city and you'll get what John offered Murray a few weeks back – you get to walk away. He said he owes you that much."

Tom fantasised about gripping the man by the throat, squeezing with both hands until his eyeballs bulged out of their sockets, his tongue lolling to his chin … but he remained still, offering nothing but his silence.

"You're finished in this city now. Who'd possibly respect you after all that's gone down?" He spoke with patience, imploring Tom to be reasonable. With one thick arm he gestured around the room. "Art is a good move for you. Tap into the finer things in life now that it's time to retire. Spend some time with the grandkids."

"*Go fuck yourself*," Tom muttered, and embarrassment washed over him. Was that all he could do, throw swear words at the man? The guy was too young, too bulked-up for Tom to take on, and they both knew it. He had to stand here and take his pity.

The man stepped a little closer.

"Old man like yourself … sons gone, wife gone, business in ruins …" He leered at Tom, "There's a lot of people speaking your name right now. Only natural in our line of work. Grudges piled up over the years, men cautious to make a move before will be feeling a lot braver now. If it were me, I wouldn't wait like a sitting duck. No … if I were you, I'd get out of town while the going is good."

He walked away, didn't look back. Tom watched his stiff stride out of the room and looked around – he found he was alone. He exhaled all the air in his lungs and leaned one hand on the wall in front of him. Salty sweat trickled into his lips and he wiped his mouth with the back of his hand. The painting came back into focus … Tom kept his eyes on the red and blue detail in front of him and stayed there for a long time.

13

Christopher O'Callaghan had agreed to meet Vivian in a popular restaurant on the Old Bandon Road. He had explained in their telephone conversation that he was heading to Killarney with his wife for the weekend, and willing to make a small detour.

Anna's stomach rumbled loudly as they pulled into a parking space.

"I'm going to *die* if I don't get a coffee soon!" Vivian complained, pulling open the door for them.

Anna groaned, her back stiff from the drive back from the graveyard.

Vivian strode forward and paused, her eyes searching the busy restaurant. She recognised the man sitting at a table for four near the window and leaned her head towards Anna's, speaking quietly as they made their approach.

"That's Christie, over there by the window. And that's his wife Francine. Cranky old hag if I remember correctly."

They walked towards their table and Christie stood up to greet them. Anna guessed he was in his late sixties; he was almost fully bald, which made his long, thick grey beard more startling. His eyes twinkled as he shook her hand when Vivian made the introductions. He was average height, not much taller than Anna, and when he sat down again he tucked his large stomach awkwardly under the tabletop.

His wife cast her eyes over them and didn't stand or offer any greeting.

"Thanks so much for your time, Mr O'Callaghan."

"Ah, now call me Christie! 'Mr O'Callaghan' makes me feel old! How's all the family?"

"Christy, love," his wife interjected, looking at Vivian pointedly as she spoke, "we really don't have long. I'm booked into the spa, remember."

She returned to sipping a cup of tea and Anna couldn't hide a smile as bright red spots appeared on the man's cheeks. He was beginning to remind her of Father Christmas.

A waitress appeared and deposited menus on the table. Aware of Francine's eyes on her, Vivian pursed her lips and gave an exaggerated sigh, her eyes roaming over the menu.

"Now, what … will … I have …" She drew each word out slowly and Francine squirmed in her seat, her eyes on her husband.

"I'll have a toasted special, Viv, they do a nice one here," Anna said, then excused herself to go to the bathroom. The display Vivian was putting on was hilarious, but the morning had been long, and she needed a few minutes to herself.

In the mirror she examined her face critically as she washed her hands. Had she always been this pale? Her brown eyes usually looked too big for her face; now they were underlined with dark circles resembling grooves carved in stone. She was reminded of the headstones in the graveyard they had left behind over an hour ago and she looked away from her reflection. Drying her hands quickly, she pulled her mobile from her jeans pocket and typed a message to Alex.

Anything?

His reply came immediately.

Not yet. All OK?

All good. Say hi to Sam & Chloe for me xx

Back at the table Vivian informed Anna she had ordered for them both.

Francine looked sourer than before. Vivian had spread the map of Cork Harbour on the table, leaving the other woman only the edge to balance her cup. She sighed in exaggerated patience as both Vivian and Christie leaned over it, his finger tracing lines to the left and right.

"So, you're saying he entered the water here, on the Western Road? The Naval Diving Unit weren't long operational then, but they would have been called in. The Search and Recovery Unit."

"Yes, that's right. There was a report from them included in the files, but I don't fully understand the terminology. Can I forward it to you? You might be able to explain it better to me."

"Of course! Send it on."

He called out his email address, which Vivian wrote quickly on the edge of the map.

"Thank you! So anyway, the bottom line is a body was never found."

"Right. Well, it's pretty straightforward. If a person entered the water here it would normally go downriver, and that's where the search would concentrate."

"Obviously," Francine muttered.

"The two branches of the River Lee join up here," he slid his finger along the map, "just beyond the city by the Port of Cork, and that would have been searched extensively. Bodies are often found around those quays – they can get caught in the uprights. Of course, a body could continue downriver, past Páirc Uí Caoimh and onwards. There are multiple places it could get stuck or it could be carried out into the harbour."

Anna shuddered. His tone was matter-of-fact, despite the nature of the details. She wondered if his knowledge had been learned the hard way.

"All those areas were comprehensively searched," Vivian said. "I mean, the guy was a killer, they *had* to find him. But he was never recovered. Does that mean he survived? *Could* he have?"

Christie sat back and scratched at his chin beneath his beard, his eyes on the car park outside. The waitress brought their coffees and a jug of water, holding the tray aloft with a quizzical expression. Vivian quickly folded away the map and dropped it into her bag beside her chair, reaching gratefully for the mug of coffee.

Christie turned back to them, nodding his head slightly. His wife sipped her tea quietly and watched him.

"It's possible he survived the jump," he said.

"I *knew* it!" Vivian thumped the table, making Francine jump.

"He was a young man, probably fit." Christie carried on, "There's nothing dangerous about jumping into a river, per se. Think of it as jumping into the sea from a rock or diving board."

"But he was handcuffed," Anna interrupted.

"Ah," Christie nodded, "that'd be a problem, for sure."

"Surely the current would have taken him?" Francine interrupted. Her interest in this case was growing, despite her earlier indifference and her appointment in the spa.

He smiled at her. "From what you've told me, Vivian, the water level was high and no-one saw him emerge from the water after he jumped. People would have been scrambling to the wall, yes? Gardaí and anyone on the street? So assuming he *did* survive, then we have to agree the current bore him away, out of sight."

"And then?" Vivian prodded.

"And then, who knows?" Christie folded his hands on top of his stomach as he gathered his thoughts. "I remember it – opinion was divided across Cork on whether he survived. He was young, running from arrest, fired up. I think luck could have been on this guy's side."

Anna shook her head. "In handcuffs though? And was he handcuffed to the front or back? That's the part that bothers me most of all."

"Front or back? That would make a significant difference, of course. I can't help you there. But I'm sure you two will get to the bottom of it. It's certainly intriguing!"

The waitress returned with Anna's toasted special and a chicken wrap for Vivian.

"Very interesting, girls. But we really have to go." With a nod to Christie, Francine signalled the lunch was over. They stood up in unison and Christie reached to shake their hands again.

"Well, this has been very interesting! Thanks for consulting me. I enjoyed that! And do let me know how it pans out. I'll help with that report too, so email it on. Lunch is on me now, no arguing."

Then they were gone and Anna moved to the other side of the table, to the seat vacated by Christie, where there was more space, pulling her plate with her. She observed Vivian closely as they ate, noting her friend looked more confused than before they had arrived.

"What do you think?"

"I think the Boy Who Jumped is still alive. It's ridiculous, I know, but ever since I started looking into this I've been sure he could have made it."

"With his hands cuffed?"

"Yes, yes, I *know*, but where's his body? I know not all bodies are recovered but the chances are higher the earlier the search begins, and this began immediately."

"So let's say we work on the assumption he's still alive. That he survived the jump and he got on with his life, evading the gardaí and getting away with murder. How do we prove that?"

Vivian grinned. "I love that you said *we*! I think we start with interviewing the gardaí that arrested him at the time. We start with Patricia O'Brien on Monday morning. She's the female garda he overpowered before running towards the Western Road and jumping into the Lee."

Perhaps then things would become clearer.

14

As the evening wound into darkness and the city was illuminated by a clear bright sky, bodies weaved in between cars, snaking their way towards St Patrick's Street in the city centre, to the clubs and bars. William watched it all, his head angled to peer out the windscreen while he sat waiting for the lights to change. The city still felt alien to him. He wasn't yet a full year living in Cork, but lately his trek around the city was helping increase his familiarity.

Beside him Detective Garda Grace Thompson flicked through a notebook on her lap, recapping the Garda reports on the search for Dean Harris. Her dark hair was pinned off her face into a low bun, her eyebrows knotted together over serious grey eyes that scanned her own handwriting. She had pushed the passenger seat back as far as it would go, and her long legs were angled to the side as she tapped the page with her pen.

"One possible sighting in Douglas at lunchtime today that turned out to be a mistake. Other than that, *nada*. Neighbours are gunning for him, disgusted to have 'his sort' in their respectable estate – three different residents have rung the station offering to assist in the search for him."

"Anything concrete from that end?"

"No, but we're grateful to anyone that'll keep an eye out, the usual line. Clearly, several of his neighbours would only be too happy to make a citizen's arrest. His alarm-installation company, if you could call it that, is wound up. He had no employees, so everything there has just stopped."

"How's his mother holding up?"

"Remember how frantic she was at the beginning, telephoning the station every day? Now she seems to have gone quiet."

"Is that so?"

There were gardaí outside Mrs Harris's house twenty-four hours a day, every day since Harris had disappeared; her house was considered secure. Yet William was intrigued by her silence now, when once she had harassed him to find her son and help him prove his innocence.

"She doesn't get out much at all. She's getting her meds delivered from the chemist. That was arranged by her sister in Upton. Shopping comes once a week, delivery arranged by the same sister. No-one's walking the dog though."

"That's it?"

"That's it."

"He has to be *somewhere*." William moved the car forward when the lights changed to green, at a pace far slower than usual. "Town's quiet for a Saturday night."

"It's early yet."

The journey down through the main shopping thoroughfare was uneventful, just the car behind them beeping in frustration at their leisurely pace. William drove on, cruising slowly down Grand Parade, watching the crowds clustered by the fountain and near the city library. He was certain the man he hunted wasn't among them. He drove on to the South Mall, the speedometer never climbing higher than twenty kilometres. There were people standing in groups, talking and smoking, dressed in the heels and designer trainers and jackets he associated with the club scene. His eyes scanned over them quickly – Harris was not among them, but then he hadn't expected him to be. They stopped again at the end of the South Mall at a red light, and he turned to the right, to a cluster of drinkers gathered on wooden benches. All men, all middle-aged, but none of them Harris, he was sure of it.

"Colin has exhausted the search of the city hostels." Grace was reading from her notebook again, "and he thinks we should look at known squatting houses next." She was watching the left-hand side of the South Mall as she spoke, at the still winter-bare trees outside the tall, multi-storey offices.

Detective Garda Colin Forde was working extra hours to show Harris's photo at as many hostels and guesthouses as he could.

"It makes sense to me," said Grace. "Harris is a public face for all the wrong reasons. He needs to lie low. Plus he's not touched his bank accounts since he disappeared. Granted he could have had his pockets stuffed with cash but I still think he needs to stay out of sight."

"I agree with you there," William said, accelerating again. "Any sign at all at his own place?"

"Nope," Grace said with some relish. "That house is off-limits for him! The windows have been smashed in at the front and someone graffitied the word '*rapist*' onto the front door. There's a squad car outside as usual but nothing is moving. His own work van is still in Garda custody, even though the evidence is long since collected from that. He doesn't have a car as far as we know and his mother doesn't have one either, so wherever he is, he's on his feet."

"Well, my money's still on the mother. Harris is the type of man who'll drift back to his comfort zone when he can."

"But we've had gardaí camped out outside her house for days. The house was searched. He's not there."

William's blue eyes glinted in the half-light inside the car. "I'm going to pay her a visit."

"Now? She might be in bed!"

"She's not that old. What did the file say again?"

"Eighty-three."

"It's only eight o'clock. Maybe she's watching the Saturday-night movie. And trust me, she's sprightly for an octogenarian! I'll drop you back to the station for your car – I'm aware your shift ended an hour ago."

"No chance!" Grace grinned at him and the car finally picked up speed. "You're not leaving me out of this."

15

Mrs. Ursula Harris lived in Ballincollig. Lying west of Cork city, it was once a small village. Now a well-populated suburban town, they reached it in less than twenty minutes and navigated the maze of housing estates until they found her home.

As William pulled up behind the parked car in which two plainclothes gardaí were sitting, he watched the house. Mrs Harris's pristine home was starkly different to the unkempt house with a faded blue front door that was her son's. The estate comprised of two rows of bungalows separated by a narrow road. The cars parked in the driveway and on the surrounding kerbs were no more than a couple of years old, or new. The front lawns were small rectangular blocks, so neatly trimmed that William could picture retired men and women on their hands and knees with pairs of scissors. And they were *all* retired – he had checked. By default the place had become a retirement estate. It was perfect – near a chemist's and a doctor's surgery, and within walking distance of a large grocery store. The bungalows were small and had two bedrooms – ample room to hide an errant son.

William knew Mrs Harris's house had been spruced up lately. The brown wooden door had been recently varnished, the windowsills painted – Dean keeping himself busy while out on bail. His efforts had been noted in the daily Garda report.

Grace climbed out of the Hyundai first and approached the two gardaí, exchanging a few words through the driver's side window. A damp mist had descended and William saw her shiver, her white blouse and grey trousers not enough to keep out the cold. She came back to his car and leaned through the open passenger window.

"No sign of Harris all day. And the old lady hasn't budged."

William nodded towards the house, where the white net curtain was dropping back into place. "Might as well go say hello. She knows we're here anyway."

"Pass me out my blazer, will you?"

It took two rings of the doorbell and a firm round of knocking before Mrs Harris opened the door. William was again taken aback by how tiny she was. His tall, lean frame, suited and in a dark overcoat, always gave off an austere impression – he knew it could be off-putting. He offered her his warmest smile as she leaned back to look up at his face.

"Mrs Harris, I'm Detective Sergeant William Ryan, remember?" He held up his ID card, "We've met before. This is my colleague Detective Garda Grace Thompson. May we come in?"

"Is this about my Dean? Have you found him?"

"Not yet. But we have a few more questions for you."

"At this hour?" She peered around them through thick glasses, out into the dark night, at the gardaí sitting in the car outside, at the neighbouring houses. Indecision furrowed her brow and she drew in a sharp breath that rattled between her teeth. She was dressed in black trousers that were several sizes too big, sagging at the thighs and knees. To William it looked like she was wearing at least two jumpers. The house was warm, though; he could feel the heat from their position at the front door.

Mrs Harris sighed, seeming to decide she had little choice. "I suppose you'd better come in." She stepped aside, before gesturing to Grace, "You'll catch your death. Don't you have a coat, love? What is wrong with young women these days? You never wear enough clothes."

Grace shrugged at William as they stepped inside. The hallway was narrow, with a luxuriously fluffy grey carpet that half-swallowed their shoes.

"In here," Mrs Harris gestured.

William had been there twice, searching for any clue she might be able to offer as to Harris's whereabouts. He stood back and let Grace go into the sitting room first, a smile playing on his lips, waiting for her reaction.

"*Holy Christ!*" she muttered under her breath.

"Indeed," he answered softly.

The room was narrow and long and stiflingly cluttered with religious paraphernalia. A large crucifix was dominant on one wall, while the cushions on the three-seater couch featured crocheted images of the Holy Trinity. A statue of the Virgin Mary stood on a wooden sideboard at the other end of the room, brown rosary beads hung around her neck, flickering candles casting an eerie glimmer at her feet. Pictures lined the walls, of Dean at various ages and of images from the Gospels – Jesus carrying the cross, his resurrection – and a large photograph of Pope John Paul II. Most bizarre of all, in William's opinion, was the framed and signed photograph of Kenny Rogers that hung over the fireplace. He watched Grace turn, wide-eyed, and when she mouthed *What the fuck?* he decided she'd had enough time to look around.

"We're interrupting the movie. We won't keep you long, Mrs

Harris. I see you're watching *Mamma Mia.*"

Mrs Harris bent to pick up the TV remote. "I don't know how to pause it – Dean would have done that for me."

"Here, let me." William took it gently from her and paused the film. "We'd like to ask you a few questions."

"So you said! You may's well sit down."

A fire blazed in the hearth and, though the heat was welcome at first, William soon began to feel damp patches under his arms and on his back. He stood, peeled off his overcoat and folded it beside him on the armrest of the small sofa.

"Just to clear a few things up," he said with a smile.

"Again? Haven't you asked me enough? Well, I have a question for you! Why haven't you found my Dean? He must be cold and afraid out there!"

She lowered herself into a brown upholstered chair, pushing a cushion bearing the words "*Jesus Is Risen*" to one side. Pulling her glasses off, she wiped them with a tissue from her trouser pocket. She looked frailer without them, her cloudy eyes completely unfocused. When she put them back on, she seemed to suddenly realise she had company, patting her sparse white hair and straightening her lavender woollen jumper.

"We continue to search for Dean, Mrs Harris," Grace said, sitting down beside William. "Have you had any contact from him?"

"Of course not! I would have rung you if I had. I promised, didn't I?"

William didn't believe her and he was long past caring about upsetting anyone. "I think you're lying, Mrs Harris. A mother wants to protect her son – but, believe me, the best place for Dean is in Garda custody." He felt Grace's eyes on him and sensed her questioning his tone – he wasn't normally hostile, but he was tired of the lack of progress here.

Tears glistened behind Mrs Harris's glasses and she swallowed a few times before she could answer.

"I've told you, and Dean has told you, but nobody will listen! He's an innocent man! He's terrified of jail – can you blame him for running away? Inside that prison with all sorts of criminals – Dean is a good man, a kind man!"

"I'm sure he is, Mrs Harris," said Grace, her tone soothing, "but all this can't be straightened out without him. So we need him to cooperate."

Mrs Harris turned her body in the chair to face Grace exclusively, warming to the "good cop" in the room, casting derisive eyes over William before she spoke. "And then you'll help him to clear his name?"

"It looks bad for him to have broken his bail conditions," Grace answered. "If he comes in, we can work towards finding the truth. You understand that, don't you?"

Mrs Harris nodded, her hands clasped in front of her, her fingers working a phantom set of rosary beads.

William watched the rapport develop between the two women and thought he should have brought Grace here before. The older woman had clearly taken to her, whereas she remained firmly distrustful of him. He didn't blame her – he had tried to remain professional, but at this point he couldn't keep his impatience beneath the surface.

A yapping sound from the hallway broke the silence and Mrs Harris rose with surprising agility to open the door again.

"Beauty!" she exclaimed as a white ball of fur bounded past her and onto the chair, her tiny paws circling around the seat until her owner scooped her up and sat back down. She settled the dog on her lap.

"Beauty misses her walks, don't you, girl?" The dog licked at the woman's lips.

Grace reached a hand across to Beauty, who began to bark again, but then stopped as she petted her soft fur.

"So, Mrs Harris, you've had no contact from Dean whatsoever? No request for money, no telephone calls?"

"I told you, no!"

"How are you managing for groceries?" Grace asked, still stroking the dog's head.

"My sister looks after me now that Dean's not here."

"And your sister has looked after your prescriptions from the chemist too, hasn't she?"

The woman's eyes narrowed and she pulled the dog from Grace's reach. "Are you spying on me? I don't see what my shopping and medicine have to do with Dean running away. And he only did that because *you* scared him!" Her eyes were blazing behind her glasses as she turned to William.

"Dean approached the niece of one of his victims."

"*Alleged* victims. I know the law, Detective!"

"Mrs Harris, could I use your bathroom?" Grace asked suddenly, her voice light and sweet, keen to interrupt the rising heat in the conversation.

"What? *Uh*, yes, of course, it's just down the hall on the right." Her fingers burrowed into the dog's fur. She looked frightened, harassed.

Grace left the room, closing the door behind her. She moved

quickly through the hall as William's baritone echoed around the small house, asking the same questions as before, changing the words but the meaning the same – *Where is Dean?* Grace felt the man was bordering on obsessed. Even when grabbing some lunch in town, his eyes never stopped searching the streets, though it was obvious that Dean Harris would stay as far away as possible from Cork city. Whether he had ventured back to the suburbs, to his mother, was something she wasn't convinced of.

Grace found the house small to the point of claustrophobic: the short hallway, the bathroom very close to the kitchen, which was bathed in darkness, and two small bedrooms, one to the left and one to the right. She turned on the bathroom light and stepped inside – shower, with the curtain pulled closed, a pale-blue toilet and sink, with a handrail fitted beside it. Splashing some water on her face, she felt a little sorry for Mrs Harris, alone in the house, knowing her son had attacked many women, even though she refused to acknowledge the truth. Grace couldn't help but pity the woman's situation. At least she had her dog, she mused, and then she stopped, her hand on the tap.

Beauty.

Why had Beauty been so quiet for their entry into the house and for the first few minutes of their conversation? Grace had two Labradors at home, and the first thing they did was announce whenever someone was at the door. And Beauty was a yappy breed. It didn't make sense. Unless she hadn't been inside the house at all . . .

She left the tap running and turned to the shower curtain. Odd to keep it drawn closed when the shower wasn't being used. It was pink, with tiny yellow ducks here and there, more suitable for a child's bathroom. The running tap drowned the sound of her rapid breathing as she reached out a shaking hand and pulled it quickly back.

Nothing.

Had she really expected Harris to be hiding behind it? Yes, she realised with a sharp exhale, she now expected he was in this house, somewhere. Mrs Harris might look frail but she was sharp. She would never let them search without a warrant, certainly not because a dog hadn't barked when Grace thought it should. She had to search *now* while she had the chance ...

Leaving the tap running, she stepped from the bathroom and closed the door softly. William and Mrs Harris continued to speak in the sitting room at the front of the house, their voices a muffled comfort. She stood in the hallway and listened ... aside from the hum of the refrigerator a few feet away, and a clock ticking somewhere, the back of the house was quiet. She moved quickly into the bedroom on her right and found the light switch, flicking it on.

Compared to the sitting room, this room was sterile. A single bed with a cream quilt and pillow, a wooden wardrobe and bedside locker. A small crucifix hung over the bed, but otherwise the room held no personality, no personal touches. She bent down – underneath the bed was clear, just dust balls and a pair of black shoes: men's, Size 11. The wardrobe was half-empty, some hangers swung idly but others held an array of dark-coloured shirts, folded trousers and denim jeans on the shelf overhead. Grace turned to the bedside locker. The first drawer contained a brown leather book, a crucifix printed in the centre. She picked it up, flipped through the pages – a book of prayers. Inside the cover in blue ink was written in childish handwriting,

This is the property of Dean Harris.

She placed it back and quietly closed the drawer, turning off the light as she left the room. In two steps she was in the kitchen and snapped on the light: it was small, neat, and empty. She turned her back on it and entered the second bedroom, the one across the hall from Harris's own room.

This bedroom belonged to Mrs Harris. A large painting of the Sacred Heart over the bed drew Grace's eyes immediately after she turned on the light. The bed had the same cream bedding but the bedside locker was covered in religious medals and books, as well as several Mass cards. The locker drawers contained rosary beads and other bits and pieces of jewellery, but nothing that stood out as of any interest. Riffling through the contents of a chest of drawers revealed nothing but underwear and old birthday cards. Underneath the bed seemed to be where Mrs Harris stored shoes and assorted boxes. Grace figured she didn't have the time to search through them and straightened up, reaching a hand out to open the wardrobe door.

The door opened in the middle, to the left and right. She pulled the brass flowered handle and opened back the first door to the right. Sleeves of jumpers and blouses shifted lightly in the stirred air and she touched them, pushing two aside, her left hand on the other door handle.

Suddenly, before her body could react, there was a face above one sleeve, dark eyes that were strangely vacant under thick eyebrows, a mouth twisted in a silent snarl. A fist connected with her throat and Grace recoiled backwards onto the bed as a dark shape leapt from the wardrobe. A man. Her hands on her burning throat, her lungs on fire as she tried to scream, Grace rolled off the bed, onto her hands and knees on the carpeted floor. She gasped frantically for air as she became aware suddenly of a shape beside her and the sound of rattled breathing, deep and heavy. And more sounds, welcome sounds – frantic barking, loud yelps and scratching on wood. William's voice grew louder and closer, and Mrs Harris's rose in protest.

She pulled herself up to sit against the wall. The shape behind her was gone, the bedroom empty. A slamming door at the back of the house told her Dean Harris had fled again.

16

"Are you sure you're alright?"

They stood in the dark outside the house. Grace turned her face up to the falling rain and let it soak her skin, let it wash away the fear that had been strangely paralysing.

"Yeah, I'm fine."

"You don't sound fine. You sound like you smoke fifty cigarettes a day!"

She forced her mouth to smile – she really was fine, and she'd really like it if he believed her. The blow to her throat had been clumsy, more like a man lashing out than one intending to do serious harm. She would have some soft tissue damage but nothing to worry about, according to the retired doctor who lived next to Mrs Harris. She had declined William's offer to drive her to Cork University Hospital. She was *fine!* She was more interested in getting the rest of this night over with.

The Garda Technical Bureau were on the way – Dean Harris had been living inside this house, or at least visiting it, and William wanted everything documented. Nobody was allowed back inside until they deemed all the evidence collected.

"His mother knew he was in the house all along. What a show she put on!"

"And we fell for it." William kept his hands in his trouser pockets as he watched two gardaí escort Mrs Harris to the back of their car. They kept their eyes cast down, unable to bear the fury in his – his words from earlier ringing loudly in their ears. "*Back at the station I expect a full report on how a fucking multiple rapist slipped past you!*"

Mrs Harris had turned from a confused old lady to a screaming, shouting mass of fury. "*You can't do this!*" she shrieked at him as she was led to the car. "*I'm an innocent woman! And what about my Beauty?*"

"Not my problem," William said, his voice cold. The dog would be alright; he didn't know much about Grace's personal life, except for the fact she was an animal lover – she picked enough sandy-coloured hairs from her trousers most mornings to let him know she had at least one large dog. He knew she had already made plans with a neighbour to keep Beauty. Not that Mrs Harris needed to know that.

"*You can't do this! This is all your fault!*" Mrs Harris spat on the ground in front of him.

"Now, Mrs Harris, how about you pray on things for a while and I'll see you back at the station shortly?" He sighed as she was guided into the car.

He watched it pull away from the kerb, neighbours turning back to their front doors, shivering in the cold. The spectacle was over, until the Tech Bureau arrived at least.

"I think he's sick." Grace's fingers massaged her throat as she spoke.

"Harris?"

"Yeah." She swallowed and winced. "His breathing sounded … rattling, like he had fluid in his throat or something. Like he has the flu. And he didn't seem very strong. I mean, he hurt me, but not to any great extent."

"*Hmmm*. He could be sick if he's been living rough." He turned to face her, tired eyes scrutinizing her face. "Go back to the station, Grace. If you're well enough to make a statement, one of the lads will take you – might as well get the paperwork over with. Then go straight home. And take tomorrow off."

"But I don't need –"

"You won't sleep tonight. This is your first attack on the job, isn't it? So don't expect any rest. Lay off the coffee and the alcohol – trust me, it won't help. I'll see you Monday."

Grace didn't argue with him – she had worked with him only a few months, but knew it would be a waste of energy and her throat burned with every word.

"What will you do?" she asked.

"Oh you know me, I'll keep busy!" With a parting half-smile, he strode away towards the house.

In Mrs Harris's bedroom he switched on the light and stood in front of the wardrobe. It hung open still, hangers and clothes spilled onto the carpet. The cream bedding was crumpled and he closed his eyes, breathing deeply, picturing Grace lying there, gasping for air. When he opened them he stepped to the end of the bed where he could see the space between it and the wall, where Grace had crouched on her hands and knees, desperately trying to breathe.

William stepped to the back door and with his sleeve pulled over his fingertips he pulled it open. Harris had run through here, jumped over low hedges and was gone. Gardaí were searching the area right now, but William didn't think they'd find anything. The back of the garden opened onto another estate, separated by a wall that a man could easily scale. Harris had been swallowed by the night and had disappeared again.

He sighed roughly, his breath a little cloud drifting into the dark night. This house was off limits now – however Harris had been slipping in here, this option was over for him. The noose was tightening and William looked forward to watching him choke.

17

Tom Gallagher pulled his eyes away from the streetlights twinkling on the dark street outside, and watched the man approach his table. He had chosen this restaurant nestled among hundreds-of-years-old buildings on the South Mall for its privacy as much as its exquisite steak. He resisted the urge to pointedly look at his watch. His solicitor was late. Though always small-statured, Victor White had lost weight in the last few months, and his dark hair was peppered with grey around the temples. Now he looked to Tom to be a shrunken, aged version of his old self. He weaved quickly between the tables with a harried expression on his face, watery blue eyes flicking to the left and right, flitting around at the diners as he moved, as though he didn't want to be seen here. His nervous energy made Tom smile in satisfaction.

"I'm surprised you bothered to show up." Tom finished his whiskey and raised a finger to the waitress for another.

"I'm surprised you're sitting by a window. The gardaí are parked outside in a squad car." Victor sat down stiffly.

"Yeah, they probably have the table bugged and all. There are two other cars parked down the street with plainclothes detectives as well – you didn't spot those?"

"Sarcasm, Tom? Really? What do you want? You can come to

my office at any time for a *legitimate* meeting. Why summon me to a restaurant on a Saturday night?" He looked around at the diners sitting close by. "Where's Marco?" Victor had rarely seen Tom in public without the bulk of his most trusted man beside him.

"His mother died," Tom answered simply. He accepted a menu from a waiter and indicated for Victor to do the same.

"I'm not staying," Victor said, ignoring the leather-bound menu. "Just a Jameson, neat."

"Aren't you worried about getting caught drink-driving?" Tom asked.

Victor frowned at him. "Spit it out, Tom."

"Alright, fine." He leaned back into the seat, swirling the amber liquid in the glass on the table, "As you know, I have men on my side in Lee Street. Not enough, obviously, but still enough to prove useful now and then. One of them told me Alan Ainsley was lifted in London this morning."

Victor's grey eyebrows disappeared into the creases on his forehead. "Are you certain?"

Tom nodded slowly.

Victor exhaled heavily, turning a silver fork over and back on the white tablecloth, his tongue probing his teeth. When he looked at Tom again, he looked deflated, exhausted under the weight of this fight. He had enjoyed being in Tom's inner circle for decades. Now he seemed like a man who wished he was sitting anywhere else. His shoulders sagged as he said, "There'll be an application to extradite him. He and David were in it up to their necks."

When David Gallagher had stolen classified security data, it had been Tom's long-time associate Alan Ainsley who assisted him in finding a buyer, leaving Tom out of the deal. It was a risky move and must have been worth hundreds of thousands in cash. Maybe more. Tom would never know the finer details. David was dead and, until this morning, Ainsley had been on the run.

"How long would he be looking at?" Tom asked.

Victor exhaled heavily, shaking his head. "There's a *range* of charges to choose from where Ainsley's concerned." He lowered his voice and leaned closer to Tom, "He was involved in an attempt to compromise national security, in stealing classified data ... hard to say where the prosecutor might stop. His record is otherwise clean but the evidence is airtight."

He looked at Tom as the whiskey was placed in front of him, a small crystal glass on a white paper coaster.

"Is this why you called me out here?" he asked then. "You're worried he'll talk?"

"Naturally. The guards have searched everywhere but they've nothing on me. But now they have Ainsley ..."

Victor eyed the diners around them nervously. "Ainsley will cut a deal and give them all they need to keep his neck off the chopping block. We can take that as a certainty. He'll offer enough to seal the case against you. It's what any good solicitor would advise. You might want to think about what we discussed." He sipped the whiskey slowly, relishing the heat of the first swallow, and waited for Tom's reaction. It was an unpopular subject between them. He was reassured by the fact that this was a public place. "Let me remind you, there's no honour in your line of business once you get caught."

Tom sucked air between his teeth, looking around the room at the faces of couples and groups, lovers and friends. All enjoying their meals without a care in the world. The colours, their shapes, the noise, it all became one, swirling and blending together, like when he had been in the art gallery. He shook his head roughly to try to clear his thoughts.

"That's it? Your best advice is to turn on men that respect me?"

"My advice has always been sound up to now. I've spoken to a few old friends that specialise in defence in your line of business. They agree with me. It's time to cut a deal. I can get you the best legal counsel to work through this. But it's the only choice you've got."

"There's no chance of me squealing to Lee Street or any other station for that matter and you know it. I've made that clear! John neither! That option is off the table."

"There's nothing else I can say. It's a matter of time, Tom. I can protest and stall only so long. And if they have Ainsley, it only takes one interview from him to blow this all up. Trust me."

"How long?"

Victor exhaled heavily. "If Ainsley was lifted this morning then you have days, at most."

"So we're fucked."

They eyed each other, the unspoken words hanging between them – Tom's days might be numbered but being a solicitor for criminals that fancied themselves as legitimate business men wasn't a crime. Victor would earn his hourly rate and walk away when Tom was inevitably sent down.

"Have you been to see your son? He's being transferred on Monday."

"Yeah, I know," Tom said sourly, flipping open the cover on the menu and feigning interest. His eyes didn't move over the black ink listing the food choices, but fixated on one spot, his vision blurring again. He blinked rapidly in frustration – he didn't have time to worry about why his surroundings turned kaleidoscopic every now and then – there was too much else going on. "John has made his bed."

"It would appear that way. Still … Mae will want to know he's OK."

"He's the fucking reason Mae is in the funny farm, and we both know it!" He snapped the menu shut, spittle flying into the air between them when he spoke again. "She begged me to keep him close, to keep him safe! What a laugh! All along he was plotting ways to kill random people with two lunatics, and film it! For what? Money? *I had plenty fucking money!*"

Victor leaned across the table, his hands flapping in a frantic shushing motion. Diners were beginning to stare at them. "For Christ's sake, control yourself, man! Half of Cork is out to get you, the press are lurking everywhere, not to mention the Guards. Keep it together!"

Tom grabbed his glass from the table and gulped. His hands were shaking and he felt heat in his face, sweat on the back of his neck. He consciously tried to steady himself, to breathe more calmly, to keep unwanted attention at bay. It seemed to be all he was doing lately.

"You good?"

Tom didn't answer, just raised his finger again, indicating another drink was needed.

Victor had had enough. Draining the last of his Jameson, he tied the button on his suit jacket.

"I think I can keep you out of jail, Tom, but you need to meet me halfway. Go home. Visit your son while you still can. Phone your wife. And keep a low profile." He pushed the empty glass into the middle of the table. "One other thing. There's progress in Spain."

Tom sat up straighter, his eyes darting to the Garda car parked outside. His comment that they had probably bugged the table had been tongue-in-cheek, yet he was still cautious.

"My man put pressure on the owner of a coffee shop she went to regularly." *She* being Kate Crowley, but no need to say the name. "He stayed quiet but his sister was keen to talk when her brother was black and blue. She spoke about a phone call and a message telling the woman to run. Seems you have a rat in your house."

Tom gaped at him, his jaw slack. Who would *dare?* Victor stood up, smoothing non-existent wrinkles from his tie again, and pushed in his chair.

"Call to my office Monday morning and we'll talk. I'll find out what I can about Ainsley."

He turned and left quickly, his shoulders hitched around his ears. At the door he stopped to greet a prominent politician and his wife as they entered, his smile broad and natural. Tom watched him, his eyes narrowed. Victor White was the *real* psychopath, he mused, not John Gallagher as the press had labelled him. Victor could switch it on for the political elite with ease. He stood there now, pumping the man's hand and, if he felt Tom's eyes boring into his skull, he hid it well.

Tom finally ordered surf and turf and another drink. He was glad he was alone now – he had a lot to think about. With one son dead and the other about to be sent down, it seemed that all that was left for Tom and Mae were their granddaughters. Rachel and Rhea. And they could all be together *anywhere*. It didn't have to be here – Cork had been good to Tom, but he wasn't a man that ever suffered the weight of sentimentality. Every city offered opportunities, even if that opportunity was to disappear and live a quieter retirement. They could start over – he had done it before. Like a muscle memory, he knew he could do it again.

His enemies were circling. Ainsley would sink the metaphorical knife deep into Tom's back to save his own skin, of that he had no doubt. Ely Murray wanted to take the business, to steal more from him than he already had. They were like vultures circling a corpse. Years of loyalty to both men already wiped out, as if it had all meant nothing. Who else was out there, rubbing their hands together as his life and business crumbled?

He smiled then, thinking about the nature of men. When a man was too close to victory, too close to gaining what he wanted, he lost all sense of the danger lurking in the shadows of the battlefield. He grew cocky, certain of success, and overlooked minute details that could tip the scales in his enemy's favour.

Tom would not allow men he had elevated to kick him when he was down.

But first he had a rat to kill.

18

Anna pushed her way through the throng of dancers inside the club, through the bodies swaying to the disco beats and those standing in clusters, shouting over the music. The Mad Hatter club wasn't a place she had thought she would go again, not after what had happened here with Kate last November.

Was it really only a few months ago? It felt like so much more. She had seen in a file at work that Kate had arranged to meet someone in the Mad Hatter nightclub late one Saturday night, at the time when she had been the prime suspect in David Gallagher's death. Kate had been trying to buy a passport and Anna often wondered if she had eventually succeeded – she had disappeared, after all. Sometimes, late at night when she couldn't sleep, she had wondered if Kate had fallen into Tom Gallagher's clutches, but the gardaí were certain she had left Ireland. And from her encounter with John Gallagher last month in her home, where he had interrogated her on Kate's whereabouts, Anna was reassured they didn't know where she was.

She didn't like to think of that now. Instead she focused on the fact that this club was the venue of her first date with Myles. They had gone to see a band whose name she couldn't even remember now. When his call had come through thirty minutes ago, she'd left

Vivian and gone to speak to him outside. Missing his easy smile, his messy dark curls and the way his eyes twinkled behind his glasses, was a growing frustration. She wasn't sure this long-distance thing was going to work.

Four wide glass panels separated the dance floor from an outdoor smoking area where Anna could see Vivian standing in a group beside some tall potted plants, an assortment of glasses in front of them at a tall table. She made her way to their group, feeling a little self-conscious. A cold wind whipped at her hair and she was glad of her tan leather jacket, a gift from Myles. She loved how it set off her cream dress underneath, and loved thinking about him every time she wore it. God, she missed him!

As she approached, Vivian turned to her with a warm smile, stubbing out her cigarette in an ashtray on the table.

"How's Myles?"

"Grand. Still too far away."

"Are you ready to meet everyone? Christ, the whole team is here!" She pulled down the hem of her sparkly dress and ran her hands through her long brown hair. "Do I look frozen? Because I'm *freezing!* But I look good, right?" She grinned.

Anna laughed. "That dress is totally worth hypothermia! You look stunning!"

Vivian grabbed her hand and stepped back to the table. "Anna, this is my work crew from Banba Productions!" she said loudly. "Everyone, this is my best friend Anna Clarke. Anna, meet my boss Carol O'Connor."

Anna shook hands with a woman she guessed must be at least six feet tall without her heels, with shimmering red hair that almost reached her waist. The woman's wide grey eyes crinkled in a smile as she greeted Anna. "Gosh, don't you have a face for TV! Those eyes! Such a dark-brown shade! Stunning! Vivian, don't call me your boss, it makes me feel ancient!" She swatted Vivian's arm playfully.

Anna realised Carol was much older than their late twenties, possibly in her early sixties.

"Carol's so experienced, Anna," Vivian gushed. "She worked in America for a long time on lots of network shows. She was a producer for them before starting her own company here. She told us stories in the office once – oh my God, the things celebrities have producers do for them!"

Carol threw her head back and laughed.

Vivian wasn't done. "She's really talented and has loads of connections. She has people from RTÉ interested in my documentary series and she's talking about the UK channels as well."

"Vivian, please! All I do is nurture talent and bring stories to the world." Carol beamed at her.

A man beside Anna stuck out his hand and grasped hers firmly. "Luke Daly, good to meet you."

His eyes roamed over Anna and he smiled broadly at her, pumping her hand. He was dressed in drainpipe jeans, heavy black boots and a black motorcycle-style leather jacket.

"Nice jacket," he murmured appreciatively. "I'm a big fan of leather, as you can probably tell – this was my dad's." He gestured to his own, the asymmetric zip closed to meet a red scarf wound around his neck. "Can I get you girls a drink?"

"Thanks, Luke, that'd be amazing!" Vivian caught his arm and leaned closer to his ear, telling him their order.

He moved off into the main bar.

"*Amazing?*" Anna whispered teasingly to Vivian, who elbowed her in the ribs.

Carol O'Connor stepped closer. "Vivian's told me a lot about you, Anna. You were in the Lee Street station? That's a handy contact to have, Vivian!" she said with a wink.

"I'm taking some leave at the moment," Anna answered, quickly steering the conversation away from herself. The last thing she wanted to do was discuss the reason for her break from work. "Banba Productions is lucky to have Vivian – she's a brilliant journalist. And Luke is your producer? I thought Banba Productions was for women, run by women."

"Unfortunately, that's 'discrimination' apparently," Carol made air-quotes with her fingers, "so we had to let some in. But, just between us, we outsource several services, and the suppliers are *all* women. We've female photographers and scouts all over Cork working freelance and they're the best in the business."

"Oh my God, I *know* you!" A loud squeal pierced the air as a young woman rushed to their table and gripped Anna's arm. Her face was flushed with alcohol and excitement. Blonde curls framed her face and bounced as she spoke. "You're the woman who fought off those serial killers last month! In her own *house!*" She squealed loudly and several people looked in their direction. "There was a photo of you in the paper. And you had something to do with that Lee Street detective getting arrested just before Christmas! I can't believe it's *you!*"

"Anna, this is Sheena." Vivian smiled at Anna through gritted teeth. "She's Banba Production's receptionist. She keeps us all in line and is a true-crime enthusiast. She's always this excited."

Sheena apparently didn't hear a word Vivian had said, too busy reaching for Anna's hand. She squeezed it hard, her fake nails digging into Anna's wrist. "I'm so excited to meet you! I've *so* many questions!"

Suddenly, Anna found it hard to breathe. She rubbed the skin at her throat with one hand, aware Sheena was expecting a response, but found she couldn't think of anything to say.

Her eyes found Vivian's, fixing her with a '*help me!*' stare.

"Let's go to the ladies, Anna." Vivian stepped forward and pulled Anna's arm, muttering to Sheena and Carol that they'd be right back, her words lost in the chat and muffled music from inside.

Sheena called questions after them as they pushed through the crowd and, for a brief, terrifying moment, Anna thought she might follow. Vivian pressed on quickly, and Anna exhaled as Sheena faded into the crowd behind them. Once they had stepped inside the ladies' she turned to Vivian.

"Sorry, Viv – I don't know what just happened! Sheena just ambushed me and I …" Water flooded into her mouth and she leaned over the bathroom sink, suddenly fearful she would throw up.

Vivian rubbed her hand in circles on Anna's back. A young woman at the mirror eyed them nervously as she reapplied her lipstick.

"Don't worry about it, Anna! I had no idea Sheena was following your story so closely – I mean, your name was only mentioned in the papers once or twice. It's bizarre! But she's like that – full-on and hyper about true crime. She swears she's distantly related to Jack the Ripper."

Anna straightened up and stared at her reflection in the mirror. Regret flooded her – this was an important night for Vivian, and she had just fled from Vivian's work colleagues. Why was she so upset? Sheena's interest in her had overwhelmed her to the point she felt trapped, unable to breathe, as though she was under attack. The therapist her boss had made her go to had said this could happen, this sudden overwhelming feeling of panic and insecurity.

She cursed the timing – she wanted to be there for Vivian – but knew it was understandable.

John Gallagher had made her a prisoner in her own home, trapped between two killers in her living room. And her visit to the nursing home, where her dad's friend Bob Evans had completely destroyed any remaining hope that her parents were alive, had broken her heart. Every time her mobile phone rang, she couldn't breathe in case it was Alex with news she dreaded to hear. She was barely sleeping. When sleep did come, it was destroyed by horrifying nightmares. She suddenly realised how fragile she felt. Was it really surprising a true-crime fan who had recognised her so enthusiastically had pushed against her strained self-control?

"Anna?" Vivian asked gently, "Are you going to be OK?"

Anna turned and hugged her friend, holding her close, and after a few seconds she felt her tension unfurl, just a little. She nodded and wiped her eyes with the back of her hand, turning back to the mirror.

"Oh God, I look like death," she groaned, pinching her cheeks. She frowned at Vivian, who had pulled a hairbrush from her bag.

"No, you don't!" said Vivian as she ran the brush through her hair. "But, look, tonight is the launch party. The press pack will be arriving soon, executives from all the TV channels. It's a big deal. It's going to get really crowded. Do you want to go home, Anna? You don't seem in the best mood for a party – and, believe me, with everything going on, no-one could blame you. I swear I won't mind."

Anna met her eyes in the mirror. "Are you sure?"

"Absolutely!" Vivian hugged her again quickly. "How's my hair?"

Anna laughed softly. "Every hair is in its rightful place!"

Vivian kissed her on the cheek. "I'll see you later. Don't wait up!"

Outside, Anna breathed in a deep lungful of air so cold she gasped. It was eleven o'clock now, and she had no desire to be alone on the city streets, in her short cream dress in temperatures that were surely just above zero.

She hailed a passing taxi and sank into the seat, calling the address of Vivian's apartment to the driver as she fished her ringing mobile from her bag. The screen was bright in the dark car, and her chest felt tight when she looked at it. It was Alex, calling so late at night that she *knew* there was news from the dig-site. Bile rushed up her throat and his name blurred on the screen in front of her, but she jabbed the screen and held it to her ear.

"I'm so sorry, Anna. They've found something."

19

When Michael and Helen Clarke disappeared following a car crash en route to a concert in Dublin in 2009, the whole country was baffled. Nightly news bulletins appealed for witnesses, for any information that might help the gardaí piece together one of the strangest mysteries many of the country's detectives had ever encountered. Blood was found in the car, a positive DNA match to their two children that waited in their house in Kinsale for news. Seatbelts in their car had been cut, all belongings cleared, no coats or overnight bags were found. The country held its breath, waiting to hear of bodies perished nearby. Vigils were held in Kinsale, where they had lived with their two children, sixteen-year-old Anna and twenty-five-year-old Alex.

But no bodies were ever found.

Background checks were done, of course. Who were the couple that had disappeared so mysteriously? Michael Clarke ran an accountancy firm in Cork city, and his wife was a homemaker. They had moved to Kinsale from the UK sixteen years previously, just before their daughter Anna was born. Neither had a criminal record. Michael trained in Taekwon-Do with his friend Jason, and Helen was active in a local book club and Tidy Towns Committee, mainly keeping to herself. They were a regular family, and Michael and Helen were "normal" people.

Except Anna knew now that they weren't.

Her relationship with Myles had opened doors to answers and, in the dead of night, when the world was still and she was alone with her thoughts, Anna often wished she could close those doors and block out the truth. He had produced two newspaper articles just after the New Year that ultimately led to the search for her parents' bodies.

Helen Clarke was born Yelena Vasilieva in the Soviet Union and grew up to become a highly talented cellist, whose abusive father regarded her talent and beauty as the currency to achieving his ambitions. He pushed her into the path of dangerous men until she ran away, her disappearance making newspaper headlines in London. The man who had saved her, had fallen in love with her, was Michael Clarke. He had made his own enemies. One man held a grudge so deep it survived decades, and he eventually took his revenge.

Now Alex was telling Anna that their belongings had been found. Of course, there needed to be tests done, but one large leather bag and the remains of a smaller one had been found at the place the gardaí had identified as most likely to be the site of their burial. Alex told her the news in clipped words devoid of emotion. She could hear the shiver in his voice and remembered it was late and cold, and he was standing outside in a field, freezing, the rattling of his teeth betraying the adrenaline that kept him standing. She could hear voices around him and what sounded like the grinding of a machine. He promised to call her when he had more information and hung up quickly.

Anna leaned forward to the taxi driver and asked him to pull over. As soon as the car stopped, she sprang from her seat and vomited onto the footpath. The driver muttered "Ah, for feck's sake," but she barely heard him. She stood up, wiping her mouth on the sleeve of her jacket, and reached for her bag from the back seat. Closing the door, she pulled a ten-euro note from her purse.

"Here," she offered it through the driver's open window. "I'll walk the rest of the way."

"What?" He looked alarmed now, his earlier disgust at the vomit forgotten. "Look, hop back in, love, and just tell me to pull over if you need to be sick again."

"No, I'm fine."

"No, it's a long walk to Blackrock Castle and it's late. Get back in – it's not safe out on your own! It's freezing – can't you get in?"

She pulled her jacket closer around her. "I'm not drunk and I can look after myself. Honestly, I'm fine!"

His jowly face and bald head reminded Anna of Vivian's dad.

After a beat of indecision, he shrugged. "Suit yourself. Take care now." He pulled away from the footpath, not taking the money she had offered, and Anna watched him go, grateful to be alone.

She passed the Society of African Missions church on her right. She had been to Mass there a few times with her parents and Alex and was suddenly filled with a memory of a priest singing and playing guitar from the pulpit, her mother's eyes closed and lips moving along with the song.

As Anna walked on, she pulled her set of keys from her bag and gripped them tightly, two keys protruding between her fingers, one key for Vivian's apartment and one for her home in Kinsale. Would she ever set foot inside there again? She hoped not to.

When they were younger, before her parents disappeared, Anna's home in Kinsale had been full of noise and bustle, full of people. Her brother and his friends took over the back garden every day with their games, although maybe that was just how she remembered it. Vivian, Kate and her twin sister Natalie had been regular fixtures too, there so often her father had joked they were part of the furniture. The four best friends had camped out in Anna's room upstairs, her mother bringing a tray of hot chocolate and slices of banana bread, while the girls played and chatted. The house had always been full of noise and love. Their dad's friend Jason was a regular too, and when he met and married his wife Colette they often came to dinner. There had always been so many people in the house.

When Michael and Helen vanished from their crashed car, the house remained full for a while. Detectives, family liaison officers, kindly neighbours keen to help. But none of them were the people Anna and Alex so desperately needed to see, and none of them had any answers. Slowly, over time, the rooms emptied, leaving Alex to pick up the pieces. The night Jason turned up at the house and insisted Anna resume her Taekwon-Do training had saved her life, in so many ways. And Alex had done his best to make everything as normal as it could ever be.

Thinking of him now, standing in the cold, waiting for more news on the recovery of their parents, broke Anna's heart all over again.

Rain began to fall, soft and light at first, then heavier, coating her, sticking her hair to her skin. Anna raised her eyes to the cloudless sky and welcomed the downpour.

Vivian returned hours later, while the night was still dark. Anna was sitting on the sofa in a dressing gown, her hair wrapped in a towel. After sitting, numb, for a long time in the quiet living room, she had made her way to the bathroom, where she had turned the shower to the hottest setting she could bear and stood under it until the feeling had returned to her toes and fingertips.

She had called Alex again, tried to eat some dry toast, and now she sat in the dark, savouring the heat from a mug of coffee in her hands, watching Vivian as she manoeuvred her way through the open-plan living area.

Vivian kicked off her shoes and dumped her handbag on the nearby stool.

"Welcome home," Anna said, and grinned as Vivian shrieked and dropped her keys.

"*Jesus, Anna!*" With one hand at her chest, she reached out and turned on the light. "I was trying to be quiet and not wake you, and there you are trying to give me a bloody heart attack!" She squinted at her, her face softening. "Are you OK?"

"They found some bags buried in the field. Alex said they will start tests on them on Monday and see what has survived of the contents. But it looks like they're Mum and Dad's things. I mean, that's the most likely thing, isn't it?"

Vivian rushed to the sofa and sat beside Anna, her hand on hers. "I'm so sorry."

Her eyes glinted with tears and Anna was reminded that Vivian had loved her parents too.

"I guess it's good," Vivian said. "You know, it brings you closer to having them back, in a way."

Anna nodded. She was grateful to have her friend near her. She gulped more of her coffee and smiled at Vivian. "How was the launch?"

Vivian sighed, looking exhausted. Her hair was completely unkempt and dark smudges underneath her eyes were all that remained of her make-up.

"It was good. A lot of fun actually. I danced too much and drank too much and, you know … it was a good night. Although I *did* make a big mistake." She grimaced, dropping her head into her hands.

"Something you shouldn't have said to the press?" As soon as Anna asked the question she realised that was hardly it – Vivian was an experienced reporter, having worked for several high-profile newspapers before moving to Banba Productions.

"No, it's worse than that!" She groaned and cradled her head in her hands.

"Worse? Tell me!"

"You'll hate me! I can't say it!" Vivian mumbled.

"Oh Vivian, spit it out, it can't be that bad!"

With a loud groan Vivian sat up, her face crumpled in regret.

"I went home with Luke!"

20

The sun was weak as it peaked. The temperature had dropped overnight and the rain that had fallen so heavily on her walk home had frozen to ice. Anna watched the night turn to morning through the balcony doors, the frozen raindrops caught on the patio furniture glistening in the light.

Once Vivian had showered and Anna had made fresh coffee, they sat together on the sofa again, dissecting the night. Vivian wanted to know everything Alex had told Anna, and listened quietly while she filled her in.

"So it's still a waiting game, really."

Anna couldn't help but agree. She wondered about her brother – he must be exhausted, keeping things together at work and waiting at the search-site as often as he could. She considered abandoning the plan to help Vivian and going instead to relieve Alex of some of the burden. But every time she envisioned herself there, waiting in the cold, the room began to spin around her, and she knew she couldn't do it. It was too much.

Eventually, the conversation rolled around to Vivian's impromptu sleepover. She insisted it wasn't something she would repeat.

"Luke was really sweet actually. But it was still a mistake! And thank God I don't have to see him in the office this week. I'll be doing the preliminary interviews and he'll be arranging footage of a few sites and deciding on the format and that. It's best to keep it professional – I don't want to be involved with someone from work!"

The doorbell rang and they both jumped.

"I'll go," Anna said, hopping up.

She had changed into jeans and a sweatshirt earlier, while Vivian was still in a bathrobe. She checked the wall clock as she moved to the front door – quarter past nine on a Sunday morning. They weren't expecting any visitors and something in her shifted, a straightening of her shoulders, a tensing in how she carried herself.

Preparing for something …

As she pulled open the door a teenager smiled at her, acne on his chin growing purple in the cold morning. "Hey! Food delivery for Miss Anna Clarke?"

"That's me. But I didn't order anything!"

He shoved a cardboard box into her arms quickly, eager to be back in the heat of his car. "There's a note inside. Hold that steady now, there's liquid in there. Enjoy!" He waved cheerfully and turned to go.

Then Anna noticed a white envelope half-sticking out of the letterbox.

"Is this from you too?"

The guy turned back and shrugged. "Nope, not me. That was there when I arrived."

As she pulled the envelope free, she heard a click and saw Dermot step outside his apartment, his cat streaking ahead of him and down the steps. He was wearing a dressing gown over blue pyjamas, and he pulled the cord tight around his stomach.

"You're up early! Seems a busy spot this morning, lots of coming and going!" He smiled and stepped towards her, his eyes narrowed in curiosity and resting firmly on the box in her hand. As usual, he was over-eager to talk, but she was too cold and had too much on her mind. With a quick smile, she stepped back inside, shutting out the chill air with a firm push on the front door with her elbow. The cardboard box was warm and there was a delicious aroma wafting from it: coffee and bacon, maybe pancakes, and something sweet too.

In the kitchen Vivian looked intrigued as Anna placed the box on the table, the white envelope to the side.

"Let's see then," Vivian said, opening the lid.

Anna noticed then, for the first time, the logo of Victus, her favourite coffee shop on the front of the box, and she smiled, remembering a flyer she had seen at work for their new weekend breakfast-delivery service. She had been right: there were two large coffees in cardboard cups, two stacks of pancakes with bacon and maple syrup, and two pots of granola with natural yoghurt.

A tiny, folded note read: **Anna, enjoy! I reckon this will go down well after last night. I'm sure Vivian will help you polish it off. Miss you, Myles xxx**

"Well!" Vivian said, pulling the lid of one coffee cup and inhaling deeply. "That man is a keeper!"

For the first time in hours, maybe days, Anna smiled widely. "I agree with you there!" She pulled out her mobile phone and took a photo of the breakfast, sending it with a text of thanks to Myles.

"I'm impressed it's still hot. Oh wow, the *smell!*" Vivian bent and sniffed at the paper plate of pancakes. She noticed the white envelope and picked it up. "This has my name on it. No address."

"Oh, I hadn't noticed – it was sticking out of the letterbox." Anna pulled cutlery from a drawer and sat down. "The delivery guy said it was there when he arrived."

"So hand-delivered this morning. Sunday morning. That's very odd." Vivian ripped open the envelope and pulled out a small white sheet of paper, frowning as she read it.

"Everything OK?" Anna asked.

"I don't know what it is." Vivian handed her the piece of paper. "It's just a load of numbers."

Anna studied the note – it looked like standard typed font in black ink and was a list of numbers as Vivian had said, in a horizontal line.

Vivian sat down, her eyebrows drawn together. "It's weird, isn't it? And I think it's the same type of envelope that the first note came in at work. The same size anyway."

"The note with the Shakespeare quote?"

"Yeah."

Anna hopped up and rooted through a drawer on the sideboard, finally pulling out a clear plastic sandwich bag. She picked up the note and envelope at the corners and dropped them into it.

"We've already touched them both," said Vivian.

"That doesn't matter. The sender's DNA could be on it. I'll drop them both in to work tomorrow. William Ryan will look into it for you."

They began to eat, savouring the food, but the troubling note had spoiled Myles' treat.

"What on earth does a line of numbers mean?" said Vivian. "The quote is one thing but today's note doesn't make any sense."

Anna chewed on her bacon slowly, thinking. A line of numbers, with no obvious pattern … it was strange. If it was meant to be a menacing note, then its meaning was lost on both of them. Neither spoke again as they ate, both deep in thought.

Vivian's shoulders were tense, her eyes unfocused. After some time, she groaned. "*Ugh*, I've no clue what it means! It's too long to be a mobile-phone number … I'll type it into a search engine, see what comes up." She pulled her phone from her dressing-gown pocket, slid the clear plastic bag towards her and keyed in the numbers. "If it *is* the same person trying to send another weird message, it's pretty stupid to just list out num – *holy shit!*"

"What?"

"Those numbers are coordinates!"

"To where?"

Vivian swallowed hard, her wide-eyed stare chilling. "I remember them from yesterday, in your car. It's the coordinates to the graveyard where Bernard O'Meara is buried."

21

"We have to go back!"

"I thought you might say that," Anna groaned.

Vivian folded a pancake and stuffed it into her mouth as she rose from the table.

"I'll get dressed. Give me two minutes!" Her words were muffled, her blue eyes were wide, wild, and for a moment she looked disoriented in her own living room.

"Look, Vivian … this could be a waste of time," Anna began cautiously. "It could be just a – a – taunt. No-one could assume we would just go straight back to Skibbereen, to the graveyard. I mean … the note isn't exactly an *instruction* to go there. And neither of us slept last night. Wouldn't it be better to –"

Vivian held up one hand. "If you're too tired to take me, I understand. You've been up all night. We both have. But I'm going there now to check this out, one way or another."

She pressed her lips together and Anna nodded, resigned.

The journalist in Vivian was investigating what lay in the graveyard, no matter what. And after the news Alex had given her, Anna realised she would agree to anything her friend asked, if only for distraction, to quiet the growing dread clouding her mind. So she rose too, determined to help Vivian, just like she'd asked her to.

Vivian dressed quickly and they left the apartment. The concrete steps outside the apartment glistened with frost and they inched slowly down, gripping the metal banister for support.

A worried silence settled over them while they waited for the ice to clear from the windscreen. Anna plugged her mobile in to charge and glanced at the screen. There was one message, a heart emoji from Myles. Nothing from Alex. She checked the time – 9:40 – nowhere near time for the radio news bulletin and an update on the search, yet she selected a CD anyway. That way there was no chance of hearing a breaking-news item on the radio.

A while later, as the now familiar route unfurled in front of her, Anna realised that what she'd said about no-one expecting them to act on the list of numbers once they'd figured out what they represented was wrong. Anyone who knew Vivian *at all* would know she would doggedly find the meaning behind them, fast. The realisation that the sender knew Vivian well was deeply unsettling.

Vivian turned to watch the road as it passed by, huddled in a puffy black jacket, a scarf covering the lower half of her face. She was uncharacteristically quiet, her shoulders hunched over, hands clasped between her knees.

Anna had turned the heating up high in the car, and wore gloves and a scarf, yet the cold of the morning still made her shiver. She drove more slowly than she wanted to – the urge to find whatever was waiting for Vivian at the graveyard was overpowering, but the temperature this morning was hovering around zero, and the car had already skidded once. She had been awake all night and drunk far too much coffee but her mind felt clear and calm.

Whatever was waiting for them near Bernard O'Meara's grave,

she hoped it might offer something to work with. And she intended to take whatever *it* was to William Ryan.

It took over two frustrating hours to get there. Mostly silent hours, save for the CD player and the occasionally swear from Anna as the car skidded on the road. Vivian dozed off, her arms crossed over her chest, and Anna felt the tug of sleep dip her eyelids. They had stopped for coffee and breakfast rolls at a Maxol service station near Bandon, but carried on again quickly, anticipation and tension racing through them.

Finally, the graveyard was ahead of them on the road. Anna pulled in as close as possible to the wall, and they both climbed out of the car.

"If someone comes too fast around that corner," Anna looked behind the car at the dry, glistening road, "they'll plough straight into my car."

Vivian took her arm. "It's too cold to be out for a Sunday drive. It'll be fine, come on!"

Both shivered as they moved through the narrow gate and crunched up the stone path, teeth chattering, their breathy clouds wafting into the air in front of them. They stayed close together, for warmth as much as a sense of protection. Scanning the area, Anna didn't see any shadows lurking or people nearby – even the crows had deserted the place. The grass in the graveyard was white, covered in frost, and the trees stood like sentinel statues pointing upwards.

Vivian saw it first, stopping dead on the path so that Anna walked into her, before stepping around her to see what it was. For a moment, a split-second, she didn't believe what she was looking at, but quickly the reality of it was as puncturing as the cold air around her.

A wooden crucifix, as tall as Bernard O'Meara's headstone.

It had been pushed into the earth beside it and stood erect from the frigid grass. The inscription, in thick-lettered black ink, stilled Anna's heart.

HERE LIE THE REMAINS OF VIVIAN KEATING
DAUGHTER. SISTER. TROUBLEMAKER.

22

William Ryan met them in the Victus coffee shop. Anna wasn't surprised he was working – he seemed to work seven days a week – nor that he was wearing a full suit, his dark overcoat flapping behind him as he walked to their table. He smiled at her warmly as he sat down, his blue eyes bright and curious, if not a little cool, as they rested on Vivian.

They had history.

Vivian was the reporter who had made front page news of things William Ryan and his team preferred to keep out of the public arena during the series of murders several weeks ago. She had sensationalised her reports, calling those responsible "serial killers", and in William's opinion, terrified the public gratuitously. Vivian didn't see it that way – as a reporter, her job was to provide the information the people needed to know. Garda operational reasons aside, she had no regrets. Anna had debated this with Vivian many times over a glass of wine in the apartment when they relaxed together in the evenings, and they had recently agreed to drop the subject and accept their diverse objectives.

Anna wondered now if DS Ryan might feel the same.

As he shrugged off his coat and attempted to cross his long legs underneath the table, she noticed he looked more tired than usual.

And less like himself – for one thing, his jaw was covered in the beginnings of a brown-and-grey beard. He was usually clean-shaven, so Anna suspected he was working every hour possible. It wouldn't be the first time she had seen him give everything to a case.

"You look tired, Anna. Long night?"

"Kind of. I didn't realise you were working today. Thanks for meeting us."

He smiled as the waitress brought coffee to their table. "I'm technically off, but there was a development last night that required me to go in for a few hours."

"A development? Is it … Dean Harris?"

He emptied two sugar packets into the coffee and stirred slowly, not meeting her eyes.

"Yes, and no. He was in his mother's house. For how long I don't know. We might have disturbed his first attempt at entry or he might have been there all along. I'm questioning her today. In any case, he fled again."

Vivian quietly watched their conversation. Still in her jacket, she sat with her chin tucked into her scarf, her face pale. She had said nothing while Anna photographed the wooden crucifix in the graveyard, just stood behind her with her arms wrapped across her stomach. In the car they had run through every possible reason for the crucifix to be placed in the ground, every potential suspect. The list for both was short: they remained frustratingly confused.

"Well, we won't keep you," Anna said, keen to move away from the subject of Dean Harris's whereabouts now that she knew there was nothing new to be learned. "You remember Vivian Keating?"

"Yes, of course." William's tone was polite, despite his angst over

Vivian's actions mere weeks before. "How can I help?"

"Well, Vivian works for Banba Productions now, and is doing a documentary on the murder of Bernard O'Meara back in 1977. Revisiting the case."

"Yes, I read about that in the paper. You can't let the dead rest in peace?" William sipped his coffee, his eyes on Vivian.

Anna was glad that his tone was soft at least. "Well, the killer was never found. Do you know the case?"

"I'm not that familiar with it, to be honest, except to know there's nothing in the case files to warrant reopening the investigation. The lads in the office spoke about that when the files were requested. In any case, I only transferred here to Cork last year and I wasn't even born in 1977. But I *do* remember the Chief Super griping about requests for files. I'm familiar with Carol O'Connor, your boss. She must have some powerful friends. You got your files released very quickly. Quicker than usual."

Vivian finally met his eyes. "Some of them," she answered quietly. Others had been delayed but she didn't bring that up.

There was a toasted cheese sandwich in front of Vivian and Anna slid the plate closer, hoping she might pick it up and eat. She needed it. She was hungover and lacking sleep, and someone had erected a makeshift headstone with her name on it.

"Well, anyway, Vivian is making a documentary and it seems someone wants to warn her off." Anna slid the plastic bag with the note inside onto the middle of the table, followed by her mobile, open to show the photographs she had taken earlier. "The numbers are coordinates to the graveyard. The photos were taken in the graveyard where O'Meara is buried, down beyond Skibbereen – we visited it yesterday. And again this morning."

William lowered his mug and eyed the bag. "How did you receive this?"

"It was hand-delivered to Vivian's apartment this morning. Another was delivered to her office. By hand as well. I handed that in to work last Friday. It was a veiled threat, a quote and a warning to tread carefully."

William examined the note, smoothing the plastic bag so he could read it clearly. He frowned at the series of numbers before zooming in on the photographs on Anna's phone, his eyebrows knotted in concentration, seeking to gain as much detail as he could. She had taken photographs of Bernard O'Meara's headstone too, and the one in homage to The Boy Who Jumped. William looked at her curiously.

"I know the history of that second headstone, or rather, the lack of information surrounding it. It's quite something. Is there anything else?"

Anna told him how Vivian had received the first note, about how her producer had said he would sort it out. She turned to her now.

"Did you ask Luke about it yet? Or speak to Carol?"

Vivian shook her head, her eyes still on the table.

"Find out from him who he reported it to, if he did at all," William said. "Actually, just give me his number. Sometimes these things don't get taken seriously. But this *is* serious. Will you open the photos again, Anna?"

She did and handed the phone back to him. "I think the crucifix was inserted into the ground last night. It wasn't there yesterday when we visited the grave, but it was there this morning."

"Why so sure it was last night? It might have been this morning early, before you both arrived."

"Because of how easily the crucifix was pushed into the ground. The wood is thin but there's no cracks at the base or anything to show it was under pressure when it was pushed into the grass. It was wet last night, the soil would have been soft. The temperature dropped overnight and this morning it was icy – I don't think it would have been easy to get it into the ground."

William nodded as he examined the images again.

"Well spotted. I'll get on to the local detective to seal the area off and I'll send someone from the Tech Bureau down there. Send these photos on to me, will you?"

He looked at Vivian, his elbow on the table, his chin on his fist.

"Did you choose this murder for the documentary or were you pushed towards it?"

She seemed surprised by the question. She sat up straighter in the seat and thought for a moment.

"It was up to me to research and present six potential cold cases and then my producer, Luke Daly, selected the final four for the series. It's a four-part series, with each episode an hour long. Does it matter?"

"Maybe … You're still hunting out the truth then?"

She met his eyes. "Always."

Anna smiled at the defiance in her voice – Vivian was coming back to herself.

William nodded. "Good. Don't let this stop you. Tell me – aside from a possible connection to the killer, is there anyone with a grudge against you, anything that comes to mind? Perhaps from your days as a journalist?"

Embarrassment coloured Vivian's face and she looked away, reaching out to pick up one half of her toasted sandwich.

"Well, Anna doesn't agree, but my brother *might* be behind it. I mean, he could be … we haven't been getting on and he's not speaking to me. Aside from him, I don't have any other enemies. Not that he's an *enemy*, of course."

"This is a pretty extreme thing to do from someone you're not getting on with. Is it in his nature to do something like this?"

"Well … no, I guess not. But the other note references Shakespeare and Gareth is studying Shakespeare's works, and seeing as he's so angry with me lately …" She shrugged. "Anything's possible, right?"

William's mouth twisted in a noncommittal way. He drained the last of his coffee and pulled on his coat. "Send me on his details as well as your producer's, OK? I'll have a conversation with them both. After you two are finished here take the note across to the station and make an official statement – Anna, Colin Forde is on duty today, he'll see you. In the meantime, keep your friend close, and stay safe."

Anna stood up and walked with him to the door. When they stepped outside onto the street, she wrapped her arms around herself and shivered.

"I see you're getting plenty of relaxation on your break from work," William said, softening the sarcasm with a smile.

Anna grinned back. "You know me, I like to stay busy!"

Buttoning up his coat, he dipped his head back towards their table. "Seriously, you look exhausted. Use this break to get some rest." He rubbed his hands together. "Alright, well, keep your eyes open. It's public knowledge that this documentary is being made, and obviously *someone* isn't happy about it, so just play it safe, OK? If things escalate it might be worth postponing the documentary. See how things progress."

"OK." Anna stamped her feet and rubbed her arms. She didn't think Vivian would be keen on the idea of postponing, but she guessed that decision would be out of her control.

"You're freezing – go on back inside. But before you go . . . I would have called you later. Harris attacked Grace Thompson last night."

"*What?*"

"She's fine. He jumped her in his mother's house. I was there, but in another room interviewing his mother. She's OK, more shaken up than anything. She'll be back at work tomorrow. I'll find him, Anna. I guarantee you that. But he's cold and desperate now, and he's already unpredictable ... so stay alert!"

He patted her arm and then crossed the street, walking hurriedly away from her toward the city centre, his chin tucked into his overcoat.

She trusted him completely, but it made her sad to think of his determination to find Dean Harris, in a way. Dark circles under his eyes and the stubble on his face told her he wasn't taking care of himself.

Harris was unstable – was he still looking for her? Did he still blame her for his arrest? She shook her head as she turned to go back inside, wondering how a man could end up that way, so damaged, so out of control.

And suddenly, she wondered about John Gallagher. The memory of him made her shiver. He was still alive, still recovering – she knew that much. He had orchestrated several murders and intended her to be the last victim, once he had extracted everything she knew about where Kate Crowley might be hiding. But he had been shot. She remembered kneeling beside his body, pressing a towel into the blood spilling from his chest, praying he wouldn't die on her living-room carpet. Her home had been sullied enough.

She watched Vivian as she approached their table. She was eating her sandwich with vigour now, colour back in her face, and her eyes were bright when Anna sat down beside her.

"That William Ryan is lovely."

Anna smirked. Vivian had described him using very different adjectives in the recent past.

"And he's right," Vivian went on. "I'm so close to the truth that someone wants to scare me off. Well, that's not going to happen!"

"I didn't think for one second that it would. So, once you've made a formal statement I guess we spend the afternoon preparing for our interview tomorrow?"

"Yep. Bangarda Patricia O'Brien. Or *ex*-bangarda, I should say – though female guards don't use that term anymore, I think. She left shortly after the case."

Anna had never met a garda that had walked away from the job before, no matter what the circumstances. She reminded herself this was over forty years ago – times were different then, certainly for women in the force. She wondered what could have caused Patricia O'Brien to abandon her career and looked forward to finding out.

23

"Between you and your mother, all I seem to do is visit people these days." Tom sat down in the hard plastic chair opposite his son. It was good to see him out of bed, and in a few days he would be out of hospital too. "You really are like a cat with nine lives!"

Despite Tom's anger at John, once Victor White had planted the idea in his head, he couldn't stay away from visiting him. It was good to see his son. It wasn't that long ago John had been in this same hospital, recovering from the severe beating the Meier gang had inflicted. He had healed well then, and fast. Youth was on his side. Gunshot wounds were different though, especially one that nicked past his sternum and punctured one lung. Yet still he lived, and it looked like he was recovering well.

John was sitting in the chair opposite his father, dressed in a tracksuit, a book on the wheeled table. His blue eyes were sharp in his pale face, a light glistening of sweat coating his skin. He needed a haircut; it fell in a thick dark mass around his ears and over his forehead, and he needed a shave. But Tom thought his son looked good, all things considered.

"What about David?" John asked, a smile itching for release on his lips. "Do you ever visit him?"

Tom shifted in his seat. He knew this side of his son well, the part of him that wanted to hurt the world. Whoever was nearest would be dealt a gently spoken yet acidic taunt while the poison in John ached to spread to everyone around him. He couldn't blame him, it was just how he was made.

"Of course I do. I'm his father, aren't I?" Tom didn't add that his graveside visits to his younger son had stopped once he had clocked two plainclothes detectives walking slowly between the headstones behind him. "Your mother said to pass on her love."

This was a lie – Mae had been "sleeping" the last two times he had telephoned her, her mobile answered by a nurse or a care-assistant. Unease twisted sourly in his gut, but he couldn't be in two places at once.

"And Marco's mam died," he went on. "I didn't make the funeral. But I sent a card from all of us."

John leaned back into the seat, panting at little. "You look troubled, Dad."

"And why wouldn't I? You're facing a long stretch, John."

His son rolled his eyes. "I'll do ten years, max. I'll keep my head down and be out on good behaviour before you know it. Or maybe I'll plead insanity. Either way, I'll deal with Murray in the next few years, if he's still alive!"

Tom eyed the door to the hospital room, half-open, a young, uniformed garda standing outside, his hands clasped behind his back. No doubt he'd been instructed to listen in, but the man looked bored to Tom, shuffling his feet now and then, shifting his weight from left hip to right. He was supposed to be alert, yet he looked anything but.

"I've spoken to one of Murray's men," he said. "Someone new."

John raised his eyebrows.

"He's linked up with a gang in the UK."

"Which gang?" John asked quickly, leaning forward, his eyes pinning Tom.

"From London. An up-and-coming bunch. Murray wants a meet. He's after the city."

Tom had digested this news for over twenty-four hours now. To John, it was an unpleasant new reality. After a few moments he began to laugh, a guttural, rattling sound in his chest that was short-lived. He winced in pain and shifted his weight in the chair, reaching for the plastic cup of water on the locker. He sipped through a straw slowly, his eyes closed, fighting waves of pain. Tom watched his struggle, admiring his son's strength. He had always been able to rely on John ... now, what was left of him? What was left of them all?

"There's more," he sighed, hating to continue. "Ainsley was arrested in London yesterday."

"*Jesus Christ!*" John leaned back heavily into the chair, watching his father under hooded eyelids. "You came here to depress me?"

Tom sat forward, his fists bunched between his knees, his head hanging.

Pushing himself up, grunting with the effort, John placed one hand on his father's arm.

"Dad, what's wrong with you? It seems like you've given it all up already! Where's your fight? I can't do shit from here but you can. Get the men behind you, get ..." He ran out of strength, his voice failing.

Tom raised his head slowly, his eyes on the window and the view of the Wilton shopping centre outside, lanes of traffic inching slowly. Life moving on, regardless.

"In five months everything I've worked for throughout my life is gone. Can you understand that? Everything I've built up! And David is dead." His met his son's eyes. "*Dead!* Have you even grieved for your brother? Did you ever even visit his grave or were you too busy plotting those snuff movies in your bedroom?"

"Dad ..."

It was a warning. John was weak, his voice a fragile rasping cough.

"Your mother was drinking herself into an early grave, worrying herself to death about keeping *you* safe, her only surviving son. And what did you do all that time? Some money-making scheme on the internet! Killing people for money! I gave you everything but it wasn't enough. *Are you some sort of animal?*" He was distraught now, aware that his hands had closed into fists.

Everything he had built up was in ruins.

"You think drugs and stolen goods is more honourable?" John whispered. "And you're not afraid to kill a man when you have to!" His watery eyes bulged around his words and his hands gripped the armrests of the chair.

Tom was reminded of a caged dog, lashing out, wounded but still full of fight.

"I killed when I *had* to – most recently to bring you safely home. Or did you forget all that when you were playing with your friends on the internet?"

John looked away, putting one fist to his mouth and clamping his teeth onto his knuckles. Tom saw a sweaty imprint of where his hand had been on the armrest of his chair.

"*And what was the end result?*" Tom hissed, keeping his voice low, conscious of the garda at the half-open door.

"Nothing! No money, no notoriety online. You blew it, because you pissed off a man who had been loyal to me for thirty years. You underestimated Ely Murray, John. He would rather have killed you and taken what was mine than walk away. *He* should have been your final target for those bloody movies, not some stupid girl! And in the end I'm left with nothing! My good name in tatters, any respect I had earned blown away. All because you were so fucking stupid!"

He pushed up from the seat and stormed from the room, his shoulder barrelling into the garda as he passed. Tom ignored the man's shouted "*Hey!*" as he strode quickly down the hospital corridor. A nurse at the reception desk turned and said something as he passed her, but her words blurred along with her features and those of the people around her. Tom knew there was art on the wall, paintings from some famous artist, and he had planned to tell Mae about them, but now they blurred too, a mishmash of swirling colour as he stalked past. Everything was jumbled, just like in the Crawford Art gallery and in the restaurant yesterday … as though his eyes wouldn't function properly any more, or his brain couldn't decipher shapes.

Was he losing his mind?

At the elevator he jabbed the button but time moved too slowly; his lungs felt like he was running out of oxygen. He was drowning. He pushed open the door to the stairwell and ran down, flight after flight, gripping the banister. The stairs rushed up to meet him and he held his breath, fearful he might throw up if he stopped moving.

Finally he was outside, gasping in fresh, cold air, his hands on his knees. Vomit flew from his mouth without warning, splashing onto his leather shoes and the concrete in front of him. When he straightened up the world was still spinning. He wiped at his mouth with a handkerchief from his pocket, stuffing it back in place once he was done, and looked at his hands. They were shaking so violently he balled them into fists. Eyelids squeezed closed, he stood still, praying the vertigo twist and turns would stop.

The cold air brought peace. Tom sucked it into his lungs and heaved again, less urgently this time. He knew the truth – he wanted to hurt his son, had almost punched him. He feared that if he hit John he might never stop.

He jogged to his car, fighting the urge to sprint. He got in, body sagging against the leather seat. The keys wouldn't cooperate, wouldn't go into the slot to start the engine, and he gave up, sitting back heavily, his head throbbing. Sobs burst from him for a few seconds before he stifled them – Tom Gallagher was always in control. Always.

If a man lost control he lost everything. And these days, it felt like self-control was all he had left.

24

"You are not going to believe this!"

Anna wiped her eyes and sat up straighter, finishing up her call with Alex as Vivian walked into the kitchen. He had nothing new to tell her, just that the bags found were being sent for analysis this morning, as the detectives had promised. All they had to do was keep waiting …

Vivian had eaten breakfast already and was dressed formally in a dark trouser suit and pale-pink blouse. Her "interview uniform" as she had called it.

"What's up?" Anna picked up a slice of toast and bit into it, her eyebrows raised. Vivian held out her mobile phone to Anna, her face flushed in outrage.

"Anna, this is freaking me out! Someone was there at the graveyard yesterday and took photographs of us. Carol just rang me – it's all over the papers this morning!"

"You can't be serious!" Anna dropped her toast and took the phone, scrolling through the newspaper articles Vivian had opened on her browser. Headlines jumped from the screen, each more sinister than the last and, as she read them, her heart began to thud inside her chest.

"REPORTER THREATENED WITH MAKESHIFT HEADSTONE"

"HUNT FOR PRESUMED-DEAD KILLER TAKES SINISTER TURN"

The photographs were more unnerving – they showed Anna and Vivian from behind, staring at the wooden crucifix. The inscription of the cross was shown close-up, and another image of Anna with her phone in hand, taking photos of her own. Their faces were not visible, not really. Their scarves and the angle of the photograph did enough to conceal them. But Vivian was mentioned: "*The Banba Productions reporter and close friend.*"

Someone had been there, behind them, photographing them. Whoever it was had likely waited for them to arrive. If whoever sent the note had banked on them turning up to a photo op, then they had played right into his hands. It would be an extreme gamble to take if Vivian wasn't so predictable in her tenacity. Anna was, again, certain that whoever had sent the note was very familiar with her.

"I don't understand this! It seemed like there was nobody there!" Vivian exclaimed. "And we weren't followed. You'd have noticed as you drove, wouldn't you?"

"Yes, I would have."

"So they must have been waiting for us there. Or could they live nearby?"

"That's a possibility," Anna murmured. "A local person."

Vivian took her phone back and pushed it into her pocket. "My phone's been ringing all morning with reporters looking for a quote. I mean, I used to work at that end. I know most of them, and they're being really pushy!"

She brushed her hair from her face angrily. Anna noticed her hands were shaking.

Picking up her toast Anna nibbled at a corner, her thoughts

racing to make sense of this. "By the angle of those images, the person was standing behind us."

Vivian paused her pacing. "So they hid behind a headstone? Were there any big enough to hide a person?"

"Maybe … there were some larger ones by the entrance gate. Or perhaps they were in the field across the road, with a very high-quality camera. But, Viv – I think this person knows you. Knows you would have rushed down there once you'd realised what the numbers represented."

"Well, I hope he froze half to death!" Vivian jumped as her mobile rang loudly in her pocket. She hauled it out. "Oh, it's my mum, she's probably seen the papers. I'd better take this."

Anna watched her go. This new development was confusing. The worry about the note quoting Shakespeare and warning Vivian to take care still hovered in her mind, yet the threat had felt somewhat remote. Confined to Vivian's work. Knowing that the second note had been delivered to her home added a higher element of risk. The crucifix had been a terrifying thing to see, distressing for them both to read Vivian's name on a makeshift headstone. She had been called a troublemaker. It had shaken them both up and, now that they had either been followed or waited for, Anna was beginning to feel out of her depth.

The more she thought about it, the sound of Vivian's reassurances to her mother reaching her from the hallway, the less things made sense. Because if someone truly wanted to scare Vivian into dropping her investigation, all they had to do was send *her* the photographs. But the person responsible had chosen to send them to the press instead. Why anyone would do that was a motive her mind couldn't decipher.

Yet.

25

The first interviewee on Vivian's list, Patricia O' Brien, had lived in the same house her whole life in the village of Glounthaune, east of the city. Once they had exited the Dunkettle Roundabout, Anna found it easy to manoeuvre in the light Monday-morning traffic.

"Has your mum calmed down yet?"

"No, not really!" Vivian had just ended her third phone call to her parents that morning. "I mean, the image with her daughter's name on a headstone was awful, as you can imagine. Especially when she and Dad read the article and saw it was a threat against me. She was crying on the phone just now. Dad is threatening to speak to the gardaí himself." She grimaced as she pushed her mobile into her coat pocket.

"Did Gareth come up in conversation?"

"Not really. Mum just said he's busy with his course work." Vivian looked out of the window, watching the passing cars idly. "Why do you ask about him?"

"I'm just wondering if you still think he might be behind this?"

Vivian turned back to Anna and threw her hands in the air. "I haven't got a clue! Carol said she'll talk to William Ryan about it this morning and for me to continue on as normal unless I'm told not to. To stay in public places at all times and not go anywhere alone, that sort of thing. I'm going to check in with my old colleagues from the paper, see who can tell me what about where the photos came from. I suppose that's all we can do really. And as the detective said, stay safe. Somehow."

Patricia O'Brien was twenty-five years old in 1977 when she and her partner responded to a call for assistance on Washington Street. She hadn't long completed her Garda training when she was unwittingly involved in what was to become one of the most high-profile Garda investigations at the time. She and her partner were the nearest to the scene. Three weeks after that day, Patricia left the gardaí, while the investigation into what had happened was still ongoing.

Vivian had warned Anna that the woman had refused to appear in the documentary. Her answer had been "Absolutely not!" But after Carol had contacted her personally she had agreed to speak to them today, briefly, and made it clear it was only to get Vivian off her back.

They pulled up outside her house, a well-kept semi-detached. The exterior cream looked freshly painted, the short, cobbled driveway dotted with large potted plants. Vivian rang the doorbell, her small, black, leather satchel over one arm with her notebook and voice recorder inside – there was no need for her notes, she knew them by heart.

"We're a bit early," she whispered. "I planned to be. Sometimes it's best to catch people off-guard."

Patricia O'Brien opened the door quickly, a mug in her hand. If she was surprised by their timing, it didn't show on her impassive gaze. She looked much younger than her late sixties. She wore an elegant cream trouser suit, her blonde hair piled onto her head in a stylish twist, her make-up flawlessly applied on a face that was virtually wrinkle free. The scent of expensive perfume drifted towards them, mingled with the aroma of her fresh coffee.

Anna nudged Vivian gently; neither of them had said anything yet.

"Miss O'Brien? I'm Vivian Keating. This is my associate Anna Clarke. May we come in?"

For a tense moment Anna wasn't sure the woman would move aside and let them into the house. Her face remained expressionless as she sipped from her mug of coffee, her eyes appraising them coolly. After a beat she stepped aside and swung the front door open wider, a loud sigh conveying her displeasure at letting them into her house.

"I suppose you must. Go through to the living room, there on the right."

The lemon-zesty smell of furniture polish was overpowering. Anna pinched the bridge of her nose as she followed Vivian into a small living room, Patricia O'Brien right behind them.

"Sit down, please. You'll have some coffee?"

They nodded and murmured their thanks. Patricia left the room, her expression souring further now that they were inside. Vivian sat down on a grey-leather two-seater and began to pull out her notebook and pen, then the voice recorder, putting them onto the lace-covered coffee table in the centre of the room. Heavy lace curtains blocked out the street, dimming the light inside and Anna pushed them gently aside, looking out.

"She's quite fond of lace." She looked around the room, at lace doilies on the mantelpiece and more on the shelves underneath photo frames and figurines. "This place is quite old-fashioned, isn't it? It doesn't really suit her ... spotless though." She moved to the fireplace, running a finger along it, past the small mantle clock and two candleholders – all Waterford Crystal. A three-seater leather sofa ran along one wall; it looked new. Anna moved to a large dresser against the opposite wall, her fingertips caressing a record player on one shelf.

"A Crosley! My dad had one of these!"

"Oh really?" Vivian's tone was more distracted than interested, her eyes on the living-room door. "Patricia's taking ages," she muttered. The sound of crockery clinking together reached them from the kitchen as she turned back to Anna. "What's her musical taste then?"

Anna flicked through a stack of records before putting them carefully back into their rightful place.

"Lots of Rod Stewart. Some Roy Orbison, some Queen." She leaned closer to a set of photographs and paused. "This must be her family. Patricia has two sisters by the look of it ... these photos must go back forty years! There's nothing more up-to-date. That's odd, isn't it? They all look very alike."

Four photographs on one shelf took up the whole space, showing a family of five, parents and three sisters, in a variety of poses: on the beach, outside a rundown caravan, standing on a bridge somewhere, an old-fashioned yellow car behind them.

"It's weird ... none of these photos show the sisters as adults, just as children and in their late teens."

"Maybe the others moved away? Emigration was really common back then."

"Who knows?" Anna pulled her mobile phone from her pocket and took photographs of the items on the shelves.

"*What are you doing?*" Vivian hissed. "I want this woman on side, Anna! What if she catches you?"

"Have you forgotten you're a journalist?" Anna whispered back, before putting her phone away and sitting beside Vivian on the two-seater. "Happy?"

Vivian didn't reply. Watching her friend, the way her fingers twitched in her lap, the way her eyes strayed to the door every few seconds, Anna realised that Vivian wouldn't feel *happy* until she had all the answers.

26

Patricia O'Brien pushed the door open with a tray as she walked into the room, her eyes on the milk jug that wobbled ominously as she moved.

"Right," she set the tray down on the table, "let's get this over with!" She sat opposite them and addressed Vivian. "Firstly, I don't see why the public would be interested in this again. There's absolutely nothing to be gained by dragging up the past."

"We disagree," Vivian said.

"And, furthermore, it was *decades* ago. Have you managed to find anyone else that will remember that day? This whole thing is absolutely preposterous!"

There was silence while Patricia picked lint from her trousers and glared at Vivian. Her resentment was at odds with the tray on the table, laden with fine china cups and a pot of coffee, a small jug of cream and a selection of biscuits on a doily-covered plate. Her hospitality was obviously ingrained, something even her hostile attitude toward them couldn't erase.

Now she placed a cup and saucer before each of them, poured the coffee and then continued her protest.

"I only agreed to speak with you today to get you off my back, as I said! I have absolutely no interest in appearing in your documentary. I can't stop you, of course – believe me, I've taken legal advice on that! But I will be paying close attention to how I'm portrayed in it. I'll be taking legal action if I come across as … Well, it's just horribly unfair! It was one of the worst times of my life and you're forcing me to talk about it all again!"

"With all due respect, Miss O'Brien," said Vivian, "at least one man died and you were one of the arresting gardaí. This is a public interest case, part of a series of programmes featuring unsolved crimes. Going back to the people that were there on the day in question is inevitable. I appreciate this is difficult for you – you were assaulted too by the killer before he escaped, weren't you?"

"Yes." She looked at the gold swirling pattern on the beige carpet at her feet, her anger dampened somewhat by Vivian's words. "It happened so suddenly. There was nothing I could do."

"Can you tell us, in your own words, what happened that day?" Vivian asked. "Everything you remember."

Patricia was angry again. "Why? I'm sure it's a matter of public record! What difference does it make if you speak to me – I've spent my life trying to move on, and here you sit, dragging it all up again!"

Her voice broke and she blinked back tears as she yanked her cup of coffee from the table, holding it in her hands. It trembled slightly and Anna met Vivian's eyes, discomfort bouncing between them on the leather sofa.

"I'm sorry you're upset, Miss O'Brien," Vivian said. "I understand the events of that day had a big impact on your life. A man dead, another jumped into the river, presumed dead. It led you to turn your back on your career. So believe me, I *have* thought about the impact this documentary will have on you. That's why I think it's important that you get to have your say! I assure you we will present only the truth – think of this visit as a courtesy to include *your* side of the story. Not what's written on paper but the *true* account of what happened to you that day. In *your* own words, as I said."

Anna was impressed – Vivian sounded passionate and genuine, and she could see her words were having the desired effect on Patricia. The woman sighed deeply and took a sip of coffee, turning her head to look at them properly for the first time since she had sat down. Her shoulders lowered slightly and she crossed one leg over the other, looking more like a person sharing a conversation with friends rather than a harsh interrogation.

"Back then … what exact year was it? It was difficult for women in the gardaí. I'm sure you both know that – it's been well documented in books and in the media. Not *all* women found it tough of course, but for me … it was hell, right from the start!"

"In what way?"

"I was a target from the get-go. Sexist jokes, snide remarks, comments that I would be better off having babies than pandering to the politicians in their efforts to reverse discrimination. It wasn't just me – plenty of female recruits suffered the same. I was left out of strategy talks and jokes, never asked on work nights out … it was relentless. Exclusion is a form of bullying, you know."

"Did everyone you worked with treat you the same way?"

"Well … no. I don't think so. But it was a long time ago."

"Your partner at the time in question was Oliver Cotter. How was your working relationship with him?"

She scoffed loudly, "My *partner*? That man made it *very* clear he was not happy to be paired with a female. He was so hostile it was ridiculous. And after the Bernard O'Meara affair, I just couldn't stay. Cotter was difficult to work with in any case, but things got worse after that day."

"How so?" Vivian spoke softly.

"He was a bit older than me … Anyway, he was unhappy being paired with a bangarda, in the first place, and after the boy attacked me it all got worse. I was pretty new, a bit wet behind the ears, and he really didn't hold back. He let it be known he was unhappy with me. He blamed me and made no secret of it."

"Why would he have blamed you?" Anna asked gently.

Patricia shrugged and spread her hands in a 'don't ask me' gesture.

"You call the attacker 'the boy'," Vivian said. "Did he strike you as quite young? Some of the witnesses said he was in his late teens or maybe his early twenties."

Patricia shrugged. "My memory of him is that he was young, that's it! Maybe seventeen or eighteen. But it was years ago – he could have been a small twenty-year-old for all I know."

"What else do you remember about him?"

"Oh God … dark clothes, a hood up. His jacket was black but the hood was lighter, maybe grey, and was from a jumper *inside* the jacket. That stuck in my mind all these years – isn't it strange? There was blood on his boots. They were black and scruffy and there was blood on the front of them …" She straightened up then, squaring her shoulders, and put her cup back on its saucer on the table. When she looked at them her expression was impatient, her lips pursed. A pink flush was creeping up her neck. "Like I said, I really don't see the point of raking over the ruins of the past."

"Well, there's a possibility the young man is still alive." Vivian spoke clearly and watched as her words had the chosen effect.

Patricia's mouth dropped open, her eyes bulging from their sockets.

Anna glanced at Vivian, slightly alarmed. Vivian really had no evidence to make this statement and it was a risk to verbalise her theory to a garda who had been involved in the boy's arrest. Yet she pressed on.

"The statute of limitations doesn't apply to crimes of this nature – there's still a chance we can get justice for Bernard O'Meara, still a chance his daughter can see someone held to account."

"Is this some sort of *joke*?" Patricia whispered, aghast. "You're trying to make a name for yourself – that's what this is!"

"Miss O'Brien, isn't finding the truth about what happened that day the best possible outcome? For Mr O'Meara's daughter to see justice done – it makes revisiting the case worthwhile, wouldn't you say?"

Patricia didn't say anything – she just stared at Vivian, her mouth an O-shape in a face that had grown considerably paler.

"Where was your partner when the killer attacked you?"

Anna's voice seemed to surprise Patricia. She looked startled, blinking rapidly as she cleared her throat.

"Well … I don't remember. He was nearby, certainly, and he was the one who cuffed the boy."

"To the front or the back?" Anna leaned forward, keen to get the woman's account of that element of the case. "It wasn't in the file."

Patricia sat up straighter, her hands folded in her lap, and inhaled a shaky breath. Her voice grew steadier as she spoke.

"To be honest, I don't remember. Nowadays it's always to the front, isn't it? You see these criminals holding coats over their faces to avoid being photographed. I mean, please!" She snorted. "Off to prison for life and they're concerned if the neighbours see their ugly mugs on the telly! But the thing is, they're cuffed to the front. That's *now* though, with all the do-gooders saying it's too dangerous to cuff at the back and whatnot. Back then we didn't have those concerns. But I didn't cuff the boy so I really can't answer that question."

"So he was handcuffed. Let's say his hands were cuffed in front of him. And Garda Cotter stepped away – he said in his statement he had to attend to the victim. So you were in charge of the boy. What happened then?"

Silence stretched uncomfortably until Patricia spoke again softly.

"Well, I suppose I led him to the squad car. It was parked only yards away, I'm sure … yes, we pulled up on Washington Street by the courthouse steps. So it was only a short distance."

"And he attacked you?" Anna prompted.

"Well … yes."

"Do you remember the details of the attack?"

"You know I don't – you've clearly read the files." Anger again flashed onto her face and flooded into her voice, "All I know is I was knocked to the ground and he ran. I gave chase – of course I did – down towards the Western Road. But then he jumped."

"Into the River Lee. Did he resurface?"

"Not that I remember."

"You made a statement that he didn't surface again," Vivian offered.

Patricia turned to gaze out the window through the thick lace curtains and when she turned back to them, her stern expression made it clear the conversation was over.

But Vivian continued. "Do you remember about –"

"For heaven's sake! It was *years* ago! Everything I know is in my statement!"

"Are you familiar with a grave and headstone dedicated to 'The Boy Who Jumped'?"

"That's *enough!*" Patricia stood up and piled their untouched cups of coffee back onto the tray, speaking again in a rush. "All I know is I was ostracised after that. Cotter didn't bother to conceal his disappointment at being saddled with a young bangarda and no-one offered me any support. It was made out to be *my* fault that the guy ran off and jumped. As if that was ever going to be true – there was nothing I could do."

Patricia stood up straight and looked at them.

"I've been more than generous with my time, ladies. Even *thinking* about this has been very traumatic for me. I expect to be sympathetically portrayed in your documentary – my sister is a solicitor and we'll be watching very carefully! Any blame directed towards me ..."

She stopped as Anna moved to stand beside the dresser and plucked one photograph from the shelf. "Which sister is that, Miss O' Brien? You all look so alike!"

Patricia stepped forward, snatching the framed photograph from Anna's hands. "*If you don't mind!*" Her eyes blazed and her hand shook, the photo frame wobbling in the air.

"I'm sorry if I upset you, I didn't mean to. I don't have any sisters myself – just one brother. It must be nice to have sisters. What are their names?"

Patricia's eyes rested on the photograph which captured them as young children and a heavy sigh escaped her lips. "Yes ... well ... yes, that's the three of us. Patricia, Christina and Margaret. All so alike, everyone used to say so. Not so much now, in our older years." She smiled at Anna suddenly, a sad smile that filled Anna with guilt.

"No photos of you all as adults?"

"No!" The smile dropped, the shutters to her mind down again.

"My father had a Crosley record player too," Anna said softly, hoping to rekindle some of the woman's momentary warmth. "The sound is beautiful from them, isn't it? I see you like Rod Stewart."

Patricia sighed again, anxious to have this conversation over. "He was my mother's favourite."

"So she played his music often?"

Patricia nodded impatiently, but at least she answered. "We always played Rod Stewart on a Saturday night after supper – a family tradition. Things were simpler then." She smiled, and it lit up her face. "Actually, my mother's maiden name was Stuart – it was a bit of a family joke that she loved Rod's music."

"That sounds really nice," Anna whispered, seeing the other woman was close to tears. She realised she wasn't the only one who missed good times with the people she loved.

Patricia wiped a hand across her face and cleared her throat. "I'll see you girls out." The gruff, business-like exterior had faded, but she didn't smile as she held the front door open for them.

Vivian turned to her. "If you change your mind about speaking about your experience that day –"

"I won't."

"Well, should I have a few more questions –"

The door closed in their faces, cutting Vivian off mid-sentence.

Back in the car Anna turned up the heat and let the car idle at the kerb for a few minutes.

Vivian was discreetly watching the house. "Well, she's definitely not behind the threatening notes – she wants absolutely nothing to do with the whole thing. And she's not a curtain-twitcher either.

I thought she'd be watching us but no sign of her."

"Those curtains are a thick lace – I doubt we'd see her if she's standing behind them watching us." Anna pulled gloves from the pocket in the driver's door and pushed her hands into them. "She looks well for a woman in her late sixties – she could easily pass for ten years younger."

"Definitely. And the house is perfect. No expense spared. Leather couch – real, I'd say – and did you see the size of the TV?"

"What did she do after she left the Guards?"

Vivian shrugged. "I've no clue. There was no sign of a significant other in the house, nothing we saw anyway so however she made her money she did it herself."

"Did you notice that she answered the door holding a mug, but served us our coffee in fine china cups?"

"So?"

"So she was putting her best foot forward with us. Wanting to give a good impression."

"I guess …" Vivian eyes were still on the lace curtains.

"Isn't it strange she has no adult photographs in that room? Just childhood memories." Anna opened her phone and browsed through the photographs she had taken. The three sisters, she guessed at aged twelve, ten and eight, and then older, perhaps Patricia in her late teens and the others a little younger. Anna focused on the youngest sister's face – Margaret, Patricia had called her – and angled her phone to Vivian.

"Does she look familiar to you?"

"Yes, she's a younger version of Patricia O'Brien!"

Anna sighed and waved the phone. "Be serious! I feel like I've seen her before."

Vivian shrugged. "She looks like a lot of people, to be honest. Maybe she was your mum's friend?" Suddenly she covered her mouth with her hands.

"What's the matter?"

"*Oh, for feck's sake!* I never switched on the voice recorder!" She groaned and leaned her head back. "I suppose it doesn't matter, we got nothing new here. Come on – it's cold. Let's get some lunch and go home."

27

The office space inside Banba Productions could best be described as sterile in William's opinion. White tiles covered the floor, so shiny he wagered he could see his reflection in them, if he chose to. Glass desks were clustered in the centre of the room, separated by glass and steel partitions. High-backed black-leather chairs stood like wheeled watchmen, guarding the documents that were bound in piles of cream folders, sparse on some tables, ready to topple on others. At the end of the large room was another desk, wider than the others, and turned to face the floor, but otherwise unremarkable. Except for the woman sitting at it.

Carol O'Connor stood up as William and Grace approached, holding out her hand in greeting, her smile warm. Her hair was a deep red and wound in a coil on the top of her head, pulled tightly from her face. Her lips matched the colour, stretching around teeth he found oddly small for a grown woman. Her nails were long and curved and scratched his wrist softly as they locked hands. She gestured to them to sit in two black-leather chairs that were in front of her glass desk, and they did so. She appeared utterly relaxed to have two detectives sitting in her office.

"Detectives, welcome to Banba Productions! May I offer you tea or coffee, some water perhaps?"

William shook his head and settled into the leather chair. He found it strangely hard and unyielding. He introduced both of them and they produced their identification, Carol's eyes scanning both quickly.

"You're alone in the office?"

"Aside from Sheena, who you met at reception, it's just me here right now, but the staff come and go. We have to be adaptable in this business. Investigative reporting is very flexible. Sometimes the story takes my crew out onto the road. I don't keep tabs as long as targets are met."

"Are there many people employed here?" Grace asked, flipping her notebook open and clicking her pen, her eyebrows rising expectantly.

"Four staff at the moment in-house, with several positions outsourced to specialist companies and freelancers. We're just getting off the ground. But things are building very rapidly." She smiled broadly. "So, you're both here regarding the photographs in the newspaper. Vivian mentioned she had spoken to you – with my full support, of course." A flash of those tiny teeth again; her smile was fixed in place now.

William nodded. "You're obviously aware of the threatening nature of the notes Vivian Keating received, and of the wooden crucifix near the grave of the man she plans to feature in a documentary. And someone photographed her and a friend at that location. We traced the photos to an online website. Within a few hours they made their way into the print media. Are you familiar with a Bill Simpson who runs 'Cork News-Linx' online?"

"Vaguely," Carol answered with a wave of her hand. "We've met at functions now and again, but I don't know him personally."

"He was reluctant to give up their source for the photos but we insisted." William smiled and watched her face for a reaction, finding nothing but expectant interest.

Grace picked up the thread of conversation. "Simpson eventually provided everything he had. It appears he published the photographs on foot of an email received from you."

It took a moment for her words to sink in. When they did, the smile instantly vanished. "I beg your pardon?"

William opened the folder in his hands and slid a printout of the email across the table. "The email he received with the photographs attached appears to have come from your personal email account."

"Well, there's obviously a mistake." Carol sounded uncertain, her hands snatching up the page in a blur of red. They watched her eyes move over the words, her jaw drop, watched her chest rise as her breathing became laboured. Her composure had completely evaporated.

"The sender asks the editor to run the photographs as a personal favour to increase publicity for Banba Productions and generate publicity for the documentary series Vivian Keating is making. It goes on to say you'll give the news-site exclusive first access to interviews and screenings."

Her eyes kept moving, left and right, as she attempted to digest the words on the page.

"What ... no ... it's not right. I didn't send this! It's not even how I *phrase* things. That's not even my email address! I don't know what to say!"

"The email address is fake," William said quickly, "or rather, set up for this purpose and then deleted. Our experts in this area have looked into it already. It was set up a few minutes before the photos were sent and disabled shortly after. Finding a footprint and tracing it to an IP server will take some time. Sometimes results never materialise from these investigations."

Carol dropped the page as if it was burning her fingertips and sat back into her chair.

"If you know I didn't set it up, then why are you here?"

"We never said we know you didn't set it up," Grace said quietly. "We said we believe the email address was created for this purpose and then deleted. There's a difference."

They sat in silence for a few moments, Carol rubbing her hands over each other in a soothing motion, obviously trying to gather her thoughts.

"Do you actually think it was me?"

"*Was* it you? Did you send the notes, put the crucifix in place, photograph your employee and send the images to the press?"

Incredulous laughter burst from Carol's lips. "Of course not! Why on earth would I?"

"For publicity. Like the email said."

Carol leaned forward and placed the palms of her hands on the table. Her face had grown considerably paler but her eyes flashed with anger.

"I had nothing to do with this! And I wouldn't do this to any of my staff! If you think *this* is how I need to drum up publicity then you underestimate me – I've *years* of experience in this business. You are barking up the wrong tree!"

"Can you think of anyone that would do this?"

Carol shrugged and shook her head. "Honestly, I've no idea. This doesn't make any sense!"

William observed a shiny line of sweat glistening on the woman's upper lip. There was motive here – to drive up publicity for the fledgling company. And if the general manager of the company wasn't behind it, who else would be invested enough to do it? But she had a point – with years of experience, why would tactics like this be necessary?

"We'll need a list of names and contact details for all the investors for Banba Productions and for the board of directors, and of course all the staff as well. Are you aware of any grudges against Vivian Keating among the staff, among any third parties connected to the company?"

Carol shook her head emphatically, the topknot on her head shaking violently.

"No, she's just a kid. She's ambitious, she can rub people up the wrong way sometimes, but she's a hard worker. I'll look into it. I'll ask around. Discreetly, of course!"

"We'll also need a list of all your social media accounts, email addresses and so on," Grace said crisply, tearing a piece of paper from her notebook. "You can send them through to me on this email. Make sure it's a *comprehensive* list – we need to move fast on this – we take threats of this nature seriously. And we'd recommend pausing the investigation Miss Keating is conducting until this gets resolved."

William smiled tightly and rose to his feet, Grace taking her cue to do the same.

"We'll be in touch," he said. "If you can think of anything that can help the investigation, contact either one of us. And consider the safety of your staff, Miss O'Connor."

Carol stood at her desk but didn't offer her hand this time – she looked to be in shock, gripping the edge of the glass table.

As they moved back through the room the outer door opened and a tall leather-clad man stepped inside, his hands full of cardboard coffee cups and a brown-paper bag. His eyes met William's, then swivelled to Grace's, and he smiled. He placed the coffees and bag on the nearest desk, his eyes roaming over Grace's face, his smile broadening.

Carol moved quickly around her desk and stepped towards them, her red heels loud on the tiled floor.

"Luke Daly is my chief producer – he's working on the same documentary as Vivian. Luke, these are detectives from Lee Street, looking into the situation with the notes Viv got in the mail." She sounded breathless.

Luke stood straighter, pulling down the end of his leather jacket. "Oh right. The thing with the wooden cross?"

"Yes, and the first note Miss Keating received was the one you said you'd take care of but never did. Glad to have met you here today – pull up a seat!" William gestured to the nearby black-leather chairs and Grace smiled widely, flipping open her notebook again.

28

"Any plans for tonight?"

Anna smiled at Jason and accepted the bottle of water he offered. They had packed away their sparring pads and rolled up the mats; the punch-bag hung steady, the hotel-gym in Kinsale quiet this Monday evening. He had pushed her hard this session and she had relished it. They would concentrate on patterns for her black-belt grading after class on Thursday night. For the rest of the week, they planned to keep their training to their little square in the gym, concentrating on fitness and small-space self-defence manoeuvres. Lately, that had been her safety-net.

"No plans," she lied. Jason would worry if she told him what she wanted to do tonight. "How's Colette?"

For a few minutes they chatted about his wife's new stationary business and what Anna's plans were for her break from work. She deliberately kept things vague. Jason didn't ask about Alex, or if there was any update on identifying the bags discovered buried in the cold ground in the field in Portloaise – he knew she'd tell him what she could. He remarked that she seemed lighter, more focused on the training, and Anna felt that too – working with Vivian was good for her, she'd concluded. Revisiting the killing of Bernard O'Meara was distracting, and the mystery stayed on her mind the more she involved herself.

Jason brought up the newspaper article he'd seen this morning, with Anna and Vivian examining the crucifix in the graveyard in West Cork. "Didn't you promise me you'd stay out of trouble?"

Anna resisted the urge to remind him she was twenty-seven years old and could take care of herself. She outlined the case briefly, asking if he remembered the story from the news back in 1977.

"Jeez, Anna, I was only a teenager then. I *do* remember it though, mainly because the young fella drowned himself in the River Lee afterwards. It was bizarre – it was all anyone in Cork could talk about for a while. The killer was like a celebrity."

"Do you think he *did* drown? Vivian wonders if he could have survived."

Jason drained his bottle of water and tossed it into a nearby recycling bin, shaking his head. "No way. Not possible, in my opinion. Everyone argued about it back then but, if you ask me, that young fella died that day."

Anna conceded that he was probably right. They said goodnight, each heading to the showers. She took her time under the heat of the water, allowing it to pummel her shoulders and neck, loosening the muscles. She thought again of the threatening notes Vivian had received and her concern that her brother Gareth might have something to do with it all. Anna had known Gareth for as long as she'd been friends with Vivian – they'd been neighbours, school-friends, part of each other's lives. She knew things had been hostile between brother and sister lately, but there was no way Gareth was behind this. She was sure of it, and tonight she hoped to put an end to Vivian's theory, once and for all.

She had expected to feel apprehension, perhaps fear, as she pulled up outside her childhood home in Kinsale. Up until this afternoon when the phone call had come, she had been firmly determined never to set foot inside it again. When she left a few weeks ago, the attic empty, the walls bare of paintings and photo-collages, she had happily walked away. Her memories came with her, wound around her like ribbons moulded to her skin. She would never be free of them, and she was OK with that now. Her childhood here had been happy – the first sixteen years of her life had been full of love and laughter. More recently, loneliness and then fear had become so powerful within the walls of the house that all other emotions had faded too far to be remembered. She'd *had* to leave.

But earlier, as Vivian typed up notes of their conversation with Patricia O'Brien, Anna had received a text from one of her former neighbours in Kinsale.

So sorry to bother you, Anna! But Dave was cleaning the upstairs windows and noticed your attic skylight is slightly open. With all the rain we've been having, I'm sure you'll want to sort that.

Alex had cleared out the attic when she'd left the house, and he must have left the window open. They planned to put the house on the market soon. She really hoped the recent rainfall hadn't caused any damage.

Anna had considered asking the Pearsons to sort it out. They had a spare key, and she couldn't even contemplate going inside the house, especially the attic. But she knew that was selfish of her; they were elderly, it would be asking too much. A hard spike of dread had pierced her when she realised she'd have to do it herself. Vivian had plans. She could have asked Jason to accompany her – to go inside alone would be far too unnerving – but then she remembered that Gareth lived nearby, and an idea had formed.

It was time he and Vivian patched things up.

When she pulled into the driveway she waited for a while with the engine idling, looking at the house. It was set in darkness, which wasn't a surprise. In the light cast by the car's headlamps she looked at the front door. The red paint was faded; it had been that way a long time. Her father had painted it in the summer before he disappeared, and neither she nor Alex had done anything to it since then. Realising that soon the house would have new owners, people that would change everything, brought sudden tears to her eyes. The emotion surprised her – she had said goodbye to the house weeks ago.

She switched off the engine and climbed out. The streetlights in the estate cast shadows around her and illuminated parts of the approach to her house. Her driveway was narrow and some of the plants either side had grown out over the concrete. A tiny wooden birdhouse hung from a tree branch in the garden; the sight of it hanging there suddenly reminded her of Kate. They all had made those birdhouses in school when they were about ten years old – hand-painted, coat after coat, giggling with Vivian, Kate and Natalie. It felt like a lifetime ago.

The sound of approaching footsteps drew her attention. Gareth.

She was surprised he had agreed to meet her, considering it was almost a year since they had spoken and he still steadfastly refused to speak to Vivian. Although Gareth and Vivian were both adopted, they could easily pass as brother and sister. Gareth was younger by two years and taller, lean, years on the running track etched in his physique. Both had light-brown hair, blue eyes and creamy skin. Gareth had a full beard now, and Anna was reminded of William Ryan yesterday.

"What's with everyone growing beards these days?" she said with a smile as he stopped beside her at the front door.

"Is that how you say hello, Clarke?" He reached for her and pulled her into a quick, unexpected hug. Gareth had always called her by her surname growing up and the familiarity of that now was as comforting as the tight hug he offered.

"Thanks for meeting me here."

"No prob." He smiled, his eyes twinkling in the semi-darkness. "Are you gonna let me in? It's bloody freezing!" He rubbed his hands together as she fumbled with her keys at the lock, stamping his feet.

She laughed, her breath dancing in the cold air in front of her face. Vivian always said Gareth was like a cat – he hated to be cold and complained even more if he was caught in the rain. She pushed open the front door, her eyes on the security alarm on the wall just inside. It remained silent. Alex must not have turned it on.

A waft of stale air greeted her and her stomach lurched. They walked through the hall and into the living room, Anna turning on the lights as they went. Everything was different – of course, it was, she knew it would be – but it was still a shock to be back here. Her sofa and lounge chair were gone. The bookcases too; all the books were in the boxes that lined her bedroom walls in Vivian's apartment. Her father's record player and his collection were in Alex's house, along with boxes of their family photographs and all the things that formed the stuffing of a family's memories – fridge magnets from every holiday they had ever taken, framed certificates of school and sporting achievements, the noticeboard from the kitchen wall. It was all gone, boxed away, to be dissected later when they could bear it. The walls were repainted a plain white, the carpet replaced too – Vivian had overseen that.

Last month, John Gallagher's blood had splattered the walls and stained the carpet. Once the Tech Bureau were done with collecting DNA evidence the house had looked even worse. Anna had been unable to return to turn it into something marketable and Vivian had taken over. She owed her friend for how the house looked now – fresh, a blank canvas for a new family. She hoped whoever bought it would be happy here.

Standing with Gareth in the centre of the living room, her body trembled only a little, and she told herself it was the cold. The house was warm, the heating set to come on every few hours. Yet still Gareth shivered dramatically.

"This cold shouldn't happen indoors, Clarke!" He looked around at the empty living room, his lips quivering a little in the cold. "Aren't you trying to sell the place? No-one will part with their money for this house if their first impression is that they'd freeze to death!"

"What are you like?" she laughed.

"You said you had a job for me to do?" he asked. "And I take payment in pints, by the way. Or a heated blanket." He stamped his feet on the carpet, his hands tucked under his armpits.

Anna kept her eyes on his face. She wanted to see his reaction to her questions, and she really wanted to be anywhere else but here. To focus on Gareth would keep her memories at bay.

"No problem, pints it is. I'll even drive you home after. But first I want to talk to you about Vivian."

His smiled slipped. "What do you want to talk about?"

Anna decided to get straight to the point.

"*The Tempest.*"

"What about it?"

"That line, '*Hell is empty and all the devils are here*'? Vivian got a threatening note warning her to tread carefully. And then a crucifix with her name on it. Are you messing with her?"

Gareth shook his head, disbelief and anger vying for position on his face. "Is that supposed to be funny?"

"No, it's a serious question." Anna met his eyes and folded her arms, waiting.

The look on her face was one Gareth had seen many times growing up. He gritted his teeth and threw up his hands.

"Fine! I saw the newspaper article on her new job and this whole crucifix thing, and Mum filled me in. What's happening is creepy, but nothing to do with me. You disappoint me, Clarke. Scaring my sister with notes and messages on wood is not my style. It's pretty messed up. Are you saying Vivian thinks this crap is my doing?"

"Well, you haven't spoken to her in almost a year!"

"That doesn't mean I'm some weirdo sending her notes and freaking her out. I'm not trying to scare her or anything. I don't even want to –"

"Be near her?" Anna stepped closer and, seeing the sadness in his eyes, she touched his arm. "I know you've had a tough time lately. But you must realise it has nothing to do with Vivian! Her relationship with Brenda is not a reflection on you or your parents. She's not rejecting you."

Gareth looked away, his eyes roaming the empty room. "Look, I know, I do! I've been ... things have been tough. My head was messed up for a while, you know?"

"Vivian told me that when you reached out to your birth mother it didn't go as you'd hoped?"

She hoped her questioning was gentle, that he didn't find it too intrusive.

Gareth stepped towards the window, parting the curtain slightly, looking out into the night.

"Kathleen, yeah. She was a friend of my dad's. Did you know that? Mum and Dad took care of me when she couldn't. She moved abroad, started a different family a few years later. When I started asking questions they had her contact details and encouraged me to write to her. That turned out to be a waste of time."

He turned from the window to face her again. He attempted an ironic smile, but sadness pulled at the corners of it and it became a lopsided frown.

"She didn't want to know me. She had moved on; she said she was a very different person, and she wished me well." His shoulders shook, as though shaking off the sting of her rejection, and he smiled properly then. "Things are getting better. I'm looking into lecturing in English Literature as a career and getting accepted on the course feels like a new chapter. Pun intended!"

His grin was infectious but Anna wondered how he could switch from downcast to upbeat so easily. Was he really OK?

"I'm happy for you! But, please, Gareth – please reach out to Vivian – you need to patch things up with her, because she is seriously entertaining the idea that you're behind these attempts to scare her."

Gareth placed one hand on his chest. "This is actually offensive! I know we've had our ups and downs but I can't believe Vivian thinks I'm some sort of lunatic."

Anna resisted the urge to hug him. She didn't think he'd welcome that just now. But she was glad he had opened up to her and she believed him – he wasn't the person trying to scare Vivian.

"Well, I believe you. And, please, call her! Now let's go for that drink – but first, I need you to close a window in the attic. The neighbours contacted me about it."

"Is that it? When you said you needed help with something in the house, I expected something a bit more demanding on my manly physique, to be honest." He grinned at her and she rolled her eyes.

"I don't know if you know this, but I hate enclosed spaces. The smaller the space the more freaked out I get. So, you're up."

She walked into the hallway and up the staircase, Gareth at her heels. Once they reached the landing, Anna stopped and looked around. The house was silent and still. The upstairs hallway was dark save for a sliver of moonlight on the carpet, coming from her open bedroom door. She peered inside. The curtains were open. Snapping on the light she moved into the room and drew them closed, Gareth behind her.

"You really cleared out, didn't you? Where's all your bedroom furniture?"

"In Alex's garage." It felt like she was moving through an unfamiliar space, not the home she had lived in for twenty-six years.

She gently pushed him backwards in the direction of the pulldown staircase that led to the attic. Suddenly, she really wanted to leave.

"Up you go!"

Last year, in search of Christmas ornaments to decorate the house with her niece Chloe, she had spent some time in her attic – before that, it had been a long time since she'd ventured inside it. She hated enclosed spaces; she had no memory of any trauma that could explain it, but her claustrophobic fear had been debilitating. The wooden attic floor was covered with linoleum. Anna had made it a storage room, and as comfortable as possible, adding a skylight to add a sense of space. Still, she had avoided it as much as possible.

"I hope there's no water damage," she murmured.

The metal pole to open the pull-down staircase had been left propped against the wall underneath it. Gareth stretched up to slot it into place but turned to face her again.

"It's open. The door isn't properly pushed in."

Anna shrugged. They had left the house as quickly as they could, and it wasn't surprising some things had been left unfinished.

Gareth pulled down the small door, unfolded the stairs and ascended quickly.

Looking up, Anna saw that the space was partially lit, moonlight spilling in through the skylight window.

"The light switch is on the left beside you!" she called to Gareth and he switched it on.

She waited at the foot of the stairs. Hearing Gareth's "*What the fuck?*", apprehension was a sour taste in her mouth. "What is it?" she called.

"I thought you said this place was empty?" he called down.

It should be, Anna thought, it *is*. Yet, clearly Gareth could see that it wasn't.

Placing a shaking hand on the metal support banister she ascended slowly, willing her legs to keep going. Nausea crept further up her throat and liquid flooded her mouth but she swallowed and she did her best to ignore it. Her nose itched at the dusty air and, when she reached the top of the stairs, she gasped.

Gareth stood in the middle of the attic, his neck bent to avoid hitting his head on the ceiling. Around him were scattered tins of soup and canned meat, some towering in large piles, others lying on their side on the floor. A sleeping bag was spread out on the left-hand side of the space, a coil of brown rope and a roll of black masking tape on the floor beside it. An open toolbox rested nearby.

Anna shook her head in confusion. This wasn't right! The house was empty, the doors were locked …

And then, like a physical blow, realisation dawned in a gut-churning pull. She cradled her spinning head in her hands and gulped in the stale air.

"Are you OK?" Gareth asked.

"*Don't touch anything!*" she croaked, reaching for the wall for support. "*I know who all this belongs to! Don't touch anything!*"

They waited for William Ryan in the safety and warmth of Anna's car. When the detective arrived, with Detective Gardaí Grace Thompson and Colin Forde in tow, along with several others Anna recognised from the Lee Street station, they joined him inside the house.

While Colin led the others upstairs to the attic, Anna watched Gareth talk to Grace, who stood with her notebook open, her pen moving quickly across the page. She listened to Gareth's statement, to his animated retelling of their time together. He had been inside the house barely ten minutes, yet so much had happened …

William touched Anna's arm and she followed him to the sliding double doors at the back of the kitchen. His height and the intensity of his mood dwarfed the small space.

"The intruder alarm was disabled. It's Harris's speciality."

Anna nodded, feeling numb.

"Everything will be photographed in situ before being taken away for testing – you know the drill. We can't prove yet it's Harris but we both know it's him. The question is – where is he now?"

Anna's eyes found William's, her fear unmistakable, and he offered her a reassuring smile.

"You're still safe, Anna! He's not here, but all his gear is. His food, sleeping bag, and so on. So he was probably planning to come back here for shelter. He won't now, of course – the house is lit up like a Christmas tree." He sighed and adjusted the cuffs on his forensic gloves, "He won't come back here. If he's near the estate he'll lie low."

Anna nodded. She couldn't speak. *How could this be still happening?*

Suddenly William placed both hands on her shoulders, bending to look into her eyes. His blue eyes were so chilling, so earnest, that Anna could no longer contain her tears.

"Harris is a desperate man now, Anna. He must be feeling like he has no hope, no options. Men in that position don't think straight – his days are numbered and I'd bet he knows it. I'm warning you now – lock all doors. Your car, your apartment, everything. Got it? Stay safe, stay in public spaces, and *stay alert!*"

"Or course." She wiped at her face, roughly drying her cheeks with her gloved fingers.

He shook her shoulders a little. "Change your routine. Nothing about your day must be the same as usual, do you understand? What do you do each day – is there anywhere he'd expect you to be?"

William was frightening Anna now. His fingers gripped hard through her coat and his eyes were wide and wild. Her shoulders were beginning to ache.

"*Think, Anna!*"

"I … well, I train in Taekwon-Do most mornings and I teach that on a Thursday night."

"Where?"

"Here, in Kinsale," she answered quickly.

"That stops now."

"But –"

"But nothing! Give Grace an address for the classes, please, and a number for your trainer. He'll need to be on his guard too. Who knows where you live now?"

"Just … just my brother and a few friends at work. And Vivian's family, I think." Her thoughts were whirring wildly, trying to answer him quickly.

William released her shoulders and pinched his lower lip between his thumb and forefinger, forgetting his forensic gloves, his eyes unfocused. "Yes, that should be alright," he said, so quietly Anna thought he had forgotten she was there.

Suddenly he moved away, walking quickly through the living room. He mounted the stairs, leaving her alone in the middle of the kitchen.

She wrapped her arms around herself and watched the team of people in her house; it was full again, of people in uniform, people that would leave it cold and empty once their tasks were completed. The air was cold around her, not warmed by the extra bodies but made cooler by the open front door, through which white-suited men and women were now walking, their shoe-covers making a strange noise as they moved up the stairs.

She became aware of a pulsing over her left eye, a tightening feeling at her temples … a migraine was looming, and she moved outside to her car to fetch some tablets from the glove box. She swallowed two tablets and sat a while longer in the peace of the car.

Watching her little house lit up and being forensically torn apart – *again* – Anna felt overwhelmingly tired. Tired of checking her phone for updates from Alex. Tired of wondering if Kate was safe, if she had made it to Natalie and was happy now. And tired of wondering when Dean Harris would make his appearance. Because she knew it was no longer a question of *if* he would find her but *when*.

29

Tom stood at a large bay window overlooking the heart of Cork city. The "reading room" had been one of Mae's favourite places with its heavy oak shelves lining the cream wallpapered walls, crammed with literary classics and romance novels, whatever had taken the interior designer's fancy. Tom certainly had never pulled anything from the shelves and he doubted his sons had ever spent any time in the room to advance their literary understanding. In fact, they had used the room to their own advantage, in a way that brought a smile to his lips now.

Years ago, John and David would take their penknives and carve shapes into the pages of the books, then replace them on the shelves, with Mae none the wiser. They never chose her favourites, the ones she might reread, like her Maeve Binchy collection and Daphne du Maurier's *Rebecca*. The boys were too clever for that. Instead they chose the books Mae kept on a high shelf, visible to their guests but not to her taste. Mark Twain's *The Adventures of Huckleberry Finn* had been butchered, a rectangular shape gouged out of the pages to hide a cigarette packet. J.R.R. Tolkien's *The Hobbit* had been defaced to hide a small hipflask. The list of books mutilated by the boys grew larger the more they had to hide. If Mae might suspected her teenage sons of drinking, or if she smelled weed or nicotine in the air around them, nothing would be found when she searched their bedrooms. Tom had admired his sons' ingenious way of hiding contraband under their noses, never letting on that he knew their secret. His fingers trailed the books – he missed those days. They were more innocent times. In later years there'd been no need to hide. David moved out and delved too deep into the drugs that were meant only to be used to turn a profit. John never dabbled. He had more than enough self-discipline for both sons.

This room had brought his wife comfort; it had been her safe space. In recent weeks, it was the room in which she drank away her days and prayed for absolution. It was decorated to Mae's taste, as was most of the house. Wide armchairs of floral upholstery, in different pastel shades, were dotted around the room in ways she had explained was "feng shui". He still hadn't a clue what she'd meant, something about the energy of the room. Sheepskin rugs on the hardwood floor, watercolours and framed photographs of the southern Irish coastline, all chosen by Mae. All waiting for her to return home.

A drinks cabinet in curved oak-wood filled one wall. Tom had purged the whole house of alcohol recently when Mae had been at her worst. Once she'd left for rehab or respite or whatever the hell he was paying thousands a week for, he had instructed Jessica to refill the decanters with the finest whiskey. If he was to be alone in this house he would need comfort. And distraction while he waited for news from Spain. He filled a large glass, several measures deep, and raised a silent toast to his wife – he missed her, more than he'd expected to.

Holding the glass, he turned to the window and stared into the darkness. Marco was due, their first meeting in days. Tom needed someone to talk to. John was out of his life now, as much as David was in many ways. Marco was all that was left to him. He had never been the brightest man in his arsenal, but he was loyal. Tom thought of the times Marco had been by his side, his loyalty blind and deaf to anything other than what Tom needed. Of all the men Tom had known over the years in this business, Marco was the only one he truly trusted. He was the most reliable, most faithful of his men. Was that still the case?

Marco was early. Tom was glad of it, of the interruption from his own company. He pressed the electronic fob and watched the gates swing open slowly, watched Marco's dark jeep manoeuvre inside. There had been security men once, four of them. Now Tom relied on electronics to keep his enemies out. Jessica had left for the day and so he opened his front door himself – how times had changed! – watching the road for flashes from newspaper cameramen, waiting for the slow cruise past of a Garda car.

Once inside, Marco shook off his raincoat and hung it on the stand in the hall, frowning, not knowing what to say or where to look. The silence of the house without Mae's friendly hospitality was deafening.

"We'll go into the reading room, have a drink," Tom said and Marco nodded, muted by the strange atmosphere in the house he had known for almost thirty years.

Inside the reading room, a space Tom had never allowed his men to pollute, Marco settled into a pink-and-cream floral-upholstered chair. His muscular thighs pressed heavily into the fabric, his bulk dwarfing the chair. His large hands worried at the fabric, rubbing it, pulling invisible threads with his fingers. He couldn't sit still.

Tom passed him a glass of whiskey and topped up his own.

Marco cleared his throat. "Mae's still … not here?"

"No."

"And Jessica?"

"I gave her the evening off. Listen, I'm sorry I wasn't there, at your mother's funeral." He had let Marco down, he knew that. Attending a funeral was an obligation between even casual acquaintances – he should have been there. The fact that he didn't go had a lot to do with his Garda shadows and the fury that swelled inside him at the sight of them. He just couldn't make himself shake hands and nibble salad sandwiches, make small talk with strangers and gawkers, curious about the Cork businessman the gardaí were so interested in. The man with one son shot dead a few months ago and another arrested for his involvement with those serial killers. They might ask about his wife, about where she was, how she was holding up. There'd be whispers and dipped heads and eyes looking anywhere but at him. Or worse, the gloating smiles of those who thought he'd finally got what was coming. His mind felt too frayed for that. But he knew it would have meant a lot to Marco – he watched tears flash in the man's dark eyes. They were pushed away with a rough hand.

"Not at all, boss, it's completely understandable. The filth are watching your every move. And you kept Mam as comfortable as possible, God rest her, paid for the best of everything! You treated her like your own mother. I won't forget that." His voice broke and he looked away, wiping his nose on the back of his hand.

Tom nodded. Marco was OK with it, but it still niggled at him. "I should have gone. She was a fine lady."

Marco smiled widely. "That she was! She had notions, my mam. Marc with a C!" His eyes were brimming with water again and he shook his head. "I never lived that one down in school." His smile faded. "She went quick in the end. A small mercy."

Tom raised his glass and Marco held up his own. "To your mam, to Mrs Carmel O'Regan, a lady!"

They nodded at each other and swallowed the liquor, sucking air between their teeth as it seared their throats.

"Tell me, what did the doctor say?"

At this Marco lowered his eyes to the sheepskin rug on the floor, kicking the edge of it gently with a heavy black boot. "He said – he said something about tumours – no option of treatment. Best to go quickly."

Tom nodded and pulled a decanter from a nearby shelf. He refilled their glasses. "I expect that's true."

They sipped the second drink more slowly this time. Tom watched the man's lowered head, his broad shoulders hunched in the armchair. A loyal man, deserving of a fitting end in this game.

"How many men are there left, Marco?"

"Four by my count," he answered quickly, his eyes on Tom.

Tom knew he wasn't the only one searching for distraction; Marco relished the thought of some action.

"Six went with Murray and two – PJ and Jimmy – they're lying low," Marco continued. "They want out. Best to cut them loose, if you ask me. The heat is too much for them and, if the gardaí get wind of their names and haul them in, they'll crack like soft eggs. So, four, plus us."

Tom frowned into the liquid in the glass. "Not a lot of loyalty there."

"No money coming in now. Murray has ruined it, split the group apart. And John's not around. Most of the lads stuck around him like flies on shit – he always kept things moving. No-one expects to see him anytime soon."

Tom stood and placed the crystal tumbler onto the nearest shelf. "Murray wants the city. He's made an approach."

Marco straightened his bulk in the armchair, heat rising in his face. "*Are you fucking kidding me?*"

"This isn't something I'd kid around about! He's joined a bigger group using my gear and cash to buy his way in. Now he has the men behind him to take Cork city."

Air whistled loud between Marco's teeth.

"I got a message this afternoon," Tom said. "Murray wants to meet by the end of the week."

"Where?"

Tom turned to him and shook his head, his hands in his pockets. He felt calmer now, talking this through. "I don't know where yet. I'll let him set up the meet – he wouldn't trust anywhere I suggest. But my days are numbered anyway. Ainsley's been lifted and no doubt is talking to save his own skin. We're not entertaining the idea of prison. My solicitor is talking about cutting a deal – rolling over on men I've dealt with to save my own neck." His mouth twisted in disgust. "Tom Gallagher is no grass!"

"So what will you do?"

He smiled then, a grin that lit up his face.

"I'll do what I always do! Figure something out. I always come out on top, Marco, you know that." He fixed him with a dark, piercing stare. "If you want out, now is the time to go. I'll hold no grudges against you."

Marco shook his head vehemently; everything good in his life had come from this man. There was no way he was walking away now. Adrenaline was flowing inside him; the idea of a plan, of something to take his mind off his own problems, was making him feel more alive that he had in weeks.

"No chance. What do you need?"

Tom sat down, drumming his fingers on the armrests of Mae's favourite chair.

"Locating Kate Crowley remains my top priority. Everything else is lost now. Cork is part of the past. I'm moving on and taking Mae and my granddaughters with me. So I need that to progress. Murray owes me. He's a problem we can work together to resolve. But one other thing. There's a rat in this sinking ship." He paraphrased Victor White's words, his mouth curving in disgust at the very thought of it.

He watched Marco's face for any tell-tale signs, any indicators of guilt. Any twitch of his muscles or flick of his eyes to the left or right, anything to convey discomfort.

"Crowley was tipped off in Spain. She knew we were coming for her. Someone told her to run."

All Tom found in Marco's face was disbelief.

30

Cork

"You owe me that drink, Clarke!"

Gareth's parting words were offered with a smile as he walked up his driveway. It was the middle of the night. Anna could have gone inside with him to catch up with Vivian's parents, but she was exhausted. Instead, she waved at Gareth and drove away.

Vivian has messaged earlier: **Hey, hope training went well. I'm meeting some of the girls from college for dinner. Don't wait up!**

Anna grimaced, knowing that an empty apartment with only her own thoughts for company were all that awaited her.

As she drove towards the city and the apartment in Blackrock she kept the radio silent and the heating in the car off. She needed the stillness of the car and the icy air – she wanted to *feel*. Because for the past two hours she had felt completely numb.

Dean Harris had made a home for himself in the attic of her house. It was a stark reality, a difficult thing to accept. And in a lot of ways, now that her mind was clearing of the numbing shock, it was quite a clever move. The house of the woman he had attempted to attack was the last place anyone would think to look for him. She laughed out loud, thinking about Harris finding the house empty of all her possessions and furniture. He must have been confused. But the short burst of laughter died on her lips – he was still out there.

* * *

It took less than thirty minutes to reach the apartment in Blackrock; traffic was thin on the roads at this hour on a Monday night. Anna found the silent apartment a strange relief – she wasn't ready to go through the whole thing with Vivian just yet. She had spoken to Jason, briefly, as she drove. On the advice of Grace Thompson he had cancelled the Taekwon-Do Tykes class this Thursday night. They were both disappointed but understood the need for caution. She wasn't happy about missing training too but Jason reassured her she knew what to do, and to keep at it in her own time, whatever way she could.

Climbing into bed, Anna felt thoroughly fed-up of the hold Dean Harris had over her life. She missed her niece; Chloe was the brightest spark in her life, and she missed their chats over hot chocolate, their bedtime stories. It was too long since she had been at her brother's house for dinner, all because of Harris.

Unable to sleep, she propped her pillows behind her head and sat up, switching on the bedside light. Scrolling through her mobile phone, she caught up on the daily news and eventually selected the photographs she had taken earlier in Patricia O'Brien's living room. The record player and the selection of records were first. She zoomed in closer, remembering Patricia's description of the family settling on the sofa to listen to Rod Stewart – it was often the simplest things that formed the strongest bonds.

She swiped her finger, moving on to the family photographs on the shelf: parents and three daughters. Patricia's father had been a handsome man, tall with fair hair and dark eyebrows. Her mother seemed faded in the photographs, either standing in the background or turning away from the camera. And her sisters ... they were all quite alike. Large oval eyes and fair hair.

The youngest sister held her interest, the one Patricia had called Margaret. In the images she was a child and then a teenager, and Anna felt certain she had seen her face before. But where? Perhaps she had been her mother's friend, as Vivian had suggested. They would have been about the same age.

The phone rang shrill and loud in the empty room and Anna gasped in fright.

Myles.

She smiled, thankful that the day would end on a positive note.

31

Casares, Spain

Kate found the nights in Casares warm and bright. Darkness crept into daylight slowly until eventually the sky was sprinkled with stars, like fairy-dust. It's what they told the twins each night. Rachel and Rhea fell asleep in their hotel bed with their heads full of stories about fairies jumping from star to star, sprinkling dust to make a pathway to the moon. Kate told them the fairies were lighting up the sky for two brave girls that were on an epic adventure. She told them their grandmother lived in America, a place they had never been, but that they would go there as soon as they could. It was a safe place where they could make a fortress in their grandma's garden and watch the stars from there. The twins loved the stories, believed her promises, but, increasingly, Kate needed to be alone.

Once Natalie fell asleep she left the room and went downstairs to the hotel bar. They had decided to remain in Casares for a few more nights – Kate needed time to plan, not roam aimlessly on buses around the Spanish coastline. They had upgraded to the most expensive hotel available with the highest star-rating possible. There was a golf course not too far away; business men keen to unwind were the hotel's preferred clientele. It was not the type of place you'd expect to find young children. It seemed a safer choice to Kate – thugs looked more out of place in upscale places, in her experience.

She selected a stool in the corner of the bar and sat with her back against the wall. She had a view of the whole room – a restaurant with a long bar counter at the top, a musician at a grand piano in one corner. The space opened onto the pool deck. Kate could see every person in the space both inside and out. She had no interest in being here among the hotel guests except to check them out, to know each face so that at breakfast in the morning she could spot any newcomers, anyone different. She needed to stay alert and familiar with everything in their new surroundings.

Though the temperature wasn't quite hot enough for swimming, the twins were drawn to the hotel pool each day. It made Kate smile to think about it now. With her daughters shrieking and splashing in the water Natalie began to unfurl, to laugh. She spoke less to Kate about what they should do; there were no more snatched conversations when she thought the children were out of earshot, no more questions about their future and their safety. Natalie seemed happy, for now, to give herself over to the sun and the pool, the temporary reprieve both offered. Each day Kate smiled back at the three of them from a sun lounger but never joined their fun in the water and Natalie didn't press her. Natalie might be happy to switch off for now, but she only allowed herself that because she knew Kate was still on alert.

And, for Kate, it never ended. Behind her sunglasses her eyes never stopped examining every entrance, every person in sight. She rarely walked in a straight line – going to the breakfast buffet this morning she had found reason to twist and turn her body at different angles: tying a loose sandal, fixing her niece's braids, turning to read a poster on the wall. To a passer-by she looked like a diligent aunt, an excited tourist – to Natalie she looked like her ever-vigilant sister.

Kate sat now with a soft drink in front of her and her back pressed against the wall behind her. She observed four couples dining in the restaurant, all middle-aged and tanned. It occurred to her that should Tom Gallagher send a man and a woman after her she would be completely caught off-guard – she was expecting the stereotypical hard man to be searching for her, because that was what his gang had looked like. Shaved heads, muscular, dark clothes, scars – she remembered one guy, Murray or something like that, with a scar that ran from his ear to his lip. She shuddered at the memory of the things Natalie had told her. Her sister had witnessed things when she was David Gallagher's partner that still left their mark.

"Are you cold?"

A man stood beside her at the bar – where had he come from? Kate frowned. He was a good deal shorter than her with receding sandy hair and a gold watch that looked several sizes too big for his wrist. He saw her looking at it and ran his hand through his hair, twisting it into the light.

"Aw, such a pretty lady! You should turn that frown upside down! Let me buy you a drink!"

Kate watched his hand rest again on the bar, a little closer to hers this time, saw the pale line on his ring-finger on his tanned hand.

"Does your wife know you try to pick up women when you're away playing golf?"

The man's eyes narrowed a little and he frowned, moving away to the end of the bar. She was alone again and she intended it to stay that way. Sipping her drink, Kate scanned the small crowd of diners again. Nothing different. The man had received his drink from the barman and moved to sit at a table with three other men, turning his back to her. She smiled. Compared to what the Gallaghers got up to, picking up women for an extra-marital tryst on a golfing holiday made him look like a Boy Scout.

She sighed and checked her mobile phone for any messages or missed calls. She had reached out to their mother and stepfather in America, even though it was the last thing she had wanted to do. She had false passports and enough money to stay hidden for a long time, and her mother had promised to work on ways to get them into the States … if that were possible.

The screen on her phone looked the exact same as it had ten minutes ago – nothing yet. Despite the distance with her mother over the years, Kate was sure she would come through for them. And there was something else that sparked hope that they could survive this – they had someone within Tom Gallagher's circle that was willing to tip her off. She was banking on that person staying on her side. Their lives depended on it.

32

"Can I get you anything? Some water, perhaps?"

Mae shook her head. She didn't need anything; it was comfort enough to be sitting here across from Susan. Sunlight was spilling into the room but the blinds had been drawn to shield their eyes. Mae could see dust motes dancing in the slats of light. She watched them float peacefully as she waited for their session to begin.

Her therapist had made a good impression on her right from the start – Mae guessed the woman was about thirty, with glossy black hair she always wore in a low ponytail. She had the most beautiful sky-blue eyes and the softest voice, with a very distinctive Dublin 4 accent. She was flawlessly put together each time they had met. Today she wore a cream blouse with a delicate string of pearls resting at her neck. Her black trousers skimmed her ankles and her heels were just high enough to cause Mae a little concern for her safety. She loved it! Susan was the whole package, someone Mae could see as a daughter-in-law, someone to go shopping with in Brown Thomas and have cocktails after … in another life, they could have been friends. She smiled at her own foolishness – her mother had always said her head was full of "notions".

"How are you feeling today?" Susan probed gently, smiling. She always smiled; even when Mae had told her the worst of herself, Susan had been unperturbed.

"Fine, much better, thank you."

Mae had learned that this response, followed by a bright smile, was exactly what the people working here wanted to hear and see. It reassured them, made them feel they were good at their job. It made them feel effective. She hadn't always been so eager to please other people, but she was beginning to miss home. To miss Tom. And she wanted to visit her son. Sons. One in hospital, one in a cold grave. So every day she was "fine" and "feeling better" and her smile was stretched so tight her cheeks hurt, in the hope that she could convince herself, and them, that she was ready to go home.

"We spoke last week about your son David, about his death. We touched on Kate, the woman you hold responsible. Do you feel able to continue that discussion?"

"Yes, of course," Mae's hands were folded in her lap, her fingers clamped together. As much as she enjoyed her time with Susan she had noticed the woman's eyes follow her body movements and write things down in her notebook. She didn't want to give anything away. "*Stay in control and you rule the world*," had been Tom's motto. Mae usually thought Tom was right.

"Can you tell me how you feel about Kate today?"

"Well … I've had time to think about her a lot actually."

Susan never rushed the conversation, just smiled and waited.

"Kate is probably what I'd describe as a 'good sister'. I've family but we aren't close anymore. Well, not really. I guess you could say that's Tom's fault, the life he led, you know. But Kate, well, she and Natalie are twins, aren't they? And she needed to take care of her sister."

"In what way?"

"Oh, I'm sure I already explained. Natalie was David's partner." Mae swallowed; talking about David was difficult. "David was using drugs around the time he and Natalie's girls were born. They're twins – Rachel and Rhea. Isn't it funny, Kate and Natalie are twins as well … anyway, David wasn't at his best when he was with Natalie."

"How so?"

"I hate to say it, but there's no other way … It's the truth! He was abusive. I knew it, Tom knew it. I assume John knew but that's not something he would have cared to do anything about."

"Did you and Tom try to do something about it?"

"Yes! It was senseless, and completely unacceptable! Tom treated me like a queen in front of the boys, never even raised his voice! He's always wrapped me in cotton wool. He might be a difficult man but, to his family, to the people he cares about, Tom is a saint. There's nothing he wouldn't do to protect the people he cares about. So it's not like David had a bad role model or anything. He had no excuse!"

"You sound angry with him. Are you?"

"Angry with David? Well, yes! I was then. But … now … I mean, how could I be? He's dead. Kate shot him in the neck, did I tell you that?"

Mae's fingers touched the left-hand side of her own neck; she watched Susan's eyes follow them and was glad she didn't write anything in the notebook on her lap.

"Have you given any thought as to *why* Kate shot him? It can help us to try to understand the actions of another, if we hope to reach a place where we might forgive them."

Mae shrugged, her hands back on her lap, her fingers coated in sweat now.

"I'll never know why she killed him." Her voice was a low whisper. "They must have been in some sort of fight. He was in *her* house, and God knows why because they hated each other. Tom says she stole things from him and, knowing David, he went round there to get them back."

"You said David was violent with her sister. Do you think Kate could have been in fear of her life?"

Susan's words were soft and Mae felt her lower lip begin to tremble. The room didn't feel so peaceful anymore.

"You know, I nearly killed myself with drink trying to block out what she did. Trying to forget – it was just too painful. Day after day, night after night. I couldn't eat, I couldn't sleep. I wanted so badly to kill her. Some days I still do. I know that's a terrible thing to say – I know how that sounds."

Susan watched her silently, her expression impossible to read. For the first time since she had arrived, Mae was beginning to grow weary of all this talking. Of worrying what Susan must think of her and hating that she even cared. Yet she felt compelled to keep going.

"I wonder if the part that hurts the most is knowing that David probably gave Kate no choice. He wasn't a gentle person. I know who my son was! But still – she killed him! I can't forgive that!"

A sob burst from her lips and she pressed her fingers to them, stifling it. Her whole body was trembling violently in the chair. Tom would hate this loss of control, she thought, and then hated herself for thinking it. Fuck Tom, she thought, fuck the whole business and their whole life. Everything was a complete mess!

"If Kate were in this room, if you had an opportunity to speak to her, would you take it? Would you like to speak to her?"

Tears spilled unchecked down Mae's cheeks. She nodded. Her face was wet with tears and snot and she pulled a tissue from her sleeve, scrubbing her skin clean.

"What might you say, do you think, if you had that opportunity?"

It took Mae a long time to compose herself.

Susan leaned forward and pressed some more soft tissues into her lap, waiting with a patient half-smile.

Though her mind was full of words, and questions, Mae couldn't say anything at all.

33

Vivian clasped an espresso with both hands, inhaling the aroma deeply, her eyes closed. When she opened them, she jumped and spilled some of the hot liquid onto her fingers.

"Christ, Anna! Where did you come from?"

"My bedroom. What's wrong with you? That's twice in the last few days you've jumped out of your skin seeing me! Should I take it personally?"

"No, it's these journalists – my phone is ringing off the hook and my nerves are in shreds! Everyone wants an exclusive. And Carol is phoning me non-stop. I'm not answering – I think she wants to pause the documentary." She winced and sucked her fingers, moving to the kitchen sink to fetch a cloth. "For God's sake, you nearly gave me a heart attack!"

"Well, maybe you *should* pause things for a little while." Anna knew William Ryan had called to the Banba Productions office yesterday. Perhaps Vivian's boss had realised the situation was serious.

"No chance! If someone is trying to scare me off the case then it means I'm close. And, besides, I have you with me!" She beamed at Anna as she sat back down at the counter.

Anna frowned. She wasn't surprised Vivian was being her usual headstrong self, but she'd much prefer if her friend would listen to advice urging caution.

After a long conversation with Myles, which soothed her nerves and made her happy but only reignited the longing to see him in person, she had fallen into a deep sleep. She woke late, no alarm clock this morning. It took only seconds into wakefulness to remember that Dean Harris had invaded her house again, but she dressed quickly in her training gear, determined to push him out of her mind. Outside, rain lashed heavily against the windows, running down the glass in angry streaks. A jog was out of the question. The next best thing was sparring and Vivian would have to do as her partner.

"Aren't you going to be late for your training session with Jason?"

"I'm training here this morning."

"Why?"

"That's a long story and I don't want to ruin your day."

"Fair enough." Vivian closed her eyes and resumed inhaling her coffee.

"Heavy night?" Anna rolled out a yoga mat onto the floor and sat down to pull on her trainers.

"We went for a few drinks after dinner. There's plenty of people out on a Monday night – town was jammed! Bloody students everywhere. I know it's not Freshers' Week but there must be something on in the college." She screwed her eyes shut and gulped deeply, a tiny moan escaping her lips.

"You look like you joined them! How are things going with Luke?"

"I'm ignoring his calls, to be honest." Vivian opened one eye and looked at Anna. "What are you doing?"

"I want to practise some sparring manoeuvres."

With a surprising jolt of energy Vivian turned her body on the stool to face Anna, her face lit up in excitement. "*Ooh*, this should be good! I've never seen you in action, so to speak!"

Anna straightened up and threw a padded chest-protector at Vivian who caught it with one hand, holding her coffee aloft with the other.

"This is for you. And the helmet is … somewhere around here."

"Excuse me?"

"It's for sparring, and I'm concentrating on kicking this morning. This gear will keep you safe – *up you get!*"

Two hours later, showered and dressed in their professional "interview clothes", they headed to the South Douglas Road, to the small bungalow where retired garda Oliver Cotter lived with his son. Though he was reluctant to speak to them, he was keener than Patricia O'Brien had been. But only just – Vivian had already told Anna that Oliver had said the whole thing was a blight on his career, an event he had tried to forget for half his life.

"I wonder what Oliver Cotter will be like. Patricia O'Brien certainly painted a grim picture of him. A grumpy man who was unhappy to be working with a female garda. Sounds like he made her life hell."

Vivian rubbed her upper left arm where a wayward kick had landed during their sparring session. "*Mmm,* it sounds like it was a nightmare for her. Thankfully female gardaí don't suffer through that anymore. Generally speaking. I've spoken to a few that I met through reporting for the paper and they seemed happy enough."

"I guess there's misogyny in every workplace, to an extent. But Patricia O'Brien's story would make you sympathise with why she left, wouldn't it?"

"Absolutely." Vivian rubbed her arm hard. "Christ, Anna, you're stronger than you look!"

"My dad used to say that." Anna grinned at her. "Sorry – I mean it. I normally don't miss the target."

She kept her eyes on the road and tried not to remember last night. The sight of *his* things in her attic still made her stomach lurch: the tins of food, the rope and tool box. He was set up to sleep and eat there, to stay there as long as it took. To do what, exactly, she dreaded to think about.

"Has Detective Ryan contacted you with any update on the wooden cross?" Vivian asked. "Luke texted earlier, asking me to call Carol, which I ignored! He was a bit miffed actually, said the detectives gave him a right roasting yesterday over not reporting the first note."

"I'm not surprised they did, to be honest. When Luke said he'd handle it he did nothing at all!" Anna couldn't keep the accusation from her voice.

Vivian was keen to defend him. "He didn't think the first note was important. Then when the second note arrived and led to the graveyard, it was already being dealt with." She met Anna's eyes and held up her hands in surrender. "I know! I know! His handling of it was a little inadequate. He's a work in progress, I guess."

"But you like him?"

"I do. He's fun to be around. And I like working with him. He's a really great guy."

"I'm sure you're right." Time to change the subject. "Let's hope William finds something. Otherwise it's just another dead end."

"This whole case is full of dead ends! Pray that Oliver Cotter offers more hope of finding answers!"

34

Oliver Cotter lived in a bungalow set back off the busy road. His son Noel greeted them at the front door, snapping a lead onto the collar of a small Jack Russel as he ushered them in. The bungalow was almost midway in a row of houses that looked too small to accommodate two grown men and a dog. It was low-ceilinged with two small windows set close to the front door.

"Go on through to the kitchen, he's in there."

The day was seasonably gloomy, the sky heavy with bloated dark clouds; the light outside was almost as dim as twilight, though it was close to lunchtime. Rain was pouring heavily again, but that appeared not to bother Noel and the dog. He stepped outside the house, the dog yanking on the lead in front of him, and waved goodbye, pulling up the hood on his rain jacket as they walked onto the main road. Anna and Vivian watched him go, feeling some level of shared apprehension at being left alone in the house with the elderly Mr Cotter for company.

"Right then," Vivian said with a tight smile, pushing the front door closed, "the kitchen it is!"

The hallway was narrow and short and smelled of stale tobacco, as though fresh air hadn't filtered through it in a long time. Vivian led the way to the kitchen, pushing open the white-painted door.

It squeaked and the bottom of the wood got a little stuck on the linoleum on the kitchen floor, causing Vivian to put her shoulder against it and push.

"Give it a good shove, love, the blasted floor is uneven."

Oliver Cotter rose from a small table as they entered.

Inside the kitchen the smell of tobacco was fresh and overpowering, in stark contrast to the zesty-lemon freshness of Patricia O'Brien's house. The small kitchen table and four chairs was just in front of sliding glass doors, the garden outside was neat and small, a wooden shed taking up most of the space. Anna longed to open the doors, just a little, for fresh air, but said nothing.

Oliver was tall and thin, his body cocooned under layers of wool. A gas heater was nearby, the smell of singed dust competing with the nicotine. Anna knew he was eighty; Vivian had told her everything she knew about him already this morning. He had three daughters and one son, Noel. His wife had passed away four years ago and, after a year on his own, his son had moved in to help out.

He sat back down slowly, one hand gesturing to the chairs opposite him and they sat, Vivian pulling her voice recorder and notebook from her bag. A near-full ashtray rested on the table, with Oliver's hand hovering near it, a cigarette clutched loosely between his fingers. The skin on his forefinger and thumb was stained yellow, the rest of his skin a sickly pallor. Sparse white hair stood in tufts on the top of his head and poked out from the collar of his jumper. The whites of his eyes were bloodshot, and the skin around his thin lips was puckered and lined. A popping sound as he sucked on the cigarette and a dripping tap nearby were amplified in the otherwise silent room as they looked at each other.

"It's Miss Keating, isn't that right?" His eyelids drooped a little, as though he needed to rest, but his voice was strong.

"Thank you for speaking with me, Mr Cotter. This is my friend Anna Clarke – she's helping me out in preparation for the documentary."

Oliver nodded his head to Anna and exhaled the cigarette smoke to his left. Anna doubted there would be tea and biscuits offered this time. She remembered Patricia O'Brien describing him as surly, sexist, a man who'd excluded her from things and been openly hostile, disappointed to work with a woman. Anna noted that he hadn't smiled yet, but he seemed welcoming enough, open to their discussion at least, and had addressed Vivian formally. He'd done his best not to exhale his cigarette smoke in their direction. He didn't seem like a man accustomed to treating women badly. Maybe that had changed with age.

"As you know, from our previous conversation over the phone, I'm working on a series of cold-case documentaries and Bernard O'Meara's death in 1977 is being featured. You were the first garda on the scene, along with your partner at the time, Patricia O'Brien. This is one of, I hope, two discussions and I'm going to record our conversation if that's OK and you can request a copy if you'd like." She pressed record. "Will you tell me in your own words everything you remember about that day?"

A rectangular-shaped folder lay beside him on the table and he slid it across to them.

Anna saw that it was actually a scrapbook. She opened it; the pages were curling and worn at the edges and the smell of Oliver's cigarettes wafted up from the pages, as though trapped within. Each page was covered with newspaper articles, with handwritten notes along the edges. Anna had read many of the articles in the files

Vivian had brought home from the office, but she found the handwritten notes illegible. The faded newspaper cuttings covered Bernard O'Meara's death, the escape of the killer and his jump into the River Lee, and finally the discovery of a headstone for 'The Boy Who Jumped'.

"They sensationalised him, made him more than he was." Oliver's tone was heavy with disgust. "He was just a kid who killed a man. Made to look like a celebrity. 'Twas an absolute disgrace!"

"We agree with you one hundred percent, Mr Cotter," Vivian said, peering at the newspaper articles. "You made this scrapbook?"

"My wife did. She told me to write down everything that had happened too, every word I remembered, every image, and so on. It helped for the investigation. It's all there, beside the newspaper clippings. In the beginning we didn't think it'd go on for as long as it did. Unsolved for so long, like. And the headlines kept on coming."

"It's so fortunate that your memories of that day are recorded."

"Still crystal-clear in my mind too, in any case. Forty-odd years ago now." He had watched Vivian as she spoke but now he looked down at the table. "A long time. A terrible thing to happen. Ruined my career – I was never promoted, never given the opportunity after that day. I worked the same plodding streets for the rest of my time in the Guards. Security work after that in supermarkets – boring and low-paid work. I had dreams of making detective."

His bitterness echoed loudly in the small kitchen.

"I'd appreciate as much detail as you can give me for the documentary."

His eyes were wet when he looked up again. He ground the butt of his cigarette on top of the remains of the others and pulled another from a packet on the table, tapping it a few times in the palm of his hand before lighting it.

"I'll tell you everything as I remember it. The mind is sharper than the body in my case." He sucked on the cigarette and exhaled again. "It was a wet day but nothing we weren't used to. We were quiet enough in the station. I was based in Lee Street. Anyway, I was following up on a stolen bicycle when the call came in. There was an assault in progress on Washington Street." He paused to draw deeply, his lips pursing around the cigarette. "Patricia O'Brien was assigned to me for duty. She wasn't long in the door. Anyway, off we went. Made it to the courthouse in no time at all with the sirens blaring. Usually the sounds and the lights would stop a fella in his tracks and cause him to leg it, but not this time. I remember herself beside me whispering 'Jesus Christ!' as we pulled up. I remember that well, her shock, like. The fella kept on kicking. The poor man on the ground never stood a chance."

"Your memory is very clear, Mr Cotter."

"Not something a man is likely to forget." There was regret in his voice, but defiance too – Anna had the impression he had been waiting a long time to tell his story.

"Of course. So even as you approached the perpetrator, the killer, he continued with his assault?" Vivian needed to be sure Oliver's version of events matched the official report, especially if she could convince him to speak on camera.

"That's right." His voice was detached; the memory was so old now the emotion had been stripped out of it. "A young fella losing his mind. Dark clothes, hood up. That's all I remember of how he looked. I stopped the car and we both got out. Herself stood back at first but I jumped right on him and pulled him off. A bad bastard he was, mad as a March hare. The look in his eyes was like something you'd see in a pack of fighting dogs. He was spitting and kicking the air and I subdued him a bit."

"*Um*, what exactly does that mean?" This part hadn't been in the official report.

"Punched him in the stomach, hard. Quietened him down. Good enough for him! He bent over on the ground and stayed there for maybe thirty seconds, I suppose, or it could have been longer." He shrugged – it didn't matter now. "He was coughing and spluttering, you know how it goes. I hauled him up then and cuffed him."

"To the front or the back?" Anna interjected. "The cuffs – was he cuffed to the front or the back?"

He looked at her with his wet eyes and took another long drag on his cigarette. "What?"

"It might be significant. He jumped into the river. If he somehow was able to use his hands he could have –"

Oliver interrupted with a firm shake of his head and sat back in his chair. "No-one got out of the water that day. No-one. He drowned. Got what he deserved and that's that. I always cuffed to the back then and I made sure they were good and tight – it's impossible to slip 'em off if they're put on right in the first place. And I never had a pair of cuffs fail me in my whole career."

Touching Anna's arm, and with a small shake of her head, Vivian warned her not to pursue it.

"So, Mr Cotter," she continued, "you placed the handcuffs on the young man and led him to the squad car?"

"Yes, but I had to let Patricia take over. The man on the ground, O'Meara, he had started to, sort of, gargle. Choking on his own blood. I let her take the lad to the car and I tried to help the man. An ambulance was called for and I put him in the ..." he waved his hand around, the cigarette swaying in the air between them, leaving a trail of smoke in its wake, "what's it called now? Ah yes, the recovery position. But it was too late for him. God rest his soul."

"Can you tell us when you realised the young man had attacked your partner?"

Oliver rolled his eyes, his tongue clicking loud inside his mouth. "*That* should never have happened. It was easy – all she had to do was walk him to the car! The lad was winded as well as cuffed. I don't know what the fuck happened!" His eyes darted up at their faces. "Excuse me! I don't like to use bad language. But she was something else!"

Vivian shifted in her seat and locked eyes with Anna, their memory of Patricia O'Brien's words hanging between them.

"Can you describe your working relationship with Miss O'Brien?"

"Why? It has no bearing on anything. But sure, we got on grand, I suppose. She was a young one fresh out of Templemore and I got stuck with babysitting her."

"We understand times were difficult for female members of the guards then," Vivian said pointedly.

Oliver sighed and his shoulders rounded as he looked at them sadly. "That what she told you, is it? That I was hard on her? Maybe I was. But let me tell you something – I have three daughters of my own, and I've never treated anyone badly just because she was a woman. Patricia O'Brien was incompetent, plain and simple! Like a little princess who didn't want to get her hands dirty. That case left a stain on my career and she's to blame for it!"

"She was assaulted by the –"

"She shouldn't have been!" Colour was rising now in his cheeks and he coughed hard, clearing phlegm from his throat. "The lad was winded. I hit him hard – and it was only a few feet to the car! She was trained for handling violent offenders. No, what happened her that day was she got spooked by the whole thing. The blood on the steps of the courthouse, the rain and cold, the man jerking and coughing … She got scared and she let herself open for an attack. She had no place in the Guards!" He coughed again and swallowed a few times before continuing. They could see he was riled up at the memory of Patricia O'Brien's actions that day. "And another thing – the lad got a head start on her! It took her a bit too long, if you ask me, to get after him. She was in shock! I remember it well, crystal clear! He ran slowly at the start – at least that's how I saw it. Although my wife, God rest her, used to say maybe I just remember it that way. Whichever, Patricia O'Brien took her time running after him. She let him get away!"

For a moment, they all sat silently, his words almost reverberating around them.

"She left the gardaí shortly afterwards, didn't she?" Anna asked quietly, hoping to diffuse the anger in the man. She didn't want to upset him further; it was enough to rehash memories of such a horrendous time in his life. She remembered William Ryan's question to Vivian when they'd had coffee with him the previous Sunday, "*You can't let the dead rest in peace?*" She was beginning to feel uncomfortable at the man's growing upset, and she wished Oliver's son was in the house to comfort him, at least.

"She took a few weeks' leave after the assault. I can't remember how many but she was out for a while. No loss to us. Claimed her shoulder was injured, and something else too, I don't remember. Then she was back at work, back in my unit, although she didn't last long. Turned on the waterworks for the inquiry, claimed PTSD or something. We worked only one other shift together and that was a disaster! Then she was gone."

"I'm sure she felt a huge amount of guilt, and responsibility for the fact that the killer escaped?"

"As well she did," he said quietly, looking at Vivian defiantly. He calmly popped his cigarette into his mouth, his eyes unfocused. His feelings about Patricia O'Brien were clear.

Anna shifted in her seat as the kitchen tap dripped on, unbearably loud, the stench of cigarette smoke and the heat from the gas heater making her feel nauseous.

"Your final shift with Miss O'Brien – why was that a disaster?"

He rolled his eyes before looking at them, pulling something from his lip as he spoke.

"A robbery in Roches Stores. A young one stealing scarves and bags from the shelf. Herself, O'Brien, she was hesitant. Like she was scared of getting hit. I told her to cuff the lass as my own cuffs still hadn't been replaced after that day on Washington Street and I didn't have a spare set. And she did, but a bit reluctantly like. Then we got back to the station and we couldn't uncuff the girl."

"Why?"

"O'Brien had only gone and lost her key!" He gave a small laugh, a rasping sound betraying years of chain-smoking. "She was mortified, her face like a tomato. She searched everywhere but no joy. I mean, a garda *never* separates their set of handcuffs from their key." He grunted in disgust, as if she had violated one of the sacred Garda rules. "It was no bother, one of the lads was able to use his key, but it was another example of how bloody useless she was. Begged me and the other fella on her shift to keep it quiet, said she'd been in enough trouble already. We did – like, nobody wanted to draw more heat on to our unit. But thank God she left soon after. Resigned or pensioned-off, who bloody cares? No-one had any faith in her after all that. And you could say it's because she's a woman if you want to play that tune, but it's not! Definitely not! She was just useless at the job."

35

A little while later Anna and Vivian left Oliver Cotter to his memories. The rain was relentless, a steady assault of cold water that pounded their skin like icy needles when they ran to Anna's car, the ominously dark sky threatening to unleash a downpour even heavier than before. Anna hoped Noel was on his way back from walking the dog. Oliver seemed very tired by the time they were ready to go. Their visit had drained him.

She parked in Douglas village and they walked to a pub, heads bent low against the rain that showed no sign of letting up. She shivered, feeling chilled to the bone. Mulling over all of Oliver's words had sparked something inside her, a niggling feeling that was coiled in her gut.

"We've two more people to speak to this week but I doubt they'll remember as much as Oliver Cotter. That scrapbook was a bit much, wasn't it?" Vivian said as they stood in the porch outside the bar entrance. "He's been ruminating on it for years! Really helpful to keep his memories fresh though!"

They stepped inside the bar, the heat engulfing them in a sudden rush.

"You're awfully quiet." Vivian slid into a booth in the centre of a row that were lined against one wall and smiled at the waitress, taking a menu from her outstretched hand.

"*Mmm.*"

She watched Anna, sitting hunched into her coat, the collar still turned up, staring at the shiny table top, her eyes unfocused. Even when Vivian shrugged off her own jacket and began a discussion of the lunch options, Anna didn't respond.

"I think I'll have a whole bottle of Pinot Noir for lunch. How about you? Anna? What do you think?"

"Sure, sounds good."

Vivian laughed aloud and reached across the table, flicking her fingers against Anna's forehead.

"*Hey! What the hell?*"

"Snap out of it! You just agreed to a whole of bottle of wine for yourself for lunch!" She laughed again but her concern was rising. "What is it?"

"I don't know, something … but maybe nothing."

"Spit it out!"

Anna sighed and flexed her neck from side to side. "I think I agree with what Oliver Cotter said – about Patricia O Brien, I mean. That she shouldn't have allowed the boy to attack her and run. He's right, dealing with violent assault is part of her training and she should have been able to handle him. He was injured and cuffed, and we can be certain now he was cuffed with his hands behind his back. It doesn't make sense."

"Well, that's not very fair! She was in shock at the situation, obviously."

"I guess. But the situation she faced is a basic part of Garda training, as Oliver said. And the boy had been punched hard in the gut by a grown man. It *shouldn't* have happened."

"Well, a person can be trained for something and still freeze when they come upon the *actual* situation. Or maybe Oliver's right and she really was useless at the job?"

"I don't know if I agree with that part." Anna exhaled deeply and rested her hands on the table, her fingers knotted. "It's the handcuffs element of it all that bothers me the most."

"Yeah, you've been going on about whether he was cuffed to the front or the back since I pulled you in to this."

"Well, now we know. Oliver was certain he cuffed him at the back. Handcuff keys are universal. Every key opens all handcuffs, it just makes life easier for transporting prisoners and so on. And Oliver just said that another guard opened the cuffs on the thief a few weeks later, after Patricia had lost her key."

"OK … so, you think the killer had a key? Oh my God!" Vivian's mouth dropped open. "You think the killer took the key from Patricia O'Brien when he assaulted her?"

Anna shook her head. "That'd be nearly impossible. Mid-assault, to locate the tiny handcuff key and steal it? And then, somehow, open handcuffs behind his back? The report said that the assault lasted mere seconds. No. I don't think he robbed her."

"Then what?" Vivian threw her hands up, exasperated.

Anna took a deep breath, aware that what she was about to say could change everything they thought they knew about the case.

"We need to explore the possibility that Patricia O'Brien opened the boy's cuffs mid-assault."

At some point in their discussion the waitress appeared. They ordered soup and sandwiches and large coffees and returned to their conversation.

"I'm really trying to calm down here, Anna!" Vivian said, one hand on her chest. "If you're right then our investigation isn't just going to reignite people's interest in the case. It could actually solve it!"

She kept her voice low. Despite her excitement at the possibilities Anna's theory opened up, the weight of the case was never far from her mind. A man had been beaten to death. And a *garda* may have helped his killer escape.

"Are you OK?"

"No." She took a long swallow of coffee, smiling weakly at the waitress as she placed their food on the table. The high-backed booth separated them from the other diners and Vivian was glad – she felt cocooned with Anna and she wanted privacy. She dipped her sandwich into the soup and began to eat, feeling revived. The bar around them was growing busier, low music overhead was slowly being muted by chat and laughter, by clinking glasses and the clatter of the entrance door nearby.

She looked around at the clientele, mostly men and women in warm coats over business suits, chatting over bowls of steaming soup and carvery lunches, umbrellas and briefcases on the ground at their feet. They all looked professional, but perhaps a business suit was the armour they wore. When that was stripped back, who were the people nearby?

Artists perhaps, longing to shed their dull, dark clothes in favour of overalls, to ditch the keyboard on their office desk in favour of a paintbrush. Or were they horticulturists, keen to sink carefully manicured nails in the damp earth? Some of the loudest laughs in the bar that lunchtime might be from people longing to retreat to the safety of their living rooms, to draw the curtains and sink back into the depths of isolation and solitude. Or maybe some of them were killers, hiding their real selves behind expensive suits and professional nine-to-fives, keeping their true nature in the shadows. Was that who Patricia O'Brien really was? A woman that had helped a killer – possibly a woman that was helping him still?

Vivian turned back to Anna, feeling as confused as Anna looked. "Perhaps everything Patricia told us is true – I'm sure she had a difficult time at work. But her story cast her into the role of a victim. We didn't question that, and I should have. I'm a journalist, questioning things is what I do! In fact, I felt really sorry for her. Now I'm just not sure about that anymore."

They ate in silence for a while. The waitress refilled their coffees and remarked upon the foul weather, receiving only nods and half-smiles in return. Both were lost in their thoughts, thinking about that day, picturing the assault on Patricia O'Brien and how it might have been feasible for her to aid the attacker.

"The report of the assault is in Patricia's own words," Anna said eventually. "Oliver Cotter didn't see it, he had his back turned to them. And none of the witnesses on the street observed more than a scuffle. Patricia said the young guy knocked her to the ground. Then he got a head start running away. But as Oliver said, he was winded from the punch he gave him."

"The cuffs were never recovered. If she opened them, wouldn't he have shaken them off before he ran?" Vivian sounded hopeful, as though she didn't want to believe the possibility Anna had suggested.

"Not if she only opened one cuff – they have separate locks, you see – and she probably wouldn't have had time to open both. He could have made a run for it and managed to open the other side later – there are ways and means. But her key went missing so she could have opened one cuff then put the key in his free hand – or in his pocket. It's all possible."

"Or it could be all wrong."

"Only Patricia really knows. But she left the gardaí before the investigation was even completed. That in itself is a bit odd – wouldn't you want to see it through to clear your name? What were the findings?"

"More or less that they acted reasonably and the outcome was regrettable but unavoidable. No blame attached to either party, officially."

Anna pushed her plate to the side of the table and added milk to her mug of coffee. "There's two big questions we need answered – *did* she help the guy? And *why?*"

"Yes, exactly – why would she do that? She was a Guard, for heaven's sake! They came upon a serious crime and, what, she just opens the handcuffs to help him escape?"

Anna shrugged but pressed on. "Maybe she knew him?"

"She has no brothers. I guess he could be a relative but, God, this doesn't make sense!"

"Well, the only way we'll get any answers is if we speak to her again. It's too weird that she had 'lost' the keys to her own set of handcuffs. I don't like it. We have to speak to her again."

"I'm not sure …"

"We don't have any choice, Viv! There are holes in her story – how did she let a winded, handcuffed boy overpower her and escape? When did she lose her cuff key?"

"If you're wrong then it's an awful accusation and she's already reluctant to be involved in the documentary. She said her solicitor will be keeping an eye on things as well."

"That's another thing!" Anna exclaimed, one fist pounding the table between them. "Oliver sees this as a blight on his career and seemed upset talking about it; no justice for the crime and a man killed unlawfully. Innocent people have no trouble recalling a tragic event. But Patricia wants to forget this whole thing and is threatening you with her solicitor if she doesn't appear well in the programme – she said as much!"

Vivian rubbed the space between her eyebrows, wincing. "Have you any painkillers, Anna? I can feel a headache coming on. And it's got nothing to do with the cocktails from last night."

Anna found the packet in her bag and slid it across the table. She watched her friend pop two from the foil sleeve and down them with her coffee. She didn't want to verbalise her next thought but she felt there was really no choice.

"Vivian, if the person who killed Bernard O'Meara is still alive, if he *did* escape the River Lee and has been lying low all these years, then we need to take the notes you received a lot more seriously. The Shakespeare quote, the crucifix, the photos – someone wants you to stop looking into this."

"I know," Vivian groaned, "and maybe we've just figured out why."

36

Casares, Spain

The temperature had risen and the poolside bar was the busiest it had been since they arrived. Kate watched it from her sun lounger, counting, noting details – four couples and three solo men, plus one woman reading her book on a chair in the shade of a parasol. Some had been at the bar last night, others looked unfamiliar, but no-one caused her any concern. All were tanned, or pink, all dressed as tourists should be. There were drinks by their sides, cocktails with little umbrellas and wedges of fruit, or cups of coffee resting on blue-rimmed saucers. Golf bags, with metal-tipped clubs glinting in the sunshine, rested against the white-tiled wall of the bar beside the three men, who checked their wrists periodically – waiting for their transport to the nearby course, she assumed. Everything looked safe to her, no-one looked out of place. She returned her eyes to the magazine on her lap. She had started to read the article about four times since breakfast but realised it might be a waste of time.

Shrieks from the pool drew her attention and she smiled at the twins. They had armbands on and matching green swimsuits. The plan to dress one of them as a boy had been met with refusal and complaint and was abandoned in the end. Kate didn't push it. They felt safer here, in the hotel, than on the streets.

Natalie stayed close to the girls, as she always did, focused on their games and their smiles. She laughed then, the easiest sound Kate had heard from her in days, and she squealed as Rhea splashed water on her face. Kate resisted the urge to shush them. It was too long since they'd had any fun. Yet a part of her wished they would have their fun in a quieter, less attention-drawing way.

Rachel stopped laughing and splashing and Kate heard her call "*Mommy!*" in a familiar whine that meant she needed the toilet. She had grown used to the sounds and needs of the twins in the last few weeks; it was as though the girls had two mothers. She stood up and stretched out her hand to her niece in the pool.

"I'll take you, come on, out you come."

"Are you sure?" Natalie pushed strands of her newly dyed blonde hair from her face.

"Yeah, sure, I'm dry." She noticed the cleaner enter the poolside toilet and carefully place the yellow cleaning sign at the door. "Oh, they're cleaning the toilets. I'll take her up to the room – you stay here with Rhea."

Kate preferred to nip back to the safety of their room whenever possible anyway – she knew it was irrational but she liked to reassure herself that their money and new passports were safe. And it was better to keep an eye on who was staying in the hotel. Anyone new had to be assessed. She had given her mother her new mobile number and the hotel number as well, to contact them when she had information that might help. She made up her mind to check for messages at reception as she helped Rachel from the pool.

Kate pulled off Rachel's armbands and quickly dried her with a towel, holding her steady while she slipped her tiny feet into a pair of sandals.

"Can you hold it until we get to the room?" They could go to the restroom near the reception desk if they really had to.

The little girl nodded and took Kate's hand.

"To our room it is so!"

Together they walked quickly into the lobby where Kate paused briefly at reception to ask if there were any messages for Lucy Robinson – her new name. There were none – so no progress yet from America – and they continued on to their room. Inside the elevator Rachel bounced and crossed her legs.

"*Aunty Kate!*"

Kate gritted her teeth and promised they'd be at the room any second now, her eyes watching the numbers creep up as the elevator ascended. Their room was a short walk from the elevator and once the doors pinged open they hurried along to it, Kate using her key card to open the door. Rachel ran in ahead of her, darting quickly to the bathroom and slamming the door closed. Kate stood in the doorway and sighed in relief.

Their room in this hotel was spacious and clean; it was expensive but worth every cent. Kate stepped inside, the door swinging shut behind her, and walked to the safe, dialled the code and pulled out the four passports and her money belt. There was over eighty thousand euro inside … so much had been spent on false documents and accommodation so far. It was necessary, she reassured herself, all of it had been necessary. Putting it all back in place and securing the safe door she really hoped her mother would come through for them soon, because the money wasn't going to last forever.

She heard the toilet flush and running water from the bathroom taps and called to Rachel, "*All set?*" as she pulled open the door to exit their room.

Pain exploded and blood erupted from her nose as a fist pounded into the middle of her face. Kate staggered backwards. A shape, a blur of colour, rushed towards her and something slammed into her stomach. She fell, her head bouncing hard on the tiled floor. A retching sound, spluttering gasps for air, was loud in her ears and she realised *she* was making the noise. Panting, a strangled cry of "*Rachel!*", she turned onto her side and tried to blink the darkness from her eyes, spitting blood onto the tiles. Suddenly, more pain, in her side this time – she had felt this before. Kicks to the ribs. She knew she had to get on her feet but the blows kept coming and her body sagged onto the floor. "*Rachel!*" it was a whisper this time, lost in the sound of heavy grunting, her attacker exerting all energy into each kick.

Fists in her hair at the back of her head. She was turned over to lie on her back and her head slammed onto the tiles again. Thick fingers clenched around her throat and panic spiralled in her. Her legs attempted to kick but were useless. She gripped the hands around her neck but her own fingers were weak and slick with blood. Her eyes wouldn't focus, wouldn't see the face of her attacker, but she could see the shape of a little girl standing near the bathroom door, watching, frozen.

Suddenly there was sound: an animal grunting and screaming, and a flash of red. The hands at her throat went slack and the blurred shape over her fell forward. Kate pushed with all her strength and the body on top of her fell to the left. She felt hands pull her upwards and her body slid in her own blood on the tiles until she was at the foot of the double bed.

Soft hands roamed her face; her nose and side ached. She sat up slowly and leaned against the bed. She needed oxygen but each lungful hurt. She gasped for air as a wet cloth was wiped over the skin on her face and neck. Her eyes focused again.

Natalie was sitting beside her, her face wet with tears, her chest jerking in shocked spasms. A woman lay on the ground between them and the door, a red fire extinguisher – like the ones that lined the hallways of the hotel – lay on the ground beside her. Rachel was still standing at the bathroom door and Rhea stood beside her now, holding her hand. Kate looked away from the shock on their faces, unable to bear it.

"*Kate!*" Natalie whispered urgently. "*Kate! Can you speak?*"

She rose shakily to her feet and sat on the end of the bed. Pain seared in her side like hot knifes piercing her flesh.

"Lock the door," she said, her voice a harsh whisper.

Natalie darted to the door and locked it. She stood with her back to it, the wood offering support, her hands on her chest.

"What happened?" Kate felt along her side, along her ribcage. Surely something must be broken – her nose definitely was.

"It was the woman, the one at the table, under the umbrella." Natalie was still crying, but her hands motioned now to the twins and they darted to her, wrapping themselves around her, keeping their eyes away from the woman on the floor and the blood on their aunt. "She followed you as soon as you left. It was … at first I wasn't sure." She gulped, struggling to speak, tears drying on her cheeks. "Who is she?" She rubbed her hands on her daughters' backs in circles, an unconscious movement, attempting to soothe them, but perhaps to comfort herself.

Kate sat still, trying to focus on her breathing and steadying her heartrate – she needed to think. The fire extinguisher on the tiled floor was a slash of red on the stark white. Natalie had saved her life, she realised. She had been so focused on searching for Gallagher's men, searching for the cliché hard-man look, she had completely overlooked a woman having coffee under a parasol. It was a mistake she would never make again.

"We need to get out of here, OK? *Now.*" She rose to her feet. The pain was breathtakingly sharp but she was steady on the ground. Touching the back of her head, she was relieved to find it wasn't cut. There'd be a lump, for sure, from where her head had hit the tiles, but she didn't need stitches. "Gallagher knows where we are again."

Natalie nodded. There was a look in her eyes that hadn't been there before; something less passive. She nodded at the woman on the ground.

"Is she dead?"

Kate shrugged – she didn't care. "Help me move her, OK?"

She was aware that Rachel and Rhea had turned to watch them from the door. Her heart was heavy for them; all they had witnessed and heard, the fear they carried – she'd explain it all to them when they were safely away from here.

Urgency descended on them, as though a clock was ticking loudly in the room. The woman was working for Gallagher in some capacity, Kate was sure of that, and it was doubtful she was working *alone.* Together with Natalie she pulled the woman by the ankles until they were all inside the bathroom, Kate pushing past the pain to get it done. She looked at her as they shoved her body up against the bathtub. Mid-twenties, dark hair, a pretty face, and a gash on her temple that was matted with drying blood. Dressed in a sundress and sandals, leather bracelets at her wrists and two yellow pineapples hanging from her earlobes, she looked like a tourist, not a hired killer. With one last look Kate shook her head at her own foolishness – she had been so easily caught off her guard.

Natalie left the bathroom, not looking behind her. Kate heard her pulling open drawers, murmuring to the girls. Inside the bathroom, Kate knelt beside the woman – she was alive. She wouldn't be unconscious for much longer. Kate was relieved – to leave another dead body behind her wasn't part of the plan. She pulled the cords from a dressing gown hanging on the back of the bathroom door and tied the woman's hands behind her back and bound her feet as tightly as she could, then stuffed a small towel into her mouth. This would buy them time. She kept her eyes from the woman's face. Nothing about this game between them was personal, just something to get done. There was no need to remember the woman's face later when she closed her eyes.

Before she left the bathroom Kate washed the blood from her hands and examined her face in the mirror. Her nose was swollen to three times its normal size, at least, and her lips were split right in the centre. She wet a towel and cleaned the blood from her face and neck as best she could, roughly dragging the cotton cloth over her skin. Red marks on her neck would be bruises soon. This reminded her so much of her fight with David Gallagher; he had tried to choke her too. Well, she had walked away from that fight, just like she was walking away from this.

In the bedroom she changed her clothes, leaving her bloodied T-shirt and shorts in the waste-bin between the two double beds. She pulled open the safe again and secured the money belt around her waist under a fresh T-shirt. Natalie had their clothes and belongings stuffed into two shoulder bags, the twins had their blue teddies under their chins. Kate ignored their pale faces, their shaky steps as they walked to the elevator again. She was keeping them safe, she told herself, all this would turn out OK in the end. The four of them were silent as the elevator descended, silent as they moved through the lobby with heads down and quick steps.

"Miss Robinson?" a young, female voice called out. They kept moving until she called out again, a little closer this time, and Kate stopped. Natalie's eyes met hers, wild and fearful, and she shook her head. *They needed to keep moving!* But it was too late; the young receptionist was beside them.

"Oh my goodness!" she exclaimed, taking in Kate's injured face. "Did you fall? Do you need assistance?"

"No," Kate tightened her grip on Rhea's hand, "I'm fine. We're going out to do some shopping now."

"Oh, OK." The young woman nodded, clearly unconvinced, but determined to get on with why she had approached them. "Well, I won't delay you." Her accent was upper-class British, not a local employee. "You asked if there were any messages for you earlier, and I said no. But I've received one just now, and the caller was quite insistent!"

"What caller? When was this?"

"*Um* … just now, as I said."

Kate's injuries and her urgent, almost angry manner were unnerving the receptionist.

"The caller didn't use *your* name. She said Kate. But she did describe you and the children and your friend." Her hands gestured to the others as she took a step back. "You are the only family in the hotel! So it must be for you! Yes … *um* … she just said to tell you Tom was sending someone to meet you. Does that make sense?"

"*She?* The caller was a *woman?*"

"*Um*, yes."

"Did she leave any details? Any name or phone number?"

The receptionist shook her head.

"No. Nothing. I think she got cut off. Are you sure you don't need medical assistance?"

Without answering, Kate turned away and walked quickly through the revolving doors and into the bright sunshine, the others close behind her. She led the way to a taxi rank she had noticed days before, her sunglasses in place and her eyes focused straight ahead.

Someone was on their side, only this time the caller had been too late. A woman. It had to be Anna. Who else in Cork would help them? But how could she possibly know Tom Gallagher's next move?

All Kate knew for sure was that Gallagher was closing in and they were running out of options.

37

Cork

The next morning Vivian left the apartment while Anna was in the shower – she suspected that it was to avoid becoming her sparring partner, or as Vivian had called it her "human punchbag" again. The morning was dry and warmer than the previous day, so Anna decided on a run. The route beside Blackrock Castle, alongside the River Lee, was familiar to her now. She nodded hello at a few faces she recognised as she passed, club classics beating loud in her ears. She didn't allow herself to think about the last few days but decided to focus on controlling what she could – so all the things that were directly beyond her control were off-limits.

She finished her jog at Blackrock Castle and ordered a bottle of water and a coffee-to-go, thinking about a call with her aunt later that day. Her *aunt*. A woman she hadn't known existed until recently. Her relationship with her mother's sister was still so new. It was precious to her.

The newspaper article Myles had provided had detailed who her mother really was. That had opened the possibility of finding members of her family, people Anna and Alex had long been led to believe were dead or didn't exist in the first place. To find an aunt, a woman that had been alive in America all this time, had been as exciting as it was shocking. Annika Vasilieva had married a Texan named Daniel Garcia; she had two grown sons, the only cousins Anna had. She hadn't spoken to them yet. It had only been weeks since she had first contacted her aunt. But her relationship with Annika was growing stronger every time they Skype-called.

Anna walked home quickly. There were mundane things to do before their call, laundry and some emails she wanted to send. The idea of an empty apartment all day was unnerving but she told herself that being alone wasn't such a bad thing. She was used to it, and so few people knew she was living here now, she felt safer than she had in weeks.

As she climbed the steps to Vivian's apartment, the door to the neighbouring one opened and Dermot stepped out, his cat at his feet. She sighed. The man had a knack for knowing when one of them was approaching. His cat was winding itself between his legs as he began to rub a cloth over the brass numbers on his front door.

"Oh hello, love, we finally get a chance to have a proper chat! Are you Anna or Vivian?"

Anna smiled but groaned inside. She had no choice but to give the man the time he wanted. She guessed he was in his late fifties, and she wondered what he did for a living. He always seemed to be skulking about his front door with plenty of time to chat.

"Where are you coming back from then?" Another question before she'd had time to answer the first.

His eyes roamed over her and she gritted her teeth as his cat watched her with pale yellow eyes.

"I like your cat," she said, ignoring his inquisition. "A tabby, isn't it?"

"Her name is Pirate," he beamed, glowing under the attention she was giving him. "She's got a darker patch over one eye, see?"

Anna nodded, though she couldn't see much of a difference in the colour of the cat's fur.

Pirate arched her back and began to meow loudly.

"I don't think Pirate likes the cold much," she said, hoping he'd take the hint and go back inside.

"You're right there – a proper princess, she is. Listen, I was meaning to call in. I'm having a few pals around for drinks later in the week. Will you both join us?" He smiled expectantly at her, his round face full of hope.

Anna's smile froze on her face – she wondered what she and Vivian might have in common with his "pals" and what type of party it might be. His hopeful eyes pierced her in a way that made her uncomfortable.

"*Um* … when exactly were you thinking?"

"Friday night, if that suits you. Unless you both have other plans? I know you young people like to party at the weekends."

Anna cringed at the hope in his voice. "I'll check with Vivian, see if she's free."

"Great!" He appeared to have taken her answer as agreement. "I'll call in for you, shall I? Around eight?"

"*Mmm*," Anna turned to Vivian's door and pulled out her keys.

"Oh, did your fella get in touch?"

"Sorry?" She felt she would never get inside.

"The lad making the delivery the other morning?"

Anna remembered feeling Dermot's watchful eyes on her as she'd received the Victus takeaway breakfast.

"Oh yes, all sorted, thank you!" She left him polishing his door and stepped inside to the heat of the apartment.

38

Annika Garcia was always punctual for their Skype call, never keeping Anna waiting. It was a trait her own mother had had; she had hated to be kept waiting and it had bothered her even more to waste other people's time. Anna guessed it was behaviour they both learned in childhood.

So it wasn't a surprise that at exactly three o'clock their Skype call connected. Annika was sitting in her living room, streams of the morning sun poking through the open curtains behind her chair. Anna wondered if it would ever get easier to see her – Annika looked so much like an older version of her sister, it offered Anna an image of the woman her mother could have grown to be, had Robert Evans and Roy Eastly not caught up to them in Kinsale ten years ago. Seeing Annika's silver hair fall in soft waves to her shoulders, her bright-blue eyes shining amid the frame of fine wrinkles, the wide smile that had been her mother's, Anna always took a moment to compose herself before she spoke.

"Anna, my love, it's so wonderful to see your face!"

Annika no longer cried through their conversations. Discovering that her sister was dead had been a blow to her, softened only slightly by the knowledge she had a niece and nephew halfway across the world.

"I received the box of photos you sent a few days ago." She clutched her hands to her chest, "Oh my goodness, you have no idea how it made me feel! To see almost thirty years of my sister's life laid out on the table was so incredible. Dan had to force me to look away and go to bed!"

They laughed together. Anna was glad to have been able to offer her aunt the comfort of knowing her younger sister had been happy.

"Tell me how you are," Annika instructed.

Anna laughed. She was growing used to her aunt's direct way of speaking. She wondered what to say. How was she really? Tired of waiting for life to move forward would be an apt description, but she didn't think it was fair to burden the woman. What could she possibly do to help from the other side of the world?

"I'm fine."

"Why don't I believe you? I'll tell you why!" Annika leaned forward, her face filling up the laptop screen. "Your brother has left his house in a hurry because a man escaped from prison."

"Well, technically, he didn't escape, but –"

Annika waved her hand to shush Anna.

"He's out! He scared little Chloe and your brother, but not you? Why are you still in Cork, waiting for him to find you?"

Anna laughed again, although she didn't find anything funny – what was wrong with her?

"Maybe I *want* him to find me!" She smiled broadly to show her aunt she was kidding, but Annika didn't get the joke.

"So you can kill him? Is that what you want to do?"

Her eyes seemed to penetrate the screen and the space between them, and Anna could no longer meet them. She looked at her hands in her lap instead.

"You are like your mother, you know? You look like a kitten but you are a tiger, yes? Look at me, please, Anna."

Anna raised her eyes; this wasn't how their conversation was supposed to go! She had hoped for a warm, affectionate exchange of pleasantries, had hoped for more information on her cousins and their home in San Antonio. The last thing she had expected was a scolding from her aunt, or questions that made her feel so uncomfortable she was now squirming in her seat.

"So you are waiting, to see if he finds you. This pervert, this Harris."

"No ... I just don't see why I should leave Cork! This is my home! I'm being careful but I refuse to go into hiding! I've already left Kinsale, and our house there. I'm staying with my friend in the city. He won't find me." As she said the words she instinctively felt that wasn't true. She knew that deep down she was *waiting* for their confrontation.

"And if he does? If he does find you, what then?"

After a pause, Anna shrugged. "Then I'll be ready."

Annika observed her quietly for so long that Anna wondered if their connection had actually frozen. Eventually she nodded. Her mouth was a thin line and she muttered some words that Anna couldn't understand, except for the name "Yelena", her mother's name. But the moment passed, Annika seeming to decide to drop the subject.

"I spoke to Alex. He updated me on the progress at the site. I'm glad you're not there too, so much time taken up with it. Such a terrible thing to have to go through. He told me you have two weeks off work – will you spend some quality time with your friend? Or perhaps travel to see your boyfriend?"

Their conversation moved on to lighter topics. Anna didn't

mention the documentary series she was helping Vivian with but spoke of Myles and Banba Productions in a vague way, keeping everything light and casual. Time raced forward, as it always did when they spoke, and soon Annika expressed regret that she had to end the call soon.

"Before we say goodbye, tell me what you decided about the money."

Anna sighed. This was a difficult thing to think about, and she was glad to have her aunt to talk it over with. When her parents had disappeared, her father's friend Robert Evans had visited their home in Kinsale, expressing his concern. Anna and Alex hadn't known him prior to that day. Bob, as he had introduced himself, was English and claimed to have worked with their father. They now knew this much was true. He told them about a trust fund their father had set up and made arrangements for the money to be transferred to Alex's account. They each received two hundred and fifty thousand euro. Here, the truth ended. At the time he had been so concerned for them, so caring. Now he was helping gardaí with the attempt to locate their parents' bodies. He had been instrumental in their death. Anna understood the money he had transferred was his own – it was guilt money. She wanted nothing to do with it.

"Well, I haven't said anything to Alex, so please don't. He's already spent his half, when he bought a house with Sam. And I know he'd want me to use it to buy a house and have some security for myself. But it's tainted. Bob Evans is a criminal. He's already destroyed my past and I don't want any part of him in my future. Does that make sense?"

Annika nodded encouragingly.

"I've found a charity that I want to donate it to. It's for victims of sexual violence. There's about two hundred thousand left because I bought a car and spent some on the house in Kinsale, but the rest is there. I must figure out how to go about it."

"You'll need a solicitor. Separate to your brother. I assume you'll split the house in Kinsale when it sells and you need to get your own legal counsel. He or she can advise you on how to donate the money and make sure it's all above board. I think it's a marvellous idea!"

When they said goodbye, after scheduling their next Skype call for a week's time, Anna packed away her laptop and moved into the kitchen to make coffee. After the warmth and companionable conversation with Annika the apartment felt still and quiet, in a way that reminded her of the house in Kinsale and why she had been so desperate to leave.

Once her parents were legally declared dead the house, their family home, could go on the market. Neither she nor Alex wanted to live there again. Initially Anna had intended to buy somewhere in Kinsale, close to the sea and the home she had known all her life. Now she could see the advantages of city life too.

One thing she was certain of was that she enjoyed living *with* someone. Vivian was chatty and fun and the apartment felt empty without her. The weekend Myles had stayed with Anna in Kinsale had been one of the happiest she could ever remember.

Feeling restless she moved to the balcony and stood in the chill air, wind stirring her hair. The mug of coffee offered heat and she pressed it close to her chest. Her loneliness was still with her. She missed Myles and dreaded the thought of moving out of Vivian's apartment to buy a house on her own.

For years she had had so many questions. She had assumed that knowing where her parents were, and what had happened to them, would bring her peace. The truth was, that even after all her questions had been answered, she still felt lost.

39

Tom Gallagher didn't believe in coincidences. The universe offered opportunity if a man was prepared to take it – that was all. There were no nuances, no faint shadows of meaning to be found in random occurrences. He couldn't have cared less when two chance events happened that appeared to have a connection, some tenuous link invented if someone tried hard enough. Mae used to speak about it, in the days when she was up to having a conversation with him. She used to exclaim "What are the chances of that!" whenever the universe connected two things in even the most remote of ways.

Still, he smiled a little when the phone rang and it was John. He had just been reading a report from Victor White about John's transfer to Cork prison. That his son had called while he was reading about him was meaningless, he knew, although he could almost hear his wife's excitement – "What a coincidence!"

He missed her – this would be an amusing anecdote when he saw her next. Although, considering the circumstances, perhaps not.

"They're allowing you phone calls already. You *must* be being a good boy."

John grunted something into the phone that Tom couldn't make out. He hadn't expected to hear from John – he knew anything his son needed could be dealt with by Victor White. Their solicitor was the only man who could help him now. Tom remembered their last conversation, beside John's hospital bed, and was saddened again at how he had felt that day. Like he'd wanted to hurt John. He was his only living son. Concern edged into his voice as he asked how things had been since his transfer.

"Fine, not bad at all." Bravado had always been John's preferred emotional response to a difficult situation. "Some of the lads in here are sound. And I'm known in here already. Respected, like. Word spreads."

His voice was low and Tom could hear background noises, jovial yells and slamming sounds. It sounded like John was calling from a recreational hall, but Tom knew it was probably just a corridor in the prison.

"I have news," John said.

"Oh, yes? What sort of news? Some sort of deal with the DPP?" If this were true Tom would scarcely believe it – the Director of Public Prosecutions was loath to cut deals with murderers, as far as Tom was aware. He liked to keep a close eye on the Irish judicial system. Perhaps Victor White had convinced John to grass up their contacts the way he had tried with Tom.

"Nothing like that. It's about Murray." John spoke so low his voice was almost inaudible.

Tom sat up straighter in his office chair, not daring to breathe too loud in case he missed what John would say.

"He's made a few enemies in here. So have the gang he's linked up with. I just heard he's on his way to Cork."

"When?"

"Tonight. To the house."

"*What, here?*" Tom could scarcely believe what he was hearing. Murray would come to his home, the place he had shared with his wife, where his granddaughters used to play and eat dinner. All without prior arrangement. Such lack of respect – after thirty years of loyalty and trust, the man would ambush Tom in his own house. After all he had done, he was intent on sinking the knife in deeper. His hand scrunched the papers on the desktop.

"You're sure about this?"

"I wouldn't be calling if I wasn't."

"Do you have a time frame?"

"Fella in here overheard a conversation … basically, I'd guess he's twenty minutes out."

Tom was silent. Aside from shock at the speed Murray was moving, he felt nothing. He realised a man in his situation might expect to feel apprehension that his enemy was about to descend on his home, about to take from him that which he had built up his whole life. He might expect to find his heart race as adrenaline spiked through his nervous system.

Yet all he felt was peace.

He stood up and stretched his arms to the ceiling, feeling the joints in his back creak. So Murray was on his way to the house. Tom decided it was time to send his housekeeper home. And he'd tell her to leave the electric gates open – he was expecting company.

40

It was dusk when they arrived – John's estimation had been ten minutes short – and Tom opened the front door wide when Ely Murray stood on the front step with two other men. Tom had expected it to be a bigger group that sauntered to his front door, but then he figured Murray, despite having several men inside the various Garda stations across the city, was loath to draw too much attention to himself. Especially among the squad cars and unmarked cars watching the house.

Manoeuvring his way into a new gang suited him. Murray carried himself with a new authority now. He nodded a confident greeting to Tom, hands in the pockets of his dark jacket.

"Tom. You know why we're here. Let's not make it a public spectacle."

Tom stepped aside and Murray entered the house, followed by his men. They were strangers to Tom, each one tracking wet footprints from the driveway onto his new hall tiles. He watched their stiff-backed walk, their gaze unfocused as they passed him and followed their leader – despite himself, he admired their professionalism. They had no interest in goading him with comments and smirks and weren't here to mock and sneer. They were here to do business.

"We'll have a drink," Tom said, and walked ahead of the others into the reading room, into the one place in the house his business had never touched. Mae's room. Murray had had the run of the house before, but never this room. It was private, family only. If he was surprised at being led there now, he didn't say anything.

When they stepped inside, Marco jumped quickly to his feet, an indecipherable roar bursting from him. Murray's men quickly gripped his arms.

Tom strode forward and placed a hand on his shoulder. "Calm down, Marco. No cause for alarm."

Marco met Tom's eyes, then shook the men off, and fixed his gaze on Murray.

"You understand we need to search you," Murray said softly, a pained expression on his face. He wasn't enjoying this.

His men briskly patted Tom down, finding nothing.

Marco glowered threateningly, but surrendered to be searched with a grunt. Nothing was found. Eventually he sat down, rearranged his shirt and pushed back his dark hair.

A book was perched on the armrest beside him – Stephen King's *Misery*.

"I didn't take you for a reader, Marco, lad," Murray said, smirking. "The soccer fixtures in the paper, maybe, but never a whole book."

Marco's hand rested on the hardback cover and he glared at Murray, a man he had often worked alongside for Tom. How things had changed.

Tom scanned the two men that had accompanied Murray, watching them position themselves strategically by the door. They were tall and well built – two skinheads with oddly vacant eyes.

"Do your new friends speak or are they just moving statues?" he asked.

Murray didn't respond. Then, at a nod from him, one of them left the room.

Tom heard doors open and close. Searching the house.

Tom moved to the drinks cabinet, poured drinks into crystal glasses and gestured to Murray to take one.

Murray took a glass and sipped. He stared at Tom for a beat, then said, "You don't seem surprised to see me."

"You sent a man to tell me you wanted a meeting." Tom shrugged. "I'm surprised you wanted to meet *here*. In my home. In Mae's home. Was this really necessary?"

If Tom's calm acceptance of the gang in his house, at seeing the man who had shot his son and robbed him was unnerving Murray, he hid it well.

"You're being watched around the clock. You know it, I know it. If I suggested a place you'd be followed there, and then what? I don't have enough gardaí on my payroll to prevent the obvious ending to that story."

"The house is being watched too, surely you know that? This meeting will probably be logged into some evidence book, your reg number traced, or papped by the press. Are you sure this was such a smart move?"

"I can't do a thing about the press. My man in Lee Street keeps me well informed. There was a change in the guard tonight – the men parked outside will turn the other way. No-one will be logging this visit, trust me on that. And the vehicle reg won't lead anywhere. You see, Tom, you taught me well."

"Yes ... you were like a son to me."

"But I wasn't your son, was I?" His voice was brittle with regret. "I was never going to be allowed to step up!"

Tom swallowed a mouthful of liquor and felt nothing, the burning sting of it lost on him.

In the cosy light of the reading room the scar that tracked from Murray's ear to his lip was shrouded in soft shadows, making him look less threatening. Tom wasn't fooled – he could see the bulges in the waistband of his jeans. He was armed. They all were.

Murray's man re-entered the room and nodded to his boss before taking up position by the window. Tom's eyes strayed to the waistline of his trousers, bulging where the weapons he had removed from Tom's office and bedroom were now pressed against his flesh. Murray knew the hiding places inside the house where Tom kept guns and knives for emergencies. Not that he'd had to use them much; after one or two minor skirmishes in the early days, no-one had dared to bring their fight to his home.

"Anyone else here?" Murray asked quietly.

Tom's man shook his head.

"*You've some fucking nerve!*" Marco made to stand up again but thought better of it, looking away, muttering to himself.

"Marco's right," Tom said. "After thirty years together, you shot my son. Left him for dead. Robbed me and now you're taking my business. That's why you're here, isn't it? You've had your pound of flesh. Yet you want the rest."

Tom could feel something stirring in him – finally. Anger or bitter regret, he wasn't sure. Perhaps it was anticipation of how this night would end.

Murray watched him carefully from the opposite wall, leaning with one heavy boot against the cream wallpaper, swirling the liquid in his glass, his other boot making a deep indent in Mae's favourite sheepskin rug.

"John doesn't get to tell me to walk away." Murray seemed calm and spoke as though he was explaining a simple maths problem to a child, but Tom noticed a tremor in the hand holding the crystal tumbler. "Not after thirty years. I took what was owed to me and, yes, now I've come back for the rest. It's inevitable – it was always going to end this way. David's dead, John's as good as. You're an old man – it should be me taking over now!" He wiped spittle from his mouth and when his eyes met Tom's they were hard and cold. "It's over for you in Cork. You're facing jail time and the city needs to be run. You can't hold it against me for seizing an opportunity! There are others, small-time, straining at the bit, but it's *my* city, and I can continue what you started."

Tom stared at him, hatred twisting his face.

"You've no sons to carry on, Tom." A hint of earnestness edged into his words. Pleading with Tom to see reason. Even after everything, he respected the man in front of him, and he wanted him to understand. "I can pick up where we left off. It's a younger man's game."

"And if I refuse?"

Murray shook his head. "I wouldn't advise that. The people I work with now are something to be feared. Think of your wife." There was excitement in his eyes. "It's your choice. You step aside or you will be made to. Believe me – I don't want to see it end that way for you. Or Mae."

Murray looked around him, at the books lining the shelves and plush furniture against the walls.

"You can keep this house. I'll run the club and you and Mae will be looked after in your retirement. I owe you that. But you're out – you hand over control of everything. The port, all the contacts, the business portfolio, everything is turned over. Men that need telling will be told and then you're cut loose. Any interference from you, or John for that matter ..." He shrugged and let the sentence hang unfinished.

Tom understood.

"I negotiated this for you, by the way. They wanted you dead. Properly out of the way."

"Do you want a thank-you card?" Tom drained his glass and stepped forward, setting it onto the coffee table in the centre of the room. He heard the click and grind of his own teeth, loud in his ears ... he was so tired of it all.

"Fuck this – I need air!" he said and moved to the door, pulling a cigarette packet and lighter from a nearby shelf.

Murray stepped forward but stopped in the middle of the room, seeming undecided.

"Allow a man a cigarette, for fuck sake!" Tom said. "Or will you deny me that too?"

The skinhead at the door looked to Murray for instruction and after a brief pause he nodded, seeming to have decided that there was actually nothing Tom could do. "Two minutes, Tom! And out the back, not the front." He pointed at his man. "Stay with him."

Marco was on his feet again. "You've no right, none whatsoever!" He was nose-to-nose with Murray when Tom turned from the door.

"It's OK, Marco. Two minutes – just give me two minutes." Then he left the room.

The skinhead from the doorway followed him through the hallway, into the kitchen and to the back door. He had an issue with eye-contact, Tom thought. Or perhaps he cared so little about Tom that he didn't see him as a person, just an obstacle to be moved aside.

He stepped out into the night. The bulk of the other man remained in his peripheral vision, silently waiting by the open back door.

Tom moved toward the centre of his garden and lit a cigarette. The air all around him was cold and he was wearing only a thin shirt, but he felt nothing. The chill couldn't penetrate him. The sky was starless, dull and grey, not yet fully dark. God, he was tired … He took a drag but it was as if the cigarette was filled with air. He tasted nothing, felt nothing. His hand was steady as he brought it to his lips again, drawing deeply. It was a waste of time and he flicked it away onto the damp grass.

Tom lifted his wrist, flicked his eyes to his watch. Suddenly there was noise, a commotion from inside, and Murray's man swung around and moved into the house.

Alone in the garden, Tom took a deep breath. It was now or never.

41

He walked into the kitchen and stopped, listening. He heard it then, as expected. Loud bursts of sound, one after the other. Was Marco's aim accurate, he wondered? He doubted it – anger would have betrayed his hand. But perhaps enough damage would have been done. He heard a groan and a shuffling sound, as legs were dragged along the ground, someone pulling himself forward, trying to get out. Would the gardaí sitting in their cars a couple of hundred metres away have heard the gunshots? He assumed so. He had to move fast.

Tom blinked, shook his head, stepped forward.

At the gas hob he pushed in and twisted the silver and black knobs, all four of them. As the sound of groaning from Mae's room grew louder, he turned away and stepped through the back door again, closing it behind him, sealing in the fumes.

It was growing darker, his visibility reduced, but Tom could have found his way around his own property blindfolded. He moved quickly to the side of the house, stayed low to the wall, crouching past the shuttered windows of the reading room. He dipped his hand into a bush and pulled out a two-litre plastic bottle from the foliage. Unscrewing the top, he pulled a handkerchief from his pocket and doused it in the contents of the bottle, then stuffed it into the top. The stench of petrol hit him and he noticed his hand shake a little but he pressed on.

Running to the back door again, he pushed it open. His thumb slipped once, twice, over the wheel of the lighter but he managed to ignite it. He threw the bottle into the kitchen, then ran to the concrete wall that surrounded his back garden, scaled it and leapt down into the alleyway behind. Pain jolted through his legs and his breathing became laboured. He wondered how long he should wait – but then a massive bang made him jump. Splinters from his home exploding hit the wall behind him. Tom crouched low, hands over his head. The ringing in his ears slowly subsided as he sat on the ground and pressed his forehead into his knees, his breath coming in short spasms. He felt nothing. All he knew was emptiness. Only one thought came to him – he had to move.

He ran in a crouch to the end of the alley and as he reached the footpath beyond he dropped lower, crawling to a beat-up silver Nissan that Marco had left parked there. It was his late mother's car. The keys were attached to the rim of the passenger wheel with flimsy string that snapped easily between his fists. He snatched up a baseball hat from inside the door, wedged it onto his head and started the car with a steady hand.

He pulled into the road. Traffic had come to a stop as passers-by stepped out of their cars, mobile phones pressed to their ears, watching the flames leap from the house and light it up like a beacon. Gardaí, in uniform and plain clothes, were already on the scene – they had been parked nearby for weeks, watching him, waiting for the day their arrest warrant would be granted. Now they could do nothing but wait for help from the fire department.

Tom did a U-turn, his eyes on the rear-view mirror, darting

between the faces of the people on the street – as far as he could tell, he had gone undetected. The peal of approaching sirens was loud. He picked up speed.

Murray had got what he deserved. In fact, it was an easier death than Tom would have liked for the man. His stupidity was his undoing – all the planning, to steal from one gang and infiltrate another came to nothing in the end. Tom had vowed to himself a very long time ago that anyone who underestimated him would live to regret it. Or die.

It was only after he had put ten minutes between him and his home that he allowed himself to think of Marco. The idea of a getaway car had been his, a rare bright suggestion from the man who had always been more loyal guard-dog than strategic planner. But it had been ingenious. Pack a bag, new identities, passports, phones and money at the ready, and go out fighting, whenever that day might come.

He remembered Marco's words a few days ago, when they had shared a drink and planned for Tom and Mae's future. A future that Marco could play no part in.

"*Tell me, what did the doctor say?*"

"*He said … he said something about tumours … no option of treatment. Best to go quickly.*"

Tom had been saddened then, to think that Marco didn't have long left. When Marco had raised the idea of killing Murray and his men, and how they might go about it, Tom had protested fiercely.

"*Absolutely not!*"

"*It makes sense. Let me do this, Tom. I can't face the treatment, not after seeing what my mam went through. It'll be better this way.*"

His plan to block the door of the reading room, book in hand, was simple.

To Tom, hiding a gun in the gouged-out pages of Stephen King's *Misery* felt like a homage to David and John – in their own way, his sons had helped him in the end. Three shots was all it took to buy Tom enough time to really end this. Murray's men were armed and would have returned fire. Tom was consoled that it had been a better end for Marco than dying from his illness the way his mother had, knowing what suffering lay ahead of him.

It was almost over.

42

Vivian and Anna sat on the patio chairs on the balcony, light from the night sky illuminating the small space enough for them both. Neither felt much in the mood for harsh lighting or conversation. A glass of wine each sat on the small table in front of them, blankets around their shoulders. The wail of sirens had finally stopped.

Gloom had hung heavy around Vivian since she returned from her meeting with Carol and Luke. With a scowl she picked up her glass, staring sullenly into the depths of the dark-red wine, churning it absentmindedly.

"I hope no-one's badly hurt," Anna murmured. "It sounded like the whole of the city's fire service was out there!"

Vivian shivered. "I hate fires!" Her voice was barely above a whisper. "I covered a house-fire once for the paper. Two people died and there were two survivors, but their injuries ..." she shook her head, "The worst thing was the smell at the scene. Certain things *stink* when they burn. One of the fire-fighters explained it to me. Worst was the smell near the human remains."

Anna shuddered, her thoughts straying to her brother and his vigil in a cold field. Thinking of him prompted her to tell Vivian about Gareth and Dean Harris. A suitable moment hadn't arisen yet, but she guessed now was as good a time as any.

Vivian reacted exactly as Anna had imagined she would, her shock at Dean Harris's boldness written all over her face.

"I can't believe it!"

"I know. The nerve of the man! Camping out in my own house. William Ryan said –"

"Not that – although, yeah, *that* – but I can't believe you contacted Gareth behind my back!"

Anna shifted in the patio chair. The hard metal was uncomfortable in any case, but now her discomfort was amplified. Still, she decided that enough was enough.

"I'm sorry if you feel betrayed. But the fact you were suspecting your brother of threatening you had to stop. You and he need to talk. Whatever is going on between you both is ridiculous! Family is precious, Vivian."

Vivian looked a little mollified, and Anna could make out the pink of her cheeks in the half-light.

Vivian pulled the blanket closer around her shoulders and looked out into the night, into the dark. "I'm glad your chat with Annika went well. She seems really nice."

Anna appreciated her friend's attempt to change the topic and was glad Gareth was no longer part of the conversation.

"She is! I really want to travel to San Antonio to meet her. It'd be weird though – she looks so much like my mum I'm not sure I could cope with seeing her."

Vivian smiled at her sympathetically.

"Has there been any news from Alex?"

Anna shook her head. "No updates. He's thinking about coming home actually – Sam wants to get back to work."

Vivian refilled their glasses from a bottle of red wine on the ground beside her seat. Her face looked pale in the moonlight, her features unable to uncoil themselves from a scowl. Anna reached across the table and touched her hand.

"Are you able to talk about it yet? What did Carol and Luke say? Will you speak to the gardaí about our suspicions about Patricia O'Brien? Sorry!" She grinned. "Too many questions!"

Vivian shook her head and blinked rapidly, clearing her throat before she spoke. "Don't worry. Well – it was a tense meeting. It's a 'no' to speaking to her. They don't think it's enough to take to the Guards. Carol is adamant that we pause the investigations on this case for a while."

"Oh, I'm sorry – you must be disappointed!" Though she was surprised, Anna was glad, in a way. It would keep Vivian safer, although she knew her friend was hugely disheartened.

Vivian sighed. "Carol suggested I get to work on one of the other cold cases and we come back to this one another time." Suddenly she groaned loudly, "*Ugh!* It feels like we had just made a breakthrough, Anna! And now I have to pull back! I really want to speak to Patricia – and *fast* – and it might give us the answers we need. But Carol's pulled the plug!"

"I think the chances of getting a confession out of Patricia are slim – she had a wall around her. You won't penetrate it. And she has a sister who's a solicitor, remember? You need to watch your step."

"That's what Carol said!"

"Well, maybe she has a point."

Vivian lowered her eyes to her drink again. It was clear this wasn't what she wanted to hear. Anna looked away from her, into the yard underneath them, the hulking outline of bins and containers making ominous shapes in the dark.

"Someone's been threatening you, Viv," Anna said softly. "That's something to take seriously. And I agree with you – the investigation is stalled. Without Patricia admitting to helping the killer escape, there's nothing you can do to move this forward."

Vivian folded her arms across her chest and huffed, her breath a little cloud in front of her face. "Well, there's fat chance of that – she won't even answer the phone!"

They fell silent, each turning over recent events in a case that had consumed them for days – weeks for Vivian.

A noise from the yard below drew Anna's attention and she peered into the darkness, jumping as a cat or some other small animal darted from behind a glass recycling bin and ran into the dark.

"You really need to get lights put in down there."

Vivian was scrolling through messages on her mobile and didn't respond. She threw her phone onto the table with a sigh.

"Nothing is coming together for this documentary! I'm *weeks* at this and all I have are questions! But we are *this* close to something, I can feel it! Just when Carol tells me to step back!"

"On the bright side, there's been no further threatening notes or anything. That's a good thing, right?"

Vivian drained her glass of wine in two gulps. "If you think *not* getting threatening messages is a 'good thing', the last few months have *really* messed you up!" She pushed up from the chair and walked into the apartment.

Anna thought she saw tears glinting in Vivian's eyes as she passed. She let her go; she knew her friend well. Sometimes when she was overwhelmed, she lashed out. She was better off being alone right now.

She wondered about what Vivian had said. Maybe she *was* messed up. Perhaps a person could only take so much pain and fear and dashed hope before those feelings hardened into something else.

Anna stood up and looked across the rooftops and the skyline towards Mahon. She had lived in a housing estate in Kinsale all her life, with plenty of buildings around her. But the city seemed different; the number of houses, of people and cars, felt endless. It was a city full of darkness and light, shadows and alleys, good and bad. *Was* 'The Boy Who Jumped' still alive? She was beginning to think they'd never discover the truth. What she did know for certain was that Dean Harris was out there, somewhere in the city. She had been afraid of him once, but she had changed in the last few weeks. Now something inside her wanted to experience what she knew was inevitable.

"*Come out, come out, wherever you are!*" she muttered into the night.

43

It was always Victor White's job to lock up for the night. He had made a routine of it. Once Nora mounted the stairs to bed he rose too, promising to be up shortly. A quick nip from the brandy bottle in the sitting-room cabinet and the day was complete. Then he made the usual circuit of the downstairs rooms. Sitting room French doors, living room and kitchen patio doors, back door, front door; his fingers found the locks and pressed against them. In the school term every door was mostly locked anyway; once the kids were home from boarding school that would change. What was it about kids and doors? It was enough to get them to *close* the bloody things after themselves – to turn the key was too far a stretch into *effort* for his and Nora's offspring.

He'd had a day spawned from hell and he was keen to close his eyes and shut it all out. Pausing at the foot of the staircase to switch off the hall lights his attention was drawn to his office, at the far end of the hallway. He didn't spend much time there – he had a plush, spacious one in the city. The spare room downstairs had been converted a few years ago to store some of the more nefarious files and reports he'd rather not leave lying alongside the legitimate side of his filing cabinet.

The office light was on now – strange, he thought. He had spent a little time in there this morning but was sure he wouldn't have needed the light then. There was an abundance of natural light in the room, owing to yet another set of French doors that led onto the garden. Victor turned and walked down the hall, wishing this long, arduous day would end. He pushed open the office door and reached out a hand to the switch, only to stop still, his fingers suspended in the air beside him, his jaw comically hanging open.

Tom Gallagher was sitting in the chair at the small desk, looking more wretched than Victor had ever seen him. His face was a shade of grey Victor associated with his kids and a stomach bug, and sure enough the smell from a small wet pool on the carpeted floor drifted towards him. Tom's face and neck glistened with sweat or rain and his dark hair was pasted to his head. His body sagged, as though someone had cut the string to hold him upright. Victor noticed a little pile of shards of broken glass on the floor. Tom had broken into his home.

"*Jesus Christ Almighty!* Tom Gallagher – you're supposed to be dead!"

"I hope you're not too disappointed." It was a defeated whisper where before it would have been a snarl – he was half the man he had been when they last spoke.

Earlier, Victor had telephoned Tom to tell him the gardaí had finally made their move. He was to attend the station in the morning to be interviewed under caution. He had ended up holding the receiver away from his ear to mute the angry, curse-riddled response. Then, mere hours later, the same detectives informed him that his long-time client was suspected dead, his house the cause of the wailing sirens across the city. Now here he sat, in Victor's own house, alive but looking like an extra in a zombie movie. Victor wondered if he was in the middle of an actual nightmare. He stepped inside and pushed the door closed – no need to upset his wife.

"But your house! I saw the footage on the internet – it's a charred shell!" Realisation dawned on Victor then, a cold grip around his throat. "How many bodies will they find inside, Tom?"

"Four," he answered easily. "How long do I have?"

"What on earth do you mean?"

"Until forensics figure out they were shot and that I'm not among them – how long?"

Victor shook his head feebly. "I haven't got a clue!"

"Days? Weeks? You *must* know!"

Victor thought of his mobile phone, charging in the kitchen. There was a panic button in the bedroom, but it was so long since he'd had it installed he found he couldn't remember the details now. Was it the gardaí that responded when it was activated, or a private security company? And if it was the latter, had he paid his yearly subscription? He couldn't think straight, and the room suddenly felt very small.

Tom was panting now, staring at Victor with eyes so intense he felt his heartrate begin to jitter in his chest. He breathed through his nose, fighting to stay calm.

"Let's go with days. Are they four *men*? Or are there any … women?" His throat felt raw and dry.

"Men, yes, similar enough to me. So it'd come down to fine details, DNA and whatever."

Victor cleared his throat. "Well, I'd say you have longer than days then. What – what are you planning?"

Tom's smile was a watered-down version of the self-satisfied one Victor was used to.

"Best you don't know – that's the way you prefer it, right? I'm just here for two things – your wife's car and Kate Crowley's current location. I presume we have her now."

Victor felt exhausted. He should have gone straight to bed, like Nora had suggested earlier. Although he didn't like to think how this conversation might have played out with his wife beside him in their bed. She tended to get hysterical, and Tom didn't look like someone with the patience for hysterics.

"You want Nora's car?"

"Less conspicuous than yours."

"Right, sure." Victor would do whatever it took to get the man out of his house. "And Crowley's location?"

He watched Tom inhale deeply, his chest rising, and knew it as a sign of the man's impatience. Victor dreaded what he had to tell him now.

"I don't know where she is, Tom, I'm sorry."

"*What?* You said she'd been found again. You sent me the name of her hotel!" He closed his eyes and kept them shut, unnerving Victor even more.

"She's gone. I assume she was tipped off again. I'm sorry."

A sudden roar reverberated around the small room, a sound so deep and raw, Victor wasn't sure it was human at first. But it was Tom – he was around the desk in seconds. He gripped Victor's neck between his hands and hauled him to his feet.

"How the fuck did this happen? You'd better have a good fucking explanation!"

Spittle doused Victor's cheeks and eyes. The stench off Tom was overwhelming – vomit, sweat, something stale – and he felt an explosion of pressure at the base of his skull. Tom's eyes were bulging, and so close to Victor he could see red lines snaking through the off-white. Tom squeezed a little harder, before roughly releasing the pressure, shoving Victor back into his chair.

"*I'm not leaving this house until I know where she is, do you hear me? I want to know every damn thing you know!*"

Victor clutched at his throat, but it was his head that hurt the most. He hated the fact that his hands and legs were trembling, but there was nothing he could do to stop it. He had worked with Tom for a very long time, and he was a seasoned man himself, in many ways. He wasn't easily scared. But he had never seen Tom Gallagher anything other than calm and measured. That had always been menacing, in its own way. This complete loss of control was terrifying.

He scrambled to the other side of his desk, pulling open a deep drawer, and hauled out a folder. Tom sat in the chair Victor had vacated – for all his anger and apparent strength, he looked exhausted, defeated. Victor was glad to have the safety of the desk between them.

"This is all I have. I've already sent you most of it. It's Vinnie's report from France, then Spain. He has three people working with him, a woman and a couple." He cleared his throat and spoke louder to hide the fear vibrating in his voice. "Here – you haven't seen these. It's some photos of their apartment in Mijas, and of a few places they used to frequent. The coffee shop where they were tipped off … it's all here. Most recently she was in a hotel in a small town called Casares, and one of Vinnie's women made a move."

"And?"

"And the woman was left unconscious in the bathroom. Her partner found her. Kate is gone."

"But you don't know for sure she was tipped off?"

"That's true, although it seems likely. Vinnie is trying to get information from the hotel staff but it's not as easy to question people in a top-end resort as it was in a tiny café."

Tom flicked through the photographs, barely interested. He didn't care where Crowley stayed, he only cared where she was *now*. But his eyes stopped at a photograph, enlarged to A4 size, of the note the coffee-shop owner had written down.

"Tom has found you, you need to run," he read softly. Tom … "This was the first time? The first tip-off?"

Victor sat down in his office chair, his legs finally done with keeping him on his feet.

"Yes, in Mijas." He could barely speak, his teeth chattering together in fear and adrenaline. He rubbed at the back of his neck where it joined his skull, wincing as his fingers probed what were surely damaged tendons and muscles.

"*Hmm* …" Tom pulled at his lower lip. "It says *Tom* has found you. Not *Gallagher*. A man would refer to me as 'Gallagher' not as 'Tom', don't you think?"

"Sure." Victor would agree to anything to get him out of the house, but now that he thought about it, he guessed Tom was probably right. "Actually, yes. 'Tom' is very personal, very female."

"Someone that knows me well – someone with access to my own office …"

Tom rose to his feet and held out one hand.

"Car keys. I'll be on my way."

"Where are you going?" The tremor in his voice was back but Victor thought it was from relief this time.

"To kill a rat. Keys!"

"They're hanging by the front door. I'll show you out," Victor led the way, Tom at his heels. He noted the man had no coat on and that his clothes were soaked through. How had he got here? All he could think of now was calling the Guards – Tom Gallagher had been his best client over the last three decades, but in the space of fifteen minutes Victor was ready to sell him out.

"What's the plan, Tom?" He felt a little braver as they stood at the front door and he handed over the keys to Nora's Passat. "You've faked your own death, is that it?"

"I just need a little time. I'll deal with the rat, collect Mae, and lie low. Once your man delivers my granddaughters to a safe place, you'll never see or hear from me again. But I expect you to fulfil your obligations to John."

Victor gripped the edge of the front door as he held it open. "Of course!" Anything to get rid of the man.

"This is for you." Tom handed him a piece of paper. "Read it immediately."

With a broad grin, looking more like his old self, he was gone.

Victor sank into his leather sofa. His legs had held him up long enough to pour another measure of brandy, to fetch an icepack in the kitchen, and had carried him to the sitting room. But then, they'd given way. He leaned his head against the leather and breathed deeply, the icepack wrapped around his neck. He had read the piece of paper as soon as Tom drove away. He had no choice but to pretend this encounter had never happened.

On paper embossed with Victor's own company letterhead, Tom Gallagher had written down the names of Victor and Nora's children, the address of their boarding school, even the name of their dorm house. He had written the times and days of the week their son trained at the school's rugby pitch and their daughter attended her piano lessons. Underneath it all, in his spider-leg scrawl, Tom had warned Victor, "*Don't disappoint me.*"

Victor saw how the future would play out now. There would be no phone call to the Lee Street detectives. In the morning he would report Nora's car stolen and he would call the window company and sort out the office doors. He would express his sadness at his client's death in a house fire and pay his respects to his wife Mae in the convalescence centre. He had no choice but to carry on representing John Gallagher in his trial, if that was what he wanted.

What Tom wanted.

He had always enjoyed being on Tom's side. Now he felt claustrophobic inside his own house. Worse still, Tom was seeking to "kill a rat" that night, and there was nothing Victor could do about it, except feel pity for whoever it was.

Even when his body was supposedly turned to ash, Tom Gallagher was the deadliest man he had ever met.

44

"Anna! Wake up!"

Gentle but insistent shakes on her shoulder roused Anna from sleep. Remnants of something dark and foreboding faded as she opened her eyes, but a feeling of dread remained.

The nightmares had returned.

"I'm sorry." She was aware of how groggy her voice was as she sat up, propping herself up on her elbows. "What time is it?"

"It's half six. If you get up and get ready now we can be at Patricia O'Brien's before she leaves for work. Assuming she has a job and leaves before nine. Come on!"

The light was snapped on and Anna squinted at Vivian. She was already dressed in dark trousers and a wool jumper, her hair scraped back into a low bun. Her "professional" look. The combined smell of coffee and cigarettes hung in the air around her, making Anna's nose itch.

"What's happening?"

"I'm not taking no for an answer, from you *or* her! I can't abandon this case, Anna, not now! I don't care what Carol said! I've been awake all night thinking it over, and I *know* I can get to the bottom of it all. I'm *this close!* Once I figure this out it'll lead us to whoever is sending the notes, I'm sure of that! So please – wake up, get up and let's get going!"

She turned and strode from the room, leaving Anna blinking in the bright bedroom light. As the last of her sleep faded, she pushed back the covers and swung her legs over the bed. She wasn't really surprised at being woken so early by Vivian, or by her brusque manner. This version of Vivian was familiar – they had grown up together.

Vivian was known to be tenacious, never taking no for an answer, her resolve like a steamroller over everything and everyone to get to what she wanted. In this case, the truth. William Ryan had once felt the brunt of her determination, and now Anna was feeling it. In an hour or so it would be Patricia O'Brien's turn. Shaking her head and smiling, Anna had no doubt that somehow Vivian would make the woman answer their questions. She wondered what might lie within the answers.

As a peace offering Vivian had coffee and a croissant waiting in the kitchen and, to her credit, masked her eagerness for Anna to hurry up. Though Anna wasn't trying to prolong her wait any longer, she did catch up on some text messages that had come in overnight while she ate and drank.

There was a long message from Alex that had been sent in the middle of the night. The items found in the larger leather bag were confirmed as belonging to their parents. This was determined by a thin folder of documents that Michael Clarke had packed relating to a client in his accountancy practice. It appeared he had planned to do some work on the trip. Though the documents were faded and much deteriorated, enough had been preserved to identify them. Alex had confirmed the business logo and their father's signature on one of the pages. In his message he had expressed regret at texting so late and promised to call around midday when he'd be able to chat properly.

Anna wondered if on some level she had known the contents of the message – perhaps she had glanced at it when it lit up her phone at four in the morning. Surely this was the reason the nightmare had returned, though she couldn't fathom why he had texted so late. Or early, depending on how she looked at it.

The other message was from Myles, finishing up work for the night and wondering if she might be awake. She regretted that she hadn't been – she could have spoken to both Myles and Alex, and perhaps joined Vivian in her ruminations. She might have been able to talk her out of visiting Patricia O'Brien.

Now Vivian sat on the bar stool beside Anna, chewing on her thumbnail, waiting for her to finish breakfast, her eyes straying to the wall clock every now and then. As soon as Anna drank the last of her coffee she asked "Ready?" brightly and, without waiting for an answer, hopped off the stool and headed to the door.

With a sigh Anna followed, suddenly feeling a lead weight in every footstep.

45

Patricia O'Brien was stunned to find them on her doorstep and made no attempt to hide it. Unprepared, in the cold light of the damp morning, she looked entirely different from their last visit to her house. The carefully applied glamour was gone – her hair was thin and wispy, falling around her face. Without make-up she looked years older, liver spots on her cheeks and fine lines framing her eyes, her skin dry and paper-thin. She was dressed in loose sweatpants and a green oversized jumper, her shoulder-bones jutting painfully through the fabric.

"What on earth?" Even as she said it her eyes filled with tears.

"We need to speak with you," Vivian said harshly. She was tired of this case and it showed.

Patricia sighed resignedly, her head sagging so low her chin rested on her chest for a moment.

"Well, you'd best come in," she whispered and swallowed loudly. She pulled the door open wide and turned away from them, not waiting to see if they were following.

They stepped into the hallway and followed her into the kitchen.

It was a bright and tidy space that had been extended at some point, with an airy sunroom jutting into the back garden that let in the light. A large vase full of fresh flowers dominated the oval table. Patricia moved to the kettle and flicked it on, reaching for mugs and a jar of coffee, pouring milk into a jug. Her movements were jumpy and they could hear her intake of breath from across the room, heavy and rasping at times, but she was still a good hostess, despite the circumstances. It was as though she was moving on autopilot.

When she turned to them she was surprised to find them still standing and gestured to the table. "Sit, please!"

Vivian slid the vase of flowers to the end of the table and they sat down.

"Miss O'Brien, we –"

"You might as well call me Patricia."

Her demeanour was completely different from the last time they had spoken. Vivian and Anna looked at each other, baffled. It was as though there was no fight left in her.

"I suppose you have more questions?" She carried a tray over with the three mugs of coffee – no fine china this morning – and rested her elbows on the table. She added milk to one mug, raised it and held it between her hands, breathing deeply.

"Yes, yes, we do." Vivian licked her lips. "We believe you didn't tell us the truth when we last spoke. There are things that don't make sense." She pressed her lips together and fixed her eyes on Patricia's.

Patricia sagged in her chair, her eyes glassy with tears. She looked at the wall behind Vivian's head and inhaled deeply.

"I suppose you've figured it out."

Vivian's eyes met Anna's and her euphoria was evident.

She's about to confess!

"Yes, indeed we have."

Anna knew the bluff in Vivian's words but her friend sounded convincing.

"We'll have to pass this onto the gardaí, of course, and I must record our conversation this morning." Vivian placed her voice recorder between them.

"I'm not sure about the legality of that ... oh, to hell with it all!" Patricia shuddered and sipped her coffee, a single tear tracking down her cheek. She let it fall, unchecked. "I had no choice, you know. He was everything to her." It was a harsh whisper, all she could manage.

"I'm sorry?" Anna leaned forward.

"*Him!* 'The Boy Who Jumped' as he became known." She placed her mug on the table and pulled a tissue from her sleeve, dabbing her face. She was fighting to compose herself, lips quivering, chest rising and falling quickly. "I knew it was him as soon as the squad car pulled up. I went into shock, really. I'm not making excuses!" She blew her nose loudly. "I couldn't believe it – I mean, we had all tried to warn her, Mother, Father, all of us! But she wouldn't listen! And when I saw him beating that man ..."

Her shoulders shook at the memory and tears flowed down her face.

Anna opened her mouth to speak again but Vivian silenced her with a hand on her knee under the table.

Let her tell her story!

"He didn't recognise me until the last minute. He was like an animal – his eyes. I'll never forget the look in his eyes. Cotter told me to take him to the squad car. He'd roughed him up a bit first but I stood back. I just couldn't! I couldn't touch him. The man on the ground ... Mr O'Meara, he was so badly injured, his face was

… I still see it at night sometimes when I close my eyes. It was horrific. And *he* had done it!"

"Who, Patricia? Who was he?"

But she was lost now, talking through her memories. Her eyes were unfocused, staring at a spot in the air between them, as though picturing that day once more.

"I took his elbow – I mean, I didn't want to but I had to do what Cotter said, I couldn't let on I *knew* him! We all knew he was trouble. This confirmed it. It was worse than my parents had ever realised! It was all of our worst fears come true. Can you imagine if your sister was in love with a monster? When he saw me, through the rain, he smiled – I remember that. He knew it was me. He had mocked me about joining the Guards, said I was a traitor or something stupid like that, but he looked happy to see me that day. I'll never forget what he said then – he was right of course – he said, 'She'll never forgive you.' I knew she would die if let him be arrested. He was so *calm* – and he had just beaten a man to death!" She gulped and paused, closing her eyes, hands on her chest as though hoping to steady herself. "I *had* to let him go. I remember I put my hand in my pocket, but then I hesitated. I mean – I was a *garda!* But I had the key in my hand … Next thing I knew, he attacked me. It was like I wasn't in control of myself … We tousled and sort of … he was behind me, then in front of me, I pushed the key into one of the cuffs. *Oh God!* I just … turned the key in the lock. It was so quick – I've never understood why I did it, except for her. Her heart would break. But, he had killed that poor man, and I –" She stopped, unable to speak any further, sobbed into her hands, into the tissue.

They waited, meeting each other's eyes every few seconds.

Vivian's hands shook on the table. "Oliver Cotter remembers that you had lost your key a few weeks later," she said matter-of-factly and Patricia met her eyes quickly.

"Oh … yes. I remember that now. The arrest … the girl that was robbing bags. I was terrified someone would figure it out."

"You gave him the key, didn't you?" Vivian's voice shook. "To open the other lock."

Patricia squeezed her eyes shut and nodded.

"This must have been truly awful for you," Anna said softly, her voice full of sympathy. She genuinely felt sorry for the woman; she looked haunted by the memory. "Trying to figure out what to do – and you never told anyone that you knew the killer? That he was your sister's boyfriend?"

Patricia shook her head. She picked up her mug again and held it close to her face, as though the heat of it might sustain her. When she opened her eyes they were glassy with tears.

"No, how could I? The damage was done. He was wanted for murder and presumed dead. It would have broken my sister's heart if I told people who he was, and I would have been in trouble too. No, I had to keep it to myself. And I was a pariah at work – it was best I left."

"Did he survive the jump?" Vivian whispered, her eyes piercing Patricia's.

It all came down to this.

"Yes," Patricia whispered in return, and closed her eyes, unable to look at them. "Yes, and my sister married him. She loved him – she always did."

Vivian hopped up from her seat and stood behind it, gripping the wood, steadying herself. Anna saw the elation on her face and felt her own heart begin to race. Vivian had been right – a violent killer had lived in the shadows of the city ever since that day. Justice had not been served on him for killing an innocent man – yet. She thought of the photograph of the three sisters in Patricia O'Brien's sitting room, and about how she felt that she knew the youngest sister, how her face was familiar but the memory of how or why she knew her refused to slot into place.

"It's Margaret, isn't it?" she said softly, and Patricia opened her eyes and stared at her. "Your youngest sister, Margaret?"

"Yes, but we haven't called her that for a long time."

She smiled a little and her eyes misted over – they had lost her to memory again.

"My parents used to call her Maggie ... their little Maggie. We stopped calling her that when she was about eleven or twelve, I think. It was all Rod Stewart's fault really." A full smile then but tears came afresh. "That song came out and it was all my mother would listen to. Piled into the sitting room the lot of us, listening to that bloody song, over and over every evening. And of course Maggie insisted on being called Maggie-Mae. Eventually the Maggie was dropped and we just called her Mae. She liked the sound of it better." She shrugged and put down her cup again, blowing her nose loudly, sagging into the back of the chair.

Anna's hands began to shake, vibrations that rattled the table. Her skin felt tingly, as though pins and needles were prickling all over her body, adrenaline pulsing as the dots finally joined and the pieces of her memory slotted into place. The girl in the photo, the young child and then the image of her as a teenager – she had seen her face so many times in the last three years in files at work. Surveillance of a suspected criminal enterprise included *all* members of the family, even those that might seem removed from the filth and grime of it all.

Even the wives.

"Mae Gallagher," she said and Patricia squeezed her eyelids shut. "Your sister married Tom Gallagher. He's the killer, 'The Boy Who Jumped'. And he's been living in this city the whole time."

46

Patricia was relieved to unburden herself, crying heavily as she told them of years of fear and disappointment. How her sister Mae had eventually turned her back on her sisters and parents to be with a man they all knew was a monster.

"It killed my father in the end," she sniffed, "and my mother pined after him until she passed away shortly after. Mae kept up some sort of relationship with Chrissie in recent years. But she and I haven't spoken in a long time. I wanted nothing to do with Tom Gallagher, and that meant having nothing to do with my sister, unfortunately."

"But why didn't you tell anyone?" Anna couldn't help the incredulity in her voice – all the years the city detectives had tried and failed to shut down the violence around the man and his sons. It could have been stopped.

"Because I *know* him! I know what he is – it killed my parents, it ruined my career. I lost my sister to him and so I ... I moved on. I *had* to!"

Her voice was heavy with fear and Anna began to understand. What had started out as loyalty to her sister had become fear for her own safety.

"This is the family home. Chrissie is a solicitor and not short of money and she was happy to let me live here. Mae, well, she has plenty, doesn't she! Clubs and bars and whatever else Tom set up."

Drugs and illegal imports and stolen goods. Anna thought about the searches on his businesses and home. She knew the detectives had been frustrated again. Tom Gallagher had a knack for wriggling out of trouble.

But not this time.

Patricia carried on, the tissue between her fingers shredded on the table.

"He was a bad egg, right from the start. He was just ... different," she sniffed. "His parents were alive then but from what I heard he was practically an orphan, on the streets day and night. I heard they were pretty useless, drink and drugs and whatnot. I suppose that's hard for a child. By the time Mae and he were an item he was in his late teens. A handsome lad, tall and broad and bright blue eyes. But there was something off about him. Like a wild cat. Drugs, my father said, but we could never be sure. We didn't understand. And Mae was just besotted. We tried everything to keep them apart but she changed for him, disobeying our parents, sneaking out at night. She didn't care about anything else. The day Tom killed that man – Mae wouldn't listen. She was like one of those people you see on TV, you know? Possessed. Brainwashed. Convinced he could do no wrong."

Vivian sat down again, her face pale. She had hoped for this but the reality of confronting the truth was a little terrifying.

"I don't know where he got out of the river or where he went. He had friends all across the city, he used to gather people to him like one of those cult leaders you see in films. People helped him and he lay low for a week or so. Mae was beside herself. My poor father – when Tom turned up looking for Mae he nearly died right then. He forbade Mae to speak to him again and told me I had to make a statement. Mae warned him he would never see her again if we did – she was the baby, his youngest child. Her reaction, her lack of disgust at what Tom had done broke my father's heart."

"So you never made the statement?"

Patricia shook her head. "I couldn't. I left the guards and suffered a breakdown. That breakdown was real, a state doctor certified it. It's just that everyone assumed it was post-traumatic stress from the attack."

"And Mae?"

"She left. With him. She told me and Chrissie that she felt his survival from the river was a rebirth, that he was born a new man, a better man. I think he believed in her theory too. They loved the hysteria in the press, thought they were something special, you know – even put a bloody headstone in the ground to mark the death of the boy he once was." She shook her head and when she spoke again, revulsion at the memory dripped through her words. "They put it in the same graveyard – how low can you get!"

She picked up her coffee again, rolling it between her hands, her mouth twisting.

"Time just passed, you know? Decades, and I tried to put it behind me. Until you came along." Her eyes rested on Vivian and they were full of regret.

"How long is it since you've seen your sister?" Anna asked. So many families were torn apart by secrets.

"We haven't spoken in years. She's in a rehab facility, I believe – she tried to kill herself."

"I'm sorry, it must be awful for you."

A deep shiver rocked Patricia's body and her eyes were wet with tears again. "I'm still terrified of him. *I'm* the one who saw what he did that day. He kicked that man to death. God knows why."

"You know we have to report this – he's guilty of murder."

But Patricia shook her head. "It's too late. He's dead."

"*What?*" Anna's breath caught in her throat – Gallagher was dead? After years focusing on him, trying to find an angle to arrest him, willing his hold over the streets to come to an end, he was *dead?* She thought of the office in the Lee Street Station and could just imagine the flurry of activity, the stress that would surely be bouncing from the Chief Superintendent in waves if this were true.

"His house went up in flames yesterday evening – it's all over the news. Four dead bodies apparently. I'm glad my sister is safely away from him, even if she doesn't see it that way. Tom Gallagher is dead, and good riddance is all I say!"

47

Jessica Rossi had been in Tom's employment for over ten years. She was here illegally, at least she had been. He didn't know if she had ever sorted that out. When he first met her there was something about her calm nature that appealed to him. Whatever might trouble her on the inside never penetrated the surface of her serene face, and there were few character traits he admired more than self-control.

She could keep her mouth shut and her head down, and he liked that about her. Her oval eyes, her creamy skin and her soft curves were an added bonus. She had a teenage son. Tom had offered him a job but she had politely shaken her head in refusal, those beautiful eyes wide and fearful. He understood; she needed this job, but Tom's world wasn't a life she wanted for her son. He was a meek boy anyway, in Tom's opinion, perhaps it was for the best he stayed in school. His own sons had been a lot harder, more capable for this business – but then, look how they had turned out.

Jessica had always been quiet and respectful of Mae, the woman of the house. Tom had never heard them have a conversation, save for Mae issuing instructions about the upkeep of their home and Jessica asking for direction when necessary.

He liked her – he had enjoyed her presence in his home – and trust had come with time.

He should have known better.

Jessica was the only woman with access to the location of Kate Crowley. When the Lee Street detectives came knocking, he had trusted the files on Crowley to Jessica to hide in her own home. A safe place the gardaí would never think to search …

So here he was, standing outside her house in a large housing estate in Carrigaline. He knew the house was rented and he also knew that Jessica would shortly leave to walk to the bridge in the centre of the village, where she'd catch the 220 bus to take her to the city. Then she would walk the rest of the way to his home, assuming she didn't know about the fire. Assuming she didn't think he was dead.

Tom felt exhausted. He had succumbed to sleep as soon as he had parked the car at the entrance of the housing estate, although a few hours in the cramped driver's seat had done his back no favours. Now he moved up the driveway quickly, keen to stay out of sight. He saw a shadow move to the front door through the yellow frosted glass, made out an arm rise to the latch, and as the door was pulled open he propelled himself inside. Jessica was pushed backwards from the door and onto the foot of the stairs. On seeing him her face blanched and she scrambled up, attempting to crawl up the carpeted stairs away from him. With a grunt of anger he grabbed her hair and dragged her – she was surprisingly light – into the kitchen, where he flung her into a chair. She looked at him, eyes wide and terrified, a small whimper escaping her lips.

His eyes always moved, darted, found what he needed – he'd had years of practice. He saw the block of knives on the counter and pulled out the first one his hand touched, a black-handled chef's knife, the largest blade in the set. Throwing himself into the seat beside her he stabbed the table between them, the knife standing upright, the black handle wobbling.

"I'm only going to ask you once and if you lie to me I will cut off your fingers, do you understand?"

Jessica began to sob, her teeth chattering in her mouth, tears streaking her face. It was the most emotion he had ever witnessed from her. The oval eyes he found so beautiful flicked to the ceiling – her son – and she nodded quickly.

"Did you tell Kate Crowley I knew where she was? Did you warn her I was coming?"

Jessica shook her head quickly, tears rolling down her chin and onto a wine-coloured scarf wound around her neck – a present from Mae, if Tom remembered correctly.

He reached out and grabbed her wrist, yanking her hand forward as she screamed *"Please!"*

"Don't lie to me!"

He held her hand steady on the table with one hand and with the other picked up the knife.

"I don't want to do this, Jessica. But you're the only one who could have known where she was. I'll ask you again – *did you warn Kate Crowley?"*

She shook her head again. *"Not me, please, no, I beg you!"*

Tom sighed wearily and gripped the knife tighter. Her screams and pleading were irritating him now, a buzz too loud inside his head. The smallest finger first, he decided, the pain would make her talk. She was the only one who could have –

"Tom, that's *enough!*"

The voice behind him cut through the noise in the kitchen and inside his head. He dropped the knife, his grip on Jessica's wrist slackening.

Mae stood behind him at the kitchen door. She looked freshly showered, wearing a dressing-gown and slippers, her hair still damp on her shoulders.

"*Mae?*"

When Jessica had looked to the ceiling he had assumed she was worried about her son. But instead she knew his own wife was upstairs, the woman he had secured in a recovery facility weeks ago, the woman who had been sleeping every time he'd called lately. What was going on? His wife's robe was a pale colour that began to blend into her skin and the wall behind her; he shook his head to clear his vision, to try to think coherently. *Why was Mae here?*

"Jessica, leave us," Mae commanded.

Jessica yanked her wrist free and scuttled from the room, slamming the door behind her.

"Mae – what are you doing here? What in God's name is going on?" Tom didn't recognise the sound of his own voice.

"I could ask you the same thing!" She moved to sit where Jessica had been, clasping her hands in front of her on the table. She looked younger, somehow. Her face was less puffy, less lined than he remembered. He looked at her hands and the steadiness of them surprised him. Tom knew he should feel glad, relieved, at how good she looked. Yet all he felt was numb.

"Aren't you supposed to be dead?" she asked, in a tone that told him she had never believed it in the first place. "The fire is all over the news. The house, Tom ... *our home.* How could you?"

He wanted to tell her it was just a building, just bricks and mortar, but he knew how much it had meant to her. Still, it had been necessary, all of it; he would make her see that! As necessary as killing the Myers to rescue John, as necessary as tracking down

Kate to heal the pain she had caused, as necessary as sacrificing Marco …

"I did it for us …" His voice trailed away. The tightness in his chest was morphing into pain, an embedded knife twisted inside him.

Mae looked at him accusingly. "Who was inside it, Tom? Who was in the house? I assume you were there and escaped. Were you the one who set the fire?"

He opened his mouth to speak but she held up her hands.

"Actually, I don't want to know. I don't want to know any more of this life you live. I don't want this anymore!" She burst into tears and covered her face with her hands.

He watched her shoulders shudder and for the first time in his life he felt completely powerless. "I just want a *break*, Tom! From all of this, all of the madness around you! Look at our sons. *David is dead!*"

She was glaring at him now, screaming the words at him, her eyes flashing with an anger he didn't recognise.

"And John … John is a *monster!*"

She tried to compose herself, wiping her eyes with the heels of her hands. With a final sniff she was back to glaring at him, calm and steady again.

"*I'm* the one who tipped Kate off."

He stared at her aghast and leaned heavily into the back of the chair. "It was you?" he whispered. "But *why?*"

He remembered the morning he had visited her to tell her he had finally found the woman that shot their son. It was all Mae had wanted, all she had seemed to need to move on. Now he knew she had tipped Kate off. But the second hotel … how had she known about that? Jessica, he assumed. They had both betrayed him. All he wanted to know now was *why*.

She threw her hands into the air and they landed on the table with a thump.

"*Why?* Because this can't go on! Everything is destroyed – our children are dead or just slightly better off. Our good name is ruined. Our home … you've destroyed everything, Tom! *Everything!*"

He sat still, stunned. She had never spoken to him like this.

"I believed in you, right from the beginning. I was your champion! I always knew you could make your mark on the world. And I was right – except the mark you made is violence and death! I've turned a blind eye to the women at the club, I've ignored John's bruised knuckles over breakfast, new tiles in the hall after the Meiers …" She pressed her fingertips to her lips. "I always defended you, you know? To my family, but mostly to myself. But my eyes are open now – I don't want this anymore! And I don't want our granddaughters to be a part of this family. They are innocent!"

"They are David's children!"

"Let them be with their mother! Let Natalie have her children like I should have mine! Let them stay away from this mess of a life! I've given you my whole life, Tom. But I've paid a heavy price." She balled up one hand into a fist and pressed it against her mouth as though trying to stifle the dam of tears and outrage he could see bubbling inside her.

He *knew* her – and this was the first time in their whole lives together that she had turned on him. Once she had fought fiercely to protect him, to shield him. She had stood beside him as he scraped a life from nothing, always encouraging him. Now she had betrayed him.

And yet, a part of him understood. He looked at the edge of a fresh white bandage on her wrist – yes, she had paid a heavy price. She was still paying it. And she wanted nothing to do with him.

No! If he lost Mae he had lost everything!

"So let's go away," he pleaded and stretched one hand across the table, hoping she'd touch him. But she pulled her free hand onto her lap. "Please, love! Let's leave Cork behind and go abroad. I've money put away; we could live out the rest of our lives somewhere far from here, somewhere warm and exotic. Put it all behind us. I agree about the girls. Leave them with their mother." *Whatever you want Mae... please!* "What do you say?"

"You would leave our sons?" she whispered. "David's grave. John in his prison cell?"

"*What else can I do?*" he shouted, in fear and frustration, and instantly regretted it, but he needed to make her see reason. "Mae, Ainsley has talked. Lee Street want me for questioning, not to mention the fire ..."

"Where's Marco?" she asked quietly, her eyes fixed on his.

He looked away. He couldn't bear it.

She knew; her eyebrows drew together and her lips disappeared into a thin line.

"Is there no-one you won't use? No-one you hold higher than your own ambition?"

"*I did it for us! To get us out of here! Please, Mae!*"

She rose to her feet so fast the chair clattered loudly onto the tiled kitchen floor.

"I want you to leave, Tom. I never want to see you again."

"You don't mean that!"

"I've never meant anything more in my life."

He stayed in the chair, staring at her face, at the woman who had been his fiercest supporter for almost fifty years. She wanted him out, not just of this house, but out of her life.

"Please, Mae." He closed his eyes, unable to look at her anger.

"I won't leave Cork with you. I won't leave our sons. Just go!"

When he looked at her the resolve in her eyes frightened him – she was composed and steady, no trembling, no sweat on her face, no fresh tears. She was certain and in control of herself. For a fleeting moment his heart constricted so tightly he was sure it might stop. He rose to his feet and moved to the doorway; what else was there to do?

"Mae ..."

She turned her body from him and his last view of her was her shoulders shaking as she leaned her palms on Jessica's kitchen sink.

48

"What happens now?"

Patricia O'Brien walked them to her front door. She had grown hunched as their conversation progressed, her shoulders rounding and slumped. Towards the end of her retelling of the past she became withdrawn, as though the memories were just too painful, or perhaps she felt fear of the future.

Anna watched her draw deeper into herself and felt sorry for her – she had carried this secret her whole life.

Vivian, in contrast, was shaking with adrenaline. Her hands fumbled with the zipper on her coat as they approached the door, and she sounded breathless as she answered Patricia's question.

"I'll have to take everything you've told us to the Guards. You do understand, don't you?"

Patricia nodded, her eyes on the wool mat at the front door. "Yes," she whispered, "I understand."

Anna placed a hand on her arm, hoping the woman found it comforting. Tom Gallagher had destroyed many lives and, in Anna's opinion, his sister-in-law was another of his victims. "It might be a good idea to contact your sister Christina. You should have someone with you when you speak to the detectives in Lee Street. In fact, I'll contact a colleague of mine right now – he'll be fair, I guarantee you that."

Patricia smiled warmly at her, the first real smile she had mustered since they arrived.

"Thank you. That's kind of you."

She opened the front door and closed it behind them without another word.

"Jeez, Anna," Vivian muttered as they walked quickly back to her car, "why did you give her the idea of getting a solicitor involved? Her sister will probably tell her not to say another word!"

"I think her sister is the first person she'll contact right now – she doesn't need me to prompt that. Her sister is implicated in this too, remember – they all knew Gallagher was guilty of murder." She paused, considering all the ramifications this could cause to the O'Brien sisters' lives. "Couldn't you tell Patricia's been terrified of him her whole life?"

"Yes, that's obvious," Vivian agreed, "But even so – I need her to make a statement! At least I recorded it all."

"Look, you have all the facts you need." Anna unlocked the car and they both climbed in. "You can connect Patricia to Tom Gallagher's wife. You have Oliver's testimony that she had lost her handcuff key. You have enough to make a convincing argument."

Anna plugged her mobile into the car charger, scrolling through her last call list in search of William Ryan's number.

"Tom Gallagher is dead, remember. He can't exactly sue you for defamation. Anyway, it all fits. The age, the family connection, it's all there."

She selected William's mobile number and dialled, starting the car so their call would be connected through Bluetooth.

Vivian swivelled around in her seat to watch Patricia O'Brien's house, noting that the lace curtains of the sitting room remained undisturbed.

Anna drove away from the kerb as William answered the call.

"Anna, is it about Harris?"

"No, but I –"

"Everything OK?"

"Yes, I'm fine."

She heard shuffling and the slamming of his car door, followed by another, then the kick of a car engine – he and a colleague were going, or leaving, somewhere.

"Are you at Lee Street?" she asked.

"No, Grace and I are in Carrigaline actually. We've been interviewing Tom Gallagher's wife, would you believe?"

Anna and Vivian locked eyes for a moment.

"Oh yes? I heard he was killed in a house fire last night."

"Apparently not! Mrs Gallagher is staying with their housekeeper in Carrigaline and Gallagher visited them this morning. Scared the life out of his poor housekeeper. Mae called the station."

"To make a complaint?" *Against her own husband*, Anna mused. It seemed the O'Brien sisters had had enough.

"Not quite. They fought, she said things she regrets now. She effectively told him their marriage was over. She's quite frantic. He didn't look well when he left the house and he's switched off his mobile. She wants us to go look for him."

"And are you going to?"

"We most certainly are! But not because his wife is concerned over their argument – if he's still alive he has a lot of questions to answer over the fire in his house. Fire-fighters are still there this morning and talking about arson. Looks like there's at least four bodies inside."

"Not to mention the various units within the force that want to speak to him. He never showed for an interview under caution," Grace interjected from the passenger seat. "Too busy killing people in that house fire!"

There was silence for a moment. The events of the last twenty-four hours of Tom Gallagher's life were whirring through Anna's mind. A blaze at his home, a place that until recently had been his fortress, had killed at least four people. She remembered surveillance images of the house from the files she had worked on in the Lee Street station; the house had been his pride and joy, his stronghold. A place he never allowed a Cork detective to set foot inside, until he'd had no choice after his son's arrest. It had been his refuge when the city's press hounded him lately for photos and interviews. Now it was burned to the ground, still burning, yet he wasn't inside it. She shivered, wondering what had prompted him to scare his housekeeper in her home in Carrigaline, what had caused the argument with his wife – the woman that had turned her back on her family to be by his side. She assumed that losing the love of his wife would be hugely traumatic for Gallagher – his sons were gone from his life, his business over, his house destroyed. And the woman who had been by his side for years had told him their marriage was over …

She was pulled from her musings by William's question.

"We're a bit tied up here, do you need something?"

She cleared her throat, "Actually, the reason I called is because I have information on who killed Bernard O'Meara. Remember, the case Vivian is working on?"

"Look, Anna –" Grace again, sounding closer than before, leaning toward the dashboard, "we don't have time for –"

"It was Tom Gallagher," Vivian interjected before they could cut her off. "We've interviewed Patricia O'Brien this morning. She's the arresting garda who was attacked by the killer that day. Turns out she's Mae Gallagher's sister. No-one ever made the connection because they were only kids at the time, dating, not married. She's identified Tom as the one who beat Bernard O'Meara to death."

Suddenly, Anna thought she knew where Gallagher might be. She heard the rev of William's car as he too realised the same thing.

"What part of the river did he jump into back then?" he asked. "Where exactly on Washington Street?"

"It was the Western Road section, where the two roads meet."

"Right. This one you leave to me, Anna! I mean it!"

They could hear Grace on her phone already, calling for back-up, for all cars to go to the Western Road, that the man was considered dangerous and possibly armed.

Vivian gripped Anna's arm.

"There's no way we are missing out on this, Anna!"

As Anna turned the car sharply, earning a loud beep from the car behind, she muttered, "I thought you might say that."

49

It had started to rain again, fat drops pounding onto the windscreen so fast the wipers had trouble keeping up. Anna gunned the engine faster that she usually dared, weaving between lanes on the Dunkettle Roundabout on her approach back into the city. The route to the Western Road was frustrating, each lane congested, each red traffic light against them. At the junction onto Washington Street she ignored the lights and pushed her foot hard on the accelerator.

They saw him as they approached the end of Washington Street where it merged onto the Western Road, a tall, broad figure standing by the low wall, looking into the river. He was the only person in sight without a coat, the only person not hurrying to get out of the rain. Anna drove the car onto the footpath beside the road and braked hard, blocking a shop entrance. She reached for her phone as she turned off the engine.

"What are you doing?" Vivian demanded.

"Calling William Ryan!"

One thing she had learned over the last few months was to trust her gut – this was a dangerous situation. Tom Gallagher was volatile, a man with nothing left to lose. Anna had had enough trauma lately. She planned to let the detective know he had been spotted, and nothing more.

But Vivian had other ideas. The reporter in her, the woman who was desperate to finish what she had started, flung open the car door and bolted. She ran towards him, holding her mobile phone aloft, recording. Anna groaned. Vivian was going to approach him, going to seek a statement. She was going to tell him she knew he had killed Bernard O'Meara in 1977.

And she was going to get herself hurt.

"*Shit!*" Anna hissed, sure that Vivian was in more danger than she could ever imagine.

She saw blue flashing lights in her rear-view mirror, and more up ahead by the entrance to the university, and her panic subsided a little. Still, Vivian was getting too close to the man who had turned his head to face her, his mouth moving in an angry outburst.

Anna jumped out of the car and ran towards them.

She reached them in seconds, just as Tom Gallagher was stepping towards Vivian and she had taken two steps back.

"*Put away the camera, Vivian!*" Anna shouted, keeping her eyes on Tom, watching his movements. Her hair was instantly flattened onto her head by the rain which dripped down her neck and under her collar, seeping down her back. She pushed wet strands from her face and tugged her friend's arm.

Vivian shook her off. She held her mobile phone steady, her face flushed and determined. Here was the killer she had sought, had become obsessed with, and she wasn't going to miss a second of this.

"*Why did you kill an innocent man on the steps of the courthouse?*" she shouted through the rain.

Tom stared at her blankly, not understanding.

"*Bernard O'Meara. We know you killed him!*"

Tom wiped a hand over his face, blinking the rain from his eyes. He looked confused, and then suddenly he began to laugh, a short brittle burst of sound.

"That old fool! That was over forty years ago! Is that why you're here?" He looked amused, "What makes you think he was an innocent man? Dig deep enough and you'll find he was a pervert with access to too many kids in that school. He deserved what he got."

Vivian pressed on. "*We know you're guilty! We have Patricia O'Brien's testimony.*"

He threw up his hands. "So fucking what! That was so long ago it doesn't matter anymore."

"*It matters to Mr O'Meara's family! It matters to the detectives investigating the –*"

"No!" he shouted again. "*Nothing* matters anymore!"

He stepped away from them, towards the wall, and rested both hands on top of it. Anna shoved Vivian behind her. "*For God's sake turn that thing off!*" She looked at the river, churning underneath them, rushing and galloping fast away from them. The water was brown, full of mud and debris dislodged in the recent heavy rainfall.

"*Tom! Mr Gallagher!*" Anna called.

He turned to face her.

She stepped forward and they were so close she could reach out and touch him. His blue shirt was soaked and made darker by the rain. It clung to his skin. She knew he must be freezing but his body didn't show it, it didn't shiver or shake like hers. He blinked rapidly as he looked at her.

"I know you. Anna Clarke. You saved John's life."

"Yes." She couldn't think what else to say.

"I know all about you!" Tom said roughly, wiping water off his chin again. "You're Kate Crowley's friend."

Finally, some emotion. It seemed to Anna that his body vibrated as he said the words. Her eyes strayed to movement behind him: gardaí rushing down the street, others directing drivers and pedestrians away from the scene. She saw a tall figure, the tails of a long coat flapping, as he ran towards them. William Ryan was close now.

"Yes, I'm Kate's friend."

"I know about your parents."

This surprised Anna. How could he know this? The news bulletins, she supposed. Why would it matter to him?

"I know you've suffered, the same way I have. We both lost loved ones, both have people that hurt us." His shoulders slumped as he looked into the water. "I chose to make my enemies pay for how they hurt me." His voice cracked with emotion.

"Was Bernard O'Meara the first person you made to pay?" She didn't care if he confessed or not, she just wanted to keep him talking until William reached them.

Tom looked into her eyes. He seemed to be having trouble focusing on her face. After a few seconds he nodded, or swayed, she wasn't sure.

"Would it make you feel better to think I didn't just kill him for the fun of it?" He shook his head violently. "I lost control that day, for the last time. Everything else ... the person I became then ... *he* was always in control. But now ..."

He gasped and rested his hands on his knees. Anna resisted the sudden urge to reach out and put an arm around his shoulder – he had lost everything, and he looked broken.

"It's true we have loss in common. But you can … *um* … move on." She felt pathetically inadequate, her mind scrambling for something to say that might delay the jump she felt sure he was gearing up to.

He looked up at her face and smiled – he was old enough to be her father, in another life, and she imagined that that thought bounced between them. She reached out her hand, shivering now from the cold and the fear of anticipation, and touched his arm.

"Please, come back from the water."

He didn't seem to hear her.

"*Your wife contacted the guards!*" Vivian shouted.

Anna had forgotten she was still there.

This got Tom's attention. He stepped away from the wall and moved towards her.

"She'd turn me in?" He looked aghast.

William Ryan stood behind him now, a few steps away, chest heaving.

"*No! No!*" Too late, Vivian realised her mistake, taking a step backwards, her phone still held aloft. "*She rang them because she was worried about you!*"

Anna stepped in front of Vivian. She could see water pooled in Tom Gallagher's eyes and she didn't think it was the rain.

Anna leaned around Tom to William, her eyes pleading. Tom turned his body to follow her eyes. For a moment he stood completely still, pummelled by the wind, taking in the uniformed guards and the detectives beside him and the blue flashing lights, as if he hadn't seen them before, as if it had never occurred to him this might happen.

William raised his hands, opened his mouth to speak.

Tom turned to Anna again. His face was dripping with rain and tears, and suddenly she felt a desperate panic. She knew what was going to happen and there was nothing she could do about it.

"It's too late for everything," he said so quietly she was certain he felt completely alone now, that she had faded into the background of the street.

And with a loud groan he pushed himself up and over the wall, leaping into the river below. It was clumsy, one hand slipping, his body awkward. His head jerked back and struck the wall as he fell. They watched in horror as his body disappeared beneath the dark water.

50

The street was awash with people, their bodies blurred at the edges by the rain that fell in sheets of grey. The patrol boat of the Garda Water Unit was on the river and Anna could make out members of the team both in and out of the water. The beat of a helicopter overhead, muted by the wail of the wind and the surrounding street noise, told her the Air Support Unit had been called in. She could picture her colleagues in the Lee Street station, replicated across all the major Garda stations across the city right now; it would be organised chaos.

At some point Mae Gallagher had arrived, accompanied by Grace Thompson. She was thinner than in the surveillance photos Anna remembered. Her coat was red, her face grey, and she stood as close to the river-side wall as she was allowed to, her arms wrapped around herself, watching the water below.

Vivian and Anna sat in the back of a squad car that was pulled up onto the footpath alongside a nearby hotel. Both had been given blankets and the windows in the car were fogged with condensation.

"I can't believe he jumped!" Vivian had said this over and over since they sat into the car, time doing nothing for her shock. "I didn't expect him to. I mean, who'd have thought he was suicidal!"

Anna winced. "Why did you think he went to the river if not to jump in!" She wished Vivian had stayed back, stayed quiet. Her obsession with this case had clouded her common sense, but there was nothing they could do about that now.

Trying to help had gone so horribly wrong. She wished she were back at work, in her warm, bustling office. She would go on a coffee-run to Victus and Lauren would have an up-to-date account of what had happened by the time she returned. They'd share croissants or muffins and sip their lattes until someone called out that the Chief Superintendent was on his way down the stairs; then they'd scuttle their chairs back to their desks and get back to work. The horror of the story of Tom Gallagher's jump into the River Lee would be the same, but she would be safely removed from it, cocooned by the knowledge it had nothing to do with her.

But she wasn't at work. She was sitting in the back of a squad car, her teeth chattering from the cold, waiting to be given the green light to go home. Or to the station to make a formal statement. She hoped William Ryan would take pity on her and it would be the former; a hot shower seemed like heaven right now.

Grace Thompson opened the driver's door and sat onto the seat, lowering the hood on a navy raincoat. She turned to face them, her eyes on Vivian, and held out a clear plastic evidence bag.

"I need your phone. And I'll need the password to open it too." She shook the bag a little, in a hurry.

"Sorry now, but I've been trying to get through to work, so much has happened and –"

The scowl on Grace's face stopped Vivian mid-protest. With a sigh she reached forward and placed her phone into the bag.

"Password?" Grace prompted, pulling a notebook and pen from her pocket. She looked soaked through, despite her raincoat, and in no mood to wait.

Vivian cleared her throat and called it out. "How long will you need it?"

"I can download the video you took back at the station and you should be able to have it back today. Right!" She started the engine. "I'm taking you two to Lee Street. I need you to make formal statements."

Anna groaned internally – this was the third time she had made a statement this week. At least while she was in the Lee Street station she'd have an opportunity to chat to Lauren and some of the others she worked with. It would be familiar ground.

"Can I use your desk phone, Anna?" Vivian pressed. "I really need to speak to my boss."

Traffic on the Western Road was still restricted, which meant that once Grace drove onto the street that ran parallel, back into the city, they were almost immediately stopped in heavy congestion. She muttered curses under her breath.

"I suppose Tom Gallagher was behind the notes and the crucifix," Vivian mused.

Grace met her eyes in the mirror and shrugged, offering a non-committal "Time will tell."

Anna didn't feel at all sure it was him; it didn't seem like his style. Too subtle – if he had wanted to stop Vivian researching the killing of Bernard O'Meara, then he would have made sure she did. Sending threatening notes seemed a bit too delicate for Tom Gallagher. But she said nothing, huddling further into the blanket that was now almost as wet as she was.

"What do you think are the chances of finding him, Grace?" she asked as they waited for a red light to change.

"Alive?"

Anna nodded, wondering if Tom could survive the jump into the river twice.

"Slim, I'd say."

"He's done it before. He managed to get out of the river without being spotted. Maybe he can pull it off again."

"Maybe, but I don't like his chances. He's older now. Mid-sixties." A sudden dump of rain was loud on the windscreen and Grace flicked the wipers to a higher setting. "And his wife said he was in a bad state of mind. He's in serious trouble – there are four dead bodies in his house and I bet he started the fire. And didn't you say it looked like he struck his head off the wall? No, I reckon he's dead this time. But it's Tom Gallagher we're talking about and, as you said, he's done it before. If he's alive, we'll find him."

It was growing dark outside by the time Anna had finished answering questions and recalling the events by the river. As she signed her written statement of the events of the morning, she enquired about where Vivian was and was told she had already left the station. To Banba Productions, Anna assumed. She had solved the cold case. Once the gardaí gave her the go-ahead to use the evidence she had uncovered, she knew Vivian would waste no time in getting the documentary out there. She doubted she'd be able to use the video footage she'd taken today though, which no doubt she would protest loudly about.

In the open-plan office, Anna found comfort in familiar faces. Lauren had a bag of gym clothes at her desk that she offered as an alternative to the wet clothes, and Anna gratefully accepted.

Knowing Lauren, she was relieved to have an excuse not to use them herself after work.

Lauren braved the weather to run to Victus, returning with coffees, filled rolls and pastries. Eating at her desk, whispering with Lauren, it felt like she had never left.

"Mae Gallagher is in interview room four," Lauren told her.

"That poor woman – they had a fight this morning and she told the detectives she said things she regrets."

"*Wow* – she'll regret it big time if he doesn't survive."

"Is there no news?"

Lauren's dark bob swished around her ears as she shook her head. "No sign of him. I just can't believe he jumped."

"Vivian kept saying that ..." Anna remembered how her friend had provoked him on camera at the riverside, telling him she knew he had escaped justice years ago. William Ryan wasn't impressed with her – again – and Anna worried there'd be repercussions for the unintended outcome of her friend's actions.

"I guess he knew the alternative was going to prison." Lauren switched off her computer and began to pull on her coat. "Everyone was after him – the Drugs and Organised Crime Unit, the Criminal Assets Bureau, you name it. They were planning to bring him in yesterday for official questioning but then his house burned down and everyone assumed he was dead!" She leaned towards Anna, lowering her voice further. "You should have seen Frank Doherty! He nearly burst an artery when he heard Tom Gallagher's house was on fire and there were bodies inside. And when he got word he was still alive and somewhere in the city, you could hear him shouting two floors down!"

Anna laughed. Despite all that had happened today, tales of the Chief Superintendent's legendary temper delivered some comic respite.

"Come on," Lauren held out her hand, "you look exhausted. Let me drive you back to your car."

Anna gratefully accepted her friend's offer. As she stood up to leave, her whole body felt weary, her legs ached and the joints in her back creaked stiffly. She longed for nothing more than to stand under the shower in Vivian's apartment, turn it up to the hottest setting and try to forget this day.

Which is exactly what she did. The apartment was in darkness when she pulled into the parking space beside the concrete steps. She muttered a quick "Good evening," to Dermot as she made her way to the door. He was standing on his side of the porch in the dark, with Pirate at his feet. She ignored his called out "Party is all set for tomorrow night!" and let herself in just as tears began to fall. Closing the door behind her she leaned against it, her hands on her knees, and sobbed uncontrollably for several minutes.

Her tears ended as suddenly as they had started. Wiping her face she walked through to the kitchen, turning on all the lights as she went. It had been a dark day, the rain never letting up and the clouds were heavy and low all afternoon. The heat of the apartment and the warm lights were soothing but her whole body was shaking. She kept moving, telling herself it was better than stopping. Pulling a pizza from the freezer she turned on the oven to heat, jumping in fright at her reflection in the kitchen window.

"Get a grip, Anna!"

Her fingers shook and fumbled on the cardboard box and she had to resort to using a knife to free the pizza. As soon as it was in the oven she trudged to the bathroom, each step feeling as though she was plodding through quicksand. It took such effort to peel off her clothes she contemplated abandoning the idea and just going to bed, but the rising heat from the shower was too tempting to resist. After a few minutes' effort she stood under the water and slowly, after several painful minutes more, her body stopped shaking.

Her encounter with Tom Gallagher earlier became a film-reel inside her head that wouldn't give up. She wished she had shut her eyes when he had jumped, but she hadn't. Instead she had leapt forward, her hand outstretched, grabbing the air where he had been, and watched his head hit the wall and his body hit the water and disappear. She saw the river swell around the spot where he entered, then close around him, as though sealing him into its murky darkness. The sound of his voice – the *pain* in it – kept returning to her. She couldn't imagine how his wife must be feeling now.

The beeping oven told Anna the pizza was cooked. Regretting having to leave the heat of the shower, she got out, pulled on her dressing gown and wrapped a towel around her hair. But her shivering had abated and the apartment was warm – she was feeling normal again.

In the kitchen she turned on the TV and waited for the evening news bulletin to start, wondering if today's events would feature. How could they not?

She brought the pizza to the breakfast counter and settled onto a bar stool, realising she wasn't even hungry. With her fingers she pulled pieces of pepperoni into her mouth, barely tasting anything. But she did jump violently when her mobile phone rang on the counter top.

"Anna! Thank God you're safe!"

"Hi, Myles."

News had reached him in Brussels; she wasn't too surprised.

"Are you hurt?"

"No, I'm fine. Just shaken up."

"Do you feel like talking about it?"

She felt too tired to sit up straight on the stool any longer. Abandoning the pizza she walked to her room, climbed into bed, and told Myles everything she could remember, hoping that by saying it aloud, she might begin to forget.

51

Anna opened her eyes and grabbed her mobile from the bedside locker. Sleep had been a welcome relief, a dream-free respite from her thoughts. She registered the time with surprise – two-thirty in the afternoon! She had slept right through the night and into the middle of the following day – she didn't think she'd ever done that before.

She could remember that sounds had punctured her sleep, though not enough to wake her; Vivian returning home at some point, the shower turning on, the coffee machine humming before the front door closed behind her again. Anna sat up and saw a full mug of coffee on her bedside locker – it was freezing cold, but evidence that Vivian had come to say goodbye this morning. Shaking her head she marvelled that she had been in such a deep sleep. Dreamless, too. She was glad of that, at least.

Her phone showed no messages from Lauren or William Ryan, which meant there was no progress on finding Tom Gallagher. She swallowed hard and reminded herself there was nothing she could have done, and nothing she could do now.

After a few minutes she made her way into the kitchen, where she found a note attached to the fridge.

Gone to work, see you later, sleepy-head, Viv xx

She made coffee and stepped out onto the balcony. The rain had finally stopped and the sun was shining. Though it was still cold, the sun bounced off the concrete in the yard underneath her, fine spider-webs with tiny raindrops caught in the light between the balcony railings. She closed her eyes and inhaled deeply. Her body felt renewed from so much sleep, but her legs were restless. She'd have some food, she decided, before going for a run. And later, when Vivian came back, they could dissect everything that had happened together.

Turning at the sound of her ringing mobile she stepped back into the apartment. It was Alex. In all that had happened over the last twenty-four hours, she had somehow forgotten about him.

"Hey, Alex." There was noise in the background, voices and passing engines and something that sounded like a low-pitched siren. "I've been meaning to call you."

She heard him draw breath before he spoke and she knew. She knew deep inside her. Her hands shook until coffee splashed from the mug onto the floor and she placed it on the counter with a rattle.

"Anna, we've found them."

Vivian returned to the apartment sometime after six in the evening, a take-away bag in hand.

"*I'm back! I brought dinner!*"

When she didn't find Anna in the living area she stuck her head inside her bedroom door, her smile of greeting quickly turning to a frown.

"Oh my God, you're leaving?"

Anna turned from her suitcase on the bed and reached for

Vivian, pulling her into a hug. She needed to feel something firm and warm, to be held by her friend. Vivian returned the embrace tightly.

"What happened, Anna? You're shaking!" she whispered.

Anna sniffed and sat on the bed, pulling the remnants of a tissue from her sleeve. She dabbed at her nose and eyes. "Alex phoned me earlier. They found bone fragments at the dig-site. Long story short, it's probably Mum and Dad." Her fingers worried at the tissue, little pieces falling onto her lap.

Vivian sat beside her and placed a hand on her back. "I'm so sorry!"

"To think, yesterday when we were tied up with Tom Gallagher, pieces of my parents were found in a field." Anna gulped and pressed the tissue to her mouth.

"Where are you going?" Vivian asked softly. "Wherever it is, I'm coming too. I'll go with you."

Anna shook her head and reached for her hand, squeezing it. "Thank you! But there's no need. I'm going to join Alex in Dublin. It's something Annika said to me the other day – she said I should be with him, and I've been thinking about it ever since. Alex shouldn't have to do this on his own. I've booked into a B&B near the site and I'll stay there for a few days."

"Let me come with you! You might be glad of the company."

"I appreciate that, Viv, I really do. But I wouldn't be good company right now, and Alex needs me. Besides, aren't you going to be really busy now at work?"

"I guess so … when do you leave?"

"Tomorrow, first thing."

"OK, well, for now let's have some noodles and fried chicken. I'm going to open a bottle of wine and we can talk."

As Vivian left the room to set up their dinner, Anna pushed herself up again, feeling weary. Her clothes were almost packed, enough for three nights. Would that be enough? The weight of her grief felt it could crush her, but there was nothing she could do about it. With a deep breath she followed Vivian into the kitchen, longing, once more, for distraction.

"So, it looks like we'll run the documentary as soon as possible," Vivian paused to suck the last of her noodles into her mouth and reached for her wine glass, "which will still take weeks."

"Have the gardaí said you can go ahead?"

Vivian swallowed a mouthful of wine and frowned. "They can't really stop us. The details of the case are decades old. But there are limitations Carol has to suss out. For example, if Patricia O'Brien is to be considered an active witness, we can't feature her yet. Realistically, we're looking at a two-part documentary. One to lay out the crime, and the second to lay out the new evidence that came to light that implicates Tom Gallagher. Carol's legal people are looking into it."

Anna placed her empty wine glass on the table and sat back into the sofa. Vivian had certainly offered her the distraction she'd craved.

"So what do you do in the meantime?"

Vivian rubbed her temples, looking tired. Anna remembered she had barely slept; while Anna had been lost in hours of deep sleep, Vivian had been working almost the whole time.

"I have to write up everything we've learned over the last few days. Luke will help with plotting a timeline and will outline the direction of each section of the documentary. The sooner we get on with it, the less likely any injunction Patricia O'Brien files will affect us. Apparently."

She unfolded her legs and stood up, stretching her back from side to side.

"What about the notes and the crucifix? Do you think that's over now?"

Vivian shrugged as she moved into the kitchen.

"Carol and Luke assume it was Tom Gallagher behind it, or maybe his wife. I mean, they are the ones with the most to lose, so it *must* have been one of them. And it brought a lot of publicity to the case already so they are keen to get things moving as fast as we can. Seize the opportunity and all that."

"I guess," Anna agreed, though it didn't feel right to her. The anguish on Tom Gallagher's face was something she wouldn't forget in a hurry. And Patricia O'Brien's too.

Vivian dipped her head, rooting through a kitchen drawer. When she straightened up she looked a little sheepish. "No judgement, please, Anna, but I need a cigarette! It's been one hell of a few days."

Anna held up her hands. "Hey, it's nothing to do with me – knock yourself out."

Vivian grinned at her and turned to the sliding door that led onto the balcony, her hand flicking the switch beside it for the overhead light. "It's so dark out! No stars tonight – when do the clocks go back again? We need more light in the evenings, it's so gloomy!"

"End of the month, isn't it?" Anna asked as the balcony was illuminated in pale yellow light. "Is it?"

Vivian was still turned towards her as she unlocked the door, slid it open and stepped outside.

She didn't see what Anna saw.

She didn't see the bulky shape of a man standing beside the small patio table, watching them through the glass, until it was too late. Vivian's eyes met Anna's in confusion that quickly turned to shock, as a rough hand grabbed her wrist and a cold blade was pressed against her neck.

52

Anna couldn't recall pushing the coffee table aside, nor hear the smash of her wine glass as it hit the wooden floor. She wasn't even aware she was moving, but suddenly she was standing on the balcony, staring into the face of the man she had feared for too long.

Dean Harris had retreated to the far side of the small balcony. He'd kicked one chair aside and dragged Vivian backwards. He stood now with his back pressed against the wall, his right arm stretched around Vivian's neck, the small circular table between them and Anna. The blade of the knife in his hand glinted in the overhead light.

Later, she would wonder why she hadn't felt anything standing opposite him, even while he'd held a knife to her friend's throat. Perhaps it was because she was already completely exhausted, her emotions wrought for too long in the last few weeks. All she felt at the point of realising Dean Harris had found her was acceptance and relief. It had been inevitable; she had *known* this moment would come.

There was nothing Dean Harris could do to her in such a confined area that she hadn't already dealt with lately. And so her heart beat steadily, her hands itching to do what she had trained to do for years. Her breathing was measured and calm. The only thing she needed to happen was for her friend to move to safety. Sparring in the close confines of the apartment kitchen with Vivian had been a form of training for this moment, and she regretted now that she hadn't shown Vivian any self-defence manoeuvres.

Vivian was crying quietly, her eyes on Anna, a silent *"Help me!"* pulsing from her.

Harris appeared to be struggling to breathe; Anna could hear him gasping for air as though he had run a marathon. His chest heaved behind a heavy dark-blue coat that was grimy on the sleeves and crusted white at the wrists. He coughed, a brittle phlegmy rattle, spit bursting from his mouth. Anna watched as he shifted his feet, swaying from side to side, unable to stop moving.

She looked over the railings quickly, seeing the green refuse bin pushed against the wall beneath her. The bin only reached so far, barely to the end of the balcony railings; he would still have had to pull himself up the railings and climb over, and the exertion seemed to have tired him out. His face was a sickly pallor behind the sheen of sweat.

"Don't you want to know how I found you?" he said, unable to hide a smile of victory.

His voice was surprisingly soft. It trembled. Was he nervous? He spoke through clenched teeth, his mouth not opening properly. She remembered the night he had crept into her house and she had fractured his jaw. The memory gave her faith that she and Vivian could survive this.

"I don't really care." Anna pushed confidence into her voice. The last thing she would do was indulge his gloating. She shivered in the cold of the balcony, the cool night wind a chilly embrace. "Let my friend go. We can talk alone."

Step closer to me.

He shook his head roughly and pressed his arm harder around Vivian's neck. She whimpered in pain and fear as the knife pierced her skin and a trickle of blood dripped down her throat. He shuffled forward, bumping into the patio table, then back again. Anna figured he would stab Vivian if she pushed the table aside and invaded his space. She took a small step to the right; he didn't seem to notice.

"I'm not letting her go! She's the only thing keeping me safe from you. You're a lunatic! You broke my jaw!"

"*You broke into my house!*" she screamed at him, the volume of her voice echoing around them, surprising them all. "*You planned to rape me!*"

He shook his head violently, "No! No! It was a game. You wanted me to!"

What on earth was he talking about?!

"You're delusional!" she said angrily.

"*Shut up!*" he roared and stepped towards Anna, dragging Vivian with him.

Vivian stumbled forward and he yanked her up, using his arm around her neck.

Vivian cried out in pain, her eyes beseeching Anna for help.

"What do you want?" Anna said, forcing herself to speak calmly, to hide the raging anger and panic that finally flared inside her.

"Ask me how I found you!"

She looked at him aghast, her lip curling in disgust. While he held a knife to her friend's neck he needed his ego stroked. He wanted her to see how he had outsmarted her.

"Fine." She sought for appeasement. "Tell me."

"The Pearsons," he sneered.

Anna's neighbours in Kinsale, the people who had needed a security alarm last year after a break-in, which was how Harris had targeted her in the first place. "I had to stay in their shed after you found my stuff in your house. I was watching you that night, walking into your empty house with a man ..." his eyes narrowed and he spat the word "*Slut!*" When she didn't react he carried on with his story, revelling in outsmarting her and the gardaí. "Mrs Pearson was collecting your mail – I knew that much – could hear her collecting it every few days when I was in your attic. She put it all into a big envelope and left it in the kitchen before she posted it. It was easy to slip into the house and read the address on the label. Led me right to you!"

Anna closed her eyes. William Ryan had asked her who knew where she was living now, and she had forgotten to mention her neighbour.

"Fine, you're smart." There was no emotion in her voice. "What do you want?"

He scowled at her and she knew he had hoped for more.

"I want ... I ..." He looked about him, stepping left to right again, Vivian rocking in the grip of his arm. "I want this to *end!*"

Anna jumped, a whimper from Vivian reaching her, making her heart sink.

"Do you know my mother is in a prison cell? *My aunt told me – that fucker Ryan arrested her! An old lady! It's all your fault!*"

Screaming at her had exerted him and he paused to cough, wiping his mouth on the sleeve of his jacket.

With her hands on the patio table Anna leaned closer to him.

"You caused your own problems! And this is only making it

worse. I've pressed a panic button and the gardaí will be here any minute. Just leave!"

The panic button in her living room in Kinsale had saved her life last month and the sudden lie had just popped into her head – there was none here in Vivian's apartment, but Dean Harris didn't know that. He stopped moving and watched her, his chest heaving. She could see a battle raging in his eyes – did he believe her?

With a sudden twist that made Vivian yelp he used his free hand to pull a piece of paper from his pocket and tossed it to Anna. "I want you to sign this."

She unfolded the square of paper into an A4-sized page and began to read his thin, scrawled handwriting. The page was heavily creased and soiled, as though dirty fingers had folded and unfolded it many times.

"*I, Anna Clarke, hereby wish to apologise to the court for wasting everyone's time. Dean Harris did not enter my home by force but was in fact invited in to participate in a sexual fantasy …*"

She could read no more. She looked at him incredulously and laughter burst from her unchecked.

"You can't be serious! This is bullshit!"

Vivian muttered, "Please, Anna!" at the same time as Harris grunted in frustration. "*Sign it!*"

That's it, she thought, that's all he wants? She had been readying herself for more. But looking at him she could see he wasn't capable of more – his body shook when he stood still, his face bore the sheen of a man running a temperature.

She shivered, chilled to realise he was so far over the edge of his sanity that he was grasping at such weak straws. It made him even more dangerous than before.

"If you sign that the judge will understand why I came here tonight. He'll see that I was being stitched-up! Anyone would understand I was desperate." He jerked his arm again and Vivian moaned in pain.

"*Alright, OK!*" Anna said. There was no point in doing anything other than what he wanted, even though any sane person could see it was madness.

He tossed a blue pen at her and it clattered to the ground. She had to move the patio table to one side to retrieve it and used the chance to push it further out of her way.

Crouched on her knees she looked up at him.

It was now or never.

As if reading her mind he extended his arm and angled the knife so the tip was pointing into Vivian's neck, his meaning clear. *Come closer and I kill her.*

Anna's stood up, straightened the paper on the table and signed her name at the end of the page. She didn't bother to read the rest – it was a waste of paper, and this was a wasted mission. No-one could help but see it for what it was, a man so desperate to evade justice for his crimes he had deluded himself.

His body was wracked with a violent, spasming cough and when he was done he wiped at his chin with his free hand.

Vivian had her eyes closed, her lips moving in a silent prayer.

"Hurry up!" His breathing sounded more laboured than before. "Pass it over!"

"No," Anna said firmly. "Not until you let Vivian step inside. Once she's safe I'll give it to you."

It was a gamble, but it was all she had.

He looked at her, unblinking, assessing his options. He appeared exhausted, as though confronting her had drained every ounce of his energy.

Eventually he nodded slowly and looked at the ground, speaking only to himself, "Yes, of course. It'd be better for me. I didn't mean to scare her. I just needed the truth to be told. Yes, that's what they need to see."

Suddenly a loud pounding noise startled them all and they each looked to the source of it – Vivian's front door. It was loud and insistent, a man's voice shouting something that barely carried through to the balcony. Anna recognised Dermot's voice – his party was tonight, he was probably annoyed they hadn't turned up.

Harris's mouth dropped open, his eyes wide, and his arm around Vivian slackened. Before he could regain his wits Vivian pushed his arm aside and darted quickly away from him, moaning as she stumbled into the patio table, her hip colliding with the metal. With a loud sob she staggered into the safety and warmth of the apartment.

Anna kept her eyes on Harris as he resumed his quick shuffling from foot to foot, unsure of himself now. His advantage was gone. It was just the two of them on the balcony and he had nowhere to go. With the table now pushed up against the balcony wall there was nothing between them but air.

Watching him now she could see how ill he really was; sweat glistened all over his face and neck, the whites of his eyes were a sickly yellow and his skin was mottled with spots and sores. A sour smell drifted from him.

She could step back inside the apartment and lock the door, but then he would leave the way he had come, and disappear again, and this nightmare would drag on even longer. She was tired of waiting. And she wasn't afraid of him, now, here, face to face.

"Vivian will call the guards now," she said calmly, "so it's time to end this. You need to give yourself up."

He squeezed his eyes shut, closed his fists, the knife held tight, and began to pound his fists against his temples, shaking his head, muttering "*No!*" over and over. Suddenly he opened his eyes and stared into hers. "*I won't go back! No-one will find me!*"

He raised one foot onto the patio chair beside him and without a word hoisted himself up and over the railing, straddling it for a moment, watching her. Hatred twisted his face – she knew he wished he had never set eyes on her.

He heaved himself off the balcony railing at the same moment they both realised his mistake. The refuse bin he had pushed against the wall to access the balcony was nearer to *her*, at least a foot from where he had jumped, and he was leaping into thin air. He shrieked in fright, a loud cry in the quiet night. Instinctively she lunged forward and grabbed his hand.

Yesterday she had failed to reach Tom Gallagher in time – was this why she had lurched forward now without a second thought? Harris was heavy, and immediately the muscles in her shoulder and back were straining in protest, pain pushing the air from her lungs.

"*Help me!*" he wailed.

She looked down at his face, cast in terror beneath her. The eyes … she had thought they looked dead before, but now they were alive with fear. His hand was slippery with sweat and she groaned, the metal railing digging into her chest.

"*Integrity Anna! It's one of the five tenets of Taekwon-Do.*"
"*What does it mean?*"
"*It means to be morally strong. Always try to live your life with integrity. Always try to do the right thing.*"

Her father's voice had come to her often lately when she was in these situations, when she was fighting for her life and needed to remember the things he had taught her. She knew what he would want her to do.

She looked at Dean Harris, felt his hand heavy and wet in hers. His face was full of panic and he twisted his body and pulled, so that her chest and shoulder ached. The wind whipped at her hair and the cold of the night pressed into her, right into her bones. It felt like time stood still as her eyes connected with his.

"Sorry, Dad," she whispered, opened her hand, and let him fall.

53

The sun fractured the night sky as the detectives finished their examinations and readied to leave the apartment.

Vivian had been taken to hospital in the first ambulance, a dressing at her throat and a shiny silver solar blanket wrapped tightly around her. She'd needed oxygen in the apartment – her level of distress so high she was hyper-ventilating. Anna had never seen her friend this upset. She'd sat beside her, holding a wet cloth to her neck while they waited for the ambulance, reassuring her as best she could.

"It's a small cut, really. I'm sure it hurts but it won't need more than a few stitches and I'm sure it won't scar."

"It's not that," Vivian had gulped around her tears, "it's … I mean, the smell off him, Anna! That knife can't have been clean! Oh Jesus! I thought … I thought I was going to be stabbed. Or worse. I thought it would never end!"

"It's OK now. It's over! We'll make sure you get a tetanus and anything else you might need."

"Oh God!" Vivian had buried her face in her hands, shaking and crying, and had remained that way until the doorbell rang ten minutes later.

Anna had been glad to concentrate on comforting her friend –

the energy of it kept the full realisation of what had just happened at bay, for a little while anyway.

While two paramedics assessed and attempted to reassure Vivian, Anna had wandered outside to wait for the second ambulance, grateful that for once Dermot didn't seem inclined to join her. She stood on the porch and waited for them – they'd need to be shown where Harris lay. Not that they wouldn't be able to hear him – he had alternated between moaning and cursing at the top of his lungs since he made impact with the hard ground.

William Ryan and his team, filling three cars in total, had arrived at some point overnight. Anna couldn't remember if he had spoken to her, but knew he had gripped her shoulders hard, searing her face with his eyes. With a nod he'd reassured himself she was OK. Then he'd followed the sounds Harris was making and travelled with him in the ambulance. It seemed that now that Harris had been located, William was reluctant to let him out of his sight.

Anna had stepped back inside the apartment while his stretcher was led to the ambulance – seeing him, hearing him, being anywhere near him was the very last thing she wanted to do.

Inside the apartment there were still too many people for comfort. Members of the Technical Bureau were still collecting evidence from the balcony and she wondered if she should leave. Her bags were almost fully packed – Vivian was safe. There was no reason for her to stay.

"Not at all," Grace Thompson answered when she asked if she was in the way. "The Tech lads will be done shortly. Harris didn't take up too much space while he was here."

Anna sat down heavily on the sofa. Someone had cleaned up the smashed glass from the wooden floor. Apart from the extra people in the apartment she could easily fool herself that she had dreamt the whole thing.

"He seemed broken, you know?" Anna shivered and rubbed her hands together, as though to bring feeling back into them. "Weak and broken. He wanted to hurt me but he didn't have the strength."

"That makes sense. He was sleeping rough, probably not eating properly. Are you OK?" Grace leaned against the counter and watched her carefully.

"Not really. I need to tell you something," Anna took a deep breath and met the detective's calm, grey eyes. "I let him go."

Grace nodded. "I'm sure you did. He weighs about three times you do. Don't sweat it, Anna. Anyone would have done the same."

"No, I … I *let* him go." Her voice broke and she suddenly felt claustrophobic, needing more oxygen than she could gulp into her lungs right now.

Grace crossed the space between them and sat beside Anna, surprising her by taking both hands in hers.

"OK, listen to me! Listen carefully, OK? Regardless of anything you felt or thought, the fact is that Dean Harris was going to fall either way. He is too heavy for you to hold him for long, and certainly too heavy to have pulled him up. *Do you hear me?*"

Anna pulled her hands away and wiped her nose, nodding. She wondered if Grace understood what she had told her.

"Besides, he only broke one leg. And maybe his pelvis. But bottom line is he's going to be fine."

"That's it? Just a few broken bones?" Anna whimpered, flooded with relief. The hatred she had felt for him had been overpowering, and still was – yet she was glad he wasn't seriously injured. She really didn't need anything else to worry about.

A woman in a white suit and shoe covers stepped inside from the balcony.

"Detective Thompson? We're done here."

"Right, thanks." Cold air had blasted the apartment when the tech officer had opened the balcony door, rousing everyone. Grace pushed herself up and stifled a yawn. The two uniformed gardaí with her took their cue to go. Three others had already returned to the station.

"We'll leave you to it, Anna. You have my number if you need anything. William Ryan will be in touch with you tomorrow."

"Is it OK if I go to Portlaoise for a few days? I need to join my brother. There's been a new development there and I … I need to be with him."

Grace's eyes were sympathetic as she pulled on her coat and wound a scarf around her neck.

"Of course. I have your statement. Just answer your phone, OK? We're all very relieved to see this over with but there'll be more questions, I'm sure of that."

Anna led the way to the front door, the gardaí trooping behind her. The Technical Bureau officers smiled in goodbye, kitbags under their arms. Anna noticed Dermot had decided the commotion was too interesting to ignore any longer and, with his cat protectively in his arms, he peered from his front door. She sighed; though she was exhausted, she would have to fill him in on what had happened and thank him for his part in things. He'd already spoken to the detectives.

Grace stepped towards him. "Can I help you with anything else? Have you something to add to our investigation?"

Dermot ducked back into his hallway and slammed the door closed.

Grace chuckled and shook her head, stepping back towards Anna.

"Nosy neighbours have their uses, *eh*? Are you sure you're OK? You're awfully pale – I can arrange for a doctor to stop by."

"Oh, I'm fine." Anna smiled at her, hoping it looked reassuring, "I just want to check in with Vivian at the hospital. She was really distressed when she left."

Grace shivered and buttoned up her coat. "Yesterday's events at the river were tough on her too. She was quite insistent about getting her phone back actually. Come to think of it, she seems feisty enough, I'm sure she'll be fine."

Anna laughed. "She certainly is that!"

"I think she'll go far in journalism. She has all it takes. Not so sure about her colleagues though."

Anna remembered that Grace and William had interviewed some of the others at the Banba Productions office, namely Carol and Luke.

"What did you think of Luke?" she asked, keeping her tone light. Grace seemed like a good judge of character to her. If he was to be part of Vivian's future she really wanted to like him. Her heart sank as Grace grimaced at the mention of his name.

"Not my cup of tea. Something a bit off there."

"Really?"

"Yeah. But that's just my gut instinct. Alright – I'll go. You take care of yourself, OK? We'll be in touch."

She turned and jogged lightly down the steps to the waiting squad car. Anna stayed in the doorway, her arms crossed protectively against the wind. Grace's words began to pull on her adrenaline, ramping it up until it flowed fast in her veins, pushing away the tiredness that was threatening to overwhelm her. Something was stirring inside her mind, a thought forming that she was sure was important ... She turned and closed the door. The apartment was quiet and cold. After hours being full of people it was eerie to stand in the silence again.

In her bedroom she riffled through her suitcase for her trainers and pulled them on. She needed to think. After all the night had brought, she knew she needed to run. Headphones out this time – she didn't want to forget anything, to dull the feelings and reality of what had just happened. Or what was to come.

But, first, she needed to speak to Dermot.

54

William shifted his weight in the hospital-room chair while he waited for Dean Harris to wake up. Sweat was building in sticky beads between his shoulder blades and on the back of his neck; he had removed his overcoat and suit jacket over twenty minutes ago. Now he rolled up his shirtsleeves and considered opening the window. He would never understand why hospital rooms were so warm.

He rose and moved to the window, moving aside the slats on the blind, and pushed it open slightly. It was enough. Cooler air drifted into the room and he stayed there for several minutes, inhaling deeply.

He turned when he heard rustling from the thin, stiff bedsheets. Harris was rousing. William watched him lick his cracked lips and blink in the light of the fluorescent bulb overhead. He saw the man turn his head slowly to take in the room, watched his chest heave as memories of the night before returned. William waited for comprehension to come and, sure enough, when he groaned and yanked on the handcuffs that bound him to the bed, William knew that fate had truly revealed itself.

"Hello again," he said cheerfully and smiled as Harris jerked in the bed with fright, his handcuffs rattling. "Do you remember me?

We met the last time you were in hospital, funnily enough. A fractured jaw that time. Leg and pelvis this time, but it could have been worse."

William chuckled as Harris watched him, pain creasing his face.

"You really should stay away from Anna Clarke! I suppose you don't need me to tell you that."

He stepped back to the chair and settled himself into it, tapping Harris's leg cast as he passed. A groan from the man was all he managed in acknowledgement. Harris closed his eyes and William watched his face – he found it easier to do that when the man wasn't staring back at him. His skin was grey and covered in a gloss of sickly sweat. The doctor had told William that aside from a broken leg and fractured pelvis, Harris was running a fever. The last few weeks had stripped all the vitality from him. Blood had dried in fine cracks along his lower lip and the skin around his nose was red and raw. Sores peppered his jawline. He looked wretched. William, on the other hand, felt revived. With Harris in custody, the world was put to rights again.

"You know … nobody ever asks the right questions," William said quietly.

Harris opened his eyes and watched him, remaining silent.

"For instance, when you were arrested last year, all we asked you was where you were on this date and that date, and did you know any of the victims. No-one asked you *why* you did what you did. I hold my hands up here!" He smiled coldly as he raised both palms. "I didn't care to ask you. Not my job."

Harris turned his head away to the window, his jaw jutted stubbornly forward, and muttered something, an indistinct jumble of words.

William leaned back into the chair and folded his arms, allowing the silence to stretch between them. Eventually, Harris turned back to face him.

"You think you're so perfect," he whispered, lips trembling.

"I'm not perfect," William answered softly. "I know darkness. All people do, it's the nature of being human. Some people keep their dark fantasies in the shadows of their minds, while others act on them. Why a person crosses that line is something I don't yet understand – maybe I never will. All I know is it's my job to catch them when they do."

"Great speech," Harris's mouth twisted sourly and he turned his face away again.

William sighed contentedly, giddy with the relief of seeing the man handcuffed to a hospital bed. It was time to go. He began to roll down his shirtsleeves as he spoke.

"I've heard this morning that your solicitor is going to argue temporary insanity for last night's attack – makes sense to me. So it'll be different people asking you questions this time. It won't do you much good, in the long term. Here's the thing – you're going back to prison, whichever definition of prison that is. It'll be a long time before you're a free man. Or, perhaps, something else entirely will happen ... who knows?"

He stood up and shrugged on his jacket, buttoning it up slowly.

"By the way, do you remember any of their names? Or were you ever bothered to find that out?"

Harris looked at him and blinked quickly, his lips pursed.

"What about Millie O'Driscoll? What about her?" He gripped the rail at the end of the bed, flexing his damp palms around the metal.

Harris watched him and swallowed hard, his eyes growing wider. Something in the detective was unnerving him.

"She was your fourth victim … do you remember her? Of course you don't. Perhaps if I told you her address? After all, you don't see them as people, do you?"

Suddenly he was leaning over Harris, his face stretched, his teeth bared. But he pulled himself back. With a shaking hand he straightened his tie.

"She was my best friend. We grew up together, two kids playing in the streets until dark." He smiled tightly. "Innocent times. I thought we'd be together forever but after college she married a Corkman, a nurse actually. Became Millie O'Sullivan." He shrugged, "Took me a while to get over that – losing her to a Corkman!"

Harris's body became very still.

"After you almost ruined her life I requested a transfer to Cork city. It's interesting really that asking for a transfer for 'personal reasons' doesn't arouse suspicion. Not even curiosity … everyone is too busy for such questions. Nobody asks the right thing anymore. Nobody asked why I took an interest in an unsolvable case when my desk was already heaving with files. Just happy to have an extra pair of hands. Lately my colleagues said I was obsessed with finding you, but no-one stopped to wonder why."

He patted Harris's cast harder this time, enjoying the sound of a suppressed groan, and opened the door wide.

"Private room … a nice luxury. No-one should have to share with you." His mouth twisted. "Let's see what the day brings."

Harris watched him step outside into the corridor and pause. William extended his hand and shook that of a man in scrubs before walking briskly away. The man stepped inside the room – a doctor, he assumed – and Harris turned his face to the window again. The sun had risen fully in the sky and it flooded through the slats in the blind, making him wince into the light. Everything ached, even the glare of the morning sun.

The sound of a lock clicking into place caused his head to whip back to the door. The man in scrubs turned to face him. With his blue surgical mask only his eyes were visible. His name tag read *"Staff Nurse Mark O'Sullivan"* … *O'Sullivan* … suddenly, Harris found it difficult to breathe. His world was this tiny room now, and everything in it began to fade: the wooden door, the white wall, the sounds of beeps and clicks as machines whirred beside the bed. All he could see was how tall the man was, his narrow shoulders, his light brown hair falling into deep brown eyes. Eyes so full of hate they didn't even seem human.

He yanked on his cuffed wrist and tried to scream, but his jaw ached and his chest felt weighed by panic. The scream refused to surface. There was nothing he could do but wait and endure whatever fate the detective had set in course for him.

He closed his eyes.

55

Vivian was sharing a hospital room with three other women and, when Anna pushed open the door, the sound of raucous laughter made her smile.

"I see you're feeling better!"

Vivian wiped tears from her eyes and grinned. "Anna, this is Emma – the funniest woman I've ever met!" She gestured to a woman who was propped up in bed, wearing a striped nightshirt, her face pink from laughter. The other two women in the room were still giggling and Vivian sighed. "It's a shame to have to leave you, ladies – I never expected to have such a laugh!"

Anna placed an overnight bag on the bed with a change of clothes for Vivian and some toiletries and pulled the curtain fully closed. As Vivian peeled off the hospital gown she had been given last night she winced a little.

"How are you feeling?" Anna sat down, eyeing the white dressing at her neck.

"I'm OK. It's just my shoulder is injured as well. He kept jerking me around." She pulled on her clothes as quickly as she could. "And my hip is all bruised. I needed six stitches in my neck. That bastard – I hope he never gets out of prison!"

"Did the gardaí take your clothes?"

"Yeah, it's all evidence, apparently. How does the apartment look?" She grimaced, waiting for Anna to tell her, expecting bad news.

Once Anna had finished her run earlier this morning she had scrubbed every inch of the apartment, even the places Dean Harris and the Technical Bureau team hadn't touched. It felt tainted to her, and she knew Vivian would feel the same.

"Everything is back where it should be," she reassured her, "and, aside from a very strong smell of bleach, you'd never know anything had happened."

"Oh, thanks!" Vivian's shoulders sagged in relief and she exhaled. "I think I'll give up the cigarettes now – no more going onto the balcony for a while!" She scooped up her toiletries bag. "Won't be long," and ducked out of the curtain to use the bathroom near the main door.

It was another hour before all the paperwork for her discharge was complete.

"How about a coffee before we go home?" Anna suggested, knowing her friend would need what she called "a decent hit" of caffeine soon. They made their way to the cafeteria on the ground floor and Vivian paused at the door, inhaling, her eyes lighting up.

"Oh, that smells good!"

While Vivian settled at a nearby table, Anna went to join the queue. Her legs felt a little weak and her head ached as she selected some sandwiches from the counter and shuffled forward. Vivian was OK – seeing it, believing it, was suddenly overwhelming, and she blinked away tears that blurred her vision. She had never considered that her friend was in danger but, looking back on things, while Harris was intent on revenge, *of course she was!* She had been so focused on denying the truth of everything that was happening around her that she had been blind to the danger she had put her friend in. Relief that his hold over her life was over was staggering, and she needed to sit down.

"How's it going, Clarke?"

Beside her, Gareth smiled and took the sandwiches from her hands. She wiped tears from her cheeks and grinned at him. It was good to see him.

"I see you shaved off your beard."

"Had to be done – I got a teaching gig. Have to appear presentable!"

Vivian was engrossed in her mobile phone, but looked up as they approached the table, Gareth carrying a tray with coffee and sandwiches. Her mouth dropped open. They sat down and Anna placed a large americano in front of her: a peace offering.

"Vivian – don't be mad. I asked Gareth to meet us and to take you home."

"You did what! *Why?*"

"I'm going to Portlaoise. I don't want you to go home alone. And you two need to sort things out."

Gareth grinned and pushed Vivian's mug closer towards her.

"She's always difficult before she's had her coffee. Come on, sis, drink up!"

As Vivian folded her arms across her chest his grin slipped, the bravado gone.

"Look, I'm sorry, OK?" he said. "We have a lot to talk about. And I'm hoping you might let me stay for a while."

"Excuse me?" Vivian's eyebrows drew together.

"I need somewhere to stay, closer to town. I got a job in UCC."
He couldn't keep the pride from his voice and he slurped his coffee
loudly, watching her, waiting for her reaction. "By the way, Mum
says you two should set up a detective agency – fair play on solving
that cold case!"

Vivian shook her head. She reached for her coffee and wrapped
her hands around it. They watched her in silence, Anna chewing
on her bottom lip, hoping she hadn't made another huge mistake.

"One week," Vivian finally said, "that's it, that's all you can stay
for! And you're on the couch. The spare room is Anna's for as long
as she needs it. End of discussion."

She winked at Anna as she brought her coffee to her lips.

Anna was glad she was sitting down – she pressed her back into
the hard wood of the chair and watched them speak, their
conversation stilted and uncertain at the start, then growing in ease
and familiarity, and she suddenly thought of Alex. She missed her
brother, and she needed to see him.

After a while she looked at her watch and stood up to leave.

"Are you going straight to Portlaoise?" Vivian looked pale and
tired. The coffee and carefree conversation with her brother had
revived her, but she was worried for Anna, sharing her dread at what
the next few days would bring.

Anna nodded. "I just need to meet William Ryan first." She
didn't elaborate – Vivian would know soon enough but, for now,
she was leaving hospital and working things out with her brother,
and that was all that mattered.

56

They met on the street outside the Banba Production offices. William smiled broadly when she stopped in front of him. He was also clean-shaven. The shadows under his eyes remained but his shoulders weren't hunched like they had been lately and the strain lines around his eyes seemed to have faded.

"Are you ready?" he asked and she nodded.

"Thanks for letting me do this with you."

He shrugged. "I doubt there'll by any charges filed so it's not a problem. You're one hundred percent sure?"

"Positive. And they're all here. Vivian spoke to them this morning. Even though it's the weekend, the office is full. Everyone's been drafted in to work on the documentary."

She took a deep breath and stepped inside the building. She'd never been to the office with Vivian. William led the way to the elevator and selected the fifth floor. She was impressed by the décor. A lime sofa in the waiting area was stark and bright against the cream carpet. Large, framed images from shows Carol had worked on in America lined three of the walls.

A short woman, with blonde curls that bounced around her face as she moved, stood up to greet them. As her eyes rested on Anna she beamed.

"Anna Clarke! It's you again!"

"Hello, Sheena," Anna muttered. She had forgotten about the woman who seemed to know so much about her. "We need to speak to Carol. Is she in the office?"

"Is this about Vivian? Is everything OK?" She stood still, waiting for Anna to fill her in, her hands on her hips expectantly.

"We need to speak to your boss," William said firmly.

Sheena nodded quickly, her curls bobbing. "Sure ... of course ..."

She turned and opened a cream door behind her desk, motioning for them to follow her, and led them through to the open-plan room William remembered from his last visit.

Luke was at his desk, a telephone pressed to his ear, chewing a pen. His eyes tracked them walk through the room, and when they stopped at his desk he ended the call. He slouched lower into the chair and swirled the pen inside his mouth, his body language showing he hadn't a care in the world. Anna would have believed that except for the vein that throbbed visibly at his temple.

"Anna, isn't it? Vivian's friend. What can I do for you?"

He blinked quickly, eyebrows raised. She felt like punching him right in the face. What Vivian had ever found attractive in him she would never know.

She thought of her friend, of her pale, scared face. Not just this morning, but when she had shown Anna the first threatening note, and in the graveyard when they had found the crucifix with her name on it. Anna's hands were bunched fists, her fingernails denting the skin of her palms, but her voice was steady.

"You delivered coordinates to Vivian's apartment that led us to a graveyard, where you had pushed a cross into the ground. My neighbour saw you – he's one of those nosy types. He described you perfectly, even your leather jacket. You left the first note on her desk, telling her to tread carefully, and pretended you'd sort it with the gardaí. You've been trying to scare her and I want to know why."

A lazy smile stretched across his face, faltering a little when William Ryan stepped a little closer. A detective in the room made things far more serious than an angry best friend. Sitting up straighter, he laughed.

"Oh come on – it's just a game! You have to drum up publicity in this business, it's how to get ahead."

"You threatened her!"

"I wasn't going to *do* anything!" He threw the pen onto the desk and looked to the back of the room, where Carol was standing now, her hands running over her hair. "Are you going to wade in here anytime soon?" he demanded, his face flushed.

Anna's mouth dropped open as she understood.

"*You?*" she whispered. "*You* were behind this? Vivian trusted you – she looked up to you! How could you use her like that?"

Carol closed her eyes and pressed her fingertips to her forehead, breathing deeply. She shook her head, speaking quietly to herself and, when she finally looked up, her eyes shone.

"It's how we did things, years ago in the States. Drum up a little publicity, like Luke said. The press love it and it boosts our online presence – do you have any idea how crowded it is out there? How hard it is for a new company to break through?"

"The detectives knew it was you, they just had no proof," Anna said. "After they visited you, Vivian didn't received any more threatening messages. You had to stop. The photographs – let me guess – you hired a photographer to wait outside Skibbereen, in the graveyard. One of your freelancers. Someone local, who kept quiet on the promise of more work?"

"It's not as seedy as you make it sound. It's how these things are done."

"It's ... disgusting!"

"*Oh, grow up!*" Carol screamed, anger flooding her face and neck a deep red. "No-one was ever going to actually *hurt* Vivian! It did wonders for her profile and for the documentary!"

She was suddenly aware that members of her staff were staring at her in shock from their desks. Sheena was standing against the wall by the reception door, gulping back sobs, her curls covering her face.

William had heard enough. He cleared his throat and turned his back to Carol, addressing the room.

"Show's over, folks. Take the rest of the day off. Some of your colleagues will be joining me down at the station to answer a few questions." He pushed his hands into his pockets and rocked on his heels.

Anna knew he was enjoying this. The euphoria of catching Dean Harris was still flowing through him.

"You can't be serious! I'm not going anywhere!" Luke stood up and grabbed his jacket and, pushing roughly past Sheena, he left the room.

Carol took a steadying breath.

"I'll come. I'll tell you everything." She shrugged on a cream blazer. When she reached them she looked at William with dry eyes, fully composed. "Will you be filing charges, Detective?"

William shrugged. "That's not really up to me. But, if we do, I think wasting Garda resources will be top of the list."

"And Vivian," Carol looked at Anna. "Will you tell her I'm sorry? Will you explain?"

Anna didn't answer. Carol lowered her eyes as she walked past and followed William to the elevator.

On the street, Grace Thompson was helping a handcuffed Luke into the back of a waiting Garda car. She grinned at Anna as they emerged from the revolving doors.

"Man, that felt good! He tried to run for it – needless to say he didn't get far."

Once Carol was secured in a second car, William turned to Anna.

"What about you? What are you going to do now?"

She took a deep breath, filling her lungs with the crisp, spring air. She touched his arm, her eyes meeting his, conveying her thanks and her respect. Words wouldn't come.

He hugged her quickly and turned away.

Walking back to her car she pulled her phone from her pocket and texted her brother.

Alex, see you soon. Just leaving Cork.

57

One month later

"I can't believe you're leaving Cork!"

The departures terminal of Cork Airport was busy, people hurrying along the gleaming tiles, illuminated in the sunlight that spilled in through the glass doors. Alex flexed his hand around the leather strap of Anna's duffel bag and passed it to her. She patted her pockets – passport, boarding pass – before smiling at him.

Part of her couldn't believe it either.

The last four weeks had passed quickly yet looking back she felt that all that had taken place had been years ago. Her trip to Portloaise was a hellish blur she longed to forget but the images and sounds in the field, the detectives' soft words, the shadows moving inside a white crime-scene tent, refused to leave her. When she returned to Cork and the sanctity of Vivian's apartment, things only got worse.

The nightmares returned.

Night after night, the unrelenting assault left her paralysed. She saw the horror of her screams in Vivian's haunted eyes, in the strain on Gareth's face. So she tried to stay awake. She lived in terror of falling into sleep where her thoughts had free reign. Her worst fears for her parents had come true; she had known it for a while, yet to have it confirmed shifted things inside her.

Hope was finally gone.

Two weeks after returning to Cork, acceptance began to creep in. She was sitting on the sofa in Vivian's apartment, staring at the cream wall opposite, the numbness slowly releasing its hold on her, loosening her chest. Then, the doorbell rang.

Vivian was working. So was Gareth. When the chime sounded again, Anna unfurled her body from the sofa, walked slowly through the hallway and pulled open the door.

Serious brown eyes behind his glasses, curly dark hair shorter than she remembered, Myles had always known when a phone call wasn't enough.

"Hello, you," he said, stepping over the threshold.

She stared at him for a long time, not daring to believe he was really here. His arms wrapped around her and pulled her close, and she allowed her body to sag against his. He couldn't stay away from work for long, but for two days and nights he banished the dark. She finally fell into dreamless sleep, his warmth beside her, and felt herself come alive again.

Before he said goodbye he made a tentative suggestion.

"I can't get out of Brussels until this project is finished."

"How long will that take?"

"Six months, at least."

"I understand."

"Will you – will you come to live with me?"

"In Brussels?"

"I think a break from here would do you good."

Anna had never thought of leaving Cork before. She adored Kinsale and had fallen in love with living in the city too. But Myles had planted a seed of thought that quickly grew into exciting possibilities. He had called it "a break" but she knew it was so much more than that.

It was a fresh start.

Once their parents' funerals were over and Robert Evans and Roy Eastly were charged with murder, Anna broached the subject with her brother. Alex had lost a lot of weight in the weeks they had been apart. Lines around his eyes and shadows underneath them told her he still suffered from insomnia. Perhaps he always would. Recent events had aged him and he looked more like their father now. She had been worried to leave him, the way he had always been worried about her.

"If you think it's a bad idea …"

But he had smiled at her, looking so like their dad that her heart had almost broken all over again.

"If it's what you want, Anna, then go for it. Myles is a good guy – I like him. I want you to be happy."

So here they stood, at the foot of the escalator that would take Anna to the queue for airport security. Here was where she and Alex would have to say goodbye.

"I'm surprised Vivian isn't here," Alex said. Both of them wanted to draw out the inevitable moment of parting. "No doubt she's chasing some story around the city!"

"Actually," Anna beamed, "she's meeting the investors behind Banba Productions. Carol O'Connor was fired. Vivian is the obvious choice to take over."

"Wow, I'm impressed! And not surprised. What about that Luke guy – wasn't she seeing him?"

Anna remembered Vivian's pain at learning the truth of how they had used her, how they had scared her for publicity. She knew

Luke's betrayal hurt the most.

"He left the country. London, I think. Don't worry about Vivian – she'll be fine. She's made of tough stuff!"

"And you?" Alex asked softly, his eyes on hers. "Will you be fine?"

Suddenly her chest felt tight. Taking a leave of absence from work and putting her things into storage was one thing but saying goodbye to the man who had been her only family for over ten years was something else. He had been her brother, then her father, and everything she had needed since she was sixteen years old. She had already planned a week back in Cork when his new baby was born. Chloe had made her promise. But she found herself terrified at the idea of leaving now.

"Alex, I –"

He pulled her into his arms; her face was wet against his jumper.

"I'm not going anywhere – your home is always here. And I want you to do this. For God's sake, go and be happy, Anna."

He hugged her tightly and then he let her go and walked briskly to the glass doors. Before she could catch her breath he had disappeared into the bright April morning. She turned and looked up at the metal teeth of the escalator, rising over and over. All she had to do was step on and go. Leave Cork behind for a while.

But not forever.

Her mobile phone beeped in her pocket and she pulled it out to open a text message from Myles.

I might have arrived a little early – I can't wait to see you!

He had added a selfie of himself; the background looked very like the airport she was currently standing in. Anna realised he was already waiting for her at the arrivals gate at Brussels Airport. He beamed at her from the midst of a multi-coloured bouquet of balloons and she laughed out loud.

Angling the camera on her phone, she put one foot on the escalator and clicked, her fingers flying over the keypad in reply as she reached out and gripped the handrail tightly with her other hand.

See you soon!

Epilogue

Lisbon, Portugal

In an internet café in Lisbon, down a side street off a busy tourist strip, a young barista was growing concerned. She thought about calling her boss, but then wasn't sure what she should say. She polished the clear glass coffee mugs while she mulled over what to do.

It was early in the morning, so it was quieter, with fewer customers, and perhaps that's why she felt so uncomfortable. If there were more people in at this hour perhaps the woman wouldn't stand out so much. She might blend into the crowd and her behaviour mightn't be so noticeable. But there was only that one woman and two teenage boys with school satchels over their shoulders, who had quickly given up browsing the internet and were now staring at the woman with all the horror the barista felt.

She would definitely have to call her boss.

The woman looked like she was in her late twenties or early thirties. A tourist, definitely not local. She had entered the café, paid for an hour at the computer without making eye contact, speaking in English. Her identity card said her name was Lucy Robinson. Her hair was dark and cut short; she was very thin and had the pinkish hue to her skin that the tourists always had when they first arrived and stayed too long in the sun. Her face was bruised around the eyes and one cheek. Perhaps she'd had a fall? The barista hadn't paid her much attention, then.

Lucy Robinson had sat down and opened a few web pages, browsing quietly, until she suddenly wasn't quiet at all. She gasped so loudly everyone else in the café turned to her. Then she began to wail, a sound so shrill that one of the teenage boys rose from his chair. His friend pulled him back down but they continued to watch her, as did the barista, all staring with their mouths hanging open in shock. The woman moaned and wailed loudly, her arms wrapped around her stomach as though it was aching. Was she hurt? She rocked back and forth in the thin plastic hair, crying loudly. After another minute her tears became laughter.

Now she was laughing hysterically and the barista had had enough. She wouldn't call her boss, she'd call her father. He was a doctor, and that's what the woman needed more than anything.

Before she had finished dialling the number the woman named Lucy Robinson picked up her red satchel and staggered from the café, a broad smile on her tear-streaked face. The teenage boys sighed in relief and perhaps disappointment – the entertainment was over. They turned back to their screens and the barista hung up the phone.

Shaking her head, she moved towards the seat the woman had vacated.

What could have upset her so much?

On the screen was a newspaper article, in English; she leaned in closer to read.

Gardaí have confirmed the identity of the body recovered from the River Lee earlier this month as Cork businessman Tom Gallagher. Investigations into his death are ongoing and no further comment will be made at this time.

The End

Blinding Lies

AMY CRONIN

Ten years ago, Anna Clarke's parents disappeared. The mystery haunts her, and she hopes her job in a busy city Garda Station will one day help her find answers.

The case of a man shot dead crosses her desk – and Anna is shocked to discover that the main suspect is her childhood friend Kate Crowley. Certain that Kate is innocent, Anna is determined to help her clear her name. But first she has to find her ...

Tom Gallagher's son David is dead, and Tom believes Kate is responsible. Now his older son John is missing. Unable to grieve for one son until he finds the other, desperation can cause a man to do terrible things ... Then the German Meier brothers descend on the city, intent on finding an item David had offered to sell them. Tom doesn't know where it is, but he suspects Kate Crowley must have taken it.

Kate is on the run. She is trapped in the dead man's city – can her old friend help her find a way out?

In a week where a political summit is taking place and the city is on high alert, Kate must struggle to stay hidden and stay alive. And Anna is drawn into a twisted race against time, falling deeper into danger.

Fiction with an edge . . .

Twisted Truth

AMY CRONIN

*"There's a devil on my shoulder, Anna,
and he wants a word ..."*

Violent and seemingly random murders are terrorising Cork city and county. DS William Ryan is struggling to connect the victims and find a motive. The crimes have one thing in common – they are being filmed by one of the killers. With each kill the case grows more disturbing.

Anna Clarke, Garda clerical staff, becomes involved. In her personal life, Anna is closer than ever to finding the truth about her parents' mysterious disappearance ten years before. But the path to answers is littered with heartache and it's too late to turn back the clock ...

Meanwhile, Tom Gallagher is obsessed with revenge. Last year his son was murdered, and the woman responsible slipped through his fingers. But he now has CCTV images of two women crouching in an alleyway, having jumped from a nightclub bathroom window. One of them is *her*. The other helped her fight off his men, and Tom wants to know who that woman was ...

The clock is ticking to a grand finale, as truth twists and lies turn, and it seems Anna will have a front-row seat.

Fiction with an edge . . .